The Biggest Modern Woman
of the World

The Biggest Modern Woman of the World

A NOVEL BY

SUSAN SWAN

LESTER
&ORPEN
DENNYS
PUBLISHERS

Canadian Cataloguing in Publication Data

Swan, Susan.
    The biggest modern woman of the world

ISBN 0-88619-043-6

1. Swan, Anna, 1846-1888–Fiction.   I. Title.

PS8587.W35B54   1983   C813'.54   C83-098904-8
PR9199.3.S92B54   1983

Cover illustration by Jamie Bennett
Cover design by Spencer/Francey Inc.
Text design by N.R. Jackson
Typesetting by Trigraph
Printed and bound in Canada by
T. H. Best Printing Company Ltd. for
Lester & Orpen Dennys Limited
78 Sullivan Street
Toronto, Ontario
M5T 1C1

For Sam and Tyler

Acknowledgements

A.S.A. Harrison, Marian Engel, Phyllis Blakeley, Ray L. Carruthers, A.H. Saxon, George Swan, Hugh MacLennan, Allene Holt Gramly, Robert Josse, Joann King, Eleanor Currie, Bert Ross, Steve Yager; also the Bridgeport Public Library, Nova Scotia Teachers College, Medina County Historical Society, Circus World Museum, Library and Museum of the Performing Arts. I would also like to gratefully acknowledge the assistance of the Ontario Arts Council and the Canada Council.

Preface

The Nova Scotian giantess Anna Swan is, curiously, not as well known as the other Nova Scotian giant, her friend Angus McAskill. But I knew about her as a child because we have the same name and because my branch of the family is tall. Unfortunately, neither her descendants nor my relatives have enough information on our backgrounds to establish a connection. My family immigrated to Canada from Ireland; hers came to Nova Scotia from Scotland. But—so the story goes—both branches of the families trace their way back to a Scandinavian ancestor who settled in Scotland, and whose descendants later became a sept of the clan MacDonald.

CONTENTS

PART ONE

The Land of the Blue-noses

CHAPTER ONE

Spieling

Do you know how a giantess grows? Overnight? Like the sumac bush? Or slowly, like a cedar of Lebanon?

I, Hominida Pina Pituitosa Majora, a warm-blooded, viviparous, coniferous giantess, grew as an elephant grows, expanding in pounds as I rose in inches. My body weight doubled and then tripled by the time I was four.

I did not grow straight up like an Eastern White Pine, the largest conifer in North-East America, although I sprang from a Nova Scotian floor and learned to consort with livewood throughout the world without losing my needles. The LIVING LUMBER GIRL who walked and talked and juggled the Pre-Cambrian Shield (rocks to you, sir).

But I digress from my opener. I grew *out* and up as does the BLUE WHALE, LARGEST IN THE SEA, and the AFRICAN BUSH ELEPHANT, LARGEST ON LAND. The principle that weight varies as the cube of linear dimensions—that's the proper answer.

My resemblance to other babies was amazing, but my ecstatic face was a dead giveaway: I was a hyperendocrinal nympha, with too much resin in the blood. The gummy elixir shot through my veins in uncontrolled quantities. Lifting up my tubby form, the juice propelled me HEAD FIRST past the unpainted stomach of the kitchen table, and aimed my crown of red curls at the top of the loft where chinks in the roof let daylight through in a sideways blare of light.

There was a sky-breaking crash! My head splintered the ceiling: it stuck through the shanty roof, higher than chimneys. My red-hot forehead, throbbing from the effort of growth, cooled in special breezes reserved for the forest's uppermost branches. That's how I, Anna Haining Swan, the INCREDIBLE KNOTSUCKING LUMBER LASS, confounded her first audience in 1846 in the land of the Blue-noses. This maritime region is located on the eastern coast of the diverse and infinite Dominion of Canada and its inhabitants are called Blue-noses, not on account of the northern gales that nip their faces, but because of a superior brand of potato that is grown there, called Blue-nose.

Now I am in full voice...blowing my own horn...spieling the way I used to for P.T. Barnum, Queen Victoria, and all the normals who came to my performances after I grew up into an eight-foot giantess who toured North America and the Continent. This is my final appearance and I promise to tell all. What really happened to the BIGGEST MODERN WOMAN OF THE WORLD in a never-before-revealed autobiography which contains testimonials and documents by friends and associates (from their perspective) of a Victorian lady who refused to be inconsequential.

Yes, I was a GENUINE SHOW-BIZ CELEBRITY who found no forum modern enough to suit my talents and who has written this authentic account to entertain you the way I could not during my career as a professional giantess. A good performer has many spiels and I have three up my long sleeve to delight and astound:

1. my lecture at Barnum's museum
2. what my hometown will say about me 100 years from now
3. the real time spiel

May I start with Barnum and work up? (It's the only direction I understand.)

SPIEL NO. 1: THE AMERICAN MUSEUM, *CIRCA* 1863

Welcome, dear friends and visitors. I, Anna Haining Swan, am not a hoax. I am the FIRST GIANTESS to be presented at the American Museum and I stand 8′1″ in my bare feet. My cloth boots, which you can't see because the canons of taste forbid it, are low to the ground. Mr. P.T. Barnum likes to say that if I left a slipper on the stairs of a palace, he would be hard pressed to find a prince to fit it. This is not as rude as it sounds: it is the sort of bragging I am accustomed to hearing from the GREAT SHOWMAN who will not hire or exhibit any giants unless the women are over seven feet and men higher than seven and a half.

You may be humbugged in other theatres where giants rein-

2

force their height with small stilts or elevated shoes, high hats and platforms designed to pile illusion upon illusion. But not in the Grand Lecture Hall which holds authentic curiosities such as the ORIGINAL THIN MAN, the SWISS BELL RINGERS, the WONDERFUL ELIOPHOBUS FAMILY OF AFRICA whose albino physiognomy stuns the wondering audience, and Commodore Nutt, the SHORTEST OF MEN, whom you see before you, on my shoulder.

The Commodore and I are an excellent illustration of the way extremes meet in Mr. Barnum's showcase. But allow me to return to his remark about my shoe. He is quite wrong. You have only to look around this wonderful pavilion to find a few princes whose shoes I can't fill.

On the next dais, you will see Colonel Goshen, the PALESTIN-IAN GIANT, who is an object of admiration, not only on account of his immense height and frame, but also by reason of his manly beauty and delightful manners. He is a giant in every sense of the word.

I mention extraordinary men like the Colonel not because I am flirtatious by nature, but to show you that we of extreme height are not different from you of normal stature. We share normal interests—I do shell work and the Commodore plays polo and we are concerned with the business of making a living, which some of us do best by being ourselves. My manager, Judge Apollo Ingalls, is a man of your size, and he says Mr. Barnum's prodigies have an important part to play in the human drama. But who can say it is greater than your own contributions to the public weal?

As our society becomes standardized, it grows more difficult for giants and dwarfs to fit in. Our clothes must be specially made, and our shoes, which costs a great deal of money. I find eight-foot doorways too low, carriages, trains and depots too confining. I can't visit a theatre unless I sit in the back row so my head won't block the view and unless I can stretch my legs down the aisle.

The Commodore experiences these difficulties in reverse. Just as I must be cautious about ceiling fans, the Commodore avoids large dogs and cats that could menace his diminutive form. On the New Hampshire farm where he was raised, the Commodore was attacked by one of his father's turkeys, with unhappy consequences. When I was a child in New Annan, Nova Scotia, I could eat dinner with my family only if I sat on the floor. If I sat in a chair, my head would be too far above the heads of my siblings to allow me to converse.

I mention this, not to invoke pity, but to share with you the irritation the Commodore and I face in our daily lives. We do not feel a modicum of self-pity, since the accidents of our physical natures have made it possible for us to travel widely, to converse with royalty and celebrated personages and, in my case, to study and learn many fascinating things.

Those who have paid for the additional feature of our drawing-room exhibition are invited to stay and watch the Commodore and I perform Act I, Scene VII, of *Macbeth*. The Commodore vacillates wonderfully as Macbeth while I have a been complimented by Queen Victoria on my sympathetic portrait of a mother who claimed she could pluck a nipple from her infant's boneless gums and dash the child's brains out. The playlet is an example of Mr. Barnum's belief that amusement is the best way to eliminate ignorance and destroy barriers between the world of normal size and the one inhabited by the Commodore and myself.

This concludes my lecture, which is offered every afternoon and evening in the lecture hall for a 25¢ ticket. In Mr. Barnum's world of marvels, SCIENCE is the RINGLEADER, taming NATURE, who pours forth BOUNTY for all.

Apollo wrote my lecture, borrowing phrases from Barnum's hand-bills, and rehearsed me on our walk to work through Central Park. My manager had a loud voice. "Send your voice over in a phaeton," Barnum liked to tell Apollo, who was called the AUSTRALIAN MOUTH at the museum.

Every morning, Apollo walked me past the Astor Hotel, where Yankees of fashion loitered, whispering to me under his breath to take small steps. Then his mouth yawned open and his voice assaulted the passers-by: "THE ONLY GIANTESS IN THE WORLD LEAVES FOR LONDON TODAY TO VISIT THE QUEEN. DON'T MISS YOUR LAST CHANCE TO SEE THIS ASTOUNDING CURIOSITY. SHE'LL MEET YOU IN PERSON AND INSTRUCT YOU ON THE TOPIC OF GIGANTISM. THIS OLYMPIAN CINDERELLA IS A MARVEL YOU WILL NEVER FORGET."

SPIEL NO. 2: SUNRISE TRAIL MUSEUM, TATAMAGOUCHE, *CIRCA* 1977

Have you heard the story of Annie Swan? One time more famous than the other Maritime giant, McAskill. No. Ahm. Born in 1846, she was a charming girl, ah, eight feet tall with, ahm, a Mona Lisa look there. That smile, ahm. Hard to figure it. Now she joined P.T. Barnum's museum in 1862, toured the world, entertained royalty and married for love. Ahm, that's her shoe here. And the green basque, and here's her wedding portrait.

At fifteen years of age: take a good look at the pict. . . . at her father, ahm, the one with his hands folded across his chest. Her mother was 5′2″ and her father, Alex Swan, couldn't have been more than, ahm, 5′6″. At fifteen, she could look out the window above the door of her home. Let's see, she went and lived with relatives in Truro to go to teachers' college. A regular bookworm, you know. Ahm, she was unhappy, ah, there. Crowds followed her home from school. Then she went out and married the KENTUCKY GIANT in 1871 and settled in Ohio. She was the tallest woman in the world and she got her man. Ahm, strange to say, she died a day before she was 42 and her husband married a five-foot woman. That's ah—a great difference. And, ah, Annie and the KENTUCKY GIANT had giant babies. The two biggest babies in the world. But they both died. Ahm, this is, uh-huh, a dog churn. The dog, ahm, would get inside and run and run. Over there? A baby churn, ahm, same principle. And here's the—ah, Hubert Carruthers who lived down the road from Annie's family, though in her papers, you know, Annie always called him Hubert Belcourt. He was 3′10″. Yeah, ahm, it's him in the donkey cart. He died at the age of 76 and them are his pants beside the cavalry trousers of Annie's husband, ahm, Martin Van Buren Bates.

THE REAL TIME SPIEL

It could be said of me that I'm preoccupied with scale, but I am not as concerned with body length as you might expect. I am more concerned with hand size. That's my standard of reference because experience has taught me there is a correlation between the size of the hand and the size of what makes a man a man. Besides, men's hands have helped to shape my life.

My own hand measures ten inches from the wrist to the tip of my middle finger. My index finger is six inches long and I have a span of one foot. No man except my childhood sweetheart has matched the length of my hand. You know what doctors say: big woman, big finger.

Angus had wider digits. The tufts of men's fingers are fleshier, *n'est-ce pas*? If we redefined the digit using Angus as a model, we could double our homes, children, our schools, banks...sorry. I see this would make us shrink, not grow. What could be worse for North America? Here I get into dangerous ground, tangling myself up like M.V.B. I mean Martin Van Buren Bates, the KENTUCKY GIANT, who shared my devotion to scale. Only Martin, the silly ogre, thought North Americans like us should boss the world because normals are too small and puny to know what's good for them.

I, *au contraire*, have always wanted to be a gallant giantess, a doer of good deeds, and I have spent my life searching for ways to put my size to best use.

Martin's hands were small for a giant's. They measured eight inches from wrist to tip, and his index finger was three and a quarter. Unlike Angus, Martin pampered his hands. He wore yellow kid gloves, which a reporter in the *Floyd County Times* (just north of Martin's Kentucky birthplace) said made his hands look like "pressed hams." He was flattering Martin, who enjoyed having himself described as a well-proportioned colossus.

Angus neglected his hands—as he did the rest of his imposing figure—and they hung like dejected children at his sides. A glimpse of them, dangling beneath his muslin cuffs, made a hollow clunk go off in my head. Immediately, I saw their companion image: my hands, beneath my trumpet-shaped sleeves, clasping a parasol of watered silk.

Ingalls' measurements were greater than Martin's, which was astonishing since Ingalls, my manager, was a shorter man. He was the normal fellow in my life and the only one with the name of a god. Very fanciful for an Australian whose grandparents were Essex convicts. Of course, Apollo and Martin had titles. They also shared an astrology sign, Scorpio, which they believed to be the sign of powerful men.

Apollo's literary ability showed itself in the titles "Judge" and "Captain" which he gave to himself and Martin respectively. It was customary to use military titles after the civil war in the U.S. But a real gentleman has no need to dress himself up: Apollo and Martin were not saluted thus by me.

Barnum's hands were surprisingly average.

The smallest fingers, no more than an inch, belonged to my childhood friend, Hubert Belcourt. When he was nice to me, I didn't want to remind him of the size of his hands, but during his pedantic moods, I wanted to shout to the Maritimes: HUBERT BELCOURT HAS THE SMALLEST HANDS IN THE CANADAS. His fingers were teenier than those of the Commodore or Tom Thumb, my theatrical colleagues.

And wait—in spite of family delicacy, I can't omit my father, whose fingers were a nice fit with my four-year-old mitt. By that time I realized I wasn't an extension of my mother's body and I considered my father a physical equivalent. (It is not the lot of young giants to be awed by parental dimensions.)

When I was twelve, my fingers enfolded my father's baby fist. His bantam size endeared him to me and set the precedent for my reaction to all human males. Their size makes them seem vulnerable and I confess that as a grown woman I can't meet a man smaller than myself—i.e., every man except Angus—without acting like a welcome wagon. I want to shout to all of them: SAMPLE ANNIE'S FREE EATS & TONICS! GUARANTEED TO MAKE YOU GROW.

I'm too big now to care what they say about me in Colchester County. Let small minds have their say. I know my preoccupation with size is unladylike, but at least it stops with hands and goes no farther. I truly do not care how tall men are or how broad. I don't even know how big I am. I stopped measuring the march of my head to the sky before my mother accepted Barnum's contract (which she redrafted herself so the Connecticut horse trader had to provide me with lessons in French and music as well as my salary of $1,000 a month). Why bother measuring? Clearly, I *am* large.

Barnum sent an agent up to Nova Scotia to see if I was authentic, a Quaker gentleman who measured me while I lay on the dirt floor of the shanty like a corpse. The agent scribbled notations in a book, but he didn't sing them out the way I had anticipated. Barnum is infamous for exaggerating the heights of his giants, and as he bills me at 8′1″, I am definitely less. In New Annan, my mother told friends I was 7′9″ and privately hoped I would not top eight feet. I put my height at 7′11½″. It's an educated guess.

CHAPTER TWO

The Great Event

The stomach of my reserved Scottish parent blew into a monster sphere during her pregnancy. Momma couldn't walk without help. She couldn't sit without fear of her belly splitting. Air pinned her body to the bed where she lay in a hysterical trance. Her five-foot frame was motionless for the last four months. She refused to talk and forgot to waggle angry fingers at her neighbours' children, peeking around the curtain when her chamber pot came. There was nothing for her to do except concentrate on lying on her back so her stomach was free to perform its matronly jig to the roof-beams.

I arrived as the GREAT EVENT, August 7, 1846. I weighed eighteen pounds at birth and tore Momma's perineum from stem to gudgeon, turning inside out her anal sphincter. My birth coincided with a bumper crop of vegetables in the garden near our shanty—a rude log hutch that stood in the centre of a small New Annan glen without a tree to shade it from sun or wind. The month of my birth, Poppa's little plot burst forth with mammoth love-apples, squash as big as wagon wheels, zucchinis as long and as fat as men's thighs, and potatoes the size of faces.

Poppa was delighted with his over-grown vegetables, but Momma remained downcast after she regained her voice. For three months, it was too painful for her to sit. Her stomach drooped, a crashed dirigible—the sign than an INNER DISASTER had transpired, tragic and frightening. "Look the other way," she whispered to her baby when she went to undress. "I'm not decent!" She told my father a thing or two when he watched. Caught it in the neck Alex-who-done-this-to-Mother! Her one brown eye gleamed with fury. (Momma's right eye had been pecked out by a turkey.)

No, Momma was not for touching or feeling, no kissing or courting! Alex, she didn't want your small body one week or the next! She didn't want you to remember how big a woman's body gets when it has to! If Poppa threw his hat in the bedroom, she'd throw it out. He had to wait for a year before Momma gave him the benefit of her brown eye. A sister, Maggie, was born November 6, 1848. Infant deaths were common in the 1840s and Maggie died a year later. I, myself, was the third of twelve children, and the first to live.

There I am, the INFANT GIANTESS, lying on the dirt floor, my first kingdom. I look like a pink tuber and am ludicrously fat. My cheeks are sucking pouches; my fingers are tree-toad pads. They cling and stick to what's offered. I can't hold up my hairless, melon-sized head. My mouth is sucking a table leg as if it's a wooden nipple and my eyes are glued to the floor, mesmerized by the sight of my parents' feet. My mother's foot, a dainty Queen Mab appendage, rolls back and forth, grinding clean and sharp, a tarnished needle on a sandy board. My father, Oberon, rests his backwoods clod-hoppers, sole to sole, next to those of his queen. Soon my head is going to wander off in search of the treetops where the delicate vines flower, north past the timber line, heading for the top of the world, up to the ARCTIC ZONE where no vegetation can grow.

But during babyhood my eyesight never wanders: it stays down beneath tabletops, observing the two lovely pairs of fairy feet going about their business. Momma and Poppa, the first missive is for you!

Why do immigrants have large children? Is it because *you* didn't do what your parents said and ran away from home?

Hugs and kisses, the INFANT GIANTESS.

The extent of my mother's trauma was not known to me until I was fully grown.

I wasn't aware that Momma's brown eye glistened with pity when, at the age of four, I grew to 4′6″. My instinct is to prefer joy to sorrow (the instinct is my greatest gift) so I noticed instead that Poppa and my lunatic uncle doted on me. As I crawled about in my world of boots and table legs, Uncle Geordie lay on the floor, trying to see things as I did. My admirer talked in prophecy or not at all and resembled a gay spider. His hair was white and fuzzy and he had long, floppy arms and legs and wild eyes whose pupils danced from left to right. I thought his nervous tic meant he felt happy to be with me, and when he lay on the earthen floor, I shifted my pupils to and fro in a gesture of welcome.

Momma chuckled in spite of herself. When Uncle Geordie felt the power of the little people and spoke in tongues, she put away her sewing and called Poppa in to listen. Staring at me with his crazy eyes, Uncle Geordie held me up to the ceiling, chanting Celtic sayings. Soon Poppa began to coax Uncle Geordie to conduct his trance in the midst of our potato hills, in the hope that we might get another bumper crop. Here I am, a fat toddler, performing Poppa's fertility rite: My eyes shift wildly to and fro as I crawl through the potato hills. Poppa scrambles after me, trying to catch me so Uncle Geordie can lift me to the heavens. Then up I go in the skinny arms of my uncle until I see the feathery tips of the spruce and look down on Poppa's bald spot. "Gordon, do you ken it? The power of the *sithichean* is with our Annie!" Uncle Geordie stamps his Rumpelstiltskin legs on the damp spring earth. He says the growth sap is in my veins and my young *bean-grugach* voice is drawing forth the seeds from their sleep in the mussel mud of my father's garden and I scream and scream with excitement until Momma rushes out and calls to Uncle that he is lifting me too high.

Not long after, Uncle Geordie died, but Poppa still encouraged me to play in his vegetable patch. "Come sing a growing song, Annie," he whispered if we were outdoors where Momma couldn't hear us. (Momma considered singing sinful and didn't accept my father's argument that if songs at a milling frolic speeded up the production of blankets and milking songs made cows give sweeter milk, why wouldn't the song of a giantess make vegetables grow?)

It was a sign of Momma's affection for my father that she didn't challenge his notion that my size was not a curse but a blessing, a symbol of luck and hope for all us Swans. After all, it was she, not Poppa, who was left to cope with the practical problems created by my height, such as clothes and schooling. As for me, I saw my growth as a symbol of my power and energy and expected others to envy me for it. Momma might look on in dismay but she couldn't stop my dance to the stars.

Move gaily, Annie. Only you can dance. The air can't stop you.

Tap. Tap. Up you go. Four years old and rosy as a milk maid for your first exhibit in Halifax. Weight 94 pounds and already your arms and wrists are as large as those of a full-grown man! Tap. Tap. Four feet eight inches and 100 pounds for your second exhibit in Pictou.

Annie, you're almost as big as the Basle girl seen by Platerus. She had a body as large as a full-grown woman's, thighs thicker than a horse's neck, the calf of her leg equal to the calf of a lusty man, and a waist girdle that could go around both her mother and her father. Think you'll grow that big, Annie? How's the weather up there? Don't take me serious now.

A girl who weighed as much as a sack of wheat that held eight bushels. Tap. Tap. Let's put Annie in a sack and see. Oh, watch out—her body is getting away from us! At seven years old, she is taller than her five-foot-three mother. Tap. Tap. At age ten, she is 6′6″ and still climbing. At seventeen, she is 7′6″ and 350 pounds. Tap. Tap. Her shoe is thirteen inches. How tall *are* you Annie? You better stop your dancing. You'll make the air mad. Tap. Tap. Hey! There she goes folks! Danced right out of our arms. Annie, come back! Don't you like us? Don't you want us? Did we say something wrong? Talk to us! Annie, you'll pay for your dancing one of these days.

Ladies, Gentlemen, Families, Children, Friends:
I'm sorry. It's not my fault I left you behind.
Respectfully yours, the GIRL GIANTESS.

I *am* sorry my size tortured my mother and pointed my destiny away from the pioneer life that my parents lived. As a child, it was my greatest delight. Later it became my greatest trouble, and my struggle with the two opposing views has been the chief task of my life. But in my early days I had no trouble accepting Poppa's and Uncle Geordie's vision of me as a special being with an important destiny. I wished for only one thing: that the race of dwarfs I sprang from would defy gravity and race up with me through the lower atmosphere to smell the fresh sweet oxygen waiting for those who will stretch. I tended to self-glorification, I confess. Witness the poem I wrote at age eleven.

THE INFANT GIANTESS

Anna, were you big when you were little?
Yes, I was large when I was small.

You should have seen my foot! All my toes
quarrelling for room, bent and curling, trying to wear
the landscape like a slipper.

The foot of a giant girl: it could squish house
and carriages between the roast-beef eater
and cried-all-the-way-home.

Cape Breton took shade under my ankle boss
farmers scaled my calves for thrills
swinging up on my leg hairs, fighting for the view
from my knee-cap.

Off the coast of Newfoundland,
fisher boats sighted my bones
expanding from their growing points,
white beanstalks hauling the flesh skyward
in a gush of arms,
hands, shoulders, face,
flowing from the earth up
with the determination of ants.

CHAPTER THREE

A Career is Born

Theatre was the social centre of Halifax, which was known as the best theatre and musical city in British North America. Even as early as 1800, theatrical productions were *à la mode*: in *Timour the Tartar* real horses came on stage. When there weren't American or British companies to see, there were local plays.

But in New Annan, the reputation of the acting profession hadn't developed since Shakespeare. My parents classified actors as the Elizabethans did, with rogues, vagabonds, and sturdy beggars. No doubt it would have taken my mother and father years to notice my theatrical skills if they hadn't met Jacob Dunseith—the captain of a Yankee fishing schooner who took work as a theatre agent during the off season.

The way I understand Poppa's story, my little parent was out in the cold, doing what a man has to do, when Dunseith drove by in a sleigh. In the cold weather, my parent couldn't be bothered to go into the woods on calls of nature. He preferred to stay closer to home, and amused himself by decorating the snowbanks about the shanty. He couldn't spell his name, merely his initials, A.S. It was a humble way to impress himself on the land, yet in a few weeks his daily waterings turned the white drifts into icy, sulphur-coloured Alps. My mother frowned at their hideous canary-yellow peaks and forbade me to play near them.

She angered me with her attempt to insert her small form between me and experience. And so I confess the key to this story can be found in two weasel-sized holes at the foot of my father's drifts. The day Dunseith drove by, Poppa was standing near his mountain range which was shiny all over with fresh ice dribbles. Responding to his rumbling stomach, Dunseith turned in at the shanty because my mother's hospitality was known up and down Northumberland Strait.

Meanwhile, Poppa's plenitude spilled forth in the bitter air and challenged Dunseith to a male rite. Lumbering out of his sleigh with a gigantic sword, the Yankee parted a moth-eaten robe by my father's side and set the snowbank smoking ferociously. Dunseith did not usually desecrate snowbanks as a way of taking revenge on the vast Canadas. He butchered moose in winter, driving hundreds of the starving beasts into deep snow and carving their necks open with a sweaty joy. In the spring, ships in the strait had to steer away from the site of such massacres to avoid the stench.

It was no surprise Momma despised him. Poppa never passed judgment. That day, he nodded at the stranger who had joined him in a sprinkle duet, then lost himself again in contemplation of the luxuriant vegetation beyond our croft.

I used to wonder why Poppa made restless jaunts out of doors to "see what the weather's doin'." Was he looking for a troll queen in the timber so he could thank her for the giant genes in his reproductive parts? More likely, Poppa used to think about the weather and a privy he would build later, after I left home. A pine lean-to with a lilac bush planted before it to sweeten the air.

Of course, when he broke from his daydreaming and saw my face behind a wall of yellow ice, Poppa looked horrified. The men's pee had closed off both my hand-built tunnels, sealing me up behind frozen cascades of urine.

Picture them: two toy stalactites! A miniature Niagara and Montmorency Falls in the bosom of a single snowdrift! Dunseith picked up his claymore and stuck it into the drift. The two men pushed and pulled the sword, trying to pry a hole in the ice until the instrument snapped in two. Through the yellow glaze, I saw my father kick angrily at the knoll. Dunseith, meanwhile, was unbuttoning again to see if another noble stream would undo the damage when Momma burst out of the shanty, running like the dickens. She picked up the broken weapon and inserted it into the top of the bank, plunging it up and down like the dasher in a butter churn, and she sang her churning song.

There's a click here, there's a clack here, there's a great
wet mass here. The carpenters will come, the constables will come,
the man with the yellow cap will come. The butter will
come in a rush.

15

Parts of the drift began to crumble and I popped out in a tinkle of ice and baby talk. I knocked Poppa down as I emerged, so relieved was I to escape my frozen prison. Momma clapped my cheek to stop my childish weeping and a strange voice shouted:

"It's a girl!"

"Thank the Lord," Poppa said.

"Will you listen to her," the strange voice continued. "She's a . . . a daftie!"

"Anna is no daft bairn. She's big for her age," Poppa replied angrily.

"Come on man. She's a loony."

"She is four years old, lummox. I should know. I'm the father, ain't I?"

Dunseith suddenly laughed and waved his broken claymore at his sleigh. Slowly, an enormous shape that we had taken to be buffalo robes climbed out.

"Meet the MARITIME MARVEL and the NOVA SCOTIAN HERCULES, GIANT ANGUS MC ASKILL," Dunseith said.

Above the furs was a white, freckled face. From within came a deeply hollow noise with a sweet, musical cadence.

"Glad to meet you, Mr. Swan. Is it cold enough for you?"

So in a frosty Tatamagouche clearing in 1851, I met my famous counterpart. Angus is more widely known than I even though a giantess is rarer than a giant. In British North America, where I should be famous as the nation's first female entertainer, it is here an Angus, there an Angus, everywhere the McAskill from Cape Breton.

Angus was 26 at our first meeting, a shy giant who ran his hands through his thick black hair and looked away when Dunseith referred to him as "my protégé" (a common term which managers used in those days for their freaks). Angus spoke only to ask for crowdie (a dessert of oatmeal and cream), and sat on the floor with the porridge bowl wobbling on his vast knee, winking and smiling at me while Dunseith talked.

"Folks will stare at your girl anyway," Dunseith said, making my mother frown. "They may as well pay for it."

"Folks who stare at Anna show bad breeding," my glowering

mother retorted. "She will learn to feel sorry for them as she grows up."

"Maybe. And maybe not," Dunseith argued, "but it don't matter now. A child don't understand. You can tell her the folks are coming to see her pretty face."

I was still chilled from being in the snow tunnel and so crawled off Momma's lap and under the kitchen table past the thicket of knees to the hearth fire. My seat on the floor gave me a clear view of what was under McAskill's kilt as he sat, wolfing down the sticky crowdie. Through the pillars of his bent calfs, I saw what looked to be a huge tube set off by a pair of giant cannonballs.

I crawled over to investigate. When I was just by McAskill's enormous boot, Momma called me back. I ignored her command and dove under the plaid skirts whose woollen folds gave off a smell like candle wax. The giant, blushing, had to fish me out.

"The girl knows how to get attention, all right," Dunseith chuckled, as I squealed in Angus' arms.

"Look here, you're poor as church mice and you're keeping your prize heifer in the barn."

Poppa sighed and looked at Momma.

"Ann, why shouldn't Nova Scotians get a chance to see what Colchester County can produce in a pinch?"

"All right, then, Alex. Folks here can admire Annabelle, but I draw the line at Yankees gaping at her."

Momma wearily took me out of Angus' arms and whispered in my ear: "Annie, we're going to show all doubters you're as big as people say."

Momma served Dunseith a helping of her bake-apple pie and announced she would show me in Halifax—as he suggested—but under her wing. My career would be a family enterprise. Only Momma (Poppa was too busy with his barley and oats) would be all things beneath her cockleshell bonnet—agent, ticket taker, chaperone, watchdog, and the soft Highland voice I overheard at prayer asking God to bless her Annabelle.

We met Dunseith again in Halifax, when I was exhibited at a hall by the docks. My début began at 3 p.m., March 24, 1851. I wore

17

Momma's poplin carriage dress and gentlemen from the audience paid 10¢ for the novelty of wrapping a tape around my legs and wrists. After the exhibit, Dunseith dropped by with Angus. To impress Momma, the Yankee brought me an orange and ordered Angus to take me on an outing to Water Street where the booms of the sailing ships made a roof over the dockside sheds. It was foggy and dark, and Angus slunk into doorways and back alleys to avoid staring pedestrians. Ordinarily, Dunseith had the giant stay off the street so the crowds would pay as high as a dollar to see him. That day, Dunseith wanted us out of his hair so he could try again to persuade Momma to let him show me.

Momma refused. She considered Dunseith a scallywag from the Boston States, too ignorant to share Poppa's conviction that my size didn't make me a freak, only someone different and special instead. We ran into Dunseith once more in Pictou, Nova Scotia, a large shipping centre. It was in July, during the Pictou Exhibition. Momma had put me on display a second time, and Angus was also there, exhibiting. Dunseith was preparing to take the giant to the World Fair in London, but by this time he knew better than to ask Momma if I could go along.

Dunseith was the first professional enthusiast of my acquaintance and it's difficult not to speculate how many more inches of newspaper column I'd have received if he'd been allowed to work for me. As it was, my press amounted to two pinched blurbs in the *Nova Scotian*. The March advertisement said I was bid fair to eclipse all giantesses who preceded me and failed to list the time of my exhibit. The July notice at least offered a description of me as well-proportioned and said that Momma was a woman of small size and interesting appearance.

CHAPTER FOUR

Go to Halifax!

For me, the term "go to town" is like uttering "go to Halifax," an oath which owes its association with hellfire to a guillotine that worked so sloppily it took several tries before it beheaded its victims. The guillotine belonged to the English seaport town called Halifax. I, the INFANT GIANTESS, assumed the razor was in Halifax, the capital of Nova Scotia.

An easy slip. My native land is fond of discipline. An intelligent citizen is not the ninny who upholds what is good, but the canny so-and-so who won't be fooled by what is bad. This dictum, borrowed from the Lowland Scot, is the basis of our English and French traditions. It may be said that the style of both is to punish and admonish.

Nowhere is this more true than in rural life. You think I jest? I swear to you, out where dirt paths burrow through shining stands of maple and oak, hostility adds a rich, full-bodied perfume to the tang of country air. Although I have performed in many theatres where the attitude to show business is too casual for my liking, no audience is harder to work than a rural crowd.

Go to Halifax! Go to town! I learned to associate the two phrases when I turned ten and Momma took me on a monthly shopping trip with the Belcourts to the town of Tatamagouche. It was my first trip away from the shanty. I hadn't been even to Wilson School, the small frame building in the hamlet of New Annan. Momma had told its teacher she needed me at home to look after the babies. In 1856, there were three siblings—John, one, Maggie, three, and Janette, five. (The Maggie born in 1848 died of unknown causes in 1849.)

Momma's excuse was a fib: She didn't want me to see the outside world until she felt I was ready. So until the age of ten, I stayed at home. I sat on the dusty shanty floor while my brothers and sisters scrambled over my lap or dangled about my neck and studied lessons brought to me by my next-door neighbour, Hubert Belcourt. My mentor was a fifteen-year-old dwarf who looked younger than me because of his three-foot-ten size. He drove a donkey cart purchased by his mother, Sophie Belcourt, so that he could elude the bands of children at Wilson School who jeered at his squeaky Acadian accent and at his huge face, wrinkled before his time.

The dwarf giggled nervously when I asked if school was a nice place. "It's *maudit*, Annie," he warned in his shrill falsetto. But I had confidence school would be fun because Poppa considered me a magic bairn whose voice made vegetables grow.

The morning of my first trip to town I had no knowledge of what awaited me. I stood 6′6″ but I had my share of a ten-year-old's enthusiasm and I giggled at the older Hubert who sat in the Belcourt's high wooden wagon, contorting his ungainly, wrinkled face and cliff-like brow into monkey faces for my benefit.

Momma frowned but decided not to notice Hubert's behaviour as she climbed into the wagon. Instead, she put on a cheerful manner to greet our driver, Sophie Belcourt. Sophie was of English stock and an exemplary disciplinarian. She looked most relaxed when chiding Hubert. As long as he misbehaved she could pretend Hubert was ordinary, because a bad child was a normal child, and Sophie considered it a point in her favour that she did not make allowances for Hubert's size. Her muscular wrist snapped a buggy whip with the same force on Hubert as on the posteriors of her other children. "Better a small body than a small mind," she bragged to Momma.

Momma had high expectations of my character and behaviour, and was distant and unflinching in public. But in private, when I lay curled in my bed like a drooping fiddlehead, weeping over a childish frustration, she sighed and crooned to me: "Poor Annabelle, poor bairn."

That day, our doll-sized mothers sat in the front of the wagon, gossiping in silk bonnets and embroidered basques—*deux femmes en promenade*. Hubert and I, the NATURAE LUXUS, sat in the back, Hubert on my knee. I wore a muslin skirt of Momma's and a waist of muslin with a lace bonnet. Hubert had on a hand-me-down sailor's suit once highly prized by his oldest brother.

Hubert caught my eye and made another monkey face at Sophie's back. I giggled harder under my bonnet, hoping our mothers were too engrossed in their stories about natural disasters to notice us. They liked to analyse every local calamity, noting the date, location, and names of other reporting sources. (Hubert and I were the only phenomena they failed to discuss.) On that afternoon, their conversation dwelt on the skinny Irish maid of the Macleans who had burnt to death seconds after her petticoats caught a spark from the hearth.

"A terrible thing," Momma said nervously, as if embarrassed by the edge of sympathy in her voice.

"Isn't she the one who laughed out loud and showed her teeth coming out of church?" Sophie asked.

"Yes. The red-haired girl who brushed her hair in public," Momma said. Suddenly she became openly pitying. "The poor lass. I hear steeping petticoats in a solution of zinc chloride makes them fireproof."

"A lady is never well-dressed when you notice what she wears," Sophie snapped, looking annoyed because Momma had strayed from judgment of the maid's conduct.

Suddenly, Hubert stood up on my lap and whispered in my ear: "A flaming attire is the sign of a deceitful mind."

Then he stuck out his miniature tongue at his mother's back. To our surprise, Sophie whirled about. With a look, she froze Hubert and me mid-bounce in the wagon.

"Little man, if you imitate an ape, one day you will have an ape's face."

Sophie gazed soulfully out at the forest, rolling off in all directions, before confiding to Momma the heart of her Presbyterian code: "I have told Hubert many times that eccentric behaviour is a sign of vanity but he won't listen."

"Anna?" Momma smiled at me. "Ask Hubert to play his game with you."

Hubert's game involved counting dying trees whose waists had been girdled with broad-axes. The trees had to be maple, the ones that stood like skeletons: dead, blanched, and white as snow, waiting to be harvested. Hubert marked our sightings in a small clipboard. Its sheets of paper were made from birchbark and held

21

down with the handle of a razor. He twisted a blond curl over his forehead as he wrote in his elegant script, and stopped to correct me when I identified a sycamore for swamp ash.

Through long stretches of blackened ground where woods had been burned for clearing, Hubert and I vied to be the first to spot the scarlet blossoms of geraniums pushing up among charred stumps. Or we fought to spy wood lilies in the grassy sections of the devastated land. Hubert always won. He was more alert than I. Perhaps he was smarter. As I learned later from the KENTUCKY GIANT, a midget's brain is one-nineteenth the weight of his body. Mine is one-fortieth the rest of me. With Hubert, I was unmajestic in defeat.

"There's a deadhead! The maple there! Three points for me!" I said.

"Anna, I saw it first," Hubert argued.

"You didn't!" I retorted.

"Who just spoke out?" Hubert asked in an injured tone.

"Well then, let's count dead pines, not maples. There's one! I saw it before you did!"

"That's a spruce, not a pine," Hubert said. "I know my pines."

"What colour is the bark of a white pine, Mr. Smartie Pants?" I asked.

"Pink," Hubert replied.

"No. Grey," I said triumphantly. "Nana-nana-na-na! You didn't know-oh!"

We stopped squabbling as we descended the slope into Tatamagouche. I could see a crowd gathering under the wooden awning of the inn on the main street. As our wagon drew up I found myself staring down at twenty to thirty hostile faces, some gawking openly, others, in the back rows, pretending not to gape. I was ready for dislike from someone acquainted with my faults, but I was bewildered that day by the angry loathing I saw in the young men's eyes, and the understated little smiles of contempt on the faces of the young women. My first impulse was to look over my shoulder to see if they were staring at something behind me, a man whipping a horse perhaps, and I turned to see.

When I realized it was me they were looking at with disgust, I was startled. My second reaction was to smooth my skirts in case they were torn or hiked up. Then—did they not know I was a *bean-grugach* with magic powers? Their sneering faces said they did not. Suddenly, I felt a slow and dreadful tightening of limbs which I later associated with remorse over making a spectacle of myself.

At that moment Hubert scrambled out of my lap, a scowl on his massive forehead. The crowd laughed and bulged towards us, jostling for a better position, while children ran in and out under the wagon.

"Annie, lift up Hubert and help him down," Momma said, ignoring our audience.

Hubert threw Momma a dark look and leapt to the street. The sidewalk loafers hooted and even our mothers' lips twitched as if they wanted to laugh. Jacob MacDonald, the drunken old Scot who managed the inn, stepped out of the crowd and pushed in front of Hubert in order to help our mothers down. I waited for my turn, smiling nervously and wishing the crowd would notice my face. Nobody can fault my countenance: my dark red hair and alabaster skin could attract attention on their own.

MacDonald turned to help me and I manoeuvred my enormous skirts so they wouldn't blot out his whiskered face as he stood below me. Hubert stood on the dirt beside him, looking up. Suddenly, MacDonald leaned forward and peered under my bonnet. It was an ill-bred antic and a few of the loafers tittered. As I stepped out of the carriage, my leg shot over the running board, and I looked down foolishly at my exposed ankle and my large slipper made of cow's hide. MacDonald whistled, and picked up Hubert, and thrust the dwarf's hand into mine so it looked like Hubert was helping me down like a gentleman. The crowd hooted in delight. Clasping Hubert against his chest with one arm, MacDonald pointed at us and made the sign of the cross as if joining us in holy wedlock. I barely heard the laughter and jeers. I was too shocked and ashamed. I did not intend to punish MacDonald but that is what happened for my shame caused me to lose physical control and topple from the wagon.

Local reporters of natural disaster rejoiced the day 200 pounds of me fell from the sky. Hubert's 45 pounds were unhurt, although the midget was knocked on his back so his little legs waved like a baby's. The only injury sustained was by MacDonald. His skin glowed a rueful black-and-blue where my bodice button had blazed across his brow in a trail as fierce as the Cape Breton fireball. Momma and Sophie made embarrassed noises at the sight of the bleeding Scotsman, then led Hubert and me through the surly crowds. A group of shopkeepers helped the victim to his feet.

Later, as we ate codballs at the inn, MacDonald came out from his kitchen, bandaged and grim, and Momma asked me in a whisper to apologize to him. As I struggled to rise, I felt an urge to startle the dour, weathered faces about me. Should I jump up impetuously, tipping over the table spread with MacDonald's greasy fare? I felt a tug on my skirt and glanced down. Momma and Sophie Belcourt watched with warning looks. It is a tradition in the Canadas: when in public, self-efface! The embarrassment of my carriage fall returned and my frame hummed with the effort of restriction, the pulling in of arms to the sides... the lowering of head and shoulders, the collapsed knees and chest.... But before shame clamped shut my mouth, I heard myself say:

"LADIES AND GENTLEMEN, FRIENDS AND PASSERS-BY: Forgive me. My body is showing."

Then my nerve gave out and I sat down. MacDonald and our mothers stared at me with baffled expressions. Hubert squealed in appreciation. When the grown-ups began to converse again, he winked at me and made a series of rapid monkey faces in their direction. The dwarf didn't hold my entrance against me. Hubert was pleased that I'd learned a freak must play to the audience.

A few weeks later, now that my début was over, I started school. Hubert drove me there in his cart, knowing the reaction would be hostile and that we might as well make the best of it together. After Tatamagouche I no longer expected much from Wilson School, yet I was taken aback when the children surrounded Hubert's cart as we drove it into the yard and tried to tip it over. Luckily, I am heavy as well as large and the cart didn't budge. The schoolmistress, an ancient Scottish lady from the North Shore, flew out the door, screaming, and the children scattered like sulky rodents. Unfortunately, her rescue made life worse for us. The children sneered and hissed questions about my height as I sat in the crowded little room and tried to listen as the teacher described the founding of the great Blue-nose nation two hundred years before.

At last the teacher trilled: "If you will only still your tongues, class, I will measure the Swan girl at morning recess."

I did not favour being exhibited on my first day at school. When she shook the recess bell, I rose grandly from my cramped seat on a low bench and fled the school.

"I decided to come home early today," I said to Poppa who was hoeing as I walked up the road to the shanty. He nodded and said nothing. I waited for his scolding. When it didn't come, my knees gave out and I crashed to the ground, dropping my slate. I began to weep miserably. Poppa stopped hoeing and sat down beside me. He stared for a long time at the slopes of the mountain spruce. Finally, he muttered: "So you found the world is not what it should be, lass?" I nodded and he put his dirty, calloused mitt in my bigger hand.

"Damn the lot!" he swore. "I could tan their hides, every one." He squeezed my six-inch fingers. "But more's the pity if they canna know a special person when they see her. Will you sing a growing song for me now, Annie?"

I rose slowly, Poppa nodded and stared up at me in awe. Gratefully, I parted my lips and began to sing.

CHAPTER FIVE

Growing Pains

In 1859, I was thirteen and close to seven feet. I had six younger brothers and sisters of short stature—Janette, 8, Maggie, 6, George and Mary, 3, and John, 4. The baby Liza had just been born. We were all confined together in a one-and-a-half-storey dwelling which was hot and dusty in the summer months, having no shade trees nearby, and I perspired mightily. In the winter, I shivered in drafts that always found a way into the house no matter how many times Poppa banked its sides with eelgrass.

I did not complain, for my brothers and sisters were worse off. They had to contend with me and my vast skirts and were obliged to sleep on a pile of straw before the fire. My parents and I were the only family members who had beds. We were too poor to have much in the way of furniture with the exception of a few stools and benches and a rough, bare plank. This board was our table where we ate a diet of fish and boiled potatoes, using lead spoons and knives fashioned from old iron hoops.

My height made it impossible for me to stand upright in my own home. The shanty was no more than a crude bin for the housing of young children; it was not suited to somebody of my proportions and I had to stoop going in and out its front door. I preferred to be outdoors in the open air where I could hold my head up and put my shoulders back without fear of bursting through the ceiling.

Momma spoke up on my behalf.

"Alex, Anna's a good girl, but the bairn hasn't got an inch to spare in her own house!"

At last, Poppa cut a crescent window in the shanty wall directly above the front door. The window was no more than an air-hole under the roof, but at least I could look through it at my family working in the fields on the slope below.

If shanty life was inconvenient, school was a misery. I had to sit on a high stool, and work at a table raised on boards. The rest of the schoolroom sat below me on benches and wrote on their slates. My seat set me apart from my fellow students even more than my size: It made them think I was a teacher's pet and they took my shy, embarrassed ways as a sign of the snob. Meanwhile, their stares made me feel hideously exposed—as if my body was covered by warts and infected wounds. I became extremely self-conscious and regularly returned from school with a headache.

Momma would put me to bed at once and if necessary send Janette on the six-mile hike to the Mill Brook for sweet mountain water to slake my enormous thirst. It was harder to satisfy my appetite. I daily ate the same food that my family devoured in a week (Barnum later claimed it was 32 pounds of potatoes and 24 cod) for I was still growing. The effort of growth exhausted me and I moved about the shanty in a nimbus of fatigue. Then puberty arrived and converted my physique into a turbulent mass. Tempests raged above and below my chin. My throat swelled with a goiter the size of a knoll; my central regions leaked unwanted milk; and my monthlies evoked a weatherless condition that caused me to sleep for several days.

I reacted to my tribulations by withdrawing into my magic world. I began to feel responsible for the growth of my siblings, whose small stature I took as a personal challenge. Not that Poppa expected me to work on my flesh and blood. I did it spontaneously because I hadn't learned to distrust the myth of the strong giant. (It is part of the vanity of the big that we believe our own mythology.)

At night, as my siblings drowsed on the straw heap before our hearth, I sang the growing song I had adapted from a Gaelic love ballad. (There were many ballads to choose from as the settlers in Colchester County believed the Highland proverb that if an end comes to the world, music and love will endure.) During the day, I sang to them from my peep-hole under the roof as they did their chores in the field below, watching tenderly whenever my siblings grew vexed and quarrelled with one another.

Here I am at my post above the shanty door in the summer of 1859. Threshing time. The GIRL GIANTESS in her colonial box. My

27

serious brown eyes are framed in the rebated pine of the loft window. I have a lazy eye. That is, one eye is more hooded than the other which gives me a mysterious expression. I also have a thin mouth and a Roman nose and my face would be severe if it wasn't for my best feature—my shiny, dark red-brown hair that hangs to my shoulders in ringlets. My hair is fluffy on top of my head and pinned back behind my small and dainty ears. Momma ordered my gown from Boston; she buys me a new one every year despite Janette's complaints that she is given nothing but rags to wear. My gowns are in the Princess style and modelled after the fashion engravings in *Mr. Godey's Ladies*, with fitted bodices that end in a V at the waist as well as long, flared skirts that hide my homemade slippers. Crawling under my hem is one of the twins, Mary, who responds to the safe darkness beneath me by sucking the toe of my cowskin slipper. I recoil and bump my head against the shanty ceiling. "Momma!" I bleat. She comes instantly. (In the small quarters of the shanty, she can never be far from my side.) Clucking angrily, she crawls under my gown and hauls out a squealing baby girl.

"You filthy lass! Don't you go mussing our Anna again," Momma says. She pushes around my skirt and carries Mary, then George, the other twin, out of doors. Momma glances up at me staring down at her and shakes her head. Her face under the poke bonnet looks worn. "It's a good thing you've got broad shoulders, Annabelle," she cries. "What else did He make you this size for if it weren't to look down with pity and understanding on those smaller than yourself?"

My parent parrots the Christian ideal without knowing I already have too grave a sense of my giant duties. Years later, watching the show-dwarfs of London whom Dickens described in a popular sketch, I felt nothing but envy for the little creatures dashing through the drawing room and bedchambers of their two-and-a-half-foot doll houses, firing guns, raising flags, and singing ditties. The show-dwarfs, inside their tiny homes, couldn't see their audience and so felt not the slightest responsibility for the normals whose delighted laughter at their antics must have convinced them that other beings were carefree souls who didn't suffer the way freaks do. Unlike the dwarfs, it was easy for me to see how vulnerable the normals were and, for many years, I reacted by feeling obliged to look after them.

That morning, in August 1859, I had not learned to dread being a giant. I revelled in my bigger responsibilities. Height was my religion *and* my politics for I believed that if everyone was tall like me, nobody would feel unimportant, or unhappy. Doh—re—me! I warm up my voice and smile benevolently through my peep-hole. There's a commotion about my knees: Janette, a stout child, with strong, burly arms, is begging to be relieved from her scything chores. Sol—fa! I stare enthusiastically at the bushy glens and throw back my head so that my magic solo spills down past the neat clapboard farms and meandering rivers and out to the tropical warmth of the Atlantic Gulf Stream. If I sing hard enough, little Janette will grow!

I'm often asking the folk here, will you dance up, and can you rise higher; but then each one of you answers that I'm foolish to give my power to you.

I give my power to you, and I can't deny it. It's not a love of wealth, or ambition, but a love that grew in me when I was a child, and it will never wither until you leap higher.

"Listen to Annie," Janette whines. "A fine help she is! While the rest of us have to sweat like pigs, she sings songs indoors—decked out like a queen."

"Hold your tongue or I'll give you a tanning, Jannie," Poppa says.

"Anna is tall and has to be dressed right or she looks poorly," Momma adds. "Besides Jannie, you're a fine strapping girl and Anna is a frail lass who canna do such labour."

Frail? Surely not I, the INFANT GIANTESS! Momma's worry over my health makes me more determined to be useful. Doh—re—me!

Now the power of the little people streams through my veins until I am dizzy with fatigue. It requires a terrible energy to make things grow but what do I care if I deplete myself? Dance to the spruce tips, you gravity beaters!

I warble full voice as my brothers and sisters stumble out of our shanty, chased by a cursing Poppa. They swing hand scythes onto their shoulders and Janette looks up at me, sticks out her tongue.

My solo wavers. Then my kin trudge dispiritedly off down to the groundhog meadow until their bodies are no bigger than insects' with peevish bee-sized heads.

Their voices make an angry hum as their insect whorl moves up and down the field. Suddenly, a cloud of dust appears on the dirt track running past the shanty. Hubert, in his donkey cart. I groan. Not Hubert! I've grown to dislike the dwarf because his daily visits embarrass me. Momma says he means no harm; he's being friendly as I'm the only girl near his age on the outskirts of New Annan. Nevertheless, his interest is humiliating as it draws attention to my over-sized femininity. I wish to find a male taller than myself.

Down below, the insect bodies mob Hubert's cart and I pray the dwarf is not coming to visit. Then the swarm breaks into a column which descends again to the meadow while the dirt cloud draws closer and closer to the shanty. Doh—doh—doh! My solo quavers as Hubert scrambles up the slope. A moment later, he is a ripple in my crinoline as he enters our home, stealing to the hearth where Momma is sewing. I hear the pitty-pat sound of the dwarf's tiny fists clapping time to my tune and stop singing.

"Encore, Annie, encore," Hubert squeaks.

"I have to pay somebody a call," I say sullenly.

"Again?" Hubert asks.

I duck quickly out our door, avoiding Momma's dark look. "Nobody who is decent dislikes somebody who is small!" she calls after me. Outdoors, I toss my auburn ringlets and suck in my tummy, looking about for the boy giant I pretend lives in the Cobequids. For a moment, I think I see his huge, watchful countenance smiling shyly at me through clumps of cedar: a vegetable love budding in the timber just for me. Of course, he's far too shy to step out of the woods to meet me. Instead, he trails after me behind the silhouette of evergreens and fills the mountain air with a sigh of longing.

In the spring of my fourteenth year, Hubert is still a daily visitor. The nineteen-year-old dwarf either sits like a dog by the hearth while I sing, or he runs about my skirts, calling up to me to see if I will play whist. He uses his old birchbark ledger to record our scores, and likes to repeat the word "well" on a C high note seven times as he flips through his notebook, surveying old card-game

30

victories. He makes the same noise when he measures Momma's yarn. Momma hands him the ball of wool and he jumps eagerly onto our plank table and seizes my hand which has a one-foot span. I stand, looking unhappily out my peep-hole while at my waist Hubert stretches the wool back and forth across my spread fingers, repeating "Well-well-well-well-well-well-well!" on a C high note until I want to knock the pest off his perch.

On a March afternoon in 1860, I left Hubert and Momma to tally the yarn by themselves. An equinoctial gale had washed the snow on the mountain into ruts so the caramel shanks of our dead pastures were dappled a dirty grey. The air had cooled and icicles hung clanking from the underbrush.

I was on my way to the spruce grove. It was a small clearing screened by evergreen which my family used as a lavatory so Poppa could collect our wastes in the spring and spread the nitrogen-rich fertilizer on his crops. In the middle of the glen was a huge, moss-covered log after which the ground dropped away into a swampy pool. In its mysterious depths lay the family cesspool. That afternoon, the pool beyond the log had frozen into a darkly glossy surface as large as a beaver's pond. I went about my business, standing up so the urine avoided my petticoats.

Suddenly, I felt compelled to turn and stare behind me at the shore of the frozen pool where maroon- and slate-coloured oak leaves lay in serried patterns. There I spied a fat, roan dropping steaming in the freezing wind. I glanced about the clearing. Was a wolf or some fearsome animal nearby? My throat constricted in fright. Don't be addle-pated, Annie! What woodland beast can injure a being of your size? I began to stride away from the pool with trembling limbs. My breath turned into a cloud of mist about my head.

Just past the stand of spruce, where the trees' branches interlocked, I noticed another ice cloud issuing from under a lower bough. I cautiously pulled away the prickly branch. Hubert looked up at me.

"So ye were not fibbing this time!" The dwarf began to quake with laughter at the sight of my startled face.

"I reckoned such was an anatomical impossibility!"

"Begging your pardon?"

31

Hubert rushed with a sprightly leprechaun leap to the incline and stood at the top, just ahead of the long, yellow stain left by me on the icy bank. With mittened hands, he made a showy gesture that I took to be the lifting of an imaginary crinoline. Then he bent his knees and haughtily thrust out his posterior. His wrinkled head swivelled my way and he blinked at me a look of pious concentration.

So Hubert saw me! I tittered nervously and the dwarf's powder-blue eyes smouldered beneath his wrinkled brow.

"Do you know what a boundless universe lies inside you, Anna?" he demanded.

I said nothing as I was anxious not to betray my ignorance. I knew nothing about my birth canal and other passages although, at night, I often stroked the silken bulb of flesh between my thighs until it was the size of my big toe and I thought the Cobequids would split apart and my sleeping family leap from their beds, shrieking with fear over my noises of pleasure. Some weeks before, Momma had surprised me as I rubbed myself and she had rubbed out my mouth with oatmeal soap. She told me my "sin" cheapened the love of men and women, and wouldn't explain further. I'd been eager to learn more and now here stood Hubert, promising to end my fourteen-year-old desperation. So I shook my head, putting aside my prejudice against short men.

"No? Silly Anna! We mortals have an unknown terra firma within, with many roads and rivers twisting up and down in fanciful routes.

"In the ordinary being, some of these waterways can unravel to python lengths of twenty feet. Fancy the length of your royal river—the alimentary canal, of course! A neutral head channel unlike, uh . . . other highways I could mention."

Hubert winked in a display of male cockiness.

"Oh, Annie, let me sketch for you your spill channels, the short, wide head chute of the duodenum, the ropey coils of the small intestine, and the shadowy five-foot sluice of the large intestine with its blind pouches and narrow, worm-like tubes. Still better Anna, why not measure? If I go first, will you?"

Before I could reply, Hubert began to strip a long willow branch of its suckers until he had peeled it smooth. He tried to reckon its length with his childish fingers and then grabbed my hand and calculated it as sixteen inches. Then he jumped up onto the family log, turned his back to me, and dropped his baggy limb-shrouders. I gazed in a clinical fashion at his short arms, struggling to reach round to clasp and part the fuzzy skin of his buttocks. And, feeling deeply superior to Hubert for presenting his defenceless part to me, I lifted up my hand and quickly propelled the twig into his wizened opening.

Hubert yelled in protest and I extracted the willow. Hubert nimbly quantified the end section of his alimentary canal with his hands.

"Seven inches, Annie," he croaked. "Your turn."

"Nana-nana-nana! I fooled you because I'm not going to do it."

Hubert's little mouth fell open and his enormous brow furrowed in surprise.

"You promised, Annie," he said stubbornly. "You promised."

I shook my head and he stamped his foot on the icy ground.

"Cheater! Annie—the Indian giver!"

I giggled at his childishness and he began to weep. I should have left the grove then, but the sight of the unhappy dwarf made me feel pity. His trousers bagged about his knobby ankles so I saw for the first time his stubby little organ. His head was collapsed on his chest and tears collected in the wrinkles around his eyes. I also felt guilt. I had promised, hadn't I? Ah, what a burden it is to be a giantess who keeps her word!

"All right, then. Measure," I said crossly and looked away to avoid seeing Hubert strip a fresh willow with a look of joy on his arresting, adult face. When he crawled under my skirt and probed my hindquarters, I flinched but did not cry out. Then my skin closed like water over the wooden stem and from below came Hubert's faint cry of "Well-well-well" on high C. Hubert removed the twig and scrambled out. "Twenty-two inches," he said after calculating its length. Then he looked pleadingly at me.

"Anna, will you let me measure the other highway uncurling in your great physique?"

"What highway?" I replied.

"Wait and I'll show you," Hubert said. He ran to a sumac and chose the longest in a row of icicles hanging from a bough. Hubert grasped my hand and measured the icicle—an irradiant tooth, twice the twig's length, and flowing in frozen ripples to a small ball at its tip. "Seventeen inches," Hubert squealed and ducked under my skirt. (To this day, I do not know why he picked such an unromantic yardstick, nor why my curiosity made me forget the fate of howling schoolmates, who, for a dare, left crinkled portions of tongue on the metal runners of our teacher's sleigh. I put it down to the fact that all big people are slow to react while dwarfs are far too quick.)

Hubert inserted the icicle and sent me lumbering crazily about the grove. The sting of pain took away my breath; I lurched and stumbled like a bear through the underbrush and tears rained down my cheeks. Ah, how pierced I felt! How exposed, and by a measure-mad dwarf, no less!

Hubert popped up in my path screaming for me to stop so he could undo his bungle.

"Do you want to tear out my innards?" I shouted. "Don't you touch the icicle. I don't want to be kilt by one of your measuring games!"

Angrily, I reached down and knocked Hubert over. He fell like a toddler over the log and crashed through the thin ice of the swampy pool. I did not wait to see if he drowned, and hurried back to the shanty as best I could, sobbing over the hurt in my private parts.

Pain intermingled with waves of voluptuous feeling. My senses were confounded; I couldn't tell if I was hot *there* or cold, nor could I discern pain from pleasure. The alternating sensations thrilled and frightened me but as I reached the shanty, the sensations faded altogether and I realized the icicle had melted into a puddle in my unspeakables.

I was uncharacteristically nervous-looking as I ducked inside and found my family at our board, spooning down mashed turnip with gusto. I refused Momma's upheld plate of food and folded myself down to my hemp cot to stare in distraction at the shanty ceiling.

"Feeling in low spirits, are you, Annabelle?" Poppa asked. "It's not like you to miss a feeding."

"Aye. You look worn with those hollow, white cheeks of yours." Momma smiled as she drank spruce tea from one of the cracked china cups she called "Grandmom's service."

"Growing pains, Alex. I reckon that's Anna's problem," Momma said.

For a month I lay in a weakened state, my feet lost beyond the edge of the cot, while Momma sent Janette on extra trips to the Mill Brook for water. But the mountain stream no longer satisfied my prodigious thirst and she purchased barley water for me in Tatamagouche as a treat. It was a pleasant, fizzy stimulant; one flagon a day eased my pain and made it possible for me to rise from my cot.

However, Hubert's icicle had not only ruptured my maidenhead; it had punctured my belief in myself as a magic being. I was human and vulnerable—a female who, like every other female, could be penetrated in a way that no man could. In the summer, my strength returned, and I staggered back to my peep-hole but I did not sing. I stared down at my family scything the groundhog meadow. I still felt responsible for my family of normals but I knew now that I could not make them grow or Poppa's vegetables either—no matter what I did.

CHAPTER SIX

Mount McAskill

I was fifteen when I again met the CAPE BRETON GIANT, Angus McAskill. Momma and I visited him at his store in Englishtown, Nova Scotia. She wanted McAskill's advice on offers Barnum had made us through an agent, the Quaker gentleman. We found ourselves at a wooden building on the edge of town where the hill sloped down to St. Ann's Bay. A huge stool made from a 140-gallon molasses puncheon stood by a door twice the height of a normal shop entranceway. A passerby announced its dimensions (nine feet!) and said the shop owner normally sat on the stool beside the door and greeted those entering his well-stocked establishment. Through the shop window, we saw every kind of staple and fancy good—from sugar and teapots to ribands for glazed hats.

That morning, in mid-August 1861, the merchant was out with the salmon fleet, bringing in the morning catch. We set off to the shore and were rewarded by the sight of a man down towards the head of the bay, carrying a fishing dinghy up the beach like a sack of flour. Momma shouted and I waved my parasol. The figure looked in our direction. Momma called again: "Mr. McAskill?" In the morning haze, it was impossible to tell if he heard. We began to advance in his direction, but the closer we came to the beached dinghy, the farther his form receded into the distance. Finally, it disappeared in the wriggling waves of heat.

I spotted his tracks and, on reflex, set my boot down beside them. His prints were wider and three inches longer. "I told you Annie, he's a big one," Momma said. The space between each pair of giant prints lengthened as they moved away towards the bush.

"Looks like he took off at a run when he saw us," Momma said. She sighed despairingly and walked back to the shop. Momma didn't know what to do. She didn't want to send me to Barnum, nor did she want to take me to the sideshow again that year. She had started to show me at provincial fairs the year before and I enjoyed spieling to the farmers on my overturned tub. If I was paid to perform, I found I did not suffer embarrassment. There is a side to every kind of work that asks you to feel like a worm and the ability to endure this demand is why you are paid in the first place.

I'd even grown accustomed to the measuring, and felt a little thrill of superiority when Hubert's shrill voice announced: "longest finger—five and three-quarter inches! wrist—nine inches round! from wrist to shoulder—five and three quarter feet! height—eight feet!"

I barely tolerated Hubert who acted as if he had special rights to my friendship since he had taken my virginity with an icicle. Sometimes, at the end of the spiel, the dwarf hissed, so the audience couldn't hear: "birth canal—seventeen inches—the longest in history!" Then I wept in private, ashamed of the indelicacy of my monster opening. In truth, I was ashamed of my entire body, even my head, which I considered too tiny. "Pinhead," I called myself in disgust. But there was nothing humiliating enough that I could say to mock my poor, over-grown vagina.

Yet the entertainer in me enjoyed displaying my astounding features. And I often improvised by taking the tape from Hubert and measuring my own waist and then calling out for a lady in the crowd to wrap the tape around hers. Unless a female is adipose, my waist measurement goes around her three times.

My parent managed the business side of our tour very well. She negotiated with fair owners and struck bargains with silhouette-makers who pestered us with requests to sketch me. (They had to pay a pound; for they used these drawings to advertise their skills.) Nor did Momma mind attending Hubert and me. When the dwarf had insomnia, she rocked him to sleep as if he were a colicky infant. And she often slept on the floor of an inn while I lay across three beds which the innkeeper tied up for me like a log-boom.

It was the moral strain that tired my parent. Momma agreed with the clergy who said the fairs encouraged licentious behaviour and she took her duty of protecting me from the vulgar populace quite earnestly.

When the manager blew his whistle and I hustled onto my tub in front of the sideshow tent, Momma's tense little figure darted into the shadows of the canteen tent next door. There she waited, ready to attack any spectators who took liberties with me. Their assaults were a hazard. Following a win at a livestock show, the farmers celebrated with "shrub"—an odious rum and aniseed cocktail—and then circled round to test for human skin behind my skirts, or wager on my gender. (The uneducated often doubt a woman can attain my size.)

I wore extra petticoats to catch the pins and fishhooks, but the heavy garments meant I couldn't move quickly if someone invaded my performance space. At least the gowns softened sudden kicks to my shins.

Often a tipsy farmer tried to pinch my limbs before Hubert finished introducing me to the crowd of adults and children at my feet.

"Dear Nova Scotians! The INFANT GIANTESS is happy to celebrate with you the harvest season...!"

The moment the farmer's hand reached for me, Momma rushed out from under the canopy of the nearby tent. She brandished my parasol, which was longer than a blunderbuss, in her little hand. I heard a howl, and Hubert picked up his narrative thread:

"Yes! The giantess finds it exhilarating to be with her own folk when, throughout the province, Dame Nature is going joyfully to the reaper!"

Momma dressed my bruised shins with cold cream and rose-water and asked God for a sign she was doing right. To keep up my strength, she prepared homemade bisques. The soups were made of gulls' eggs bought from a friendly old fortune teller who put on a red cap and sold fish when business was slow. Momma spoon-fed me because I was too tired to feed myself and muttered: "Maybe I should let Barnum have you. Maybe he wouldn't botch the job like your old mother."

Momma had sworn only Maritime folk would be my audience: She was against loud-mouthed Yankee braggarts having a peep at me. Barnum's agent had made two visits and each time Momma had slammed the door in his face.

Meanwhile, Barnum's showplace, the American Museum, continued to be popular. We saw the newspaper sketches that showed

38

crowds lining up in front of the museum. Its front wall displayed a huge mural known as the "Moral Spectacular Drama," which my poor parents thought represented the interior of Barnum's building until they realized it described a scenario of Hell. In it, ghastly demons scrambled out of coal-pits only to vault off the red-hot sides of the inferno into the pits below. How could this gaudy showplace be any safer than the sideshow with its jeering crowds?

But I did not hold it against Barnum that he was a Yankee. I suspected he held the answer to my search for a way to put my size to best use so I was unusually vivacious the next time his Quaker agent appeared. Momma had brewed him spruce tea in her hearth pot and listened suspiciously while he said a prayer of gratitude for the fertility of my parents and spoke on the moral probity of Barnum and his museum. I had sung "Take Me Back to the Land Where I First Saw the Light" twice because the agent claimed to admire the dear old song and my loud singing caused Momma to regard me thoughtfully.

Meanwhile, the early signs of autumn—the goldenrod ripening by the roadside, even the days of wine-and-vinegar sea winds which she loved so well—had made Momma despondent. One morning Hubert had read us a write-up in the *Nova Scotian* that made Momma remember Angus McAskill and so together she and I had set out to ask his opinion. Momma had been sunk in a mood of melancholy when we boarded the sailboat to St. Ann's. She had listlessly answered inquiries from other passengers about our destination. "Annie and I are travelling on a business matter," Momma had replied, looking sadly at me as I sat stretched out on the floor of the vessel among the knees of the other passengers. I had smiled at them, happy to have a travel adventure, and avoided Momma's face, brooding under her poke bonnet.

Half-way back to Englishtown, after the disappointment of losing Angus, Momma signalled for us to sit down on the beach. She took off her bonnet and waved the flies from my perspiring cheeks. We were weary from walking in the summer heat with our heavy garments and so sat for a while listening to the slap of waves along the shore. Suddenly, Momma pointed to a meadow behind us.

I saw a tall form, slowly picking its way around the stones and cow patties. A cherry pipe as large as a mallet smoked from its mouth. It was Angus. He had doubled back towards Englishtown through the woods.

Momma leapt to her feet.

"Don't you remember us, McAskill?" she shouted.

He turned slowly, as if in some pain, and shaded his eyes with a hand.

"The INFANT GIANTESS," Momma continued to yell. "Barnum wants her!"

McAskill began to move quickly in our direction. "Not that blackguard!" his hollow, musical voice came back.

"You don't approve?" Momma asked.

"Nothing is worth going to the city for, but least of all P.T. Ballyhoo," the voice said.

The bashful giant joined us and shook hands, advising us to squeeze lightly on account of his rheumatism. Then, winking at me, he threw back his black head and started to recite in Gaelic:

A MANIFESTO FROM THE MARITIME MARVEL

You won't catch Angus in the BIG CITY.
There's no place under the sun today where I would rather be
than on the slopes of the bay among a bunch of fishermen. I saw a
wonder today as I sailed on the sea, an ox without hair, without
flesh, dragging grass from the black earth. It's the backwoods I
give my affection to, where we who work the land and the sea are
the sustainers of life. The soot-faced farmers and the fishers with
crinkled palms, the hardy, handsome, manly lads. There's many a
delightful person has been spoiled by the BIG CITY.

Give this buckeroo the backwoods and the sheep with the
crooked horn (all sheep have milk, this one has a gallon).
Did Finn m'Cool need the BIG CITY?
I won't answer to the degenerate lords in the BIG CITY.
I'll tear the tyrannous forest up by the roots first.
I LIVE IN THE BUSH: I LOVE IT.

Momma and I eyed each other.

The giant coughed in embarrassment behind a white, freckled hand.

"Excuse me for sounding off ladies," he said. "Maybe you don't like poetry."

"Oh, Anna has literary tendencies," Momma said. "But you're wasting your words on me. I've come to find out about Barnum."

"Is he offering your daughter the life of a gentlewoman?" Angus asked. He chuckled. "That's the line I heard. The life of a gentleman. I have a swallowtail coat and a beaver hat to prove it."

He chuckled again and took us to his shop where he was distracted by a gaggle of customers. They stared at us and made whispered comments while our host measured out one pound of tea in his cupped hand. Momma studied his extravagance wonderingly. There was no doubt his customer was getting more than if he'd weighed it on the scale. When his last shopper departed, Angus made us a pot of the costly stimulant. Then he poured some rum into his "tub"—a vessel that held three glasses' worth—and drinking deeply to lessen his reserve, began to relate the narrative Momma and I had come to hear in the droll and satiric manner of the Highland bards who used to banter at a ceilidh (or gathering) in New Annan. There is nobody who can ridicule faster or more vehemently than a Scot and Angus was no exception.

CHAPTER SEVEN

Angus in New York

"I can't say I, Angus McAskill, worked for Barnum. I was educated at his institute of higher ballyhoo against my better intentions.

"For starters, the old reprobate refused to exhibit me in the lecture hall on the American Museum's third floor with the other curiosities. He wanted me to have more schooling before I joined the freaks who pontificated on the dully varnished theatre parquet. Which is where he'll put a nicely mannered girl like you, Anna, if your mother is witless enough to accept the showman's offer.

"In vain, my agent, Noah Fitfield, pressed to have me moved to the theosophical third. Noah owned a Yarmouth inn, but he was a spiritless yea-sayer and did nothing to change my dean's mind. Angus was not to have a quick graduation. Why, I was meant to be edified by daily exposure to the museum's 60,000 educational displays.

"Weren't they enough to provoke the brain of a yokel from Cape Breton? From Samuel Hurd, Barnum's son-in-law and underling, Fitfield prised the reason behind my program of studies. The old Bamboozleem was too busy to instruct me in person. I was on ice like a fresh squid until he'd be finished with his high-culture tour of the singer Jenny Lind. The Swedish swan was art; I, Angus, a biology lesson."

"What happened to Dunseith?" Momma interrupted. She wrinkled her nose. The smell of his rum evoked memories of shrub cocktails.

"We had a fight. So I hitched up with Fitfield, which was a serious mistake. Fitfield thought the way to handle Barnum was to hold him off and let him pound. That's fine if you don't mind ending up like a rock washed by the sea—I mean like sand! Only I wasn't willing to receive the higher truths Americans are eager to bestow on foreign laggards like me.

"And my lessons from Professor Humbug were few. The first was his personal tour of the American Museum, a five-storey building on New York's Broadway. We began with the murky basement aquariums and steam boilers, and moved up to the ground floor. What a sombre cave of learning I discovered in its hand-painted panoramas, its human and animal displays, and its illuminating ticket booth! Climbing to the second, we met Ned, the LEARNED SEAL, and drank in the white whales before Barnum ushered us past a room of wax figures into a honey-comb of offices ruled over by Samuel Hurd. There I saw Barnum's own display case with his writing desk and its special cubbyhole for correspondence with the showman's FAMOUS MIDGET, Tom Thumb.

"How could I learn to appreciate his scholarly lore? Could I start to comprehend the educational materials my master had crammed behind one pane of glass? In Case 794, on the third floor, beyond a cabinet of mangy toucans and stuffed monkeys, I was stunned to find: '...ball of hair, from the stomach of a sow; Indian collar, composed of grizzly bear claws; petrified piece of pork recovered from the water after sixty years; fragment of the first canal boat to reach the United States of America; bill of swordfish piercing the side of a ship; Algerian boarding pike; African pocketbook; Chinese pillow; wrought metal Mexican stirrup. . . . '

"My instructor's cheerful voice barked at my elbow—'However uncouth these unsightly attempts at sculpture appear, Angus,' Barnum said, 'They are highly revered by millions of ignorant Heathens.'

"On the fourth floor, we paused to admire a stubby lacrosse stick Barnum told us had killed Captain Cook. Among the cases of pebbles (his mineral and geological specimens), Fitfield and I spotted the GREAT MODEL OF NIAGARA FALLS. Water from a barrel gushed over an eighteen-inch replica—the same water again and again, directed in its flow by one wheezing little motor.

"Then up we went, in that tower of learning, to the Glorious Fifth. Here, with the world of knowledge beneath our feet, Fitfield and I beheld the HAPPY FAMILY, a vast cage in which one owl, two pigeons, some guinea pigs, a nest of rats, one basset hound, and two kittens co-existed.

"Across from their cage was an awe-inspiring prehistoric relic, the petrified horse and rider. A life-size boa was wound around the horse and in the act of striking the rider. Nearby a flock of gold pigeons picked ett off the gallery floor.

"Beside a case of live boa constrictors, I saw a four-foot papier-mâché volcano ringed with the stars and stripes. I recognized this to be my resting place by its emblem: SEE THE CANADIAN ALPS AND TOUR MOUNT MC ASKILL.

"At once, Barnum began a lecture on the duty every American has to master rugged environments. My blood jumped. One beat behind, Fitfield's noggin began to bob in agreement. The showman talked so loose and fast, in just five minutes I swear he bragged about his wife Charity's pumpkin pie; confided as to how he used to drink a daily bottle of champagne during lunch before he became a temperance reformer; and implied that Fitfield failed to realize my potential.

"'A big man needs a big build-up, isn't that a fact, Angus?' Barnum asked. Fitfield's head nodded yes in ever-widening arcs.

"'What I did for midgets, I can do for an unknown like Angus. By the time I'm through, the giant's cheeks will be rubbed raw from ladies' kisses.'

"Then Barnum shoved a paper into my hand and thanked Fitfield for going along like a gentleman. Immediately, I heard an explosion of vulgar noises at the far end of the room. The racket kept up as Barnum and my agent strolled towards the exit. Fitfield's nodding pate was threatening to depart from his collar-bone when Barnum suddenly stopped by a cage and hissed: 'Shut up, Zip, or I'll dock your salary.' The monkey screwed its black, hairy face up at the receding Barnum and launched into a soft 'Yuk Yuk' noise. On its barred cage, I read: THE WHAT IS IT, NAMED BY LITERARY GENIUS CHARLES DICKENS.

"It fell silent under my scrutiny so I walked away to examine the HAPPY FAMILY. As I stared at the sleeping animals, a deep pleasant voice sounded in my ear: 'Laudanum, friend. The old geezer has them on laudanum.' I whirled around and found the WHAT IS IT standing on my alp. He chattered, then bounced on the shaky perch. I moved towards him and he climbed up the wall, shrieking with fear.

44

"Zip did not reveal his true self again until a week went by—one week with a packed gallery that giggled continuously at me, striking poses on my heights. The WHAT IS IT was noisy with delight at our large audience, but after a few days his tone changed to irritation. Soon the Negro dwarf was upsetting the ladies with his vulgar 'Yuk Yuk' sounds. One fainted; several others complained; and Hurd came up to levy a fine of a week's salary on Zip for undermining customer relations.

"The next morning, when I arrived in my cutaway coat with a velvet collar, a white brocade vest, and a Highland kilt—all thanks to Barnum—a sleepy Zip swung himself out of his cage and walked over to my exhibit. He offered up a smudge of powder on his yellowy palm. 'To get through the day, Angus.' Again, his melliflu-ous voice.

"It wasn't right, and I didn't think the day Fitfield and I sailed into New York (me asleep in the hold) that I'd get into a smuggling ring. Mother still has no idea her son would do such a thing. But the twenties are a stupid time of life. I wish I could have crammed all the liquor-swilling, fancy parties, women, and wild deeds into two weeks and had done with them instead of all that tomfoolery leading me by the nose for a decade. Well, ten years ago I needed more education, didn't I?

"So I took the opium from my little black friend and ended up selling it under P.T.'s bulb nose. Zip fitted it into my act. He made a horrible ruckus, communicating to me with the forbidden 'Yuk Yuk' noise when our buyer entered the gallery. The crowds saw a GIANT AT WORK, grunting through a series of exercises that required no more effort than it took to lift Zip. Meanwhile, the powder was taped to my outside thigh. The buyer dared me to lift my kilt, and I let the crowd egg me on until he lifted my plaid and showed my full-grown cod.

"A few ladies fainted and the gentlemen were agog so nobody spotted our transaction. Even better, Hurd appeared on the Fifth to say Barnum was writing the dare into my handbills. The old deceiver sent me up one of his publicity bills with a notation that said: 'The art in humbug is creating a mystery your audience will enjoy solving, but there's no humbug about what you've got under your dress. P.T.B.'

45

"Eventually Zip mentioned the excitement my privates aroused and suggested we go elsewhere to manufacture carnival atmospheres. Our work day finished by eight and down we went to the grog shops by the wharf where sailors and bowery bums jigged to fiddles and tambourines. Zip said it would be better if I didn't talk so in we walked, Zip drawing immediate attention to my shoulder with his cigar-eating act.

"Then he asked the band to strike up 'The Blue Bells of Scotland' and invited the audience to bet on the size of my equipment. I stood, my trap shut, on a table, usually two planks strung across wood sawhorses. Zip leapt about, collecting slips of paper tossed on the sawdust floor. When the tallies were in, he whispered a word to a dolly-mop who was glad to disappear under my kilt and emerge with myself."

Momma frowned and pursed her lips at frightening angles, but Angus failed to notice. He stumbled to his feet and groaned about rheumatism. Then he fetched another tub of rum and resumed his history.

"The house bets fell short because who in the big city knows a maritime cod is three feet at maturity? Zip measured and the sailors cheered and threw coins for him to catch in his mouth; the giggling dolly-mops blew kisses and raised their colourful short dresses and we all hoisted a shot of oak juice. For the knuckleheads who saw me as the end of physical limits, I used to play jolly strongman. I'd rap a puncheon like this one and make the bung fly out, or lift it with my baby finger until it reached the level of my face and then I'd write my name in the air.

"When the mood turned ugly, Zip slipped on a pair of wings and went into his famous theatre role, the GNOME FLY. Zip was a stand-in for the great minuscule actor of the Bowery, Hervio Nano. And when Zip's wings oscillated upside down from the ceiling, the crowd forgot about fighting. It was incredible how the little bugger could hang on; his muscles were bigger than you'd think. Zip had a few other tricks I don't know if I should mention in front of ladies."

"Anna's tall for her age, but she is just fifteen," Momma said sternly. She stared at his tub which he was once more replenishing.

"She sure looks older," Angus said. "And handsome too."

"What about Barnum?" Momma asked.

46

Angus glanced my way, then his eyes slid off evasively. He put his tub down and picked up his story:

"Barnum gave me—Anna will know what I mean—what is called in the Maritime schools, a 'lesson of order.' I had a ladyfriend—you don't mind if I mention her, Mrs. Swan—who worked down on the third. Nobody at the American Museum could resist her sad-eyed shrugs, her sighs that sent clouds scudding over the horizon. . . . People ·would do anything to make Aama laugh. Me and Zip included.

"I used to light my pipe from a street lamp to coax a happy look from her great melancholy eyes. When she smiled, it was like a shaft of light piercing the night cloud and burning up the bay.

"One night, after hours, Zip and I were feeding the boas for Aama's amusement. I had the female, Hecuba, coiled about my chest; Zip held a squawking gold pigeon—Hecuba's dinner—in his hand. O, we were a writhing mass of laudanum lovelies! Aama couldn't help but grin at me and my female partner—jiggling towards Zip who was smeared yellow from the pigeon's gold dye. Jesus! Hecuba was about to gobble the pigeon right out of Zip's hand—well, I couldn't stomach seeing that poor bird go into the snake's chops, so I cuffed Zip out of her way.

"Zip fell quivering to the floor as a housefly will buzz and keel over in spring weather. The pigeon escaped so Hecuba veered towards the cage where the HAPPY FAMILY slept among withered shrubs.

"Aama's giggles caught me by surprise. I stopped Hecuba's advance and held her in my arms where she nestled like a harmless reptile. Aama laughed harder: She refused to stop although I begged her to consider Zip's condition. His gold-dusted eyes and mouth were open, producing a startling effect. Zip resembled in his coma—the GNOME FLY. I put Hecuba back in her cage and cradled Zip in my arms. And who has torn the gnome's wings? I thought bitterly. Aama hid her mouth behind spread fingers, and her broad shoulders jiggled and shook. She kept up the merriment until we arrived at a doctor's office where a nurse gave her a sleeping potion. So she was snoring loudly when the medico came out and asked me to notify the parents of the death of their son, Henry William 'Zip' Johnson.

47

"Oh, how could I endure the Glorious Fifth without my Zip? He was replaced by the FAT BOY, a repulsive piece of work whose chubby bow lips were stained from his habit of swigging cherry syrup."

"And Barnum?" Momma persisted.

A tear rolled down Angus' freckled cheek.

"The professor of human truths had Zip stuffed and mounted on a dais among the wax figures of Napoleon and Queen Victoria. But Zip's deification was only part of the lesson. My dean erected a sign on my mountain: ANGUS MCASKILL KILT THE GNOME FLY AT ONE STROKE!

"I also had a garnishee on my wages to pay for the two years of earnings Zip had promised in his contract, and my own contract was extended for two years, no help to Fitfield's spineless yea-saying. 'Only twenty-four months, think of it that way, lad,' the rolling domehead said when he showed me the document that signed me up for more courses at ballyhoo college.

"Twenty-four months! Who can blame me if I thought I had become educated enough, and stowed away on a schooner for Truro? The day we sailed into St. Ann's I put on my kilt and beaver hat and wept to think how lucky I was to get back to the land I first came to as a boy, with fourteen fiddlers playing on the deck. People are tricked by the notion you have to go to the Big City to make a success. The casual life in St. Ann's is what I like and if I could put a fence around my shop and let the world live on at its own pace, I'd do it. You'll learn: The best cure for the city is the country."

I cleared my throat. "What about Aama?" I asked.

"Hallo. She's talking to me."

"What happened to Aama?"

Angus looked boldly into my eyes, and then away.

"I heard she went back to Cuba to tend her dying mother. St. Ann's might not have been the best place for a Negro giantess and I didn't want Aama blaming me if things didn't work out."

CHAPTER EIGHT

Annie at Teachers' College

Momma took Angus at his word and came up with a new plan: teachers' college in Truro, Nova Scotia. I stayed with my Aunt Mary and Uncle Ray Johnson in a clapboard bungalow where I was subject to a frequent nightmare. It began with the ironstone pitcher on my bureau. As I grew drowsy, its shape melted into the hawk-eyed countenance of Alexander Forrester, principal of Truro Normal School.

The man-jug in my dream stood at the entrance to the college as sixty-five students filed into the examination hall looking for seats among the rows of oak desks. When I walked in, I realized the man-jug was studying me with a horrified expression. It scratched its head, rolled its eyes and then, with a hopeless shrug, suggested I find a seat. ONE TWO THREE! The examination bell clapped and all hands began to scratch in desperation. I stood back until I could no longer bear the tension. Then I took a little run with an optimistic hop and lowered myself onto a desk which splintered about my skirts like an oaken egg. As the students gathered to jeer, I lapsed into sleep.

Yes! The INFANT GIANTESS was experiencing the maggot side of the scholarly profession. Instead of the shrieking sideshow whistle, I had a bell. For a tub, I had a desk, and bands of ill-bred students had replaced the fair-goers. Here I am, returning to Aunt Mary's after class, after playing the worm in academic circles. I have on a gown out of *Mr. Godey's*, but in Truro's flat terrain the gown looks out of place. Too theatrical by half. Fifty yards behind me, a group of sneering young people imitate my walk and toss the occasional snowball at my lace-trimmed bonnet.

People in this little town follow anybody who looks different. Aunt Mary says a Negro sailor was chased through the streets because nobody in Truro had seen dark skin before. This does not comfort me. A trifle shy, I consider spieling as a way of diverting the crowd. I turn, lift my hand in a wave, smile engagingly. The group stops; one of the girls smirks. A stone pellet, packed in ice, flies past, and misses my rosy cheek by inches. "How's the weather up there, monster lass?" a boy calls in a sinister tone. I refuse to answer his unspeakable how-do-you-do. On impulse, I stick my tongue out at his scowling face, then stride as quickly as I can along the narrow cow path leading to Aunt Mary's frame house. My relationship with my audience has always been an uneven one. In Truro, I began to establish my professional attitude. No performer should expend energy for groups that offer neither pay nor applause. I wrote to Momma of my distaste for the life of a student and a letter returned, in Hubert's handwriting, encouraging me to continue my studies until the end of March.

"Dear Anna: As you know very well, a lady's conduct is at the mercy of critics when she is in a public place," the epistle scolded. "Her dress, carriage and walk are exposed and every passer-by will look at her if only for a glance to check for an unladylike action.

"Why don't you follow the example of Hubert Belcourt, your childhood friend, who is a pillar of respectability, striding in a stove-pipe hat to weddings at St. Paul's, taking Sunday sleigh rides along Basin Shore to a country inn? And by the way, how is the social whirl in Truro? Are you still punching holes in the winner's card during Aunt Mary's whist parties?"

The lecture didn't sound like Momma. I guessed it had been composed as a joke by Hubert who enjoyed adding sections to Momma's letters without her knowledge. My illiterate parent was an ideal dupe for Hubert who now worked as a clerk in a Halifax molasses business and did Momma's correspondence on his visits back to New Annan.

I shuddered to think what Momma would say if she read his first postscript, dated October 30, 1861:

"All the boys want to know how you measured up. I told them to take the word of Rabelais: one acre and two roods."

I was obliged to answer that ill-bred notation. My reply whistled off November 6 of the same year:

"I have no interest in old measurements so get lost you tiresome tidbit, you tot, you vestige, you pittance, you speck, you trifle, you drop in the ocean!''

More postscripts came from Hubert in Momma's letters (boldly promising to show me a way of love-making so our size didn't amount to a hill of beans). When I didn't respond Hubert flattered or threatened me in the adolescent style popular with male normals:

''November 23, 1861: Write, or I'll tell your mother you fell me on purpose that day in Tatamagouche. Not to mention how you pushed me in the beaver pond!''

''November 21, 1861: Guess you don't care my back has never been the same plus I got chilblains to show for my dip.''

''December 1, 1861: My back isn't so bad—only when I think about it. I got what was coming to me. Oh Anna, with your good looks, it don't matter what the rest of you is up to! My arms ached to catch you and hold you when you fell off the wagon!''

''December 10, 1861: Just a word! Your amorous Huey.''

''December 11, 1861: And I thought giantesses were different from other girls!''

''December 14, 1861: You can't do this to me you colossal cunt.''

''December 15, 1861: Did the elephant treat the mouse like this after the mouse took out its sliver?''

''January 10, 1862: Adieu Anniekins! I'll not forget your lilypads or the magnificence of your clitoral magnitude! Other women are just small potatoes to me now. Your H.''

More decorous letters came from Angus, who had started to romance with me through the mails. In Truro, I day-dreamed continually about his hollow voice, and the broad fingers that created his tiny, rheumatic script. Who could match him? He was my vegetable spirit budding in the timber and had the auspicious glamour of a romantic birthplace and heritage. From his missives, I learned the details of his early life in the Hebrides. Born of Highland stock on the island of Harris near Fingal's Cave, he was a crofter's son who, at the age of twelve, was so short he was considered a dwarf, and who grew in the New World into the TALLEST, STOUTEST, STRONGEST MAN to be entertained by Queen

51

Victoria at her palace. Alas! He was ideal except for his attachment to rural existence. I longed to escape the rough, puritanical life of crofters like my parents, while Angus kept a vigil on the shore of St. Ann's Bay for the old ways. I believe he hoped to stop the migrating flow to the city with his powers of concentration and his fidelity to the land.

The disparity in our attitudes shows up in old newspaper documents which I include. (A few testaments about my childhood appear later in the chapter.) Here are *Daily Portraits* drawn by an unknown reporter whose Canso journal, the *Maritime World*, went bankrupt before these could be printed. Galley proofs were sent us as a courtesy.

ANGUS MC ASKILL: A GIANT IN THE RETAIL BUSINESS

The day starts at 6 a.m. I wake like clockwork, before the salmon fleet goes out. Rheumatism makes it a wee hard getting started in the mornings—but it would be hard for me to rise no matter what the time was. In my bedroom over the shop, I eat a bowl of crowdie—the bilge Cape Bretoners call cereal—and watch the Bay. For me, the ocean is like a friend coming to meet me with a smile on its wrinkled face. It's by the shore I like to be, watching the ebb and flow, not at the rear of town where all you see is stumpy, crooked trees around a patch of clearing. Look here. A person can't explain it: it's just so nice.

The next part of the day I meet with the fishermen I am organizing into a commercial salmon fishery, or the women who card and weave wool for me to sell. The afternoon is more meetings at my mill. I built the little place I call home with my own hand. The mill I bought with profits from my tour of Lower Canada. All actors have to be entrepreneurs, whether it's their fancy or no. In the Dominion, many able-bodied performers don't understand the trick is to wear many hats.

I drink rum all day as a cure for headaches and nervous irritability. It provides nourishment as I'm not a big eater. A serving of blood sausage and another bowl of crowdie does me fine. I eat that on the *Christina*, a half-ton job named for the mother who raised me. Her nicest asset is the three rum puncheons I've had to stash in the bow to balance 400 lbs. of its skipper at her rudder.

I'm called Gille Mor by the fellows in St. Ann's. It means big boy. The buggers like to tease me. I don't know anywhere in the Cape that has a bigger group of jokers. One time we had a tug of war, the boys at one end of a dinghy and me in the other, and the boat broke in half. The best of the crew drop into the shop, for my generous dispensings and my songs.

I'm something of a verse-maker. I wrote a ditty about the St. Ann's potato famine in 1847 and am doing another on the wreck of the *Astrala*. Its corpses—248 of them—had to be buried before sunset on account of superstitions here. I'd never take my verses seriously though my mother thinks I'm the best in the Cape. I used to read her *Sighs from Hell* by John Bunyan, which is how I got started on poetry. Mother boosted the finer things and has no use for the mean parts of farm life. Like the day she cried to see me pulling a plough. I was trying to win a bet after our horse went lame. "A man's a man for all that," she said as she unhooked me.

In the evening, I sit around the shop and chew the fat. Then I go to bed. Every week I write a girl at teachers' college. We're courting. On Sunday, I read some psalms in the shop. My appearance in church kicks up too much fuss so I don't go to hear Rev. McIntosh do his damnedest.

Life in St. Ann's is good. More people would visit here if travel conditions improved. My only regret is that I have to control my temper. I know the bigger man has the bigger responsibility, but some days when a joker makes a crack about my appearance, I'd like to wipe the floor with him. That's my first thought. I guess it's not a very nice one.

ANNA SWAN, A GIANTESS,
TO BE AN ELEMENTARY SCHOOL TEACHER

I arise at 10 a.m. after my uncle has departed for his clothing store on the main street of Truro, N.S. My aunt is also out on shopping errands at that hour so I have the two-room cottage to myself. Then, wearily, I go about my morning toilet. It would be

53

uncharitable to complain merely because I have to put a horsehair couch at the end of my bed to support my feet. My relatives have lodged me at some expense out of family obligation.

I am one of twenty students accepted at the Model School in Truro. It is run by the Normal School whose principal is Dr. Forrester. Our fall semester began in November so the students could help their families with harvest. In my case, I was able to complete the sideshow circuit under my mother's guidance. I arrived here in a state of extreme exhaustion. I do not see the point of teachers' college when my interests lie in theatre. (Not that I dislike children.) However, my family and their advisers feel it is a more respectable living for a farm girl such as myself.

At 10:30 a.m., I trudge off to class, using a back alley to avoid crowds that like to follow me in Truro. From 11 a.m. to 3 p.m. I study reading, writing, grammar, geography, and arithmetic. The subjects are at the elementary level as Dr. Forrester is subjecting us to a thorough review before we take literature, mathematics, and philosophy in the spring.

I do my work at a desk which has been specially constructed for me, and is kept in the hall. It is Dr. Forrester's belief that the class will work more attentively if it doesn't have me to distract it. He has been very encouraging about my mental aptitude despite his constant worries over the Legislature's decision to discontinue the annual £100 grant. Following prayers last week, he took me aside to say how pleased he is at my progress with the piano. Dr. Forrester has arranged music lessons for me with a Mr. Fitch. Dr. Forrester lectures on chemistry and vegetable and animal physiology to the older students.

At 4 p.m. I leave school. It is my practice to take a long route through Victoria Park to avoid male students from the Normal School. The second day of our semester, six of them chased me down a residential street. Only when I ran off into the park and down one of its many footpaths was I able to elude my pursuers. Unfortunately, I tore my gown and my aunt was obliged to sew a piece of ruching over it. She said I must have provoked the students as a lady sets the tone of a gentleman's behaviour.

I used to read my correspondence before dinner but now I prefer to leave it until I am abed. My aunt is curious about who would write me such thick letters. She and my uncle are fond of teasing me on the subject of marriage.

"Anna's going to have a time finding one as big as herself, aye Ray?"

"A real pity the girl's so huge when her face is comely," my uncle says back.

I practise the scales before our meal on my aunt's piano. We eat at 5:30 p.m. This is the only time my aunt cooks. (At breakfast, I consume cold potatoes.)

The evenings find me in the parlour where I read the Bible or Charles Dickens out loud. My uncle slumbers by the woodstove, but Aunt Mary likes to listen as she repairs feather pillows or embroiders slip cases. I retire at 8:30 p.m. since my large person requires 13 to 14 hours sleep. If my day hasn't been rigorous, I might compose a missive for Angus McAskill (about my ambitions and hopes for the New York stage).

It's unlikely my dream will bear fruition. American entrepreneurs like Mr. P.T. Barnum will no longer exist because the civil war is bringing the democracy of the United States to an early grave. My mother says the war is God's punishment for the money-crazed Yankees. More likely it is the fault of the demon majority that overrules the minority that is virtuous. That is what Angus says and he has lived down there. He is an older giant with a worldly reputation. His parents are Scotch immigrants like my father, who says I could do worse than marry a giant like Angus, when Angus and I have so much in common.

My piano lessons, the glare of Reverend Forrester, the rude students, my melancholy evenings listening to the snores of Uncle Ray—all my grey town life finished in early February 1862. Angus brought news of the change, arriving in person to tell me Momma had decided to accept the third offer from Barnum's agent. Angus had heard about it from Hubert, whom he had seen in Halifax when he was in buying goods for his store in Englishtown. Momma had taken in four children who had been abandoned on the Cobequid Mountains, and there was now no financial alternative but Barnum who had promised Momma he would protect me from the unpleasant side of show business, which she felt she couldn't do. Angus was still opposed and came to Truro, hoping to talk me out of a career he thought undesirable for a lady.

I found his huge form lolling unhappily against a column at the Normal School entrance. His bulk menaced the pillar, yet Angus was unconcerned. His vast, white, man-in-the-moon face stared down at me in alarm, and I gazed back, pleased to find myself looking up to a man.

"You won't go will you, Anna?" he said. I smiled nervously.

"I wish to have a show business career, Angus," I said. "What else is a big person like me to do?"

"You've no brains if you think you can make a respectable living by being yourself! There are better things to do than dress up to give folks a laugh or stand still so some ignoramus can wind up and give you a swift one."

Angus did not say what the better things were, but I knew; a duty-bound life as Mrs. McAskill in the back waters of Cape Breton. I wanted Angus but I did not want his setting. I saw the problem with us clearly, yet I felt foolhardy. After all, where would I find another giant mate? Half the human race was already ineligible.

Angus frowned darkly as we began to stroll through the flat snow-bound streets. The giant wore a beaver hat and carried an old broadsword in a frayed silk sheath. This dress made him look like a refugee from the Battle of Culloden over a century before. I waited nervously for the pack of students behind us to hurl insults. Groups of them were flowing home under the leafless elms and pointing at us and laughing. Suddenly, St. Ann's Big Boy whirled about and carved the air in their direction with his enormous broadsword.

"Be gone, ye little buggers!" he yelled.

The students ran off and the giant reached down his freckled mitt to take my gloved hand.

"I'd sooner have my old claymore than a gimcrack like the Kentucky rifle," he chuckled. "Aye, Anna?" his hollow musical voice rumbled in my ear. "What's wrong with a hundred-year-old weapon?"

Suddenly, he stopped and gripped me on the shoulder with one huge, freckled mitt.

"Good lord, lass, I have to be alone with you. Could we go to some private spot?"

I thought of my Aunt Mary and Uncle Ray watching pop-eyed in their parlour as Angus and I talked, and suggested we try Victoria Park. It was known throughout the province for natural beauty spots but who would go there in the dead of winter? Who, that is, except a pair of thick-blooded Blue-nose lovers like Angus and myself?

We walked, puffing, to the park and stopped by a wishing-well whose bucket swung foolishly in the wintry breeze. A watery February sun hung over the forest of spruce. It was mid-afternoon and although the temperature was ten degrees Fahrenheit, the air was still mild enough for us to linger without getting frost-bite on our cheeks. Angus spread his plaidie on the snow and stood looking down at me. Our breath formed ice clouds between our faces.

"I reckon you know I didn't fetch you here to waste time gibble-gabbling," Angus said.

I looked up shyly at his deep-set blue eyes and just had time to notice a garden of freckles before his face eclipsed mine. On my skin, I felt a downy cheek as wide as my own. I shuddered and my large, booted foot swung up behind me in dainty self-satisfaction.

Of course, I knew that we were going to spoon. Our prudish Scots background made it difficult to speak frankly, but nonetheless Angus and I understood one another. In my case, I felt lucky my first time would be in the arms of a man like Angus. He was a worldly giant who had had carnal knowledge of a giantess before— his Cuban Aama—so I had no reason to fear that he, of all people, would laugh at my trunk-like pelvis topped off by a tiny pin-head, and my overwhelming vagina. Nevertheless, I was frightened and offered him up my secret world the way a barker lifts the tent flap on the mysteries of the sideshow.

Crooning softly to me, the giant lowered my large frame to the snow. I closed my eyes and imagined I heard it melt sizzlingly under our weight. Suddenly, Angus began to cover my neck with kisses in the same gluttonous way he wolfed down his bowls of crowdie. He was avaricious and his hands were clumsy as he fiddled with my privates somewhere far below our heads. When I felt his organ slip in, I was surprised at my lack of sensation. Why, it caused a feeling no stronger than the little ripple a pebble makes as it skips across a beaver pond. I blushed to think I had believed his story that it was three feet long. The fit was snug but not too much for my seventeen inches. A mere foot was my guess. And the diameter of a doorknob.

There were a few moments of moist thrusting as I waited for Angus to give me pleasure the way he might bring me a nosegay of flowers, then the giant moaned my name and lay still. Was that all? For a long time, I lay on the cold ground and stared in disbelief at his dark head now resting on my breast.

At fifteen, I didn't know that I was as much in charge of my sexual ecstasy as the man. I imagined it was something the male of the species did to the female and I did not connect it to the fumbling which Momma had surprised me at that night in the shanty. Had I known, I would have shown Angus how to rub me.

As it was, I could only watch speechless and surprised as a layer of baby-fine snow coated the huge form above me which showed no more signs of life than the white playground around us. The temperature had dropped and the sunset was an orange event when the giant finally propped himself up on an elbow and peered suspiciously down into my face.

"Was that the first time, lass?" he asked. I nodded. He grinned in relief. "It was for old Angus too."

"You were a virgin?" I gasped.

"Aye, lass. I've been saving myself for the likes of you."

"You are fooling with me, Angus McAskill."

"Not old Angus. Why would I let one of the New York dolly-mops sample my giant flesh just so she could brag to her friends?"

"What about your Cuban fiancée . . . ?"

"I'm not saying there weren't some who had a peep or two under my skirts, am I?" Angus grinned and I could see the gaps between each of his big teeth, like the cut teeth of the jack-o-lantern. "Now you'll have to marry me, Annie, and settle down to farm life."

I turned away so he wouldn't see how dismaying that prospect was to me. I wanted to be a show-biz personality—not a rural drudge—yet I felt scared to admit it was so. Angus would never understand an ambitious giantess like myself. He caught my chin in his hand and turned my head around so that I was forced to stare into those burning blue eyes. Then the giant threw back his head and bellowed:

"Aaaach! You'll go to New York! The old blackguard has had you under his spell from the start!"

He jumped up cursing and threw his claymore into the air. Immediately, we heard a crash and nine boys scrambled down from an oak and raced across the clearing. Angus roared again and that is when I saw a foot-long male hand reach out, pull up a pine by its roots and bat the intruders so they flew up in an arc high above Victoria Park's famous beauty spots. A second boom like a backed-up cannon went off behind my back and a stand of staunch Nova Scotia spruce lay flat from one slice of the giant's broadsword. Angus swore as six more boys ran off.

I rose and ran over to soothe Angus, but the giant waved me into silence. He stared respectfully at our impression in the snow. The outline of one giant body was visible: the arms were slightly blurred like the snow angels I used to make as a child in New Annan.

"May it last a hundred winters!" he said sadly.

Then he tossed me a mournful look. "Or 'til Eskimo dwarfs draw bathing costumes on the March snowdrifts and Annie returns to me."

We walked to Aunt Mary's house in silence. Angus did not come in. He was too full of anger and self-pity to say goodbye. I wept openly—first, for the true loss of my virginity which I felt deserved crying over even though it had been a sensationless experience, and second, for Angus, who looked so broken-hearted that I almost called him back.

At that moment Aunt Mary spoke and I realized she had been standing with me in the cold, wearing only her nightdress.

"Ain't your gentleman caller coming in?" I shook my head sadly and Aunt Mary reached up and squeezed my hand. Together we stood on the verandah and watched him lumber off until I could no longer make out his beaver hat in the blowing wind. The night had turned wild and fierce and an eerie rose light filled the sky.

"Real beautiful, if you like snowstorms," Aunt Mary said finally and we went inside.

TESTIMONIALS ABOUT THE INFANT GIANTESS

Mary Johnson: Truro was not the best place for my niece. Of course, my heart went out to her long-suffering mother who didn't understand that Anna couldn't teach school. Nobody wants a school marm that big! Anna was real shy when she came to stay with Ray and me on Thomas St. I'd have to say self-conscious. It was quite a freak thing, you know. Men used to follow her on the street and holler at her. You've no idea. I came home one night, late, from shopping, and found a young fella up in our oak tree. He was playing with himself, watching her room. Can you beat it? I called the militia. The next year that oak took sick and died. Another time a giant came into our kitchen and asked for Anna. He said he was going to talk her out of going to New York. You could have knocked me over with a feather. I didn't know a girl like Anna would have a beau. He was a big one. When he talked, the china in my cabinet shook. His words made a hollow sound, like pebbles falling down a well. He sat on my best Sibley chair, and I waited for it to snap like a kindling stick. My niece left right after his visit. So she didn't get to see how nice Truro looked when the Prince came that summer. The Ladies' Aid Society strung up triumphal arches and the air smelled sweet from the boughs of spruce. His Majesty accepted a bouquet from the mayor and rode to Pictou for the P.E.I. barge. Anna would have enjoyed herself. She was real sociable. I used to miss the songs she played on our piano. Jim put the piano on a table for her. Maybe because her fingers were so long, I thought her music had a sound all its own.

Hubert Belcourt: My family had the farm next to the Swans' back in New Annan, but truth to tell, I can't recall much about the early days. There wasn't anything for me on the farm. Of course, I heard stories about the giantess and me growing up. Mother likes to tell how the giantess shoved me into a gulley to prove she wasn't sweet on me. We were razzed on our way to school when the big girl started throwing her weight around. So Mother says. I don't recollect it. I know some of the town thought the Swans made a meal ticket out of Anna. They were dirt poor when she went off to New York. But folks up there are ignorant because Ann Swan loved her daughter. Anybody with a mother like her would be lucky.

Janette Swan: My sister was too good to scythe grain like the rest of us. She used to sit inside, dressed in a silk carriage dress and lace

bonnet I'd have traded my eye teeth for. You can't tell me she
didn't think she was better than us. Going to New York was very
egomaniacal. What did she care about her family stuck up in New
Annan? She didn't write when Father had pneumonia. Mother was
fooled by Anna's airs, but not me. I had to laugh when the two of
them set out on their trips to town. Mother used to make Anna
carry the Belcourt dwarf on her lap on account of the lack of
space. His head was bigger than hers, just like an ugly baby, and
hers was way too small for her body. Oh, she is a freak all right.
Imagining herself a famous actress. In a hundred years nobody will
know her name.

PART TWO

The American Dream

CHAPTER NINE

Annie in New York

A squirming herd in Mammon's mesh,
a wilderness of human flesh;
crazed with avarice, lust and rum,
New York, thy name's Delirium.

—Byron Rufus Newton

Who is prepared for New York, no matter how desperate the circumstances leading to that entrepôt? I, the BIGGEST MODERN WOMAN OF THE WORLD, was not ready for the chance it offered me to be inconspicuous. I blush to remember my awkward manner, my confusion in the rush-hour on Broadway. Of course, I was a sixteen-year-old farmgirl when I arrived, June 16, 1862. I hadn't acquired the polish my European tours were to bring.

Momma and I met my new employer at the Astor House Hotel. Poppa was not with us; he had returned to his groundhog meadow the day before, blowing me a sad kiss as he fled down the Astor's blue Quincy granite steps. I think he was frightened of an encounter with Barnum, who had a reputation as a Connecticut devil back in Nova Scotia. Poor Poppa! His case of nerves was unnecessary. Barnum turned out to be an ordinary mortal who looked exactly like any one of the excitable, middle-aged men we saw rushing through the Astor's gas-lit lobby. He rose to his feet like a jack-in-the-box when he spied us at the door of the hotel dining room. "Welcome to America," he said, extending a hand. "Glad to be out of the ice and snow, ladies?"

It was almost summer at home so I took Barnum's remark as a joke. We had left Halifax at the end of May—pleased to be escaping an early heat wave. The muggy breezes had driven me to bed at the Halifax Hotel where I lay, perspiring on sheets as white as

65

snowdrifts, while my parents watched soldiers drill on the common. Momma parted a drape so I could see: "Look Annabelle, they are as miserable as you."

New York had seemed delightfully cool as we rattled in by stagecoach. Invigorating breezes from Long Island Sound blew damp curls off my face as I was helped down from what Barnum must have imagined began as a fur-draped sleigh. How were we to react to this balding merchant who obviously hadn't stuck a big toe in the Canadas? Could he be the same adventurer who persuaded European royalty to kiss the midget fingers of Tom Thumb? This balding Yankee, a potentate who commanded international agents to ship him curiosities as if they were fresh vegetables?

I'd seen the cherubic face of the showman minutes before we met, painted on his museum walls. The portrait was done in the Graeco-Roman style and stared off in all directions from its vantage point on the fourth floor between flapping pennants and lavish oil paintings of birds, beasts, and creeping things. Barnum's portrait depicted a patrician who knew everything, and forgave North Americans for what he saw.

"Oh, it's pretty warm up where we come from," Momma said politely.

"Is that a fact?" Barnum replied. He stared appraisingly at me as I made my sideways entrance through another inconsiderate doorway into the hotel dining room, and steered with open delight to a table in the centre of a room ringing with the clatter of soup tureens that waiters slammed down on cloth-covered tables.

He made a signal to a headwaiter in dress coat and white tie and the man glanced our way, grinning. I suspected their exchange referred to me. I could see Barnum continuing to size me up as he spooned assurances onto Momma's demurely lowered head. Yes. Yes. New York was a busy place. No. No. No. Not as dangerous as people said. Certain areas only. You'd get used to it. So many stores. The Greatest City in the World for Lady Shoppers! The Marble House, Arnold Constable's dry goods emporium, was too wonderful! Nothing like it back home, ladies. Hahahaaaa. No, men have no genius for shopping. Nature has left their faculties imperfect in the particularity.

You and the girl don't shop? The girl doesn't like shoppers

staring? The museums then, aaah, the parks with their stands of poplar and elm, the marvellous silver light, river light, that is the wonder of the northern seaboard. Yes. Yes. We'd find something to enjoy. An asset the girl was shy. Did we know there were theatrical agents who kept their prodigies off the streets? Increased admission fees. Angus McAskill, the MARITIME MARVEL? Never heard of the giant. Couldn't be the one who exhibited at the American Museum. P.T. provided star treatment for all his troupe, no matter how big or small. And heated dressing rooms.

At that moment, I spied the object of Barnum's conspiracy with the headwaiter. A white dining table had been rigged to resemble a throne. Pillows with golden tassels and the initials "A.H.S." embroidered in gold were puffed into shape at my approach. I was to eat sitting on this table, a plate on my lap. A velvet cushion had been placed on a chair for my feet. An ordinary table was set for Barnum and Momma. A satin rope of a vulgar purple colour cordoned off the area, which was guarded by three sets of waiters who bowed their heads to their chests at a snap of the fingers from the headwaiter.

Barnum nodded, the headwaiter unhooked the cordon and beckoned at me, but I couldn't move. I was frightened by the sea of eyes fastened on me. I waited for calls of "Who does she think she is?"

Instead, the diners applauded loudly and some cried out the customary greeting to tall beings—"How's the weather up there, Big Woman?" Their voices sounded admiring. I blushed. What a surprise that the mudsills did not want to punish me for making a show of myself! New York was a different universe than New Annan! I thought of my seat on our shanty floor and suddenly felt pleased. Although I recognized in Barnum's face the crafty manipulator whom Angus had warned me about, at that moment I understood the extent of the opportunity Barnum offered—to escape the embittering experience of rural life, to spiel before approving crowds—Barnum's courtship of me could be a dream come true!

Beside me, the old showman bowed low for the diners—his diamond cufflinks and finger rings sparkling. Then he took my hand and helped me mount my throne.

"I approve of your shyness, Annie," Barnum whispered in my ear as I climbed. "A retiring nature excites a gentleman's interest."

Momma looked at us quizzically. I blushed again and spread the ruched cotton flounces of my carriage dress. How gauche I felt! My gown was *à la mode*, but not nearly as voguish as those of the women gabbing to men in lounge coats and civil war uniforms. Don't bite the hand, Anna, I thought, but truly, if my boss was presenting me as a queen, shouldn't he outfit me like one first?

The Astor's chic crowd continued to watch with admiration as a retinue of waiters presented my knees with five different types of fowl while the maître d', acting on Barnum's orders, replenished my crystal glass with barley water, Momma's remedy for headaches. It was easy to see from where I sat, staring down at diners' faces staring up at me, cheeks bulging with *timbales à la française*, that Americans were the world's strangest people.

My employer sat by my left calf, Momma by my right. She reached up and patted my knee. Barnum busied himself whistling and polishing each item of his silverware, blowing on it first. "Microbes," he said, but he didn't offer to repeat this ritual for Momma or me, and with grins and chuckles fell to tearing the wings off a short-neck snipe.

Six feet below my lap, his bald dome bobbed as he questioned Momma on her remedies for pulmonary disorders. His phobia about these diseases wasn't familiar to us since we hadn't read up on his idiosyncrasies. He endorsed Dr. Bartholomey's Expectorant Pink Sirop as a miraculous Yankee invention and rattled on about his proclivity for colds and sore throats, shuddering as he spoke. Momma's mat of curls shook in disagreement. Dr. Bartholomey! Not his sugary placebos! If he wants to treat diseases that grip the throat like bulldogs, he should use Radway's Renovating Resolvent, made in Toronto.

"A Canadian cough sirop?" Barnum's eyes glittered. "Surely your technology hasn't reached our state of advancement?"

"Mr. Barnum, we have far surpassed primitive Yankee methods," I blurted. There, it was out: the forthright lecture voice I used to divert jesters when I stood on my overturned tub at the country fairs. It was my first remark since entering the room. Immediately, the diners, who were engaged in the shouting talk mudsills call conversation, stopped conversing. The opulent chamber was silent. Behind the wall papered with brocade, where candle-lit sideboards held up the mutilated remains of our dinner, I heard the whining instructions of the Astor's French chef, talking in an irrefutable French accent. I cleared my throat and continued:

"Allow me to clear up a few misconceptions about the Canadas, which are thought to be a technically backward dominion, important only as a massive exporter of wheat and timber.

"Contrary to the opinion of the rest of the world, which sees us as a backwater of medical research, the development of cough suppressors is a major scientific field in my country as well as a philosophical principle.

"Our grain bins are dwarfed by our cough-drop warehouses whose manufacture is the single largest Canadian industry, employing more workers than lumbering or agriculture.

"Deafness, piles, chronic diarrhoea (that fatal Californian disease), or any gleet that, if neglected, sweeps away the young, the old, the lovely, and the gay, even weakness of the genital organs—there is no ailment that cannot be treated by our advances in camphor science.

"The Canadian cough drop is unequalled as an oesophageal elixir, and if administered in regular doses, along with maple leaves, our pills produce a calming side effect. In time, the user will exhibit an agreeable tendency to avoid confrontation and seek consensus instead.

"A desire to avoid war-like behaviour, a failure to sustain violent controversy such as the calamitous war you are fighting with your southern brothers—what more can a scientist ask of a drug?

"Of course, I can't speak for all my dominion." I glanced with a meaningful look around the room. "There are parts that resist the progress of medical science and I can't take responsibility for them here."

"Are Canadians infectious?" Barnum asked suddenly.

"The cold mummifies agents of disease, rendering the majority of people in the Canadas harmless. But there's no telling what goes on in the blood if a Northerner leaves his habitat," I added, directing an ominous glance down at my fidgeting employer.

Barnum shivered and the audience laughed in shocked tones. I

69

felt a pull by my right calf. It was a sharp tug that vibrated through the 27-foot circumference of my bellcage crinoline. Momma was looking up, mortified at the way I was drawing attention to myself, but I stared fiercely over her head at the nervous mudsills, willing them not to resume their yelling talk. My stern face made the atmosphere chilly. I might as well have blown an Arctic zephyr across those paling diners. (When I frown, brave men tremble.) Soon the Yankees began to cough in tiny, apologetic bursts until the carpeted room thundered with frantic, hacking barks. Barnum hurried me out, his own face purple from choking on imaginary pestilence.

"Fascinating, that bit about mummifying the microbes," he said, and avoided taking my arm as he led me away. Momma swept along behind, her rugged face anxious. "Annie, have you gone daft?" she whispered.

I shook my curls, and bent down. Barnum waited for me a few steps ahead.

"Momma, I was making your point about Yankee ignorance." I felt an afterglow of pleasure and shock that I had dared to be so bold.

Momma recoiled in anger. "Don't you know it's rude to poke fun?"

I shrugged and cast my eyes down, hoping Barnum couldn't hear Momma's whispery tirade.

"It's not like you, speaking out like that," she hissed. "What's got into you?"

When I didn't reply, she glared up at me and rushed around my skirts to take Barnum's arm. The showman looked at her and then at me and chuckled and together they walked on down the lobby. I continued to hang my head and slowed my gait—I didn't want Barnum to see how mortified I felt. Had I stepped out of place and offended the great showman? At sixteen, my confidence was easily upset. I felt acceptable in my own eyes, but so imperfect in the eyes of others that my slightest mistake filled me with self-loathing. I walked slowly by the gentlemen smoking "segars" in the lobby. They had their feet up on the white marble balustrade as they spat on the marble floor. Suddenly, one of them whistled and all together these rude fellows shot their juices my way. I hurried up to

Momma and Barnum and, with an apologetic look at my indignant parent, clasped the other arm of the showman. It twitched slightly under my fingers and was still.

So entwined we three climbed the stairs and I was astonished to find the upper passageways spacious. Our sixth-floor suite looking out on City Hall Park was twice as big as the first floor of our shanty. Barnum tested the taps to see if the hot water was working and demanded room service through a peculiar guest-to-management machine called "the annunciator." Immediately, a bellboy arrived to serve us tea on a tray embossed with a screaming eagle in pain or in its death throes, a Temple of Liberty, and a Phrygian cap on a staff.

"You have a good speaking voice for someone so modest," Barnum said from a safe distance on a divan. I felt too humiliated to answer.

"Anna learned how to behave in public when she was a child," Momma said.

"In that case, I'll ignore the introductory coaching. Anna can start work tomorrow."

"Too soon," said Momma. "We must do things properly. Let's contact the lawyers first and sign the papers."

Barnum's nose twitched at this. Lawyers were an obnoxious breed. But in the end, he did it as Momma wished: a legal document stamped together with another wounded eagle, promising three hours of lessons a day for three years with a private tutor (this included music and voice lessons), ladylike clothes (Momma's synonym for expensive gowns from *Mr. Godey's*), and one thousand dollars a month! God bless the Universal Yankee Nation—to borrow Barnum's phrase for all who share an interest in sound business practices—I was rich overnight! Momma may have disliked my bold manner but my little talk, delivered off my crumpled cotton cuff, had demonstrated I was a natural performer, leading the old showman to conclude he should pay the NOVA SCOTIAN GIANTESS anything she asked.

CHAPTER TEN

"La Loi Du Destin"

Swallowing the first American oyster is
like swallowing a baby.

—William Thackeray

In New York, Momma and I experienced the mixture of scorn and awe that the Blue-noses feel for the mudsills. New York, with its myriad of excavations and demolitions, its traffic jams and its advertisements plastered on the walls of buildings and even on the city's curbstones, astonished and disgusted us. The mood of the city during the civil war was volatile although I could not make out whether the mudsills were upset because they were anti-slavery or because they were losing commercial trade with the South.

During the day, I rehearsed at the American Museum which was located near the Astor, at the corner of Broadway and Ann streets. In the evening, I took hot baths in the waterclosets in the Astor's basement and enjoyed five-course meals which Momma ordered for us from menus printed on the hotel premises. On Saturdays, Momma took me shopping to the Marble House so praised by Barnum, and dressed me like a Fifth Avenoodle in cone-shaped skirts and fashionable military jackets. Even Momma put aside her poke bonnet and wore a matron's cap of lace and net, for although she was a farmer's wife with six children, she was still a young woman of thirty-nine when she chaperoned me in New York. Poppa wrote us about once a month but was too tactful to ask about Momma's return. Likely he was glad she was having a reprieve from rural drudgery.

I felt lucky to be out of New Annan and was impressed by Barnum's theatre company of giant and midget stars. At the American Museum, I was introduced to the other show-business celebrities by my new manager—a loud-talking Tasmanian who spoke in a rough English accent and dressed in the plaid bellbottoms and top hat of a Bowery tough. His name was Hiriam Percival Ingalls. He wore shoulder-length yellow hair and had a habit of hissing through his teeth as he rolled a pair of yellow dice that had been carved from a sheep's bone. He was a gambler and a ladies' man and everyone called him Apollo, although he preferred the title "Judge." I did not fancy short men so I was surprised when I felt attracted to him as soon as I shook his hand in Barnum's office. For one thing, he didn't joke about my height on greeting me. Instead, he studied me carefully while the showman described my background and then whisked me off to meet the other giants as if he couldn't wait to get me away from Barnum.

We met the LARGE CURIOSITIES after they'd given their spiels in the museum's third-floor lecture hall. They ambled out of the hall and across the corridor to the alcove where we stood, stopping to chat with spectators who gazed up at them like delighted children. I was amazed by the benign, almost indifferent, expressions on the giants' faces. Did I look that phlegmatic? I shivered: I did.

There were three of them: two men and a tall, monstrously fat girl in a crimson gown criss-crossed with pink sashes.

"Jane Campbell—six and a half feet, three hundred and nineteen pounds," Ingalls hissed.

The fat girl hissed. "You can't have too much of a good thing, can you, honey?" she said. Then she pinched Ingalls' cheek. "When you coming to feed, Apollo?"

"Later, Little Jane," he said and I felt disappointed because I guessed from the tone of his voice that they were lovers.

The fat girl sauntered off, swinging hips as wide as a scarlet sofa. The two male giants shook my hand. I eyed their foreheads. Was I the biggest, as Ingalls said? Even though my size could be troubling, it seemed to be the only distinction I had.

Bihin, an elderly Frenchman, had a long, rubbery neck and an imposingly large head for a giant. The height of giants is usually contained in their legs.

"Mademoiselle?" Bihin peered amorously up into my eyes and Ingalls hissed, "He's shorter by three."

I breathed a sign of relief. Simultaneously, Ingalls and I turned to size me up next to Colonel Routh Goshen. He was a Kentucky Negro who Barnum claimed was from Palestine. He talked in a whispery dialect, and he had a small head (like me) and an extremely high forehead.

"You've got him beat by an inch," Ingalls hissed.

"*Sans doute*, this is the BIGGEST MODERN WOMAN OF THE WORLD," Bihin announced, with a gentlemanly wave of his hand.

"Barnum will like that," Ingalls said. "Now come along, boys. Let's dazzle the lovely lady with a tour of the shrine."

The two giants and I tried our best to keep up with Ingalls as he led us past the glass cabinets filled with sharks' teeth and butterflies into an elegant cubicle decorated with a miniature lilac divan and wood stove. It belonged to the famous midget General Tom Thumb and its walls were papered with faded reviews. I scanned the clippings while Ingalls explained to me that Thumb had received his title from Queen Victoria and had been Mr. Barnum's top-grossing performer before he had gone into retirement the year before. Apparently the midget had no interest in continuing his acting career even though his natural comic ability had captivated New York and London during the 1840s and 1850s.

"We esteem the little fellow . . . a perfect Garrick in miniature," I read in a clipping from an American newspaper that described his role in the fairy tale *Hop o' My Thumb*. The kudos for his acting and dancing rolled on and on and on. There seemed to be nothing the midget could not do—from singing gospel songs in blackface to winning the heart of Queen Victoria.

"If he's as good as they say, why did he stop acting?" I asked. I could not imagine any reason that would persuade me to give up such a glamorous career.

"Tommie will be back," Goshen whispered. "Just you wait."

Bihin smiled knowingly. "*L'amour, mademoiselle*. He's looking for a wife. He's been too busy selling kisses to British ladies to find a *femme*."

"The little man has quite an effect on the ladies," Goshen added enviously. "They outnumber the men ten to one at his perform-ances and call him cherub, angel, darling. At the end of his show, the English ladies pay a shilling for a pamphlet on his life and a kiss."

"Poor Goshen," Ingalls hissed. "Do you wish somebody would call you 'lambkins'?"

Goshen hung his head.

"A great comic actor can't be sad, Routh boy," Ingalls said. "Anna—Goshen was wonderful as Cousin Joe, the Rough Diamond, New Bowery, 1 March 1860. Goshen and Bihin represent the two great traditions of freak drama: classical and modern."

"There's only one tradition in America: novelty," Goshen whispered.

"I'll talk for you, Goshen. It's easier to hear me. So Bihin does classical work such as the wicked giant in Old King Cole's kingdom. Goshen here plays in contemporary farce and makes hay out of his height. You follow?"

Goshen frowned and Ingalls looked up at me, asking, "Which will you be?"

Bihin spoke. "With such a serious young face, I predict Anna will be a great tragedienne. She will do *Phaedra, Macbeth*. . . ."

Ingalls made his odd hissing noise. "I'd like to see her wiping spots off her dress. Shall we look for Jane and the others?"

We found the rest of the troupe eating dessert at Delmonico's—the popular French restaurant at the corner of Fifth Avenue and Fourteenth Street. Jane Campbell, exuding a minty flavour, rose and kissed Ingalls on the lips, and my manager returned the favour by squeezing both her pillow-sized breasts. She squealed in joy and asked Bihin to order a round of French sweets.

Behind us, frantic waiters rushed about in Delmonico's torch-lit splendour. I hoped I looked presentable: I wore a new Swiss muslin, in two tones of ivory, with a bow at my neck and a tight clamp belt to accentuate my wasp waist.

"Isn't she *jolie*?" Bihin asked.

"You're making her blush, Frank," the THIN MAN said. "Hi there, gorgeous. I'm Isaac Sprague."

"And I'm Commodore Nutt. I cost Barnum $30,000 for a three-year contract so I'm called the THIRTY-THOUSAND DOLLAR NUTT," said a midget with a round, tufted blond head. The other midget, a dark-eyed woman who looked far older than I, introduced herself as Lavinia Warren Bumpus. (Later I found out she was twenty-one.) Her lips curled down in a sarcastic way although the manner in which she tossed her black curls reminded me of a *femme fatale*'s.

"And now, mademoiselle—your choice," Bihin said.

"Of the curiosities?" I replied and all laughed. Ingalls boomed, "Give her 'La Loi du Destin'." Bihin signalled for the waiter. "'La Loi du Destin' for Mlle Swan; the 'Stars and Stripes' for M. Nutt and Mlle Warren; for myself *et* M. Goshen, 'Le Monument de Washington'; for M. Ingalls, 'La Temple de la Littérature'; and for the rest—blueberry pie."

"No pie for me. I'm dieting," Isaac Sprague said. "I'll watch to see who makes the biggest pig of himself."

"Oh skinny, you've given me an idea!" Jane said, "Let's have an eating contest!"

The table of curiosities clapped noisily over the prospect of over-eating. I too was secretly thrilled. Like Angus, I had never suppressed the babyish satisfaction of putting things in my mouth. Indeed, when it came to food, I acknowledged no limiting principle. (Luckily, I remained slim because I was tall.) But my new English leather corset, custom-made in the Victorian style, would be a handicap, as would my clamp belt. That I removed when nobody was looking, and hid under the napkin on my lap. Then Jane noticed and undid the sash on her crimson gown, giggling as she dangled it above Ingalls' head for all the room to see.

The waiters ran to and fro more nervously than before but nobody came over to reprimand Jane. Likely she was a frequent customer. She certainly looked at home, standing beside Ingalls who tugged playfully on the dangling pink scarf with his teeth. At last, Jane let out a happy porcine bleat and threw her sash into the centre of the table.

"Toss your belt in too, Big One," she said to me with a wink. "You're long and I'm wide, and may the best freak win."

I blushed and set my ivory belt in the middle of the table next to Jane's sash.

"Is it just a ladies' duel?" Colonel Goshen whispered. "Or may us gentlemen join in?"

"Oh, there are no gentlemen in this town," Jane said and looked at Ingalls. "But who wants gentlemen?"

I found the devotion in her gaze annoying. Surely my manager could not admire such a noisy, fleshy lump!

"I think Jane means you can put your belt in, Routh," said the small woman, Lavinia Warren Bumpus. "I've decided to refrain. I prefer to watch excess than to commit it."

She stared coldly at me and I felt rebuked.

Then the desserts arrived with cups of "gloria" (black coffee and brandy) for us all and I was so startled by the sumptuous food that I stared at it stupidly and forgot to eat. At last I started on Ingalls' choice for me, which turned out to be a chocolate pudding with dark, runny intestines and hard white knobs of frosting, while my competitors gobbled their desserts and coffee in the gulp-and-swig style I had seen businessmen take their lunch in at New York's stand-up restaurants.

I could not eat "on the wing" and worried that I would be left behind as I hungrily devoured one after another of my "Lois" which, thanks to Bihin, kept appearing on my plate although I was too busy to notice him giving the order. Beside me, Ingalls speared his puffy white "Temples of Literature" with a knife and popped them into his bull-frog maw while crumbs fell like snow on his plaid jacket and organ-grinder's tie.

The others ate on in a frenzy as if they were swallowing oysters at some dingy oyster café in Lower Manhattan. Not a mouthful was savoured, not a dish praised for its flavour. Yet the noise was horrific. Jane swore as she masticated—cursing her pie's thick pastry; Nutt choked and complained that his mouth was too small to accommodate one wedge of his ice cream pie at a time, and Bihin and Colonel Goshen breathed loudly (as giants are inclined to do) while they matched each other—monument for monument.

Suddenly all was quiet. No jaws ground, none, that is, except mine and Ingalls'. The bloated faces of my fellow curiosities sullenly regarded me. Ingalls winked and called the waiter back.

"Two more 'Temples of Literature' for me, boy," he said. "And give the giantess one more whatchamacallit."

"Make it four for us both," I replied.

Ingalls coughed. "You heard the lady."

A moment later, four of the gooey "Lois" were lined up before my place. I didn't wait to see how quickly Ingalls ate his "Temples." Instead, I inhaled the puddings like air and signalled for another four. The others stared at me in astonishment. But I hardly cared; I had succumbed to the heady feeling of relief that accompanies loss of restraint. I might be a shy farm girl but you do not need to be sophisticated to win an eating match.

Indeed, I knew I could eat for a day if necessary; my stomach was the infinite bowl of the universe upon which the "Loi" fell and settled like atmospheric layers in space.

Beside me, Ingalls stared dispiritedly at the fresh row of plates waiting at his place. I smiled encouragement as I stuffed back another "Loi" and then another but my manager kept his eyes upon his plate. Suddenly, I felt a vise clamp about my waist so viciously that I had to gasp for breath. My hands flew to my side but I could not unfasten my corset which had become cripplingly tight at nineteen puddings.

Colour drained from my face. Ingalls chuckled as he realized my predicament. With renewed gusto, he bent his head and speared the fluffy desserts faster and faster into his bull-frog mouth. I sadly watched his nineteenth cake melt in his jaws and then lurched off to the powder room where an attendant stood on a chair and unlaced me.

When I returned, Nutt leapt onto the table top, now a battleground of cake.

"I pronounce Judge Hiriam Percival Ingalls the champion at twenty cakes!"

The waiters and customers stared our way in amusement. Lavinia raised her eyebrows.

"Anna could have done the Judge in," she said sarcastically. "She's just being modest and letting a man win the contest."

"Frailty, thy name is woman," Nutt chirped, to my annoyance. Wasn't it bad enough that I, the GIRL GIANTESS, had been outstripped by a normal? And now I had to endure accusations of faintheartedness? But ah, how could I explain that it was my corset and not modesty that had put me out of the race, without sounding like a poor loser? I glared at Nutt who stared saucily back, winking and sniggering as if I was a midget saloon girl he intended to pick up.

"I think Anna might have beat me if she had been dressed for the event," Ingalls said with an understanding hiss. He stuck his thumbs under his trousers and showed us how the material could still be stretched a few inches out from his waist. The curiosities chuckled and the grinning Tasmanian scrambled up on his chair and deposited a loud smack on my cheek. Glasses clinked, and this time the diners leapt to their feet and applauded. My companions toasted me and I heard my lecture voice thanking them. Only Jane picked at some half-eaten pie bits on her plate and was silent.

"Anna, I'm going to take little Jane to play faro over at a 'Hell' on Broadway. Why don't you come along?" Ingalls asked. "It's a Second-Class house—strictly respectable," he added, and waited for my answer. I had a 9 p.m. curfew. Already it was 8:30 and Momma would be peeking around the curtains of our Astor Hotel room, wondering where I was. I knew she would never give me permission to visit a gambling club. But I didn't want any of them to realize I was only sixteen so I said I had a stomach ache and wanted to go to bed. To my surprise Lavinia stood up and said her lodgings were near mine, and we left Delmonico's together.

On the street the small woman scurried along in front, panting and darting backwards looks at me as if she was afraid of my catching up. Finally I realized she was trying to show me that her little legs could go faster than mine, and I slowed down to make her demonstration easier. She caught her breath and launched into a description of a giantess named Miss Hardy who shared a stateroom with her on a Mississippi show boat. (I do not know why people expect you to be interested in other tall people simply because you are large!)

"Miss Hardy was slow-moving like you," Lavinia snapped. "She wouldn't have the gumption to beat a man at anything."

"I always beat men, so losing this time didn't bother me," I lied angrily.

Lavinia stopped and smiled sweetly.

"I've got a sharp tongue, haven't I?" She looked pleased at the thought. "Sometimes sharper than I intend. So there is no need for you to look offended, Anna. Perhaps we can be friends."

I stared at her and she giggled and reached up to shake my hand. Then she waved good-night and disappeared among the four-storey buildings on Fifth Avenue. A harvest moon coloured the stone façades. Autumn would soon be upon Manhattan. For the first time, I remembered the wine and vinegar sea winds of New Annan, and felt homesick. I even thought fondly of Hubert scribbling retail

79

invoices in a Halifax shop, and, of course, of Angus rocking in his ocean dinghy, waiting for me to join him in his vigil for the old ways.

A letter from Poppa on the occasion of my first New York exhibit, July 23, 1862.

Dear Annabelle:

By today New York must be getting a look at what Colchester County can produce in a pinch. It will do the Yankees good to see a Nova Scotian production. They are as rude and disorderly as their newspapers make them out. During the Prince's visit last year, a ballroom floor collapsed, and girls lacking my Annabelle's ladylike charms threw themselves at the feet of the visiting retinue, screeching "Let me kiss him for his mother!" Imagine what the Queen thought of our southern neighbours.

I fancy you and your mother are cozily housed at the Astor and have forgiven yours truly for abandoning his womenfolk. After I left you during the dining crush—the ringing gongs and agitated waiters labouring under vast soup tureens—I was swallowed in the confusion outside. There I saw dozens of hotel stages, carts, wagons, private carriages, and omnibuses with fancy names, going pell-mell in "the rush hour." It took me ten minutes to cross Broadway, a street less wide than our groundhog meadow. A city of ruffians! However, Mother will know what to do and I am taking comfort in the knowledge that pirate Hicks and his band of murderers are locked up, making the Yankee hell-hole safer than it was a year ago.

My pangs at returning home alone were not helped by the appearance of Hubert Belcourt who drove up from Halifax yesterday to hear my news. He walked into the hayfield as I was mowing and surprised me with a scolding lecture on your contract with Mr. Barnum. He said I had no appreciation of your sensitive nature and told me I was a greedy father to put his own flesh and blood on display in the American "Venusberg." The little midget claimed you wanted to become a teacher but felt obligated to help with our financial situation, now compounded since Mother took in the foundlings. I kept on with the job at hand, but he did get me thinking about our difficulties making up our minds to exhibit you. Do you recall your first exposition, Annabelle? You were exhausted. Whether from the long coach ride, or simple growing pains—I do not know. We went by Democrat to Halifax and you slept on the mail bags when you weren't counting dead trees, a childhood game of yours. Dunseith met us at the station and took us to the Temperance Hall where he had rented a room for the occasion. As is often the case, the road from the station passes through some of the poorest thoroughfares and the meanest houses whose doors and windows were crowded with dirty inhabitants. Dunseith pointed out Micmac squaws to you. They were an eyesore in vulgar colours and their great splay feet were clad in blanket moccasins. You studied their rag-tag group trudging in the carriage dust, and asked: "Poppa, how much do their families charge for people to look at them?"

Again I was mentioning our troubles, deciding whether to show you. Dunseith was a nuisance with his braggart Yankee ways, throwing a bad light on the situation. "Why keep a prize heifer in the barn?" he asked Mother. I don't need to tell you Mother had no use for Dunseith.

I never thought it a crime to show someone with unique features, such as yourself. Mother, meantime, didn't mind Nova Scotians looking at "her baby," but when you were small, she drew the line at Yankees gaping at you. I couldn't understand why it was wrong to show you one side of a border and not the other. But don't bother telling Mother I said that. Her foundlings are calling themselves by the family name although they are not real Swans. Annabelle, do you know Mrs. Sheridan's commandments to her daughters? Fear God. Honor the King [sic]. Obey your parents. Brush your teeth. Here then are the commandments of Alex Swan. YOU ARE MY ONLY GIANT DAUGHTER. I EXPECT GREAT THINGS OF YOU.

Your loving Dad.

P.S. Hubert brought over 60 lbs. of salt pork and some potatoes so our household is secure from starvation for some time to come. It is his hand that penned this.

81

CHAPTER ELEVEN

Charms from the Backwoods

August 1, 1862

Dear Angus:

Here I am, at my desk in the Astor, writing you. You would tease me if you could see my makeshift preparations: the desk placed on my knees like a tray, a jeroboam of ink, my quill pen made out of an ostrich feather from the costume of a museum dancer. And now this big person sitting amid luxury and modern conveniences can make small, delicate tracks across the page to you. (My handwriting is the one average thing about me, Angus!)

From my window, I can see all of Broadway. Across the avenue is the magnificent city hall colonnade, and the plumes of the Croton Water Fountain in City Hall Park. Wall Street lies beyond the park and so do the newspaper offices of the *Tribune*, managed by Barnum's friend Horace Greeley, and the *New York Herald*, started by the Scot immigrant James Gordon Bennet. (I know their names because Mr. Barnum asked me to make a note of them. My employer cultivates such friendships and is so wily he is able to have them print his puffs about the museum as news stories, written by their own people!)

To the south of me, in the midst of a group of tobacco and clothing shops, squats my house of work, a garish, four-sided museum, with a brass band on its second-floor balcony tootling out-of-tune marching songs on Barnum's orders because the showman hopes pedestrians will go inside to escape the noise. To the west, towards the Hudson River, are St. Paul's and the harbour docks.

Oh Angus, the view is staggering! The endless façades of rugged stone as high as four and five storeys! The spires and smoking chimneys! And the parade of life winding through in all directions, carrying along horses and carriages! That is my public, Angus. Mr. Barnum says I belong to them. He is a bit of a scallywag (as you know) but I feel a certain gratitude to the mudsills for wanting me. They have given me the opportunity to be a show-biz personality and I should like to do something to repay them. Oh yes, I am beginning to feel at home. New York is a little like living in a farm house with eight hundred thousand relatives. The walls in every building are thin: often in my room, I overhear domestic activities and, distasteful as some aspects are, it is wonderful to have company. I notice I walk faster to the American Museum; I cannot execute the amazing run-walk one sees on Broadway, but I manage to go at a good clip.

Meanwhile, Angus, you will never guess my news. I may play Lady Macbeth in the summer stock. In the winter Barnum turns the lecture hall over to popular theatre companies, but in summer the giants and dwarfs take it over. Any day now I go to be measured for a magnificent Elizabethan gown. My manager, Hiriam Percival Ingalls, wants me to wear high shoes under it so I will look even more imposing. Have I mentioned him before? He is the ogre who keeps our troupe late, rehearsing our spiels for the hall. He is from Tasmania, but years in New England working with circus promoters have made him as much a Connecticut Yankee as Barnum. A giant named Goshen is to play Macduff, and Commodore Nutt will be Macbeth.

Momma is going home once she has established me in a good boarding house. She shares my views about this exciting town where people are quick to appreciate the marvellous. I work every day. At 3 and 7, I rehearse a lecture at the American Museum. It was written by Mr. Ingalls who, as it turns out, shares my literary interests. I also have three hours of lessons with my tutor, Miss Beasely. She is from Connecticut and feels unworthy because she is small. (But you know I do not have your belief that I am better than others because I am big.) Anyhow, my height is a constant topic because Miss Beasely worships size. Miss Beasely is a friend of the Mormon reformer Eliza Farnham who holds that woman is superior to man.

She says intellect, the male stronghold, is "a coarse bungler" compared to the efficient workings of female intuition. Woman has a nobler contour, her bosom a finer swell, the upper half of her skull is more expansive, her ear quicker, her veins of brighter blue, her skin of purer white. . . . The inventory of our virtues goes on, says Eliza Farnham. Our brains are of higher quality and quicker growth: even our biological rhythms are better regulated than "the licence of mere waste in the masculine."

Miss Farnham's ingenious views will be published in two volumes called *Woman and Her Era*, according to Miss Beasely who suggested to Miss Farnham that I should be the model for the cover of her tome. If normal woman is superior, how much more superior is someone of my proportions! argued Miss Beasely. The logic is faulty, but I would have enjoyed being a cover girl. Imagine, Angus! Miss Farnham's photographer wanted to shoot me leaning up against the Home Insurance Building in Chicago. (It's a new type of building called a skyscraper.) I was to hold a tennis racket in my hand and the caption was to read: *Anna Swan:* THE BIGGEST WOMAN OF THE WORLD! Unfortunately, Momma told her my contract with Barnum forbids other commercial enterprises and she has dropped the matter.

Miss Beasely may have a high opinion of female intelligence, but our lessons seem frivolous. She uses the standard text, *Magnall's Questions*, which runs together a discussion of whalebone corsets, umbrellas, and whales in a series of questions and answers that make no sense.

Miss Beasely questions and I respond. *Par exemple*, when she asks me about Dick Whittington's cat, I am to say, "Yes, but it was not the whiskered mouse-killing cat, but the coasting, coal-carrying cat that realized his fortune."

Miss Beasely is also directing me in the making of shell boxes, seaweed albums, and wax flowers. I prefer my piano to the manufacture of bric-à-brac. Small objects give me enough trouble as my skirts constantly sweep to the floor dozens of china figurines on tables here. But I have refused to learn the art of Berlin woolwork. The stitches are too small and hurt my fingers.

Nor will I salute the American flag although I know that would please Miss Beasely. She has a tiny "Old Glory" pinned on the north pole of her atlas and she sings her national anthem to the shrivelled bit of cloth at the start of each lesson. Miss Beasely believes that to be American is the true destiny of each of us. She tosses meaningful little looks my way as she sings. I smile, and to mollify her, politely mouth the words as I watch the buzz of heads on the streets below Miss Beasely's lodgings. Their bonnets and stove-pipe hats look so fragile. Do you think they need a tall girl like me to protect them? YOUR ANNIE, WHO WANTS TO KNOW IF BIG PEOPLE HAVE BIGGER RESPONSIBILITIES.

P.S. I was a runner-up in a cake-eating contest here. Nineteen puddings in one night.

August 15, 1862

Dear Annie:

I just arrived back from a funeral in St. Ann's when the coach dropped off your letter. I was a pall-bearer. The minister's wife died of childbed fever and I carried her box to the graveyard at the foot of the bay. It is cold here, and wet, and I expect the gout will soon lay me up. One bad spell and then I'm all right for a while. This winter the minister asked me to be one of *the men*. Mother forbade it. She said the nights in the hills, meditating and praying, would ruin my knees. They are sore. I find it harder to rise from my barrel when customers come. I am 37, yet my hands and feet are still growing. I have not measured myself. It's enough I feel pain from my rheumatism and the spells of sleepy exhaustion I've had since I was a wee boy. When I came in from the service, Mother said I looked satisfied and relieved. I thought this a strange observation and yet it occurs to me as I write how accurate are her words. There is a sombre pleasure in death or some terrible anticipated thing. I feel the majesty of it—its great blankness, like the St. Ann's fields in November. How different from a cake-eating contest are my joys. You know, however, I could have beaten you hollow. YOUR ANGUS, WHO CAN EAT TWENTY BOWLS OF CROWDIE AT ONE SITTING.

P.S. I forgot your question. Annie, the world may expect more of you because you're big but don't feel obliged to provide it.

P.P.S. I've enclosed a bit of whimsy I cooked up since our last meeting.

THE LIVING LUMBER LAD'S POEM

Who carves Anna's name
on every grove of living land?
Gille Mor Gille Mor
Who frowns to hear
the splintering of
lobster casements
beneath his big boy boot?
Gille Mor Gille Mor
Who sets his clock by the slow
reliable rundown of tissue
and waxes a beguiling moon
in the bosom of his shirt?
Gille Mor Gille Mor
Who has his big toe in a snow storm
and wades ankle deep in cold spring streams?
Gille Mor Gille Mor
Whose hot dandelion head
is seeding the wilderness?
Gille Mor Gille Mor
Whose rain-soaked skin
is bleaching to fall colours?
Gille Mor Gille Mor
Who through his camouflage
watches stick girl fall
off stick boy's horizon?
Gille Mor Gille Mor
Who calls himself Annie's bake-apple baby
in the tree tops?
Gille Mor Gille Mor
Who's the one-selved mountain man
shut out of Anna's city garden?
Gille Mor Gille Mor
Whose sickle scoops empty meadows
in search of Anna's secret city selves
and finds no blade of grass
petty enough to contain him?

Who is the giant shrinking in the wilderness?
Who is drunk on dandelion wine?
Who has plucked his last lobster?
Who will bequeath the largest shell
& no vestige of his love?
Who is invisibly melting like bergs of slush
in the bush?
Gille Mor Gille Mor Gille Mor

October 8, 1862

Dear Angus:

I have joined a fiction club along with Mr. Ingalls. We meet in a
Bowery tea room, and read John Whittier and Walt Whitman out
loud. Our president, Luke Devere, a gaunt, bespectacled college
professor, is a Transcendentalist. Do you know who Transcenden-
talists are? Don't confuse them with Miss Beasely who professes a
trashy spiritualism. My tutor has replaced the Mormon reformer
Eliza Farnham with spirit faces in darkened Manhattan parlours.
Her description of prophetic voices and musical instruments that
play by themselves amuses my manager who sometimes comes to
my lessons. Miss Beasely changes her ideas as often as her carriage
dress. (Once a week.) Today it is Daniel Douglas Hume, the British
medium who is alleged to float in and out of windows while jets
of flame shoot from his head. Tomorrow I predict she will take up
the Fox sisters—those spiritual has-beens who even Barnum says
are a humbug.

Contrary to some critics, transcendentalism is an inspirational
philosophy: it recognizes the divinity in man and nature. You must
read Ralph Emerson's Divinity School Address, Angus. Even better, I will send it to you (with explanatory notes). Emerson influenced Whitman; no modern author makes sense without knowing
Emerson's work. I worry you are too cut off. We are living in the
middle of a turbulent revolution—the advent of the machine
age—and you are gone fishin'. Angus there is a wind rustling my
handbills whose name is PROGRESS. We are on a chasm. Enormous
scientific changes are coming. We must prepare ourselves.

Have you read Whitman? I have.

Do you agree with Darwin? I do.

Will you advocate the rights of women?

Are you shocked? Women do have a right to the quality of education available to men. Miss Beasely's training shrinks the mind when it could stretch it. I sound like a hard-bitten American feminist. Yet a good education will make us better companions for our husbands and more competent mothers. Listen Angus: I am not what you think. We have one of them at the museum: Lavinia Bump, and I find her manner aggressive. Now I sound apologetic. It is frustrating to attempt explanations in a letter. I wish I had you face to face so I could talk you into coming to New York. You can stay at the Astor. The manager is used to large guests and would fix you a comfortable room. I'll ask if you can get one with a view of the harbour. Oh do come, Angus. YOUR ANNIE, THE BIGGEST MODERN WOMAN OF THE WORLD.

P.S. Mr. Ingalls walked in, carrying an old handbill advertising your appearance at the American Museum. He is curious about you. See. You should come. He has cancelled rehearsal today and is taking me for a walk to the Battery to smell the health-giving harbour air.

November 15, 1862

Dear Annie,

I used to think you had a grain of sense, but in your last letter, you sounded like a twitter-pated fool. When will you learn? Darwin & women's rights are nothing to brag of. You must be hinting at something your friend here is not picking up. You think I'm stupid, but you are unrealistic, Anna.

I have seen and done everything. And learned the truth. People are pigs and the worst are not among my sex. No other species is as eager to betray her husband, brother, father, than one of your kind. The dolly-mops, pitiful creatures, don't know any better but it is the so-called ladies of society I am talking of here. They disgust me, those snake charmers with their innocent airs—that faintly lisped 'hello,' that meek smile, that slender swooning form

88

on the davenport. Let one of their men leave the room for a second, and this same tiny helpless doll will be clambering all over me, sighing and squeezing until tears spring into my eyes.

This is the suffering being to whom you would give the vote? This performer—better versed in theatre than you or me? Who makes a living by ruling the emotions of those deceived by her faint-hearted appearance?

All I can say is your letter was ridiculous. At least you are learning domestic craft, but there is more to running a house than sticking shells on boxes. Perhaps your height is an excuse to avoid female duties. Most folk take only two years of careering in New York to see what a hell-hole that town is. But somebody as naive as you may take ten!

I think I am getting the gout or I would come down and talk some sense into your thick skull. YOURS UNTIL I DRINK CANADA DRY. ANGUS.

November 18, 1862

Darling Annie:

I am sorry I went off half-cocked in my last letter, but I have been feeling poorly and as I suspected, I have the gout. Mother has installed me at home so she can look after me better. She is fussing about as I write, muttering how tired I look, and worn. Her voice makes me sleepy; it's a fine, soft voice, very like yours. (Or have you developed a hard, Yankee twang?)

I didn't know how weary I was until I heard the latch click behind me. Mother & the brothers came to fetch me at night. I didn't want the village to see how weak I was. They heaved me into the family wagon, and joked about the times when I would pull the cart for a longer period than our ox. Mother told them to hush, then reached for my hand under the pelts they had wrapped me in. I pulled away and Mother wheeled about fiercely: "You are still my baby, Angus McAskill, no different than when you were little and scared of bears in the woods."

The brothers didn't hear, lucky for old Angus, and I let her hold my hand so she wouldn't make more noise. She is the worst

worry wart, but I pay no attention and we get along fine now I am grown. What's that creaking sound? Aha! Mother's step in the hall! She has brought a letter from you! When she goes to blow the conch for dinner, I will read you. Her chattering is very tiring. "Don't mean to disturb you, Angus," she says, coming right in and sitting down with her mending. You know the way mothers are.
YOUR ANGUS, THE GIANT WHO IS HOME FOR A SPELL.

November 14, 1862

Dear Angus:

Oh Angus, is it wrong to be this happy? I came back to the Astor last night in a flush of pleasure. Mr. Ingalls walked me to the door and I let him kiss my hand. He is pleased with my work at the museum. Well, I floated in past the concierge and spent a long time staring out my window. I am still not accustomed to looking down on row after row of buildings, each row ending in a church or a monument. How different from my view at the shanty! I worry: what is required of me? Shall I sing my growing song to a heap of stones?

Yesterday I climbed into a barouche, a two-horse buggy with a crest and the name Lady Clinton on its door, and was whisked on a tour as soon as the driver learned I was new in town. He took me the long way to the American Museum through the Five Points slum.

Have you heard of it? Dickens described it as "a square of leprous houses" during an earlier visit to New York. A few buildings have been demolished but it was still a shocking sight. I felt terrible stirrings of sympathy for those mudsills. What can I do to help them? The dwellings at the "V" in the road, where the two avenues join up, were infested with strange pink shapes. As I looked, flesh reassembled into heads, legs, arms. I witnessed, Angus, what I know to be beautiful—the bodies of humans—as something repulsive and misshapen.

I think it a problem of backdrop. How can the human form be displayed to advantage in a crowd? It needs space to show it. As I deliberated, the cabbie turned his head and barked: "Isn't this something Miss! The biggest slum in the world?"

"Yes, it undoubtedly is the biggest slum in the world," I replied in a foolish voice. He told me stories about "Slobbery Jim" and "Patsy the Barber" who murder for murder's sake, and then, suddenly I was being deposited at the museum. Goshen was waiting for me at the door and shouted over the wailing of Barnum's brass band the news that Tom Thumb is going to join us.

Angus, do you think if giants like us looked after the mudsills cities like New York would be safe and happy? YOUR ANNIE, ON THE TOWN IN NY NY.

November 23, 1862

Dear Annie:

You are taking a lawless muddle like New York too seriously. You know those Yankees couldn't care about us. Good Lord. You shouldn't carry on like that. I don't know why you sound so happy. Remember you are my sweetheart and I am waiting for you to get fed up with Barnum and come back to me. Enclosed are two charms to keep you from being suckered by the city. I don't like the sound of that fellow Ingalls either. I worked with numbskulls like that; I know how little they have to offer. They think making money is the answer to a successful life. Mind you, I don't know what success is—maybe a combination of everything.

Now this will surprise you: I don't have a great affection for the folk here either. You could say St. Ann's is a miserable little town where the only thing that changes is the weather. I am attached to the sea, the bush, the view, nature in itself. I don't need people to bother me and I can truthfully say I have never cared what others thought of me. I don't know if that's fortunate or unfortunate. Say the charms each evening when the moon is up. (Not that they will do somebody as flighty as you much good.) YOUR ANGUS, WHO WANTS YOU TO STAY DOWN ON THE FARM.

Charm 1: Make a backwards turn in the service of rural route one
Make a backwards turn in the service of rural route two

Make a backwards turn in the service of rural route three and each backwards turn in the service of the backwoods and each backwards rotation made on the backwoods for the sake of the backwoods and each backwards turn in the service of the rural routes that grow us.

Charm 2: Angus stood out; he tripped over a maple wood and found it pulled apart. He placed twiglet to twiglet and trunk to trunk and the forest took care of itself. As he cured Acadia, so let Angus cure Anna's city fever.

P.S. One good thing about living here is Barnum wouldn't be caught dead in Canada. He thinks it's one long bronchitis bacillus.

CHAPTER TWELVE

The American Museum

I didn't tell Angus the whole truth about my life in New York because I didn't want to admit that I found it difficult in some of the ways he predicted. So I exaggerated the attentions of my manager, Apollo Ingalls (to make the big Maritime Know-it-all jealous), and did not mention that I was dismayed by my dramatic roles at the American Museum.

I longed to play serious drama, written by well-known Broadway writers. Instead, Mr. Barnum put me in farce and melodrama that drew unhappy critical reviews. One Yankee critic dismissed my work in an adaptation of *Gulliver's Travels* as "a wooden Glumdal-clitch to Nutt's pint-sized Gulliver." Another complained that the freak shows at the American Museum turned contemporary theatre into a circus. My role as the wife in *Jack-the-Giant-Killer* was not mentioned.

Mr. Ingalls told me not to mind the critics—"a useless clack"—and he assured me that Mr. Barnum was extremely pleased at "the natural comic talent" I demonstrated. I sometimes saw Mr. Barnum watching me—all grins and headbobs—as he sat hidden in his sedan chair in the wings by the stage. (We referred to the chair as Mr. Barnum's private box and were accustomed to his face glowing lustfully at the ballet corps. My employer was married to a sickly matron called Charity, and there were rumours linking him to the lead ballerina.) In any case, I suppose Ingalls spoke a half-truth. The mudsills are fond of mocking feminine behaviour. They see women the way they see European aristocrats—as a pretentious self-interest group out to thwart their manly pioneering spirit. So any female who is prepared to have a pie thrown in her face will be a success. And certainly my audience of 3,000 in the Museum's enormous lecture hall laughed at everything I did. I seldom received the Bronx cheer (or "boo" as Ingalls called the rude yells and jeers).

93

It was bewildering to me as I had a fear of making a fool of myself along with a desire to entertain and delight the normals and the more I made a fool of myself, the more the mudsills liked it! I also worried that the rowdy theatregoers would turn against me and I felt distressed by my roles. Truly, how could I be comfortable in the role of a large wench in *Jack-the-Giant-Killer*? Me, a slattern who tripped about and smiled when Goshen, my overweight peer, slapped my backside? Who could manage to look pleased after his hard blow and say coyly, as Goshen fell to his paper flapjacks with snorts of hunger: "Be a good boy and eat your breakfast!" My part as Gulliver's child nurse wasn't suitable either.

I wore a short cambric frock and ribboned bonnet and rolled a nine-foot hoop. The moment I stepped on stage the Yankees began to hee-haw raucously and the noise stopped me dead. Nervously, I pushed my wobbling hoop across the stage wishing I could turn into an invisible giantess who was detected by the hiss of her crinoline!

"Loosen up, loosen up!" Nutt hissed. He, Gulliver, stood to one side of me so his face wasn't hidden from the audience as he positioned a miniature ladder against my skirt. I gazed blankly down at the midget who prepared to go up on me as if I was a mountain to be scaled. He carried a small pick-axe and a coil of rope and wore a jaunty green cap in the style of the Swiss mountaineer. Once he had the ladder in place, the midget pounded up the rungs, smiling and winking at me in order to coax the look of mortification off my face. Half-way up, Nutt stuck the pick-axe under my belt and unfolded his rope. Then he tossed it about my neck and swung himself up and onto my left shoulder while the audience jumped up, screaming in delight.

"See Anna—they're at your feet," Nutt whispered in my ear.

Whenever I could, after my afternoon show, I flew across the street to St. Paul's, an ancient cathedral built before the American Revolution. Here I am in the Yankee church, five rows from the back, near the pew George Washington once worshipped in. It is July 4, 1862, the American holiday of Independence, and Barnum has me dressed to promote the Union cause. I wear the uniform of the 5th New York Zouaves, a northern regiment who copied the dress of the ferocious Zouaves. I am picturesque in the extreme. I have on a blue jacket with purple facings and scarlet breeches. On my head is a fez; its tassel swings into my eyes as I bow my head.

Oh, God, will I continue to satisfy the beast which makes loud noises when it loves or hates? That does not care for *Miss Leslie's Behaviour Book*, or Sarah J. Hale's manual, *Happy Homes and Good Society*? Whose endless eyes gaze eagerly up from under bowler hats and mops of dangling curls, waiting to be diverted by my game of hoop and stick?

Oh God, keep my knees from knocking and my hoop erect.

Oh God, let me not see the men shout and spit tobacco nor the angry frowns on the sweet, kitten faces of the women if my nine-year-old game falters.

Oh God, it is painful to pray.

My joints grind noisily as my knees hit the floor, and I examine the interior of the high, vaulted church to distract myself from my discomfort. My lips move soundlessly; my eyes climb slowly up the fluted Grecian columns and wander across the ceiling where dazzling crystal chandeliers dangle so far above the merchants and dock workers in the congregation that not even *my* head can endanger them.

Alas! It's hard for a woman like me to escape into a private world. At that moment, a vestryman passes my pew with a stack of prayerbooks under his arm; he catches sight of me and drops the lot. I reach out a long arm, and in one scoop, retrieve the leather volumes which look tiny in my six-inch fingers. I hand them back, smiling piously to charm the creature. I've been told the clergy at St. Paul's have no love for my employer. The museum's calcium floodlights shine through the stained glass above the altar and distract worshippers during the evening service. The vestryman accepts the prayerbooks and continues to stare. I bend my head in a gesture of devotion and try to ignore the tassel swinging before my eyes. I move my lips again in prayer, and the vestryman hisses softly to get my attention.

"Thank you, Miss...say, aren't you Jane Campbell, the CELE-BRATED MOUNTAIN OF HUMAN FLESH?" he asks. I shake my head, and suddenly he whinnies in delight.

"Ah, ha. I know—you're the BIGGEST MODERN WOMAN OF THE WORLD—I saw you yesterday at the museum." He's so eager to open a prayerbook that he snaps its spine.

"Will you make it out to Thaddeus Marvel?"

"Your name?" I ask. He nods and closes his eyes in embarrassment. Outside the quiet cathedral we hear suddenly the roar of an
excited crowd. The vestryman walks away to see what the fuss is
and I rise and follow him. From the portico overlooking Broadway,
we see that traffic has been brought to a halt by throngs of holiday-
goers who are watching my employer string flags and banners from
the door of the American Museum to the picket fence of the
cathedral. A gaggle of St. Paul's clergy stand on the front lawn,
staring helplessly at the old showman.

Near Mr. Barnum are Ingalls and my fellow curiosities who are
dressed, like me, in uniforms of the North. The crowd on Broadway
sees me and laughs. Barnum looks up, grinning.

"That humbugging scoundrel!" the vestryman hisses. He looks at
me in alarm. "Don't tell Barnum I said that! You'd better go. I think
he's calling you." I nod regretfully and hurry down the steps, and
past the clergy on the front lawn.

"Hail to the chief who in triumph advances!" the old showman
cries, and winks at me so I won't mind that he's mocking me with
the words of a popular ditty which the mudsills associate with the
President. I stare down at my boss, frowning, and more laughter
rises from the crowd. One of the clergy walks to the front gate.

"Mr. Barnum, will you remove your bunting at once," the
elderly priest asks, careful to stay behind the gate, on consecrated
ground.

"Remove the Stars and Stripes on the birthday of American
freedom?" Barnum shouts, "Are you Britishers over there at St.
Paul's?" The Broadway crowd roars angrily and surges in the
direction of the frightened clergyman. He quickly ascends the
stone steps of the cathedral and stands beside my vestryman.

"That's right! Retreat—you limey traitors! We'll drive you back
into the sea like our ancestors did eighty-six years before!" Barnum
chuckles and lifts a hand towards the brass band on the second-
floor balcony of the American Museum. An out-of-tune version of
"Yankee Doodle Dandy" makes the crowd put their hands across
their ears. The July breeze is hot and sticky and, down Broadway,
the shops and office buildings pulse in the heat as the curiosities
begin to march in time to the music—three abreast in military

columns—up Broadway. Nutt is in the lead. Ingalls bellows in his embarrassingly loud voice: "Fall in step, Giantess!" Barnum grins and bobs his head at me and I obey, falling into place behind the shuffling Goshen who is immense in a navy and white suit. The crowd shrieks and laughs and follows along behind as we strut our parade to the door of the museum. "Barnum's freaks give a good show," a mudsill yells. I wince at the word "freak."

Oh God, keep me safe from harm in this city of eight hundred thousand ruffians.

Oh God, am I making a fool of myself in this city of eight hundred thousand ruffians?

Oh God, save me from the mudsills.

To vent my frustrations, I composed a manual of Etiquette for the mudsills. An amateur's plaything. I did not show my canons to anyone so I was surprised when a draft titled "Giant Etiquette" disappeared from my dressing room. I had a second copy and thought no more of it. A few weeks later, the mystery was solved. The time was evening, early November, 1862. Our troops had just received a round of boos for a Shakespearean skit in which I played Lady Macbeth. I detested the sketch and dreaded the moment when I strolled on stage, wearing a baggy sultan's costume—a style which Mr. Ingalls thought resembled Elizabethan dress. My red hair was plaited in braids under a flowing headdress, and on my feet I wore strange shoes whose toes curled up in front like the tips of skis. In my arms I carry Nutt who played my infant, rolled up in silk baby's bunting like a mummy. Goshen, in a monk's robe and cowl, played Macbeth. The casting was wrong; Goshen couldn't declaim loudly enough for the audience to hear, and our speeches were dreary. The midget drew our single laugh. When I exhorted Macbeth to kill Duncan and vowed that, if need be, I could dash out my baby's brains, my child began to drum his tiny pink feet against my bosom until his bunting unravelled and he was naked in my arms except for a large frilled diaper. His savage kicks made my breasts ache and I longed to do as I threatened—and hurl Nutt to the floor. Midgets are so tiresome. They can't take life calmly as giants do. If a normal steps on my toe, why should I be angry? It does not theaten me. However, normals step on midgets' toes every day so the little creatures live on the look out for big toes to step on, to prove that they are important.

My mood was cross when we finished our skit and I retired backstage to watch the next act, Signor Donnetti's troupe of acting monkeys, dogs, and goat. That night, Nutt and Goshen didn't notice our bad reception and giggled rudely over the antics of Mlle Mimi, a monkey that performed as a female bare-back rider. Mimi's furry bottom was exposed under her frilly tutu each time she vaulted on and off the back of a trotting bulldog. I frowned sternly because I do not favour skits that ridicule female behaviour and the snickering of my colleagues ceased.

"A wonderful performer, isn't she, Anna?" Nutt said and respectfully patted me on the knee.

"Yes, ma'am. Yes, ma'am!" Goshen agreed, smiling affably. A photograph of an English bulldog rising against a backdrop of an erupting Vesuvius shone on the stage curtain and Signor Donnetti finished the act with his slide-show finale, "Magic Lantern Changes."

"After you, Lady Macbeth!" Nutt said, clicking his heels and bowing.

Our dressing rooms were a row of filthy cubicles. My employer's stinginess was notorious. The heating he had promised turned out to be a foot-warmer in each dressing room. It was our job to heat the water, scooping it from an old barrel and boiling it in pots on a woodstove in the hall. That evening it was my turn to fill the pot. Dispiritedly, I placed them on the stove, dreading the "notes" on our performances from Mr. Ingalls. When it was done, I joined Goshen and Nutt who sat on old wood boxes, leaning against the wall of the hallway. Mr. Ingalls stood silently for a few minutes, warming his hands over the stove. He liked to make us wait. Likely, he thought he looked a romantic figure as the firelight played on his fully whiskered blond face. And he was right.

"Goshen, you need work on voice projection!"

"Nutt, be yourself and stop acting like Tom Thumb."

"Anna, you were holding yourself back. What law says an Elizabethan lady can't smile?"

Ingalls grinned broadly to demonstrate the potential stretch of the human mouth. I flushed and looked down at my ski-tipped toes.

98

"We need a script written for us," Goshen whispered in his Kentucky dialect.

"It is a mistake to cast us in dramas that were not made for special people like ourselves."

"You know the answer to that, Routh boy!" Ingalls said.

"Real genius transcends its material," Nutt piped up.

"Wrong, pipsqueak!" our manager boomed.

"Show Judge Hiriam P. Ingalls a script that works and I'll let you play it all over Europe and North America."

"Anna is writing something," Goshen said and exchanged a glance with Nutt. Goshen fumbled in the pocket of his monk's robe and retrieved my crumpled, scribbled pad. He bowed towards me.

"The Commodore and I believe she's too shy to show this to you, Judge," Goshen whispered.

"So you took it upon yourselves to show me, did you, boys?" Ingalls asked. He hissed loudly through his teeth and grabbed the pad from Goshen and handed it to me.

"What is the meaning of this?" he said. The hall was silent except for the logs crackling in the stove as I waited for my limbs to tighten. Instead, my mouth opened and out popped my lecture voice.

HOW TO BEHAVE IN THE COMPANY OF GIANTS

Do not ask, "How's the weather up there?" or talk about good things coming in small packages.

Do not speak in a loud voice like Gulliver, who remained small when he appeared big.

Do not trick giants into being measured. Giants lie about their height: as a way of pleasing the world; out of politeness; sometimes through fear or humility.

Do not bribe giants to exhibit themselves unless you have left them no other way to make a living.

Do not expect giants to carry you when you can walk.

Do not make giants perform rescue operations when there is nobody to save.

Do not climb to the top of a giant's head to make yourself feel important.

Do not boil giant flesh for bones to make bridges, even in your imagination.

Do not kill giants and steal their treasures.

Do not bring giants gifts or take them out to the park because it is be-nice-to-a-giant week.

HOW TO BEHAVE IN THE COMPANY OF DWARFS

Do not try to breed dwarfs.

Do not put dwarfs in choker collars and ask them to run naked through your apartment.

Do not serve dwarfs in cold meat pies as a way of improving a dull dinner party.

Do not exhibit dwarfs in boxes or sell their bodies to the College of Surgeons before they die.

Do not fondle dwarfs in your lap or against your breast unless you have carnal inclinations.

Do not say "Hi Pygmy!" to a dwarf.

Do not wipe your hands on the hair of dwarfs sitting beneath banquet tables.

You can nominate dwarfs for the legislature; dwarfs have sharp wits and make excellent counsellors of state.

Do not make dwarfs fight turkeys for your amusement.

WHERE TO SEE GIANTS

The American Museum.

The Roman games at the Coliseum.

Civic parades, where giants are stuffed and mounted on floats.

Any schoolyard, where there is sure to be one giant who may not grow tall enough to work for P.T. Barnum.

100

WHERE TO SEE DWARFS AND MIDGETS

The American Museum, picking on giants.

Wrestling in teams in European sporting events.

Holding bridles in civic processions.

Nota bene: All giants have spinal curvature and shoulders tilted like seesaws from stooping to hear conversations at social levees. Dwarfs are small people who aren't perfectly proportioned. Midgets are perfectly proportioned small people. Unlike giants, there is no quick and easy way to spot dwarfs. No longer can they be picked out in a crowd by the jester caps, doublets, and jewelled belts they used to sport when royalty dressed them.

I recited my etiquette breathlessly, like a schoolgirl, stopping only when Jane Campbell tiptoed in, bringing into the room the smell of mint. Jane looked slovenly in a child's dress of plum-coloured muslin that didn't hide her ankles from public view. (I don't know why fat women are considered the most erotically appealing of us curiosities! Her ankles were as large as pillows in torn and dirty pink stockings and threatened to bury her small, square, shoeless feet.) I noticed Ingalls and Nutt stared intently at Jane's legs as she settled herself on the largest wooden box near the stove. Their heads moved in imperceptible forward arcs in order to see the insides of her billowy thighs while she squatted—legs akimbo—pretending to listen. I had the full attention of Goshen at least; the Negro giant stood warming his ample backside against the woodstove, and looking at me with a pathetic, self-pitying expression in his brown melancholy eyes.

When I finished, my audience showered me with applause. Nutt hugged my left knee. Goshen stamped his long feet so hard in approval that a partition wall fell down between one of the dressing rooms. And Jane slapped my bottom in delight.

"You left us fatties out!" she gurgled. "Or aren't we gen-u-ine curiosities?" All laughed and I flinched in annoyance.

Ingalls banged the side of the stove with a fire poker to obtain order. "What kind of poesy was that?" he bellowed and reached up and tapped my breastbone with his poker—too hard. It hurt.

101

"It's a manifestor," Nutt chirped. "As elevating as the *Shepherd's Clock* by Spence, if you ask me."

My manager furrowed one of his fuzzy yellow eyebrows.

"We'll converse on the meaning of Anna's...er, manifestor tomorrow," Ingalls said.

"Naw. P.T. should hear about it tonight, honey," Jane said. This time she smacked my manager's bottom and he roared in pain and rubbed his hindquarters.

"Maybe the old showman should hear about it," he said, grudgingly.

Nutt and Goshen cheered and Jane threw her arm up around my shoulder and gave me a friendly squeeze.

"Real nice, Big One!" she said. I smiled shyly. Would Mr. Barnum like my composition? Would he see the humour—and significance it held for men such as himself? If Mr. Barnum saw—the world would see! And from now on, prodigiosa such as myself and the others would be treated with the respect that we deserved! I took Jane's saggy arm and returned her squeeze. She giggled.

"C'mon, you bunch of freaks! Let's go to Del's," she cried. "The first round of desserts is on me."

The next night Ingalls escorted us to the dressing room of Tom Thumb after our performance of *Macbeth*. He would not discuss "Giant Etiquette" and told us instead that he had "a little treat" for us. Nutt, whom I carried on my shoulder that evening, hissed in my ear that the treat was the General himself. The prospect unsettled my short friend. He had a complex about the older, more famous midget, who was the embodiment of the mudsills' dream of mobility. Thumb, so I learned at the Museum, was the son of an impoverished Yankee carpenter, who had grown so rich and famous under Barnum that he could enjoy a country lifestyle at his home in Bridgeport, Connecticut, playing billiards on a miniature table and sailing his yacht in Long Island Sound. Nutt, who already envied and worshipped him for his success, developed a hatred for the older midget because Lavinia, whom Nutt adored, had fallen in love with him.

To me, Tom Thumb seemed an obvious match for Lavinia. She was twenty-one years old, thirty-two inches tall, and twenty-nine pounds—"an accomplished, beautiful, perfectly developed woman in miniature," as Barnum boasted in his advertising. Nutt, at eighteen, was shorter, slighter and younger than the twenty-four-year-old Thumb, who was reputed to be thirty-three inches and still growing. Nevertheless, Nutt refused to accept Lavinia's love for Thumb; he would and could not be comforted and made himself a nuisance by following Lavinia wherever she went.

In the summer Nutt had enjoyed a small victory over the General, which he had hoped would win over Lavinia's affection. My employer had milked a common suspicion that Nutt was really Thumb brought back under a new name. Mr. Barnum had exhibited the two men, side by side, as the TWO SMALLEST AND GREATEST CURIOSITIES LIVING, and had invited the crowds to pick out the real Thumb. Nut had been overjoyed when Thumb was booed as the impostor because the older midget had puffed through his famous interpretation of Cupid in flesh-coloured tights, a few pounds heavier and several inches taller than the crowds remembered him. Unfortunately, Lavinia didn't change her mind. Instead, her admiration and love for the wealthy midget grew until she seldom joined us at Delmonico's, spending long weekends in the country with Thumb.

All of this is to let you know how dismayed Nutt was to be in the General's dressing room. For my part, I was extremely excited to meet the celebrated midget whom I had glimpsed at a distance, whisking Lavinia out of the lecture room as soon as her act was over. Thumb looked slightly corpulent, yet he possessed the air of practised confidence that proclaims the star. As Nutt and I turned the corner to go into Thumb's first-floor cubicle, I felt pressure against my skirt and looked down to see an enormous top hat—about the level of my calf—float by me and into the room ahead.

"Save me, Anna! That's him!" Nutt whispered. The midget hugged my neck despairingly and begged me to take him downstairs to the basement so he could hide in his cubicle. Unfortunately, I could not. Ingalls walked just ahead with Goshen, so in we went in the wake of the cocked hat which absorbed all of Thumb's head and neck. Lavinia was already in the dressing room; she sat on the miniature lilac divan I remembered from my first tour. When she saw Thumb, she leapt to her feet with a loud twitter of joy, her black eyes flashing. Thumb blew her a kiss and then promptly turned and began to pass out miniature cigars and business cards to all of us. With his hat, he wore a faded swallow-tail coat, which I assumed was meant to be a replica of the uniform of Napoleon. His face, now that I could see it, was a shock—it looked oddly mature, almost dissipated, because the midget had a faint brush of mustache above his upper lip, sagging cheeks, and dark rings under his eyes.

"You are supposed to be the BIGGEST MODERN WOMAN OF THE WORLD?" Thumb asked when he came to me. I nodded, overcome to be in the presence of such a famous person.

The midget snorted and spat a stream of tobacco into a tiny silver spittoon near the divan.

"I've seen bigger women on my European tours," he said. Then he scampered up the divan and stuck his hand inside the breast of his shirt in the manner of the great French warrior.

Immediately, I felt humiliated and I stood awkwardly looking about the cubicle which I noticed was heated by an ordinary wood-stove. A pot of water simmered on its surface—in case Thumb or anyone else wanted to fill the pewter foot-warmer I spied under the divan. An enormous wooden water barrel stood in the corner by the door. The temperature in the room was toasty—an agreeable change from the damp of our downstairs cubicles—but there was no furniture except the divan, and Ingalls, Goshen, Nutt, and myself found ourselves standing while Thumb and Lavinia occupied the divan.

"Fellow players, the illustrious showman P.T. Barnum has told me that some of you are scribbling scripts because you are dissatis-fied with the material your employer has given you the opportunity to play." Here Thumb paused and looked at me. Even though he stood on the divan, his head was level with my thigh. I smiled eagerly at him and the midget smiled back condescendingly.

"Will you believe me if I say all of you will look back on your early trials with fondness when you are rich and famous?

"Yet I must warn you that P.T. and I are of the opine that your amateur drama will have no success with a modern audience accustomed to high professional standards. They come to this palace of artistic knowledge to forget the hum-drum vicissitudes of life."

Again Thumb regarded me and I felt a kernel of irritation with my employer. So "Giant Etiquette" wasn't diverting enough? So Mr. Barnum had put Thumb up to letting me down? Couldn't he inform me in person instead of telling me before my peers? I gazed miserably over the top of Thumb's cocked hat.

"Your friend and servant, Phineas Barnum, has confided to me that he wants all of you to develop the keen edge of professionalism demanded by audiences of today.

"I cite my career as example. My dedication has never faltered, not since Barnum discovered me at the age of five when I was the size of a doll and weighed no more than the showman's pet dog. . . ."

Thumb stopped and I realized he wanted us to laugh. Instead, we all stared glumly at him. Of course, Lavinia obliged with a giggle. Thumb smiled at her and looked coldly at us.

"The key to all professional success is aggressive instinct," he said. "If you doubt my words, look at the contrast between myself and Commodore Nutt. There you have a midget who is not unlike me, who, as a teenage youth, even resembles early portraiture of myself, but cannot approach the heights of stardom. Why?

"He lacks the killer instinct of the true professional which is the secret of giant success."

Thumb cleared his throat and Nutt, who still clung about my neck, hugged me tighter than ever. His blond tufted head drooped and I felt a sensation of wetness on my neck. Oh dear! Nutt was crying. How could Thumb be so insensitive to the despair of the younger midget?

"But, fellow thespians, I need not look for examples close to home to illustrate my point," Thumb continued. "I will refer now to the example of the deceased British painter B.R. Haydon.

"Isn't it a fact that this artist, born a genius, slashed his throat and shot himself in the head after Londoners ignored his exhibit of paintings at the Egyptian Hall and packed the room next door to watch performances by myself?

"And isn't it a fact that this internationally famous painter acknowledged my talent by advertising in *The Times*:

EXQUISITE FEELING OF THE ENGLISH PEOPLE FOR HIGH ART

General Tom Thumb last week received twelve thousand people who paid 600 pounds; B.R. Haydon, who had devoted forty-two years to elevating their taste, was honoured by the visits of thirty of one hundred and thirty three and ½, producing five pounds, thirteen point six. . . .

Thumb quoted the ad in a shrill English accent. Ingalls hee-hawed while Goshen gawked admiringly at the midget star.

"Isn't it a fact that a man born a dwarf went on to win the heart of the great Queen Victoria and the love of millions while a man born an artist could not cope with life and so ended his own? And the stuck-up limey tried to say *he* was of the Napoleonic species!" Thumb's voice rose to a squeaky bellow and his chipmunk jowls quivered.

"It makes me think God should bless all humans with freakdom so that they can prosper like a humble minimum of man such as myself!"

Mr. Ingalls applauded and Thumb smiled patronizingly and lowered himself to the divan. I clapped, and so did Goshen. Nutt, on my shoulder, was silent. Thumb waddled out the door and re-entered a minute later, wearing a white peruke in the style of George Washington and the same cocked hat and swallow-tail coat. In his arms, he carried an immense papier-mâché model of the White House. He placed it on the floor and climbed up onto its roof. There he sat dangling his stockinged legs between the high Ionic columns of the monument's northern portico, a ten-inch revolutionary sword hanging from his waist.

"You have heard how professionalism conquered genius," Thumb began again, "not only killing off a weaker member of our species, but creating such success that I was invited to address the limey Queen herself.

"And what did I tell this remarkable woman when we were face to face? I told her success is the cornerstone of the Yankee spirit.

" 'Queen Victoria'—and these are my very words—'every American is a Jason racing to get his golden fleece. Our great country is so

106

free—that if you run hard and fast enough you may get the biggest fleece of all.' "

Thumb paused and lowered his voice.

"I refer, of course, to the presidency."

Thumb unsheathed his tiny sword and started to whistle "Yankee Doodle Dandy"atop his Lilliputian palace.

"Excuse me, General Thumb," I said, startled to hear my lecture voice pop out.

"You refer to the Yankee superstition that anyone can become the President of the United States. With due apologies, the presidency is denied to members of my sex."

"Who cares what you think?" Thumb squealed.

I stiffened in surprise. "Perhaps I do not understand because I come from the Canadas," I persisted. "But not only is your great race restricted, it seems that the chance any boy has of becoming President is so low that your contest may well be a lottery."

"Anna! Don't insult our famous guest! We want him to come back," Ingalls hissed at me.

"I am only trying to make sense of the mudsills' beliefs," I said. "Surely Thumb knows there is only room for one person at the top?"

"Big lady, our great office is awarded to the gent with the most gumption and get-up-and-go," Thumb said, adjusting his high-pitched voice to a lower, more gentlemanly pitch.

"Why, if I had my way, it would be mandatory to ask immigrants if they believe their sons can become President! And I would only admit the lucky so-and-so's who said yes!"

"The U.S. is a land of achievers and adventurers," I agreed, hoping to show the irascible midget that I could see both sides of the question. "But perhaps it's a mistake for you mudsills to think that your way is the only way."

Thumb angrily whacked me across the thigh with his sword.

"Shut up!" he squawked. "Shut up you big vegetable! You overgrown excuse for a female!"

Nutt, who, in my ear, had uttered strange growls and cheeps while Thumb spoke, let out a shrill war whoop and slid down the front of my gown to the floor. He pulled out a bowie knife from a holster inside the vest of his Commodore's jacket and advanced on the startled Thumb. Ingalls and Goshen withdrew to the wall nearest the door and Lavinia screamed in fear. In some situations, a giantess has to do what a giantess has to do, so I quickly leaned down and picked Thumb up by the back of his trousers, lifting him high above Nutt's head. For a second, Thumb dangled from my long fingers, staring up at me in bewilderment, then his child-sized face turned purple in rage and the midget's nasty little mouth opened and closed hard on my palm, drawing blood. I shook him until he loosened his bite, and lowered him onto the top of the woodstove. The midget squealed in pain, and Lavinia flew at my knees with raised fists. Meanwhile, the smell of scorched wool rose to my nostrils; reluctantly, I lifted Thumb up with both hands and dropped him into the barrel of water used to fill his foot-warmer. Then I sailed majestically from the room—without restraining my skirts. I knew I'd done a grievous thing, but I felt relieved all the same. Let the mudsills have their ridiculous race! I, the BIGGEST MODERN WOMAN OF THE WORLD, preferred a saner pace. A moment later, I found myself outdoors near the Croton Water Fountain. I stood staring in distraction at the mudsills running off in all directions as they went about their business.

CHAPTER THIRTEEN

Barnum Considers "Giant Etiquette"

"About your material," Barnum began. "What is the meaning of its peculiar title, 'Giant Etiquette'? Don't you mean etiquette for normals?"

"My manual has a few idiosyncrasies," I acknowledged.

"Hahahaha—so you were making a little joke, Anna!" Barnum said. "For a woman, you've got quite a sense of humour."

We sat in Barnum's office on the second floor of the museum—my employer behind his writing secretary with his coat-tails folded on his lap, Ingalls and I on a horsehair sofa. My legs were curled around a marble-topped table decorated with china memorabilia of Jenny Lind and Charles Dickens. My skirts swirled about me—100 yards of satin and 50 yards of lace bought by Barnum for $1,000 following a scolding from Momma. She had been quick to remind my employer that neither the uniform of the French Zouave nor that of the Yankee soldier was in our contract. My skirt was a liability in the cramped office and I strained to keep it from knocking over Barnum's porcelain figurines. A bouquet of wax fruit under a bell-jar stood on a side table, precariously near one of my elbows.

Barnum's eyes flickered over his possessions, checking their position vis-à-vis me. Then, his baby-blue eyes sparkling, he heaved his brogues onto the marble table so all the china jumped. He was enormously pleased to be chatting with me since he had enjoyed hearing about Thumb's dunking and wanted another look at the woman who had pulled "a fast one" on his famous prodigy.

I was pleased and excited to see Barnum. At sixteen I was innocent enough to believe the showman would like my scribblings if I explained them to him, face to face. Little did I know that I had a more democratic opinion about the arts than my employer who, in the age of Jacksonian democracy, had become rich by creating a palace of amusement which challenged the British notion that museums had to be places of scholarship. You see, I was convinced the public was not really entertained by entertainment and, like me, longed to enjoy work of better quality.

"Your canons are engaging, Anna," Mr. Barnum declared. "But they are too didactic for the thrill-seeking audience of P.T. Barnum."

"I think my manual can be enjoyable and instructive, in the tradition of your great museum," I said. "I share your views that the entertainer who relieves public tedium and brings momentary excitement and happiness to the masses deserves the thanks of humanity."

Barnum chuckled. "Save your serious thoughts for St. Paul's, Anna." He leered at me. "I like women with a few things on their minds besides new dresses. But audiences don't want to think. They want to enjoy themselves."

"I found Anna's etiquette enjoyable, P.T.," Ingalls said. I stole a sideways glance at my manager who was staring at the showman with a look of impatience.

"What? You found it entertaining to listen to the views of a big curiosa?" Barnum hooted in disbelief, but looked sober when he saw me regarding him. "No, Judge. Anna's appeal lies in her size. She is a wonder, the LARGEST OF HER SEX, not a philosopher."

"Well, she is not the burlesque buffoon you're trying to make of her, P.T.," Ingalls snapped. "She is too ladylike."

Barnum raised his eyebrows in surprise.

"You're the one who put her in a fez!" Ingalls continued.

"An economy move, Judge. That hat was made for another giantess. Aama? I can't remember. The one run over by a chariot." Barnum winked at me. "Of course, the big woman must be, ah . . . refined. But her material has to divert the audience. People want to laugh because these are serious times, Judge. Men like me are risking their lives for soldiers at the front."

"I don't call your work on the Prudential Committee dangerous," Ingalls said sarcastically.

Barnum jumped up. A paranoid look slid over his affable face. He reached out and pulled a green shade down across the window of frosted glass on his door. The window was emblazoned with huge white initials, "P.T.B." Then he motioned us to lean close

"Do you know I've had threats on my life because of that vigilante committee, Judge? There are far more southern sympathizers in our great town than either of you know." Barnum groaned. "Poor Charity has had to learn how to fire the rockets Mr. Lincoln sent me in case the Copperheads attack my country home."

Barnum tilted back in his office chair. He stared at the ceiling and slowly closed his eyes. In repose, the face looked worn-out beneath a wreath of white hair. He was already fifty-two; and he had brought the Swedish singer Jenny Lind to America, made a hero out of Tom Thumb, suffered one bankruptcy with the Jerome Clock Company, and published his own autobiography, *The Life of P.T. Barnum*. My employer is an old man, I thought.

At that exact moment, Barnum leapt to his feet. The fire was back in his round blue eyes.

"Judge! Anna! We'll do a play about my life! A drama of historical realism with fire bombings, southern conspiracies, an uplifting Temperance ending ———"

"And Anna?" Ingalls asked in surprise.

"She'll play my wife," Barnum said, winking at me. "Without Charity, I am nothing!"

Barnum began to sketch his flamboyant rise from the son of a Bethel, Connecticut, tavernkeeper, talking non-stop like the clever filibusterer he was. I listened in awe—my ankles crossed, my palms flat on my knees so my skirts couldn't escape. Out of the corner of my eye, I noticed my manager start to grow. Startled, I turned sidways and saw that Ingalls' bandy legs were lengthening and curling in vine fashion—twice around the legs of his chair. I tried not to stare but I couldn't keep my eyes off his square trunk which had burgeoned into a massive zucchini that rose until his top hat split open like a seed pod. Barnum—I noticed to my amusement—had dwindled. His head looked to be the size of a Prince Edward Island spud above his embroidered showman's vest. Meanwhile, the office was filled with giant writing. Vast letters splattered the walls and furniture; they coated the gas jets of the chandelier so the room receded behind a lurid light. Some—as big as babies—sat on our laps to be held.

111

Barnum bounced the word "engaging" on his knee and looked at me curiously. His speechifying stopped abruptly.

"I don't think I've seen you smile before, Anna," he said.

I looked away to avoid giggling at his pasty potato face and glimpsed in the glass bell-jar a vast, skirted Maritime squash nestling coyly against a stubby zucchini.

I reddened; my vision was inspired by my sexual interest in Ingalls. Barnum stood and let the shade rip upwards.

"Any time you want to test another script, call on Old Barnum," he said in dismissal. He bent down and kissed my long fingers.

"By the way, Judge, there's a giant over at Irving Hall I want Anna to see. A real showman!" Barnum chuckled. "I'd like to see her dump *him* in a tub of water!"

Barnum waved us out, a little potato man with stick arms and legs.

"Glad you took my criticism so well, Anna," he said. "I can't stand temperamental theatre people."

Ingalls took me to a soda fountain on Ann Street near the museum and played in a melancholy way with his yellowed dice as I devoured chocolate ice cream. It was so pleasant to be alone with him—without Jane and her proprietary pats and kisses—that I barely thought about Barnum's dismissal of my scribblings. In truth, it was the beginning of my disillusionment with the showman and the American dream, but at the time, I was aware only of Ingalls' laced Hessian boot resting next to my kid-leather slipper. (Did I or did I not feel a square foot brush against mine under the table?) Oh, I was far too thrilled by the way Ingalls had defended me to be angry with Barnum whose childish pleasure in his ability to outdo his fellow human struck me as amusing. Later I came to dislike the way the Prince of Humbug, like many Yankee businessmen, excelled in raising noble emotions in order to produce banal products. But I never stopped to admire the daring of Barnum who taught Puritan North America that having fun could be instructive. His palaces of amusement broke with the tradition of his pilgrim ancestors and with the dour ways of my ancestors too, and gave people like me a new opportunity for making a living.

"P.T. is washed up—a has-been!" Ingalls boomed up at me as we left the restaurant. It was the first time he had spoken since we walked out of our employer's office. I glanced down in surprise.

"Barnum's trading on ideas that are twenty years out of date," he added, not knowing the showman would use those very ideas to revolutionize the circus in the decade to come.

"Oh, you mustn't disparage him like that," I admonished. "He does the best he can."

Ingalls shook his head. "You're too generous, Anna. Barnum doesn't care about anybody except Barnum."

He paused by the steps of the Astor House and took my hand in his large rough paw to stop me from hurrying inside. Then he walked up three steps so his head was on the same level as mine.

"Some day Judge H.P. Ingalls is going to fly solo and he'll be looking for a giantess like yourself to manage. Tuck that away in your big head and don't forget so you're ready when I come for you."

I smiled shyly and hoped Ingalls wouldn't notice the gaggle of pedestrians who had gathered at the bottom step to jeer at me, a tall woman with a bantam escort. He noticed, unfortunately, and ran down a few steps, shaking his fists at the youths who wore the Union blue and whose indolent manner suggested they were soldiers on leave. I called, "Apollo, I'm not offended," and the boys hooted. Ingalls whirled around angrily. He saw my worried face and slowly walked back up the steps. I took his arm so he could escort me inside.

In the lobby, we found Momma sitting on one of the immense scroll-back Astor sofas. She was sewing a lace ruching on her poke bonnet and wore the cat-who-swallowed-the-canary look of one privy to extraordinary news.

"Guess who's in town, Annie," Momma chirped. A huge form wearing a tall beaver hat lumbered towards us through the busy lobby. Angus! My lighthouse among lampposts! I fainted before I could greet him, but I maintained just enough control to collapse in an inward spiral so as not to knock Ingalls down. When I opened my eyes again, the freckled moon face was staring at me with concern. I jumped up and threw myself into his arms while Ingalls and the crowd in the lobby gaped.

"You've won lass," Angus mumbled in his hollow, rumbling voice. "Old Angus is moving into this hell-hole to be with his Annie."

"You're going to live in New York?" I asked in astonishment.

The giant kissed my cheek shyly and I smelled his wonderful candle-wax smell.

"Aaach! If I'm with you Annie, the land of the mudsills won't be so bad."

CHAPTER FOURTEEN

Angus and the Kentucky Giant

To please Momma, Angus found himself lodgings at another hotel. My little parent didn't want him to stay at the Astor House for fear his presence would create gossip about my reputation.

Her sense of propriety irritated me. (I chafed under the Scots' prudish morality; I was Rabelaisian in my giant core—and only adopted a staid manner later as a way of becoming normal.)

In any case, Angus cautioned me to be gentle with Momma who had grown up in a more religious age. He pointed out that she would return to New Annan once Angus and I set up housekeeping in the brownstone we planned to buy on Fifth Avenue. There we intended to juggle a marriage and *two* careers, as Angus had decided to take work as a fish merchant to help with the payments for our new home.

So, unknown to Momma, I stole off to see Angus between my shows at the lecture hall. Thanks to my interview with Barnum, I had been removed from the role of farce and now gave a lecture on the trials of gianthood. I had begun to understand that performance is not true exposure, and that if I acted skilfully, I could hide behind my stage presence and fear nothing. So I was in better spirits and more sure of myself as I puffed (a trifle guiltily, nonetheless) through the crowds at Ann and Broadway on my way to the giant's hotel in the Bowery. Angus' thriftiness had led him to choose cheap lodgings in a decaying area of town. Gangs of Irish toughs clustered in the hotel lobby; the giant's room was as narrow as the water-closet at Astor House, and almost entirely filled by the two beds Angus had tied together with sheets. There was no view: The window faced the stone wall of a tavern; and I found Angus staring morosely at the ceiling when I made my breathless entrance.

"Not a peep of sky, Annie," he complained as I nuzzled in his arms. "I'm a prisoner in a gaol."

Our love-making cheered Angus, though it left me with bitter-sweet feelings. The driving pressure of the giant's one-foot organ was curiously mild, like a zephyr skimming across the surface of my flesh. When he was done, and the hotel room redolent with the smell of candle wax, I felt puzzled and sad. Perhaps the nervous organism was different with large women—or was I too big to be pleased by any man?

Poor Angus. He was shy, and so was I, and I couldn't bring myself to tell him how to rub me as I rubbed myself so that the heavens opened and the clouds dropped out. Instead, I concocted fantasies to distract him from his grievances with New York.

Here we are, lying on his makeshift bed, *circa* 1862. I have on a lacy pink chemise, and my gentle giant has pulled his plaidie up about his knees. I am stroking the downy snow-white cheek with its garden of freckles and whispering into his ear that we are not in the land of the mudsills, but floating on an iceberg up to the Canadas to perform an imperial mission. Angus's sly blue eyes enlarge. The giant is suspicious of my imagination but he cannot resist listening. He brushes my hand away and checks the blanket to make sure his private parts are covered. I whisper throatily: "Angus, Angus, you and I are wrapped in silver fox, the pelt of snow monarchs. . . icicle jewellery sparkles on our heads and necks like the northern lights, our lips are cold, glacial blue, but our skin, beneath our furs, is hot! You make us Arctic highballs (mix one ice floe with navy blue Arctic sea) and we smooch up a summer storm. . . ."

The mention of "smooch" and Angus looks cross. He doesn't like me to use slang. "Aaaach Annie! Will you not blither on like a fool! What kind of mission are we on?"

"The mission is one of true patriotism, my dear," I say. "We are smuggling a growth elixir up to the Blue-noses stunted by the Arctic breezes. Two little sips and they will spurt up-up-up!"

"On an iceberg?" Angus asks.

"Ssssssh!" I put my finger on his thin rosy lips. "Our berg is not real ice but a chunk of frozen pick-me-up sap whose formula I've stolen from the Yankees. Only listen Angus, our love-making is melting our floe and we are sinking into the steamy seas, our vital elixir wastefully dispersing and later to be the reason for the extraordinarily large sharks seen in that vicinity."

116

Here Angus bellows for me to stop and begins to smack my exposed shoulder with his glutton kisses. I sigh and close my eyes. With Angus, I was inspired to day-dream about altering the face of the world, but the MARITIME MARVEL only wanted to kiss away at my large frame as if I was smeared with crowdie.

Meanwhile, life in New York sped on. Barnum showed no interest in mounting a play of his life, and our troupe carried out the performance of melodramas for the mudsills whose behaviour was more ill-mannered and unpredictable than before. The civil war grated on their nerves and made audiences eager to be diverted by novelties like the KENTUCKY GIANT, who performed in the full regalia of Confederate soldier. The giant, a southerner, had left the Confederate army as a conscientious objector, and come to New York for sanctuary. He was the showman Barnum had mentioned to me, and when I learned crowds were being turned away from his performances, Angus and I went to see what the fuss was about.

The audience stared when Angus and I took seats in the front row at Irving Place, a fashionable hall in Lower Manhattan. I had on a new grey poplin walking dress and Angus wore his cutaway coat with velvet collar, a white brocade vest, and his highland kilt from Queen Victoria. The hideous beaver hat—so *de trop* in New York— had been left at his hotel.

We were forgotten when the curtain rose and a swash-buckling young giant sauntered on stage in the white pants and dove-grey cavalry jacket of a Confederate officer. The giant twirled a pair of duelling pistols and sang "Dixie," the southern anthem. He pointed the pistols at the audience until people began to squirm in their seats.

"Prepare to receive a memento from Robert E. Lee," he said sarcastically, looking slowly and deliberately around the hall.

The guns fired—two frightening retorts. When the smoke cleared, I realized the thunderous noise had been blind cartridges.

"You bunch of Yankee suckers!" the giant said and started to guffaw, rolling his head back until his large nose pointed at the ceiling. Suddenly, he stopped and executed an army salute. "Captain Martin Van Buren Bates at your command."

The crowd booed and a mudsill yelled out, "Slave owner!" But the giant seemed indifferent to disapproval and set up an easel, mounted with charts and graphs. He said he was not in the hall to fight the war, which he had left for personal reasons, and began a lecture called "The Survival of the Mediocre," which examined the history of giants. Goliath was his starting point. Bates said the legendary figure was an normal-sized warrior who looked large to a small race like the Jews.

"The Bible says Goliath was six cubits and a span in stature," Bates roared, "but I speculate the Jewish cubit was nothing to boast of."

I started, expecting the giant to go on to make an anti-semitic remark. Instead, Bates launched into a tirade over discrimination.

"We have all heard unfortunate remarks about size, such as the proverb that a dwarf can threaten Hercules, or the term 'long and lazy.' Even an encyclopedist like France's Virey dared to call tall men tame and insipid.

"Why has largeness been scorned? In part, because of the tendency among large beings to embroider with accessory structures such as horns and bony bosses. Who would not sob over the tragedy of the hadrosaur dinosaur if they knew of its unfortunate certobsian crests? These bony knobs were not central to the animal's 'hormonic engine.' But having achieved an impressive stature, the animal elaborated on it uselessly.

"But the true reason, my friends, is that throughout history man has felt safer with the obscure and the mediocre and resented the brilliant, the exotic, and the spectacular, a category to which giants belong."

Just then the giant noticed me in the audience and smiled. Nearby, the mudsills listened, frowning. The giant's aggressive manner and his eccentric view had captured their attention.

"Now is the moment to forget bigotry and accept our destiny. In our world of plenty we can breed a superior species whose mental development will increase as the race grows in size. Provided physical development is normal."

Bates coughed and smiled at me again and I smiled back. His lack of concern for what his audience thought intrigued me. His broad, clean-shaven American face was darkly handsome although his slanted black eyes and thick brows made me think of Attila the Hun. (Wasn't the Scourge of God a midget?)

"Stop looking at that lying clay-eater," Angus rumbled in my ear. I squeezed the Highlander's calloused hand to let him know he was the only big man in my life, and Angus continued to glare up at Bates.

"Not even the infusion of foreign blood will prevent your children and your children's children from being two and three times as tall as you who sit here," Bates continued.

He pointed to a graph on his easel. "The tallest men in the world come from the northeast and southeast American states where I was born," he said. "Our moist, temperate climate is excellent growing territory for giants." Bates drew himself to his full height. "You have only to look at me to see this is the case."

Angus suddenly threw back his head and bellowed, "You hornswoggler, the brawest lads are from Cape Breton where winters are deadly fierce and the summers will suck you dry!"

Angus slowly rose out of his seat. The audience laughed and the MARITIME GIANT hoisted himself up on stage and marched over to Bates. The KENTUCKY GIANT stared blankly at this apparition. Then he bowed and obliged by standing back-to-back with Angus.

From my seat in the front row, Angus, at 7'9", appeared to stand a head taller, but the southerner bested him in weight. Bates looked to be about five hundred pounds—seventy-five pounds more than Angus and one hundred and fifty pounds more than me.

I considered both giants form head to toe. Together they made a contrasting pair who satisfied my fantasies about tall men: Bates was rude and beautiful and Angus was beautiful and kind. Idly, I wondered if Bates would be impressed when I stood up.

Then the audience roared that Angus was taller and Bates shook Angus by the hand and directed him back to his seat. The NOVA SCOTIAN HERCULES beamed as the crowd applauded him. I smiled in delight too. Suddenly, Bates called out to the crowd:

"There you have a fine Celtic specimen whose race has contributed to the nation of the great *Americanus*. But alas, my friends, I must fault the Celts for less tenacity of purpose and mental hardihood than the *Americanus*.

119

"As mercenary soldiers, Celts do not exhibit the same zeal, energy and power of endurance," Bates declared. "Celts submit with less patience to the requirements of discipline, are turbulent under hardships and given to complaints about rations and fatigue duties."

"Blackguard! Clay-eater!" Angus grumbled from his seat and started to rise. I put my hand on his arm to restrain him. Bates winked at me gratefully, and went on with his lecture.

"Unfortunately, I must also dismiss the Germanic breed," the southerner said. "They suffer severe defects of structure such as unusual weakness of the abdominal muscles, flat feet, and a tendency to varicose veins.

"The Negro has many excellent physical qualities, but has small, ill-developed calves and feet, and a tendency to the exterior show and parade of military life.

"Inferior to all is the mixed race of New Mexico whose mercurial temperament spoils the strain.

"The *Americanus* is superior not in his muscular development and height so much as in the toughness of his muscular fibre and the freedom of his tissues from intestinal fat, allowing active and prolonged movements."

"What is your opinion of the Canadian?" I ventured.

"Who?" the giant asked.

"She means our dominion to the north," Angus said grumpily.

"Ah, our friendly neighbours in the land of snow and ice," the giant smiled knowingly. "Not evolved enough to submit to my anthropometrics." He came to the edge of the stage and stood directly before me. "Though I'd say, God willing, there is every chance the Canadian will join us on the evolutionary tree!"

Following his lecture, Bates invited Angus and me to take refreshments at a booth in the hall. I was proud to notice I was at least five inches taller than the southerner who in person turned out to be expansive and witty, gulping coffee in great draughts (a tic among a nervous people like the Americans) and twitting Angus and me as Britishers for ordering tea.

"You Yankees may think a case of tea is something to float in the harbour of Boston, but in the Canadas, we drink the stimulant," I said.

"Canadiana," Bates drawled, "you've got some fine American fighting spirit in you." The giant stroked his moustache and bowed towards me. "If I may be bold, ma'am," he continued, "for a Kentucky gent accustomed to southern belles, you are a sight for my poor eyes!"

I blushed while Angus glowered beside me, tongue-tied as Bates and I exchanged complaints about gianthood—and skirted politics according to the custom in well-bred society.

"At least your height allowed you to put on long dresses and enter society at an early age," Bates joked. "What did it do for me except deliver me to a war no one wished to fight?"

The giant explained he had been pressed into service two years before, when he was fifteen, because his seven-foot frame led a squad of Confederate soldiers to conclude he was older than he said. They kidnapped the giant, threw him over a mule, and took him to a camp of the Fifth Kentucky Infantry C.S.A. Although he sympathized with the southern cause, Bates said he soon realized he was a pacifist. He asked to be discharged after he rose to the rank of Captain. Then he had gone back to his family's farm on a boonpork, a creek delta near Whitesburgh in Kentucky's Letcher County where his mother and father lived with Bates' twelve older brothers and sisters. For a few months he taught school in the Blue Ridge Mountains, but decided to leave again because neighbouring feuds had become intolerable during the civil war—fights had pitted brother against brother, and were the outcome of Kentucky's divided stand on abolition. Half the state was fighting for the north while the other half had joined the southern forces. So Bates left— trekking out through Cumberland Gap, resolving to forget politics and enter show business. He attached himself to Wiggins and Bennoit, a small Cincinnati circus, but when he arrived in New York he decided to go into business for himself.

"Quite a history, Captain," Angus said when Bates had finished, "but I wouldn't brag about deserting your army if I were you!"

Bates narrowed his eyes and Angus glared back. Suddenly Bates guffawed, and turned to me with a significant look.

"Mr. McAskill, I pray my history is only now beginning in earnest," the southerner said.

The two men walked me back to the Astor House, one on either side of me. We took a roundabout way, going down along the docks because Angus wanted to sniff the sea air. As soon as the masts of the sailing ships came in sight Angus cheered up and began to banter with the southerner who had become stiff and nervous because his suit—the uniform of the Confederate enemy—was attracting hostile attention from the passers-by who did not know he was a theatre personality.

The two giants sauntered on either side of me, Bates spitting tobacco anxiously while Angus stared at the Atlantic with a look of gratitude that was pitiful to see. It was early evening. The crowds on the teeming wharves yelled at Bates and soon a throng followed us, noisily disparaging the Confederate cause. Of course, the hecklers called out from a safe distance—the three of us must have been a frightening vision to the mudsills.

By the East River, we passed a group of Yankee sailors who had gathered on a pier to jig around a fiddler. One of the sailors spoke to Martin and the fiddler stopped playing so the other sailors could hear.

"You there in the Rebel suit! I wager your southern manhood you can't lift the anchor by our ship!"

Martin wheeled about and stared at an anchor sitting on the wharf near the American tars. It was a monster object, whose weight, the sailor told us, was 2,700 pounds. The KENTUCKY GIANT grunted and shook his head but Angus dropped my arm and pushed through a growing crowd until he stood near the massive anchor. Then he stripped off his cutaway coat and handed it to the sailor who had challenged Bates.

"I, Angus McAskill, the NOVA SCOTIAN HERCULES, will do the feat!" the giant boomed in his rich musical voice. "I am not only a prodigy of size but a prodigy of strength."

The sailors began to cheer. I smiled at Angus who cut a dashing figure standing head and shoulders above the sailors. Angus pointed to Bates who was chewing tobacco, and watching the Highlander suspiciously.

"Yon southerner says the tallest hail from his state. Well gentlemen, where I come from men are hardy as well as large, and learn to suspend 100-pound weights from their little fingers." Angus grinned at me. "And then the manly fellows write the names of their lasses in the air!"

Angus bent to the anchor and I felt a sudden chill. Why do normals celebrate feats of power and domination? What has power taught except detachment? (And in the case of Angus—reckless waste?) I looked about for a way of stopping my sweetheart, but could think of nothing that would not embarrass him. O ye promoters of male exploits, pity females like myself who must pretend to believe in our man's strength in public, while our knowledge of his vulnerability has us in anguish!

Angus grabbed the anchor. Then he braced himself against the hull of the ship behind him and with amazing ease lifted the anchor to his chest. After a pause, he traced the letters A-N-N-I-E in the air.

The sailors applauded crazily and the fiddler struck up another tune. Angus next cradled the anchor against his chest and kissed it before hoisting it above his head. Then slowly, he lowered it onto his shoulder and began to strut back and forth across the pier in time to the fiddle music. The giant's sweet moon face did not flush; his limbs did not tremble.

A group of sailors swarmed about Bates and started to taunt the southern giant. "I'll warm your butts if you don't watch it, you goddamn weaklings!" Bates barked at them. When they continued to jostle him, the southerner reached out and knocked down the closest man. Then the group rushed Bates who stormed off the pier with one of the men clinging to his back and another hugging his knee like a child.

I was relieved to see him go. Interesting though Bates was, I did not like the way he had talked to Angus back at the lecture hall. Meanwhile, Angus, in a long, flowing, overhand motion, as if he was tossing a Highland caber, pitched the 2,700-pound anchor towards another pier. His gesture misfired and one of the huge flukes caught in his shoulder.

Blood poured from Angus' chest. The crowd closed in, many of the mudsills sobbing to see Angus in pain. I pushed my way through to him and he leaned gratefully on my shoulder. A spectator found us a hack and we drove back to his hotel in the Bowery, Angus cursing softly in his Scots brogue.

"Dammit lass," he said, when I had him fixed in his room and a doctor sent for, "misfortune always strikes me in this infernal town!"

CHAPTER FIFTEEN

A Dream of Smallness in Central Park

Angus was still recovering from his wound when we attended the wedding of Tom Thumb and Lavinia on February 10, 1863. The giant was in a morose mood; he had to wear an enormous padded bandage under his frocked shirt in case a movement reopened the stitches and caused his wound to bleed again. Scowling at the staring crowds, he lurched up the steps of New York's Grace Church, wearing his cutaway coat and a new top hat, and holding one of his huge freckled mitts protectively before his injured shoulder. It hurt his shoulder to move the other hand, so it dangled uselessly at his side.

We squeezed into the last pew on the bride's side, since Thumb had no love for me or for Angus who had held him in his giant palm years before during an exhibit at the American Museum, and dropped the midget into the cage of the HAPPY FAMILY for a prank.

"Who is Thumb except a sawed-off mudsill who loves to be swanky?" Angus rumbled in my ear as Thumb and Lavinia strolled solemnly down the aisle and up six small steps to a special platform that had been erected for them in front of the chancel. Walking arm-in-arm behind the bridal couple were Lavinia's younger sister— the midget Minnie Warren—and a dejected Commodore Nutt.

"As for the Bump woman, who is she except a social-climbing school marm?" Angus continued in a bitter tone. I sighed, and smoothed the puckers out of the lap of my lilac reception gown. Angus had sunk into a fit of Celtic gloom since his anchor wound. Although Angus and I intended to announce our own wedding for July at the reception, I was also in low spirits. Each day, in his shabby room, Angus produced a fresh grievance about the mudsills, and each day it was harder for me to coax a chuckle from his sad, moon face. I longed to have his approval, but in small ways the giant let me know I could not count on it. His hatred of New York soured our time alone and Angus sometimes forgot I was a Blue-nose and lumped me with the mudsills in his disparaging remarks.

The sight of him staring miserably ahead at the crowded pews took the pleasure out of the ceremony. The church was packed with prominent politicians, actors, and business people who had been personally invited by the midgets. Their wedding was the talk of New York's social season, and some mudsills had offered to pay an outlandish fee of sixty dollars to attend. Lavinia had ignored Barnum's suggestion that she charge admission, telling him in sarcastic tones that since she and the General weren't marrying for money she saw no reason to include finances in the ceremony.

Barnum sat directly across from us, on the groom's side, at the end of a pew filled with Union generals whose pride in their uniforms made them keep on their immense navy shakos. Barnum soon noticed us and beamed our way in delight. When he heard Angus was back in town, he had tried to contact the giant at his Bowery hotel. Of course, Angus had no interest in working for the Prince of Humbug, although he was finding it hard to get started in the fish business.

"McAskill!" Barnum hissed, ignoring the disapproving frowns of the General beside him. "Long time no see!"

Angus shifted his immense bulk and pretended not to hear. He lowered his eyes to his lap where his one good hand worked a knot with a piece of string. The same hand that touched me clumsily in the afternoons between my shows now wove and unravelled the string with the deft handiwork a sailor uses to mend his nets. I stared in admiration, but Angus caught me watching, frowned, and jammed the string into the pocket of his fancy coat.

Meanwhile, the organ struck up the "Fairy Bride Polka," and the Reverend Dr. Taylor led off the midget wedding party to sign the church register. At that moment, a robust, grinning face appeared around the corner of our pew. Angus started in fright. There, on his knees, was Barnum! While the congregation goggled at the midgets, my employer had crawled across the aisle to where we sat. With a conspirator's wink, Barnum lifted his index finger to his lips and handed Angus a church calendar. The giant stared at Barnum in amazement. Then the showman winked again and reached out and squeezed the muscle on Angus' good arm, shaking his head vigorously back and forth to indicate he was impressed.

126

Once more the organ pumped out the "Fairy Bride Polka," signalling the return of the midgets. In a pivotal movement (suprisingly quick for a middle-aged fellow), my employer twirled about on his knees and crawled pell-mell across the aisle to his pew. Angus stared at the calendar with an expression of horror. On it, Barnum had scribbled a new offer:

Bravo on your anchor lift!!! Kentucky Giant is up for a rematch at the American Museum!!! It's worth $20,000 to you if you will vanquish that Confederate scoundrel a second time. Your old friend, P.T. Barnum.

The giant's frightened look surprised me. I wasn't prepared for fear, not from *him*. After the ceremony, his agitation increased as we stood on the church steps and watched the society matrons hold out their gloved hands for Thumb to kiss. Barnum and a photographer from Brady's stood a few steps below with Lavinia. The little bride waited for her groom in a frenzy of impatience; her veil was askew and her maidenly lips showed a sarcastic drag at the corners. Suddenly, Barnum spotted us and shouted above the cheering spectators: "Angus! Annie! Over here for a group portrait!"

Angus blanched but shook his head and doffed his top hat. "Let's vamoose, Annie!" he rumbled. "It's a trick! The old bugger knows I owe him $2,000."

But we couldn't move. To our surprise, neither Angus nor I was able to push through the dense crowd that had gathered to see the midgets. At least our height gave us a good view of Thumb, his jowls quivering from the exertion of his kisses as he helped Lavinia up into their miniature honeymoon carriage, driven by a pair of matching Shetland ponies. Soon their carriage was lost in the traffic of downtown Manhattan, on its way to the Metropolitan Hotel where a wedding reception was being held for two thousand guests. Angus and I fled along a side street in order to avoid Barnum.

We started to bicker irritably as we made our way to the reception. Why we fought I do not know! I guess we never believed anything was large enough to come between us. The arguing was started by Angus, who wanted us to give up New York and go home to Cape Breton.

"New York is not ideal, Angus, but it isn't time for me to leave yet," I said firmly.

"Why not lass? Must you wait until this burg kills you before you come to your senses?" Angus snapped. "Besides, the jig's up for me here. I'll have no peace until Barnum has me where he wants me."

"He may not even remember your debt," I replied. "That was ten years ago, and it's not as if he has a lack of curiosities!"

Angus glared and sullenly followed me into a parlour at the hotel where the wedding gifts had been set out for display. The giant stationed himself beside a drink table, surrounded by ladies in puffy lace dress bonnets and gentlemen in stovepipe hats screaming social chatter at each other. Gingerly, so as not to hurt his shoulder, the giant lifted up an enormous crystal bowl of punch and drained it dry. The crowd under his elbows laughed but I refused to watch his indulgent display and strolled about, looking at the hundreds of wedding presents, all custom-made in miniature for the Thumbs. Here was a silver-plated sewing machine from Wheeler's, there a chariot ornamented with rubies from Tiffany's, and what was this? A curious singing bird with Mr. Barnum's card on it. It appeared to make a strangled sobbing sound, but as I pondered the toy, I realized the noise came from beneath a food table displaying a miniature ice-cream fortress. There sat Commodore Nutt, weeping miserably. I bent down and handed him my three-foot-square hanky.

"Anna, my fruit is plucked," he moaned. "I've found the woman of my dreams only to lose her."

"It's true you don't have great choice," I said. "But your love for Lavinia may not be the elevated kind that comes with maturity."

"How would you know?" Nutt said. "Nobody has ever felt for you what I feel for Lavinia." His tear-stained face looked indignant.

"Oh no?" I said angrily. "What about Angus?"

I turned to point to the giant, but no one was there. I excused myself and hurried off, but the crowds in the lobby slowed my progress and suddenly I found myself looking down at the bulbous red face of my employer.

"Lost your giant?" the showman said, his blue eyes twinkling. "Take my advice, Anna, and find yourself a husband. McAskill isn't the marrying kind."

I started in surprise.

"The THIN MAN is partial to you, but we must have consideration for his brittle bone structure."

I frowned and Barnum chuckled. Ignoring my protests, he took my hand and led me to a lobby window. There he settled me on a love seat overlooking the broad snow-cleared avenue, continuing to stand so his head was on a level with mine.

"Annie, there is nothing wrong with a large woman if the man is up to her," Barnum continued, "and it's time you married. But not McAskill. Too lazy for an ambitious gal like you."

He looked thoughtful and offered me some calamus, which he had been chewing since he gave up his cigars. It was made from the root of sweet flag and I found it flavourful.

"Monsieur Bihin? Already a husband. At least twice. What would a girl from Nova Scotia want with a bigamist?"

"Why just curiosities?" I joked. "There are normals who would marry me."

It was true. I regularly received mail from members of the audience, asking for my hand in marriage. I found their offers odd since early in life I had ruled out most of the human race as a possibility. Yet I was plagued by males who were intent on finding a way around a biologically hopeless situation.

"Do you fancy us normals?" Barnum asked suddenly, pressing close to my seated form. I rose from the sofa at once and Barnum's expression changed to a scowl. His head was again level with my cinched waist.

"The normals you mention see you as a money-making proposition, Anna," he said grumpily, and stared out the window. After a pause he began to chuckle at the antics of the wedding guests outside the hotel, arguing and jostling over parking space for their elegant coaches and hacks.

"Marry Goshen," Barnum said. "He likes you, you know."

I looked quizzical. Goshen's preference lay with men.

Barnum shrugged. "So he's a Nigra. You aren't prejudiced, are you?"

"No. I. . . ."

"You are prejudiced. Too bad. Look what a show-business marriage is doing for Vinie! Have you seen a happier dwarf?"

"I do not wish a show-business marriage," I said. "Angus and I want some private life."

"There will be no other kind of life but the show-business life for a girl like you, Annie." Barnum patted my hand. "And you would prosper from it. I'll take you and your groom on a European tour after a ceremony at St. Paul's. You like that old mausoleum, don't you? Ponder it! BARNUM'S GIANTS OF NEW YORK: THE WORLD'S TALLEST COUPLE! Dump McAskill and tie the knot with Goshen, and you'll bless old Barnum till the end of your days."

"No! The BIGGEST MODERN WOMAN OF THE WORLD will only marry for love!" I grabbed his collar and Barnum shook slightly and made a show of kissing my large hand. "Funny bird, aren't you, Annie?" he said.

A waiter came up and whispered in Barnum's ear. The old showman spun about, and waved nervously at an aged matron sitting in a high-backed chair near the lobby door. She had a high forehead and receding chin, and looked as old and dour as a pilgrim from the *Mayflower*. I recognized Charity, Barnum's invalid wife, and chuckled as Barnum scurried off to attend a mate who was as uninteresting to him as the Yankee past he had revolted against. I left immediately afterwards.

I found Angus collapsed across his two beds at his hotel in the Bowery, sucking a bottle of rum as if it were cow's milk. Twenty or so empty bottles sat on his windowsill. As I came in, his blue eyes filled with tears, and I saw his shirt front was stained with blood.

"If that's the kind of wedding you want lass, old Angus can't do it," he said in a gloomy voice. "A man like me won't be wanting to wear his heart on his sleeve to give the mudsills a thrill."

"You didn't mind entertaining them with your punch drinking," I said crisply and immediately regretted my words.

"Aaaach, Annie, you don't understand a buckeroo like myself," Angus roared. "That was sport, which counts for nothing, but love is not for show."

"I do not wish a wedding like the Thumbs'," I said, growing angry myself as I was hurt by the giant's tone. "You aren't listening to me. You are inebriated and illogical!"

Suddenly, Angus sprang out of bed, throwing off his plaidie. His gentle moon face looked red and brutish and the cords of his neck were swollen to the thickness of a bull's. He seized my shoulders and began to bellow in a terrifying manner.

"Why, you don't care about your Angus at all," he roared with a betrayed look. "Or else you'd do what he wants!"

130

"Restrain yourself!" I said. "You don't know your own strength."

The giant frowned and dropped his hands. Immediately, he began to smash one huge fist into the palm of his other hand, his blue eyes burning with a maniacal frustration.

"You stupid, stupid lass," he yelled. "See this! This is what Angus would like to do to you!"

I shuddered at the menace in his voice, and edged towards the door, feigning a show of calm. Suddenly, the giant ceased battering his palm. A look of pain passed over his enraged face. He sank down on the bed, holding the spot where the anchor fluke had pierced his shoulder.

"You know what's the matter with you, lass?" he said slowly. "You're selfish. You are for no one except Anna Swan!"

"It's you who are selfish!" I said, my eyes blurred with tears. "You judge me as a sinner, you self-righteous old Scot, because I do what is best for me but you think it fine when you do what is best for you!"

Angus glowered, and I turned my back on his vast, flushed face and fled.

The next day he sent a message for me to the Astor House. It read:

Dear Annie:

You have me down wrong.
I am not ridiculous, but filled with ridicule.
I am not disappointed; my trust in bitterness can't forsake me.
I am not unhappy although beauty like yours pierces my over-sized heart. YOURS FOREVER, THE LIVING LUMBER LAD.
P.S. I've gone back to the Cape. If you want me, give up Barnum and come home.

True enough, when I inquired at his hotel I was told the giant had checked out and booked passage on a steamship to Nova Scotia. Without a word of apology! Not a peep of remorse! I did not write to him. And no word came from him. I learned through the museum gossip that the KENTUCKY GIANT had been kidnapped by a squad of southerners and was being held in an army camp as a prisoner for deserting the Confederate cause. So another anchor lift would have been out of the question, even if Angus had agreed to it.

Meanwhile, life in New York was anything but genteel. The city's vile anti-Negro lynchings, its draft riots, its felonies, and the drunken behaviour on every streetcorner depressed me. I was accosted once and had to slap away my attacker with my silk parasol. To help the winter pass, I took up ice skating with Commodore Nutt. The sport had become fashionable at Central Park, which was under construction in the 1860s.

As many as forty thousand skated on the park lake and Nutt always stayed close to me so I could protect him from the hilarious pushing and shoving which the mudsills saw as part of their pleasure-seeking. Here we are on a Sunday afternoon in March 1863: The red ball is posted in the bell-tower on Vista Rock, indicating the ice is safe, and calcium reflectors provide light for the skaters since a veil of snow is falling. Towards the northern section—the part of the lake reserved exclusively for ladies—a few mudsills sweep the ice with brooms in the strange Scottish game known as curling. Ice chairs with runners glide by us. Nutt's cheeks are pink apples as we coast through the crowds that open like the Red Sea to let me pass. Crinkle, go the blades of our custom-made bone skates while Nutt reads out loud a letter from the Thumbs, whose recent visit to the White House has been in the newspapers. The midget's voice is shaky with envy. Not only has Lincoln (already troubled with prophetic dreams of his own murder) fêted the bridal couple, but the president's son Tad was astounded by Lavinia's resemblance to his mother. Not thinking of Nutt, Lavinia described her ecstasy over her marriage.

" 'Truly, it is a story from dreamland,' " Nutt reads sadly. He looks up to me for consolation. " 'Imagine! Your Vinie compared to the first lady of the land!' "

I shake my head gravely, remembering the way Lavinia spouted Bible verses at anyone who doubted her intelligence, and per-formed gruelling theatrical routines to prove that her stamina was equal to a normal's.

"Poor Vinie!" I say, thinking out loud as we coast along. "She will run, clap, dance, and spout and never learn that there is no need to prove anything."

"Just because you're a lazy bones doesn't mean Vinie should be!" says Nutt, instantly wrathful.

I'm startled even though Nutt is known to be a volatile youth. To the amusement of mudsills nearby, he is skating before me with his dukes up and looking as if he will take a jab at my knee.

"You'll regret your insult to the Lady of My Thoughts," Nutt cries. "My heart will crack if I have to listen to another lecture about maturity!" All of a sudden he is weeping loudly.

The midget lowers his fists and skates off to put himself out of earshot. Away from my sphere of protection Nutt is jostled by the crowds but manages to keep a skater's stance, mittened little hands clasped behind his back, as he strokes down a pond near an unfinished hillside where construction caravans and steam engines stand idle because of the cold weather. I glide quickly after my charge, careful not to turn over on my ankles, which are the weakest point in my long frame. As I swing around a bend near Bow Bridge, a strange scene unfolds: Nutt in the midst of a flock of swans, some as big as the midget. One of the larger birds waddles closer to Nutt and he delivers a savage kick to its breast. There is a horrible noise of bird protest. I put away thoughts of my own safety, and redouble my strokes. Suddenly, the wind fills my massive skirts until my dress billows like a sail, propelling me at top speed towards the midget who has just time to glance up in terror before I blow into him. At the last moment, I restrain my petticoats so I won't tip the midget, but Nutt falls down anyhow.

My heart bangs in fear for I cannot stop; the wind pushes me through the scattering birds and on down the lake until the wintry breeze dies out and I come to rest near the squatters' hamlet, Seneca Village. The Central Park skaters are far behind me, and despite a few squatters sitting by their fires, I feel as alone as if I am on the moon. The snow has stopped and the air is astonishingly clear.

To the south I can see the spires and smoking chimneys of the city. There is St. Paul's and there the city hall cupola and flags of the American Museum, and even (am I mistaken?) the roof of Angus' hotel in the Bowery. A piercing sadness makes me catch my breath.

I truly am alone! My heart twists in disappointment as it occurs to me for the first time in my life that I am not going to get everything

I desire. I stare bleakly at the city which has ruined my fairy-tale romance, and in a trance-like way mouth the words to my old growing song, saying it backwards, willing New York to shrink with all the magic energy I can summon from the sidhe. . . .

Lower leap you until wither never it'll and child a was I when me in grew that love a but ambition or wealth of love a not it's it deny can't I and you to power my give I you to power my give to foolish. . . .

    I'm that answers you of one each then but lower sink you can and down dance you will here folk the asking often I'm. . . .

The city, from Fifth Avenue to Battery Park, dwindles to the size of a tourist trinket whose inner workings are plainly visible in Manhattan's clear river light. I can make out the tiny, rugged stone façades and the streets with the amusing traffic congestions, the needle-sized spire of St. Paul's, a minute city hall colonnade, and the uninspiring little geyser of the Croton Water Fountain. Angrily, I reach down and pick up the miniature town and in a long, ladylike toss, pitch New York as far as I can out into the Atlantic Ocean. . . .

CHAPTER SIXTEEN

Emblem Fatigue

June 2, 1863

Dear Annie:

You will never guess who I met sailing back up to Halifax. That blasted midget and his new bride whose maiden name used to be "bump" or some fool thing. (She's a pretty little piece with the airs of a school marm.) Of course, they were the last people old Angus wanted to see and do you think I could shake them? Good lord, no! They were on the first lap of their honeymoon tour and already wilting like ten-day-old celery stalks without their regular dose of public adulation. Well, I was in severe distress on account of the wound (I stained my shirt with blood three times and no doctor on board) and the little gumpers hardly noticed my condition, they were so busy making social repartee. You should have seen them Annie, chattering and bouncing, their little bodies sparkling with wedding jewels while they indulged in the ignorant generalities travellers make about other nationalities. In vain did I try to set them straight about Halifax, which they appeared to think was as far north as Hudson Bay.

"The burg you are going to is an old international port—just like New York," I said with a ring of pride. "You need to remember Nova Scotia has been run by a nation of Blue-noses for over two hundred years."

"Halifax like New York?" sniffed the f. midget. "How can a town of igloo-dwellers be modern?"

"Angus is full of tall stories, Vinie," the m. midget had the nerve to say to his little woman. "I visited the town as a boy and saw sailors who lived in ice huts and supplemented their diets with polar bear."

Annie, did you ever hear such a pack of lies? Their manager, Bleeker, was as weasely as Thumb—a long drink of water with the face of a dead man and a three-foot beard that gave me the willies (like the hair corpses grow underground). Damned if the zombie didn't inform me the Governor General was going to have an audience with the midgets when they visited Quebec. Now what would that British nabob want with those pipsqueak mudsills I'd like to know!

At the wharf, I was met by Mother, who cried for one hour solid at the sight of me and my broken shoulder. Of course, the midgets nearly knocked her over, clambering out of the launch and racing to hail a taxi. (I said Halifax was international but I never said it had a rush hour, did I?) But they ran off and disappeared into the fog. Unfortunately, Mother and I stayed at the Temperance Hotel where the midgets were giving a levee. I refused to go, but Mother went, bless her foolishness, and I slept for two days solid. When I finally woke up, Mother told me the f. midget sang "Annie of the Vale" with special gusto and I said that was likely on account of the midget's friendship with you.

And now I get to the bad part. How I disgraced myself before you in N.Y.N.Y. I have a murderous temper, Annie, that's the God's truth, but only on one or two occasions has it got the best of me like that.

Once at a house-raising, when some no-good neighbours gave one and all except Angus a rum drink, I climbed up on the frame and took down a board 60 feet by 8 inches and consigned it to the Atlantic Ocean 500 yards away. The other time was at a dance, after a fellow stepped on my toe (three times in a row, Annie)! I laid him out and prayed like a saint over his unconscious form that I hadn't gone and killed the bugger. (I hadn't, by the by.)

Of course, I've thrown a few Yanks around. Most Yanks are like the Kentucky faker who talked big but wouldn't lift a decent weight. They need to be taught a lesson before you can get on with them. Which is why I sent my three-hundred-pound ex-agent, Dunseith, over a woodpile. Another Yank had to have his ship stoned before the bugger would sail back and return the stones he and his men took from my field. They didn't ask, just sailed in and robbed me, so I called them back from the shore.

"Say Captain, get back here with those stones and rocks you took."

"What do you want them for?" the Yank skipper hollers.

"It matters not," I said, "but it was a dirty mean trick to take them without my permission."

The captain told me I might stand a chance of getting them back if I showed up on deck so I heaved a shower of boulders until I saw his crew rowing my way in a hurry.

Hundreds of pounds of stones were put back. "Over here, sir, granite lumps go by the gate," I told them. The crew ran to and fro until I tired of remembering how the meadow used to look and asked the Yanks to write my name and the date with the stones left over.

The captain said too bad he couldn't have the rocks for ballast and I said he could have, but I wouldn't put a pebble of mine on a Yankee schooner when its captain didn't have the decency to ask first. The captain said they were only rocks and he didn't think a farmer would mind seeing the last of a hindrance. I said, "Sir, they might look like worthless lumps to you but now I know they are valuable to Yankee captains and the next one that sails in and minds his manners can pay me for them."

The *Cape Breton Advocate* wanted to write up that event. I said no, I don't have a swelled head. Of course, you will hear other stories about my temper which are hyperboles, like the night my fishing dinghy on the beach at St. Ann's fell to pieces. I asked the boys on the shore to help me haul up my beauty and the buggers thought they would play a trick and carry my boat right up the beach and into a tide pool. At high-water mark, I said, "That will do gents." But they kept on pulling and so I grabbed the boat and pulled the other way and a bow plank cracked. That's all. Similarly the story about shaking a man's hand until a drop of blood squeezed out. Annie, I wouldn't do a soul such a nasty turn. Me, who carried a friend on my back thirty miles up the trail in a snowstorm and thirty miles back just because he said he was tired of walking! Also, did you know I cried during a bull-fight in Cuba? I couldn't bear looking at the torment of such a massive thing made helpless by ignorant humans. You see Annie, I am not bad throughout. I have a good nature and have done some good things in my life. Samples of Angus's good deeds: (1) standing up on a train to show my full height to frighten a band of American desperadoes so they wouldn't come and rob the passengers; (2) carrying a pork barrel under each arm to amuse the folks in St. Ann's and not minding when an ignoramus on the street called me "Big Boy"; (3) helping a poor farmer from the South Gut who was promised (by a conniving merchant) as many fifty-pound barrels of flour as he could throw up onto the deck from the hold of a sailing ship. (Sad for the merchant, I was the farmer's stand-in and tossed up six barrels which cleared the twelve-foot distance onto the deck and landed in the bay.)

Plus, I am a good son to my mother and an honest shopkeeper with a spiritual and moral character. (I am not above holding the Sunday service in my home, Annie!) I credit my good works to Father's advice that it is better to follow one general principle than abide by many rules. If men do their duties to the best of their judgment, power, and strength, it matters not whether their motives are selfish. Do you see Annie? What is good for one bloke is good for another, more or less. Maybe you still do not consider yours truly worthy enough even after all I have told you. So I hereby swear to you that from henceforth Angus will do his Annie proud. How? What would you say if I told you I am going into politics? Well, it's the God's truth. A bunch at the shop want me to run as mayor of Englishtown. They've told me Abraham McIntosh, the new minister, is going to approach me. I'm chewing it over, Annie, and would be interested in your thoughts on the matter. Not that I will glory in power-mongering (like John Munro who was defeated in the last election for provincial legislature and is going off in a huff with Rev. McLeod's bunch to New Zealand). Nor do I look forward to the teasing I'll get from the boys for taking on such a bullshit job. But I thought you might be more interested in living here if I was more prominent in the community. (Contrary to what you think Annie, I care about you in a big way.) I know you will have some problems getting used to St. Ann's because you have gone and got Yankeefied.

Everybody does once they get down there. Then they come back here for a visit and talk to you as if you were retarded. "Oh, hasn't that come up here yet?" they ask. They think living in the

United States of America is like graduating from school. They don't appear intelligent to me. Americans know how to make money, but money is overrated. Do I need it, living in St. Ann's? The Yankees aren't better than us. (Maybe crookeder.) Annie, I don't want to sound judgmental. Yanks are people too. Except for Barnum and his crew, there must be a few of them that are all right. So as soon as you can wind up your contract with the old Bamboozleem, do so lass, and come north where real people are who love you. I wish you were looking at the bay with me tonight. The sight of its silky blue water makes my heart big. Of course, nothing has changed in St. Ann's since the day you and your mother came down. Except I'm not at my shop but staying with the family again until my anchor wound mends. Mother has fixed my old bed up in the living room. It's very homey: my brothers' coats hanging off pegs in the long hall to the kitchen, the lathed walls, the braided rugs. . . . Personally lass, I don't think it's the wound that's got me, but an affliction peculiar to giants, who are always having to shoulder giant expectations from normal folk. Not even the physician of Queen Victoria could diagnose this condition of exhaustion old Angus calls emblem fatigue.

Think on it Annie: The up-down motion of living is tiring for people like you and me and what is the future but more of the same? So come home and make it up to your ANGUS, WHO WOULD WANT TO MARRY YOU EVEN IF YOU WEREN'T THE ONLY GIANTESS IN THE WORLD. P.S. Emblem fatigue is no joke. You'll see. You'll get it too.

CHAPTER SEVENTEEN

Need-fires at the Museum

April 2, 1868

Dear Angus:

I know I have not written for six years but I was so angry after our last quarrel that I felt word from me would be capitulation to your point of view. I do not feel this way any more and am sorry I let a person as valuable as you go without attempting to resolve our differences. I would like for us to reconcile and live as husband and wife. (If you are unattached, Angus. Even as I write, I have a melancholy feeling that long ago you gave up on me and married a normal from Englishtown.)

Unfortunately, the notion of moving to Cape Breton still presents difficulty for me as I prefer urban life. Can we not compromise and find a locale in between—some country air for you, some city ways for me? I do not know where to find a blend of the two styles but if you will forgive me for failing to answer your note so many years before, I would search the world with you to find it. (We are from the Canadas, are we not? where compromise is an art form.)

You were right about the mudsills and their barbarous ways. Of course, it has taken me longer than you thought to understand I do not belong among these energetic and warlike people who will sacrifice all to please their heathen god of financial gain. Yes, I agree, money-making is the Yankee Baal. Let me bring you up to date if you are still with me and have not thrown my letter away. After the marriage of Tom and Lavinia, Barnum's museums burned three times—almost Angus, as if the showman had St. Elmo's fire crackling over his shoulder.

The Disinfectant Hypothesis says Confederate arsonists tried to cleanse New York of luxury hotels and theatres. But I doubt if a few muddled southerners would be competent enough to torch a showplace like Barnum's with a bottle of Greek fire!

Another theory has it that the League of Disgruntled Pedestrians started the fires. These educated New Yorkers considered the American Museum a nuisance on the busiest thoroughfare of New York. They strode by the crowds at the museum lampposts with their hands over their breasts to keep their pocket hankies fresh! And they were the only mudsills who could not be fooled into chasing the filthy beggar hired by Barnum to entice crowds into the American. Remember him, Angus? He was the poor creature who moved a brick from one corner of Broadway to another, gathering a puzzled crowd that followed him until he led it to the corner near the door of the museum.

Hypothesis aside, here is the truth. Barnum's conflagrations were a stimulant to growth in the manner of the old fire festivals of Europe. Just as Druids set hardwood bonfires ablaze on the tops of hills, hoping to make the earth fertile for a rich harvest, so do the primitive mudsills stage fiery holocausts to make their cities grow. (Yes, Angus, I am bantering sarcastically but it was you who introduced me to the bard's tradition of satire eight years before when Momma and I visited you in St. Ann's.)

Tein-eigen, beltane fires, need-fires, the Celts called their fire festivals, which burned alive both animal and human sacrifices. The human victims were members of the village who unsuspectingly chose a piece of Beltane cake with a special knob on it. These terrible fires, Angus, were started by a priest rubbing a piece of firewood against an oak plank seasoned with flammable birchwood tar.

Do you understand me now? While I worked for Barnum, the mudsills danced around three such fire festivals, always held at slow periods during the year.

The first fire scorched the brow of winter on American Thanksgiving, November 25, 1864. The second fell on July 13, 1865, in the dog days of New York, and caused serpents to wriggle from out our stone cage, and I (in a stupor of dread) to fly. The third fire, on a frigid March 3rd night, was a Lenten hop which the mudsills hoped would bring a reprieve from cold.

Praise Baal! I stormed out of the museum in the first fire, and

141

met Samuel Hurd and a phalanx of firemen who tried to throw their nets and ladders on me so I put up my dukes and sent six firemen sprawling. Then I reeled out of the Yankee temple onto Broadway where smoke and water plumes from the fire engine obscured the views of the Hudson and East rivers and the crowd cheered to see Hurd dragging on the ground as he clung to the folds of my plaid gown.

On July 13, 1865, I presided over the mudsills' second festival from a third-storey window at the American Museum. I had no choice but to play Mama Reuss, the civic mother whose straw dummy was burnt at the old Follies of New Amsterdam, as the fire had eaten up the large doors of the museum and I was too big to exit through the small ones. Beside me, on the fiery heights, was my friend the LIVING SKELETON who had stayed behind to comfort me when the other curiosities fled.

Below us, the crowd rejoiced in the deaths of the museum animals, screaming for tastes of "boiled whale" and "fried snake" and calling out to dying Ned, the LEARNED SEAL, "How are you?" My consort and I reigned philosophically since we couldn't join the merriment over the helpless animals cooking nearby. We did not find it funny to speculate with the merry-makers on how high the kangeroo would leap to avoid the flames or if Jocko, the monkey, felt the fire was more aggravating than being fed fake nuts, or whether the owl and the white cat sang "a doleful harmony" as the flames filled their cage.

We officiated unsmiling and were pleased only when a fireman blew a trumpet to drown out the happy cheers from the crowds as the fire swept through the hat store next to the museum. "Be jabbers, now the fire will be *felt!*" a wit yelled and when the crowd laughed, the fireman blew his trumpet again.

My skinny friend was dehydrating more quickly than I, although both of us were losing quantities of bodily fluid in the heat. Indeed, our perspiration plopped onto the floor, sizzling loudly. If only we could have extinguished the carnival with our human juices, but large as I am, I am not a HUMAN FIRE EXTINGUISHER.

I begged the LIVING SKELETON to leave me while he could still move his deathly weight.

"Isaac, look what your heroics are doing to you!"

"Oh Anna, you can't even see," he said. "Our perspiration is converting to mist." He took my hand sadly. "We're in a fog, dear girl."

I looked down. The heat had intensified, so our sweat rained down on the floor, converting to steam that rose in scalding clouds about us. At last, the shrinking SPINACH SPIRIT deposited a salty kiss on my hand and fled.

I buried my terrified face in my skirts. This ostrich ruse kept me from watching the activity in the street below where, by the belching steam engines, museum employees had erected a lofty crane that had been left nearby by workmen. Eighteen men grasped the line of a harness and tackle and a fireman exhorted me with his speaking trumpet to hook myself up.

I stole a look out from my skirt and saw the tackle knock a wall away on either side of me. Yes, Mama Reuss needed wide egress so she could hang over the embers and make the profits climb. Fly for free enterprise, giantess! Swing for Wall Street—its bulls and its bears! And kick your heels up so the crowd can be fired by a peek at the steaming mystery of your unspeakables!

With a solemn face, I fastened the harness over my shoulders and down I soared—a straw maiden with a heart of stone. An enormous phaeton waited and the applause was thunderous as I was pushed in, only to lurch out the other side because the eight-horse vehicle had become wedged in the crowds. Then it was my turn to join the dash up Broadway, pursued by the heathen mud-sills who shrieked with joy because they didn't need a ticket for the spectacle! In front of me, Jane, the FAT WOMAN, made her breathless escape under burning shop awnings, and next came the bare-breasted members of the CORPS DE BALLET in scorched tights and melted tutus. I brought up the rear of the rag-tag procession, sobbing over the loss of my savings of $1,200 (kept at the museum), and my entire wardrobe, with the exception of the hideous Zouave uniform.

Behind us, the seat of warmth and disorder roared with monstrous energy; its splendid religious mural, the MORAL SPECTACULAR DRAMA, crashing in a shower of sparkling brick.

To avoid our pursuers, Jane and I and the dancers fled to an editorial room at the *New York Tribune* building. There we met Krista, the mother of the WONDERFUL ALBINO FAMILY. She was doing a striptease in a showgirl's corset on a table in the newsroom as seven reporters cheered behind scribes' desks that came up to their noses. The editor-in-chief, Barnum's friend Horace Greeley, strolled in wearing a frock coat and white hat to announce that Samuel Hurd had wired word of the disaster to Hartford where Barnum sat in his seat in the state legislature. Greeley's owlish spectacled face expressed sympathy for our distress. He politely averted his eyes from the topless corps and found us seats in the noisy room. In a few minutes, he came back muttering apologies in his squeaky voice. He said Barnum had telegrammed to ask that Krista stage her entertainment in Greeley's office for a select group of New York businessmen in order to raise funds to rebuild the museum.

Jane and the corps stared sympathetically at Krista's sad, translucent face. "The old scoundrel," Jane whispered. "Thinking of money at a time like this!"

Krista's unfortunate plight did not surprise me. There was a listless, underdog quality about the albino woman and the rest of her red-eyed family, although Barnum tried to compensate for their lack of fire with ludicrous stories about night people who lived deep in the earth to avoid damage to their pink eyes. The showman also made them stiffen their white hair with beer to demonstrate the African heritage Barnum claimed for them. They were in truth a family of Dutch musicians whose strange appearance barred them from having a traditional career.

Greeley shuffled uncertainly, as if he didn't countenance Barnum's fundraising benefit. His spindly legs quivered and then found their rhythm as he escorted the silvery lady away. By the copy desk, Krista turned, and in my direction, made a hopeful gesture with her beautiful hands.

"Anna. Don't cry," she said. "We endured, didn't we?"

I saw a rivulet coursing down my gown. It splashed onto the filthy floor where it grew into a puddle that anointed Jane's block-like extremities and the toes poking through the ballerinas' shredded slippers. One by one, Jane lifted her feet out of the water and examined the square, wood islands on the floor before the islands were submerged by the tides of my body. She clapped her heels together to dispel the water from her shoes and, smiling nervously at me, stepped down again into the lake.

The water's yellow colour bespoke urinary contamination, squeezed out by the nervous prima donna. It's unfair, however, to stress her contribution since Jane and I and the dancers were doing what we could to swell the YELLOW SEA lapping at the walls of Greeley's office. If only we had put our glands together ear-lier. . . . What tragedies we could have quenched! I sighed to think of the wasted droplets rolling from the LIVING SKELETON.

Yes! The BIGGEST MODERN WOMAN OF THE WORLD did not weep when it counted. Not till I was sitting in the newsroom with my fellow workers did I cry for the animals we had left behind. I wept for Jocko's resigned monkey face and for the rest of the HAPPY FAMILY whose glowing cage I saw when the Ann Street wall of the museum fell at 1:15, and for the whales who were roasted alive when the walls of their aquarium broke apart, and for the sabre-tooth tiger, killed by a fireman's axe. Then I wept for Jane, the FAT WOMAN, whose jiggly white arms and chinny-chins were toasted amber, and for the members of the ballet corps, splashing each other in our woman-made sea. I wept for the LIVING SKELE-TON who had almost evaporated beside me and for Goshen, the PALESTINIAN GIANT, with his case of Potomac Fever, and for Com-modore Nutt, and all the curiosities who ran the public gamut. I also wept for my mother and father who made me, and for you, Angus, who tossed an anchor in the air to please me.

And last of all, I wept for myself and the selves I was in my growth, including the AGORAPHOBIC VICTIM who cowered as the tackle ball broke the museum wall, the VICTORIAN LADY hauled like a pachyderm over the heads in the street, the GIANT ACTRESS who smiled as she was lowered to the roaring crowds and, finally, the BIG SURVIVOR who failed to convey her waters to the fiery wimbles until the festival was over.

The waters rose as I wept until the FAT WOMAN bobbed belly-up at my waist like a frightened narwhale, making indecipherable noises and pointing to a drowning ballerina. Weeping still, I scooped up the terrified chorine and put her on Jane's buoyant stomach. I placed the other two on my shoulders and strode in long, oh-so-long steps until my legs floated in pliés towards the door. Greeley's reporters dog-paddled in circles about us, or dove unsuccessfully for their typewriters and pens submerged like merchant treasures in our juicy sea. Uncle Horace himself had come back and could be seen standing shoulder-deep beside a huge paper raft he was decorating with strings of rapidly smudging sentences. I waded towards him and asked him to climb onto Jane sculling beside me but his owlish eyes only blinked in perplexity.

"Stop that crying, young woman," he squeaked across the rising sea.

The highwater mark had crept over the lintel so I was compelled to push Jane, the barge, under, submarine fashion. Then my passengers, who were clinging to my back and shoulders, pinched my nose and covered my ears, and I dove head-first after the FAT WOMAN's feet. I came out in the flooded hall to a noise of roaring and crying.

Angus, are you still with me? That was fire number two. The third bonfire, March 3, 1868, was at the New American Museum at the corner of Prince and Spring streets. Barnum reopened there November 13, 1865, with an advertising puff that displayed a portrait of the showman with wings spreading from his balding pate under the banner headline: PHOENIX T. BARNUM. When the New American burned too, my employer went out of the museum business for good. The first fire had cost him $1,000, the second $350,000 and the third, $128,000 (as Barnum's stinginess kept him underinsured).

Baal was pleased. New York's stone garden was fertile again and grew:

THREE TIMES AS HIGH as the fireman's ladders that couldn't reach the museum's second-floor windows!

THREE TIMES THREE AS HIGH as the tallest flame that bounded from the cage of the HAPPY FAMILY glowing on the fifth floor!

THREE TIMES THREE TIMES THREE as high as the beams of the calcium floodlight that made day out of night on the museum's summit!

Angus, not even Barnum could continue to see the sunny side of the mudsills' pageant, which is enough, after half a decade, to wear a curiosity like myself down. So, dearest, I hope it's not true, as that old moralist La Rochefoucauld said, that "Absence is to love as wind is to fire—a little fans the flames, a lot puts it out by and by." Do not let my bantering tone fool you. I am, after all, only carrying on our fine Celtic tradition. I love you, Angus, and want you back in my life. YOUR ANNIE, WHO'S HAD IT UP TO HERE WITH N.Y.N.Y.

TESTIMONIALS OF PERFORMERS AT THE AMERICAN MUSEUM

George Washington Nutt: Vinie thought Annie had a grand opinion of herself, but I'd say the giantess just had a naive attitude. In New York, the smart individual learns to leave well enough alone. Once I had a scuffle with a goose, and Annie, in a misguided rescue attempt, accidentally knocked me down, giving me a bad bump on the head. Annie came from up in Canada and didn't understand life in New York. It takes more than good intentions to survive in a big city. I learned fast at the American Museum that you have to look out for number one.

Jane Campbell: The giantess was never real good after the museum fires. She used to talk about shrinking New York all the time. I don't know where she got such an idea. She went so far as to say it was her tear drops, and not water from the firemen's hoses, that froze on the lampposts after the third fire. Well, I can tell you all she did was pee her pants in the newsroom at the *New York Trib*. Fancy her thinking you could shrink an international entrepôt like New York! Nobody but nobody can shrink New York!

She had the worst of it in the fires, that's why. I was with her in the dressing room when the second one started. The pantomine was on upstairs with Goshen and them. We were eating cake from Del's, unwinding after a levee, when the giantess said she saw a wisp of smoke make a finger-wag over the partition. She was on her second helping, giving it a good, slow chew. I'd mushed up my lot and was sucking it off my fingers when I noticed the air got real heavy. I could smell our perfumes—so strong. The giantess wore jasmine to liven up her northern exterior. I used to kid her about General Hooker's women in New York. "Got on your whore lure, Ann?" She never laughed. Once she told me my musk made her think of candles and roast lamb. Baaa-baaa yourself, I told her. She was real thin. I used to feed her the cake sometimes for fun and coo, mama bird to baby bird, so she'd open the hatch. She wasn't a laugher but she liked to have fun. Oh, the smells got real oppressive and then a flame stuck a red tongue at us right through the wall of Thumb's dressing room. I giggled and giggled. I don't know why. She said: "Ssssssh Jane. No need for hysterics." Wasn't she the serene big girl? When she spoke her mouth opened, showing cake crumbs down as far as her tonsils. Who wouldn't laugh?

She waited for me in the hall while I grabbed up the cake box and then, real elegant, began to walk to the first-floor entrance with me. The smell from her jasmine was terrible. She was sweating worse than me and all around the world was sliding off to hell. All I could think was: see the bodies falling down the stairs, see the bodies popping out of rooms around us, see the bodies coming out of the lecture hall, see the body trapped in a balcony seat, screaming.

And then I knew we were going to die. Because we were cut off from the exit by all those bodies and she wanted us to wait our turn, good as good can be. I kept tugging her sleeve and coaxing her to try the back exit and she kept shaking her head—real stern. She didn't want to crush anybody, she said.

I couldn't stand it so I let myself be swept away by the crowds and what do you know, in a minute I was swept back and into her long arms and the crowd pulled us in and pushed us towards the entrance like we were both light as a feather. We were a waltzing mass and the smashed cabinets kept falling—one-two, one-two, like a gavotte beat—a real glass band with a pounding rhythm and our bodies swung and twisted in the crush of people as if we were in time, and following a beat. So then the firemen came up and I let myself be carried off by John Denham but she wouldn't let the first batch near her. She sent two of the men sprawling and it took six in a second charge to subdue her. Or was that the third fire? Now I think of it, it was the first. For the second fire, she was trapped on the third floor with Isaac who was sweet on her. She had to be swung to the ground in a harness.

Anyhow, all the fires were bad. No human lives were lost but there were lions jumping out of their cages, bears on the second-floor ledge, firemen killing half-burnt snakes. I think the fireman who rescued me killed a tiger with a single blow of his axe. He was real strong. And Barnum lost most of his collections and had to rebuild every time. The third fire was nothing to speak of and happened at night so it didn't get the crowds the others did.

Isaac Sprague: Nobody believes me, they think I'm making it up because that's what Hurd wants them to think, but I'm telling you, Anna could have escaped the fire by just walking down a flight of stairs and going out the Ann Street door. Of course, she didn't know this. I didn't know this! Not till I left her and saw the ten-foot door still standing at the Ann Street entrance. But Hurd knew this. And he wouldn't send his men in to get her. He wanted her to be rescued by a derrick. For the newspapers, you know. Hurd was Barnum's assistant every inch of the way.

After the fire, a story went the rounds that I had a romantic interest in the giantess because I tried to help her escape. Nonsense! I'm not one for big women. In any case, Anna was fond of a giant from the Maritimes. McGill? A McSomething. He died of brain fever but it was some time before the giantess found out. The letter advising her of his death was lost in the mail. McAskill, that's the name! He was a legend up where he came from. The giantess was quite heart-broken, the poor woman.

PART THREE

Adrift on the Continent

CHAPTER EIGHTEEN

Anna's Journal

March 30, 1871

"I heard about Angus's little accident with the anchor," Barnum said. We sat before a blazing fire in his brownstone on Fifth Avenue at Thirty-ninth Street—Barnum in his "scolding chair," a mahogany throne embellished with puffing cupids which he used to lecture his daughters from, and I in a custom-made monstrosity: a horn chair with a cowhide seat and splayed bone feet that the old showman had purchased from Buffalo Bill. Outside his home, pedestrians and horse-driven rigs waded through two feet of wet snow left behind by a surprise spring blizzard.

"He died from a fever associated with the anchor wound, didn't he?" Barnum continued. "Why, the giant couldn't have been more than 38 years of age."

"He was dead for six years and I knew nothing of it," I replied. "Hubert Belcourt, an old friend in Nova Scotia, told me the news. The dwarf had run into Angus's brother in Halifax."

"Was the family's letter to you lost in the mails?" Barnum inquired. "Postal ineptitude is a curse in our modern world."

"No. Angus was quite secretive and his family knew neither my name nor my whereabouts."

Barnum chuckled. "So old Angus didn't consider a ladyfriend in show business respectable enough to mention to his mother."

"Ah, Phineas, I wonder," I said softly. "I still cannot believe it. How could somebody like Angus cease to live without me knowing about it?

153

"Do we pass off the side of the planet as simply and quietly as a leaf in autumn?"

"Of course not," Barnum scoffed. "But accidents that take our dear ones can be upsetting. If anything happened to my wife, I'd be a ruined man."

I gazed suspiciously at Barnum. His unhappy marriage was well known at the museum.

"For without Charity, I am nothing," Barnum said, his baby-blue eyes twinkling. He winked and pulled out a handful of sweet flag to chew.

"You and I retired after the last museum fire, Anna. I lasted without work for two years. How did you enjoy four years in New Annan?"

"I am too sophisticated for the backwoods," I replied. "I felt like a snob in my own family. Like most well-travelled Victorians I've become opinionated in matters of taste and I couldn't look at their plain ironstone china, the crude hooked rugs, and hand-carved chairs without shuddering."

Barnum nodded. "My family in Bethel is the same. They have not yet learned that the last manufactured pattern is the best."

"I thought my family's home looked like one of your museum exhibits—so rough and crude did the log house appear to me, nestling on a wooded rise above a dirt track."

"Of course, opportunities must be better now that your province is part of a nation."

"The atmosphere is charged with political hostility and suspicion. Already some leaders want the Blue-noses to separate because they think the new situation is ruining trade with the Yankees."

"The Canucks should join us and then there'd be no problem." Barnum grinned. "Stop frowning, Anna. Who wants a bunch of Eskimos to feed anyhow?"

He leaned forward in his scolding chair and the firelight made the diamonds on his fingers and cufflinks blaze.

"Now let's get down to business. Isn't it a fact that you are eager to work again?"

"Not in a museum."

"I am through with museums. Let the academic poohbahs reclaim them. I am beginning a new era and the possibilities for you are manifold."

The Old Deceiver crossed his leg on his knee and studied me with a happy, earnest look. "I want you in my circus, Anna. On April 10, Bill Coup and I are opening the GREAT SHOW ENTERPRISE in Brooklyn.

"You will become a star." Barnum coughed nervously. "Not that you weren't well known before. But in the new day that's dawning, performers like you will become as famous as kings and queens."

"Aren't you talking about the old days, Phineas?"

Barnum frowned. "What do you mean?"

"Your speech sounds like the flimflam Thumb used to give us at the museum."

I took a deep breath, trying not to giggle at the consternation on Barnum's face. "Fame—that's all you Yankees think about. You're a nation of adolescent boys who want to show our parents in the old country you're important."

"Everybody wants to be famous," Barnum replied huffily. "Don't tell me you don't, Anna."

"I admit I am a bit of a ham. But that's not what I mean. Fame is a side product of achievement—not an answer. Phineas, what do people do after they are stars? Life goes on, you know."

Barnum leaned back in his scolding chair and regarded me shrewdly.

"You think I'm interested in fame for myself, don't you, Anna?" he chuckled. "You believe I don't give a hoot for what the old country calls culture. Isn't that a fact? Culture, Anna! That is why I built up museum collections. And now I am reinventing the circus. Not, as you think, to be rich and famous—money is beside the point. You see, I know I am envied. Why? For knowing the secret of show business. The real art is not in acquiring fame for yourself, but to produce a spectacle of fame that involves everyone and offers them a catharsis such as the Roman dramas."

"You mean Greek dramas."

155

"All right. Anna, tell me how I can be wrong! Are you not fascinated to watch an individual handle a change of circumstances? How will an unknown—say the midget Tom Stratton or the giantess Anna Swan—handle the adoration every Joe Doe wants but doesn't have the gumption to get? Will Tom and Anna be crushed by wealth and recognition? Will they renounce it? Making a great star is not just making money. It's a great intellectual and cultural process that all can be part of, no matter how short or tall."

"You Yankees have a genius for making platitudes sound brand new. But the emphasis on stardom is . . ." I paused, not wanting to hurt P.T.'s feelings, "a trifle shallow."

"Anna! The celebration of the individual is what makes America great."

"Yes, but what does it do for the individual?"

"Are you insinuating that I talk nonsense?"

I nodded. "Self-serving nonsense. The individual is a business gimmick."

Barnum glared at me, his eyes flashing. Then suddenly he began to chuckle. "You're so serious, Anna." His eyes shone. "Even what I would call . . . morbidly moral. You remind me of Mother. She wouldn't let Father put a heater in our church pew. She thought discomfort made us pray better." He chuckled again, amused by his fantasy of me as a reincarnation of his religious Yankee mother. "Now Anna, will you come and work in my circus?"

"I've signed up with Apollo Ingalls for a tour abroad."

"What did you come to see me for?"

"I wanted to say goodbye before I sailed."

Barnum sighed unhappily and walked over to a red leather writing desk and reached into a cubbyhole. He took out a contract with my name on it. I noticed it came from a cubby next to the one labelled "Colonel Goshen."

"Anna Haining Swan, the BIGGEST MODERN WOMAN OF THE WORLD. Height 7'6 ½", $15,000 for a season with Barnum and Comp."

Barnum put down the contract and eyed me nostalgically.

"Anna, if I could manage you again, your family up in Canada would eat chicken pie every night."

156

"I am being handsomely paid by Mr. Ingalls."

"Oho! So my offer is too cheap!" Barnum extracted from his pocket a cheque for $18,000 and waved it under my nose. It was $2,000 more than Apollo's offer, but I didn't react, and he crumpled the cheque into a ball and threw it over his shoulder. The old showman sank to his knees before my horned chair. His determined mouth sagged and the all-knowing blue eyes dimmed.

"How would you like to play the role of public trickster, a cheap and shallow hoaxer whose prodigies desert him because they think he has no fine feelings?"

His bejewelled hands squeezed my fingers. "Anna, don't leave me for a two-bit roustabout."

He raised his arms in a parody of despair and I couldn't discern if he was making fun of himself or trying to be serious. His bald pate drooped against my knees and I stared affectionately down at the old showman. Why was I refusing his offer? Because of my objections to Yankee pageants? Or was I just getting old? Barnum sensed my conflicting feelings and squeezed my fingers.

"You'll play Glumdalclitch to circus audiences all over North America and Great Britain too," Barnum croaked. "And Lady Macbeth too."

I kissed his perspiring dome and shook my head. The prospect of repeating the hackneyed old female roles filled me with horror. "Goodbye, Phineas," I said.

In the foyer, I met Goshen waiting with a midget named Admiral Dot; both were to be in Barnum's circus. My old friend lisped good wishes for a safe voyage across the Atlantic. At that moment, Barnum reappeared; he winked and waved goodbye with this usual good-humoured and alert countenance and I felt relieved that I had not been taken in by the dramatic tricks he had learned from his years on the temperance lecture circuit.

New York is no longer satisfactory—not for a giantess such as me. The mudsills are stronger than I dreamt, and will willingly suck the life out of any large being foolish enough to entertain them. Angus is right. (I still cannot use the past tense—not yet!) All normals are stronger than they look and it is unwise to feel obliged to look after them. I must protect myself instead from those of smaller stature who wish to exploit me. (For all I know, normals have more energy since their muscles have a shorter distance to stretch.) I do not want to be worn down by emblem fatigue, like Angus.

His death is a terrible loss. Momma likes to say, "The death of a dear one is like pulling an object out of a bucket. There's a terrible sucking noise and then the water closes over the empty space and the pail is the same as before." But I take no comfort from such a grim Highland platitude. An important person is never replaced. Ugh. It hurts to think Angus died knowing me as a self-absorbed creature who was awestruck by New York. He looked so sad in the photograph Hubert gave me. The giant is posed on the front porch of his family's home in St. Ann's, wearing his kilt and beaver hat. His freckled moon face stares with a hopeless expression into the camera. In the end, Angus felt trapped in a parochial spot where nobody appreciated him. Hubert recounted in pitiful detail the story about the insensitive pranksters who floated Angus's eight-foot coffin in St. Ann's Bay the night before the giant's funeral. Meanwhile, Hubert has become a prosperous molasses merchant who is married to a normal with five children and lives in Halifax in a Tuscan villa; its design was copied from an original that Hubert saw during a summer in Italy. The dwarf has found a place for himself but I am in exile from the ways of my childhood. Angus gave up the search for a home that suited him and I am still looking. Will I be happier on the Continent where centuries of culture have taught its inhabitants a civilized approach? I wonder.

April 15, 1871

I met Apollo in front of a Broadway gambling house today. I wore a brand new solferino walking dress and feathered hat in an attempt to lift my melancholy spirits.

"How's my big girl?" Apollo's deep baritone resounded from a swarm of pedestrians. In my absence, Apollo has sprouted mutton chops. Now his blond locks flow east and west as well as north and south. The chops make him look like a prosperous New England Flatfoot (as the circus men in Connecticut are called). He appeared glad to see me and rattled his dice eagerly as the hostler lowered the coach steps. I dispensed with them and stepped down in one bound.

"The troupe has lacked something without you," Apollo chuckled.

"A little gravity," I said. "You all need it."

He reached up and caught my fingers, feeling the soft mounds on my gloved palm. A schoolgirl might mistake Apollo's bold manner for *savoir faire*, but not me. Besides, Apollo is too short. I quickly retrieved my hand.

"And love!" Apollo said. "Don't we need it too?"

"Love is a luxury and not a need, Apollo."

Apollo grinned. "I like the new Anna," he boomed. "Barnum told me you'd grown (excuse the word, will you?) into a woman although he warned me you might be mooning over that dead Canadian giant."

"The BIGGEST MODERN WOMAN does not moon," I replied. "My situation has taught me to be stoical."

I curtsied at some mudsills gaping nearby. "Of course, I wish I could be as other people, but as I can't, I must make the best of my situation and be contented with my lot," I said, quoting a line from a spiel at the American Museum.

"Well, you still know the old routines," Apollo said. "Come and meet half the troupe or do I mean one-quarter?"

He pointed to two round-shouldered mulatto girls standing behind him. They had sweet shiny brown faces with wide, thick mouths, and had piled their knots of kinky dark hair up on top of their heads. They were well-formed though short (no higher than my thigh) and wore identical orange taffeta gowns with three ribbings of lace on the hem. When they saw me look, they waved and giggled and ambulated towards us in an odd, shuffle step. The two women moved only their outer legs and held up their inner ones. They appeared to share a pelvis. I realized they were Siamese twins.

"Meet the TWO-HEADED NIGHTINGALE who has given our

touring company its name!" Apollo bellowed. "Chrissie is taller and stronger than Millie, as you shall see."

At that moment, the larger one stooped and picked up the smaller one on her back and ran with her burden in circles around us until Apollo asked her to stop. Chrissie was not the least bit out of breath, and Millie was giggling hard, as if she knew how funny she looked, lying on her sister's back, her legs dangling uselessly in the air.

I shook hands with both of them simultaneously, and they bowed their heads shyly. The four of us began to stroll up Broadway to the Astor House.

It was spring in Barnum's town. The chestnut trees were out, and I stared—eyeball to bud—at the yellow blossoms so I didn't look into second-floor bedrooms and frighten occupants who ordinarily pulled their drapes at my approach.

"How did you like working for P.T. Barnum?" Chrissie asked. Her shy voice was husky and melodious.

"Isn't he a stingy puss?" Millie added. Her voice was identical to her sister's except that it was lower in pitch. "We hear he makes his own ticket seller pay him five thousand dollars *before* Barnum gives him the job."

"He never underpaid me," I replied. The brown heads eyed one another and I added: "Forgive me but I dislike show-biz gossip."

Once again the brown heads stared at each other and their questions ceased so I was able to walk in silence, staring glumly at my feet—those neglected travellers who pedal energetically so far below. No slackards they! My slippers of quilted bronze kid streamed along beside Apollo's grimy Hessians and the four orange satin pumps of the twins.

"Isn't it morbid the way the feet move but the head never goes anywhere?" I mused. At once, the heads below my waist tilted up to scan my face.

"Sitting, I am no more conscious of my head than I am of my own womb, but walking makes me aware of its frozen weight, suspended on my shoulders like a Ming vase. It's unnerving to be aware of the body's monarch. Steady on! Mustn't spill or smash the head! Tipping it is *verboten*!"

160

"Anna is quite an entertainer, ladies," Apollo said. "A true spieler, who can outshine anyone in the business!"

The twins tittered and I felt vaguely pleased, but I kept my eyes fixed on our feet so I wouldn't have to make polite conversation. At that moment a pair of cavalry boots, with dusty wedge-shaped toes, loomed among the other boots on the crowded New York sidewalk. Lo! The boots charged—scattering the twin's pumps and closing with one of Apollo's Hessians. My slippers danced away to the side, and oops, my head bobbed like an apple cart skidding on one wheel. A massive heel came down on Apollo's toes. Apollo roared in pain.

"Excuse me, Judge! I only wish to escort this nice Nova Scotian lady!" a Kentucky accent drawled.

Before me stood Martin Van Buren Bates in the cavalry uniform Angus and I had seen him wear at Irving Hall. He appeared taller. Or was he just slimmer? His cheeks showed deeper hollows, so he looked more mature, and he'd grown a moustache—trimmed in a neat, upside down V. The eyes (which I'd thought brown) glittered blue-black, and he held his dark head a little to one side—almost deferentially—as he gazed across at me. Every part of him, from the thick shoulders and ample waist to the large head thrust out of his winged cavalry collar, looked solid and assured. Obviously, the glue that held his body together was in no danger of unsticking. Then he bowed and I smiled warmly at him. Without Angus to make me feel guilty, I realized Martin Bates attracted me.

"I told the Judge I wanted to meet you, but the little so-and-so beat me to the draw," the KENTUCKY GIANT mumbled shyly.

"Now you have met the troupe, Anna," Apollo chuckled. "What do you think? Will we win the heart of the British Queen and the love of millions?"

"With the giantess in our show, we'll knock the Limeys dead," the KENTUCKY GIANT said. I blushed. It was a pleasant shock to stand next to a large man again. Apollo realized how pleased we were to see one another and shortly afterwards he went off to gamble at a shop over on Broadway, taking along the twins for luck. So the KENTUCKY GIANT and I decided to stroll in Central Park.

We talked of how little our families understood us (like all young people, we felt they could not fathom our inner workings) and made a game of seeing who was taller by standing up against lamp posts at the gates of the park. The KENTUCKY GIANT says he is 7′7″ and I am 7′9″ and that one of these days he will catch up as his growth is not over. I told him I am five inches taller than he is but that he shouldn't worry because I like short men. He doubled over with laughter and I found myself remembering how relaxing it is to be with somebody my own size. I have been accused of being preoccupied with myself, but it is the world which is preoccupied with a giant's height and never lets a giant forget it. So big people may as well enjoy being noticed. I told the KENTUCKY GIANT this and he nodded wisely.

When we said goodbye in the lobby of the Astor House, he pressed into my hand some typewritten pages entitled "Species Development: A Tract Towards Continual Anatomical Wonders." I looked through it in my hotel room and found it is a curious sort of diary which contains research and notes, apparently written by him. His thesis argues that the human race is destined to increase in mental and physical development. I was too sleepy to read it but found it touching that he'd entrusted to me such a personal document.

April 26, 1871

I have been seasick since we sailed on the twenty-second of April. Lacking *le pied marin* as the sailors say. Our ship is *The City of Brussels*—a comfortable old steamer with the Inman line. Outside my window, the waves roll and grow into mountains while I lie strapped into my berth. At least, I have had a chance to reflect on what I am to tell the KENTUCKY GIANT about his tract on anatomical wonders. I have read it over and over, trying to find some points in his thesis that I can admire. Unfortunately, it is a long-winded work, flawed by his failure to recognize his subjective view behind his scientific idealism. I cannot read such tracts without hearing the voice of male pride and, in his case, it is obvious he glorifies size to make up for his excessive height. It is interesting to learn about the historical giants which he discusses in order to argue that gigantism is a fast-growing trend and I can always tell him that.

Yesterday Apollo came to discuss business and tried to kiss me while I lay curled up in a ball like a huge kitten so that I could fit my short bunk. I fended him off by asking about Jane and he grew huffy and told me Jane had left him for a thin man in a New Orleans circus. He said Jane was a 100-year-old story and why didn't I give him a chance to show me how much he cared instead of paying attention to show-business gossip. He swore he saw me as a goddess, like one of those big Greeks who interceded between man and God. (The Titans? I am not certain.) He also claimed he was no lady killer but a one-woman man who worshipped love and cards in that order. When I refused to kiss him back, he sat and played solitaire with an old military deck whose characters wore the uniform of Union soldiers. (He has lost his old yellow dice.) I had to ring for the steward to make him leave the cabin. Absurdly enough, I was flattered because I once longed for his attentions. But I would be foolish, indeed, to think he was sincere. Likely, he is curious about what it is like to make love to a giantess.

April 28, 1871

The KENTUCKY GIANT seems starved for my company. When I went up for air this morning, he joined me in stumbling about the deck and was kind enough to say how steady I was on my feet.

"You don't miss a step when we turn," he said.

"You talk as if you hadn't done this sort of thing with a giantess before." I twirled my parasol and he laughed so hard I thought he was sobbing. He explained he is delighted that somebody as large as me has a sense of humour. Then off we lurched, arm-in-arm, and out of step, his left foot moving

163

with my right so our hips knocked. Our concentration was intense—we might as well have been learning to do the schottische. The Siamese twins do this dance on their two connected pairs of legs, but they have the advantage of two inner legs that are slightly shorter than their outer legs. (Possibly a connecting bond is required before all promenade steps are mastered.)

Luckily, we only touched upon his tract and I did not need to trot out the tired euphemisms for rejection which amateur authors get. I did tell him I distrusted his assumption that size was the answer to everything because I felt one solution would not solve human problems. But I also confided that I liked being big and saw no reason why the planet shouldn't spring forth with giants who (as in the vision of my childhood) could dance exuberantly to the stars. He chuckled in the happiest way. Our devotion to scale is not the only thing we have in common, though. It turns out the giant also shares my interest in travel and stylish living.

During our promenade, people bowed and spoke to us as if we were taking the air at Central Park. The captain caught up to us at the taffrail where we had stopped to discuss a levee Apollo has arranged for our troupe at the end of the cruise. We must have looked striking. I was resting my elbows on the rigging, facing out. Bates had his back to the sea, leaning towards me as I gazed down at the gloves I was peeling off to hold in my fist.

The giant appeared amused by a Miss Millingham, a British lady on the captain's arm who asked a string of foolish questions and told Bates she had seen land on the horizon that morning.

Bates made much of her little observations. He congratulated her on being the first to see shore despite the fact that we are only half-way across the Atlantic. Miss Millingham's huge, inverted mouth came up to the captain's breast braid and there she nestled in the coyest way. He was a tall Scot with pop-out eyes and red whiskers. The way he bent and folded himself around his consort accentuated Miss Millingham's babyishness. I could see Bates admiring her thatch of curls which reached just below his belt buckle. I fidgeted, waiting for the predictable comparison between us. But the giant turned his attention back to me, and the captain and Miss Millingham strolled off rhythmically, in a state of semi-fusion. Chrissie and Millie couldn't have done better. I almost expected the captain to stoop and lift Miss Millingham onto his back as Chrissie picks up the shorter Millie, and race pell-mell down the deck with the Englishwoman's legs thrashing in the sea breeze.

April 30, 1871

One two—skip to my loo—after seven days at sea I have become very fond of Martin. I like the way he waits for me on the forecastle, sniffing the sea air with enthusiasm and booming out answers to questions on the future of gigantism. He looks commanding as the first-class passengers press round, touching his cavalry pants and jacket when they think he isn't watching. Who can help but admire him?

On the poop deck, before one of these curious groups, Martin followed up on my story about my Scots ancestry by praising my parents for sending me to Barnum so he and I had a chance to meet. Then, to surprised gasps (Oh, the myriad of pleased, curious noises the passengers made!) he said:

"If the Lord smiles on me, perhaps Anna's history and mine will be written of henceforth as one."

"Figuratively speaking, you mean." I laughed and continued to hold his arm. I could see the shadow of *our* connecting bond in the upturned faces brimming with pointed questions that Martin's blue-black eyes forbade them to ask. I stole a glance at Martin's cavalry pants (a man of large parts, it goes without saying) and thought I saw the tell-tale tendril winding its way out and waving its blind leaf-head. It rattled its foliage at Miss Millingham, who stood nearby with the captain, and then spun in twists to land at my feet.

Am I daft? I haven't forgotten the giant once treated Angus rudely and it is impossible to ignore the foreboding glare he uses to stare an awkward question into the ground. But his

165

surliness is a coverup for the tender-hearted man trapped inside his giant frame. Normals don't understand that giants are too big to be men. They attack a giant to prove their manhood and are ignorant of the dilemma of the giant who is called a bully if he fights back because his height gives him an unfair advantage. I suspect Martin feels bewildered by the role fate has given him. Of course, it's easier for me to notice his vulnerability. He is less frightened to let me see the soft-eyed boy beneath his mask, the child whose family nicknamed him "Baby Bates" because he was the youngest of twelve. My knowledge makes me feel protective towards the lumbering southerner. Who knows? Perhaps my presence will temper his aggressive behaviour the way the northern expanse of Canada checks the war-like energy of the Yankee nation. Yes, it's true: the BIGGEST MODERN WOMAN wants to Canadianize the KENTUCKY GIANT!

CHAPTER NINETEEN

The Route Book of Judge Hiriam
Percival Ingalls

April 25, 1871

The giantess came on deck today. I was moved by the sight of her vast form floating among the other passengers, in the shadow of sails and funnels. I thought of Charles Lamb's delightful lines on Widow Blacket of Oxford. "The gentle giantess," quoth Lamb, "goeth mincingly with those feet of hers, whose solidity need not fear the Black Ox's pressure."

The Big Woman wore an olive-coloured promenade dress and protected her upper regions from the sun with the aid of a parasol. Its finely carved ivory handle rested against a massive shoulder with utmost delicacy, as if the instrument might bruise her flesh. The giantess is overly fond of dainty accessories.

Behind her, Bates followed at a distance. His forehead betrayed the strain of concentration he was experiencing. His hands, encased like pressed hams in yellow kid gloves, swung at his sides in time with his legs.

His hasty strides soon overturned several deck chairs and an elderly occupant. The giantess heard the commotion and turned her serious young face in our direction. I went to help Bates make up for the damage and a sudden wind blew the hat from my head. Bates swore at the top of his lungs over the mishap. Meanwhile, his overcoat flapped in my face and effectively blinded me, making my rescue of the old gentleman an arduous job.

The giantess did not come to our aid. She waved instead and then gave us the small of her back. Bates and I stared after the vanishing apparition. It did not appear to dwindle as objects do when disappearing. It looked to be normal size from where we

167

stood—one hundred feet down the promenade deck. Instead of a giantess, we saw, against the stretch of sky and ocean, a curvy female silhouette that couldn't be disguised by the muslin layers of an outing dress.

I don't know what Bates made of this shift in vision. He glared her way with a palpable hunger. (Perhaps the desire of one member of an exotic species for another.)

Of course, the reduction of a woman like Anna is a hopeless illusion with dangers for the beholder. Bates will stumble on them soon enough. I have no use for the giant except as merchandise. His bullying manner is obnoxious and the grunts and groans he makes as he strains to move his bulk revolt me.

April 29, 1871

Rough weather has kept my troupe below.

I carried a flagon of barley water through listing corridors to the giantess; she is seasick and has strapped herself to the bed in her stateroom. She received me on her back, and scolded me for putting the Nightingale in the hold with the Bog-trotters.

She wore a *robe de nuit* with Valenciennes lace. "Niggers can't travel first class," I told her. Her face tightened. She tried to hide her angry feelings by making a game of watching the gulls fly by her porthole. Meanwhile, I couldn't stop myself from staring down at her breasts.

I found myself wondering if I dared approach her generous frame . . . if I scrambled up beside her on the bunk and lay my head on her chest—on those colossal udders that would befit a dinosaur—would she let me suck? Could my lips even fit about her nipples, which are the size of guinea eggs? The AUSTRALIAN MOUTH has eaten bigger things surely . . . a banana whole, a squash. . . .

As we discussed the Nightingale, the rocking vessel made a whirligig out of Anna's bedclothes. Her thin linen fell off one of her shoulders and exposed a naked breast. She was too irritated with me to notice. I contemplated the breast in silence. The boat rolled and the writing table and chair

168

slithered past the bed. The giantess stuck out an arm to catch the furniture, exposing the breast below the nipple. All done during her lecture: a surprisingly sharp talk from somebody who was stretched before me in such a helpless fashion.

I had forgotten how rosy are the nipples of a maid. Hers are a sunrise pink and break over the top of a perfectly oval mound. I doubt if a mountain can compare in glory to a giantess' breast. Where is a circle that seen from above looks like a temple of land with the blue vein over the heart running off the heights into the plain? A faint web of striations was visible; the skin must stretch and give under the play of that gland, but overall, it was amazingly smooth. The nipple is a soft pink nectarine floret not darkened yet to the wrinkled brown motherhood brings.

The giantess tried another tack and warned me the tour would lose money from postponements because the hold was ruining the Nightingale's health. It was a good point and I consented and then, God help me, placed my paw on her mammoth breast and said her name. Twice. The giantess looked at me for a moment before she said in a soft voice: "I know you fancy big women, Apollo, but please take your hand off me." Well, then she giggled and giggled like she didn't take me seriously and I could feel my privates wilting. So I got disgusted and went off to the men's smoker for a game of faro and played all night and lost £300. God damn. The giantess has developed into a fine-looking female since the day she came to Barnum's, gaping at the rest of the freaks like an over-grown kid.

Oh Anna, my dinosaur cow, there is nothing I'd refuse you if you would lift up your doughy hills and, with a stern look, position them on either side of my head, jiggling and squash-ing me until the sea rings in my bad little urchin ears. (I pray to God not to punish me for such thoughts. It is no use anyway since I want her to marry Bates. The pair will be a good money-maker. Besides nobody but a fool would let romancing interfere with business.)

CHAPTER TWENTY

Bates at the Peep-hole

(From "Species Development, or A Tract Towards Continual Anatomical Wonders" by Captain Martin Van Buren Bates)

April 25, 1871

Great fortune is mine! The NOVA SCOTIAN GIANTESS underwent a medical examination by Naughton, the ship's doctor. He is a Kentucky man like myself, who is all eyes and ears about my anatomical thesis that Americans are destined to grow into a species of giants. Likewise, he was impressed with my interest in the reproduction possibilities of the giantess and agreed to let me view his examination after we imbibed some bourbon in the smoker. "The things I do in the name of science!" Naughton said.

The next afternoon I stepped into the gentlemen's lavatory and, peering through a small window near the ceiling, saw the mountainous naked woman in the next room, as Naughton had promised. The sight of her was an eye-opener for me, used to small females. I sent a prayer up to the Almighty for allowing me to see the progenitress of the undegenerate race of the future!

The giantess was lying on Naughton's examination table. Her knees were up and slightly parted. There was no excessive growth of hair over her pubis. It was a prettily arched hillock, normal in all aspects except for its extreme size. I couldn't spot any signs of bossing, or other abnormalities about the outer lips.

She has a dolichocephalic head, about the size of my own.

170

Some enlargement of a neck goitre was present. It looked to be as big as a grapefruit. Her eyes are normally spaced. At no point during Naughton's examination did she open them (likely a sign of a refined temperament).

The doctor did not use the standard pyramidal system of mass measurement. He measured the length and breadth more or less at random and only once or twice did he address himself to width. He began with the arms and twice doubled his tape to get his figures. His exertions as he lifted and surveyed the arms were comical to see. I assumed the span of her arms to be 173 cm from the flexing of the tape. The hands and fingers were notably large, as were the toes of the extraordinary feet.

None of the distal ends had a swollen or spade-like appearance that would spell a future coarsening of the countenance. It was blatantly feminine, with a pleasantly curved mouth. I noted her baby-fine hair at the temples. The ears were as large as primordial clam shells, and curiously lobeless.

The breasts were also delightfully visible. They loomed up behind Naughton's hand, ampullaceous, boundless, with no disfiguring hair about their ruby peaks. The doctor took their circumference with a caliper, chatting in low monosyllables to reassure his patient. The tool made large arcs in the air over the chest and was then returned to a box of instruments in the table drawer.

Naughton measured the legs more easily, walking up and down by the table as he continued to unfold the tape. When he was at her knees, the giantess murmured in a girlish voice. I concentrated and caught the term "emblem fatigue." The doctor's brow wrinkled, registering surprise. He disappeared and for a moment I had her to myself. Sighing, she lowered her knees and smoothed back reddish curls which had fallen into her eyes. Then she lay still. (A large body is difficult to move once it has settled into a horizontal position.)

Naughton returned carrying a new box of instruments. He proceeded to strap the giantess down and arrange her legs in a frog-like position. This time I could see the pudenda clearly. Its magnificent foyer glistened before me, wreathed in purple

171

tissue. Within lay the mighty organ of gestation: the hope of the renewal of our species. I was giddy with joy.

From my post I saw the doctor's face contort, and realized his arm had disappeared into the pleats of skin. First the folds swallowed his fingers and wrist and then his forearm. The man achieved penetration as far as his elbow. The patient appeared unaware of her examiner's distress. Her eyes stayed shut in serene contemplation. Naughton looked around and for a second his eyes held mine.

I changed position. I was sweating in the hot little cubby-hole. Suddenly, Naughton braced himself against the table and pulled out his hand. He shook off the moisture and left the room. There was a whispered exchange with his assistant outside in the passage. Naughton said his size made an internal examination impossible. "A hand like mine can't do a proper job on her," the doc said. "She needs a big mitt!" In a moment, the other medico entered. He was a full head higher than Naughton, a gangling youth who trembled slightly when he saw the giantess. His hands were the size of footballs, and he had no trouble concluding the examination. The following are the calculations I desired, given me afterwards by my Kentucky pal:

Weight of womb $6\frac{1}{2}$ ounces (average organ only $1\frac{1}{2}$ ounces); mammae each 3 lbs., left slightly larger as is norm. Vagina 17 inches along anterior wall; 20 inches in posterior aspect, compared to $2\frac{1}{2}$ inches (a.w.) and $3\frac{1}{2}$ (p.a) of average female.

Womb $6\frac{1}{2}$ ounces! Extraordinary to think that in that half pound lies the future of man! I thanked the medico for confirming my belief that the giantess is an unspoiled natural resource. Then I allowed Naughton to calculate on me the genesis of the new species. Each of my great bollocks is four inches in length, four inches in breadth, and five inches in anter-posterio diameter. Their weights vary slightly, the left being a little larger, but the final figure is 32 drachms (2 ounces). The erectile cylinder—even on a man of my height that is of no consequence to the American system of weights. An estimate of the combined weight of the giantess' heavy equipment and mine is six and a half pounds with over half the poundage due to the weaker sex!

In centuries to come, when the great *Americanus* species is developed to its potential, our measurements will be considered puny. I look forward to showing my findings to Henry Gray, F.R.S., whose volume, *Anatomy, Descriptive and Surgical*, overlooks the trend towards gigantism in the human skeleton.

April 26, 1871

I am learning much to encourage me about the suitability of the female giant as a domestic partner. In mufti, she is a healthy being with a refined manner. Her princess gowns are becoming and her shoes and stockings beyond reproach. As Cobbett says to young gentlemen choosing a wife: "Look to see how she is shod." She wears black kid boots open at the arch of her foot in order to display her fashionable pink stockings. I have yet to see her in blue shoes or other types of vulgar accessories.

Cobbett would say the one that heaven made me is overly fond of "hardware"—she has a large vocabulary of gloves, hats, purses, parasols. But who can begrudge her feminine frills?

She shares my interest in education but admits she has no feeling for science and shows no sign of having a photographic memory. This is a Bates characteristic (which I hope will be carried on in our children). She has a few other flaws such as a fault in vision. She occasionally bumps into walls when supervising the animal motion of her frame. She is also one year older than me and five inches higher, but fortunately I am still growing. (I blame some of her height advantage on her heeled boots and the cowpads she piles on her head.) Another drawback is her appetite. It is too big for a woman. We ate at the captain's table last night and I was dismayed to see her devour four dishes of tongues. I am a practical granger, and don't think an animal's clapper is proper food for a female. To see her chew these parts of the body with relish upset my digestion.

Her hands didn't touch the tongue. She selected them from the waiter's tray with a pair of tongs and cross-sliced them into dozens of little pieces before she put them in her mouth and munched. I noticed she ate bananas in the same fashion. First she tonged them, and then she peeled back the skins with a knife and fork before she chopped the fruit into tiny, identical segments. Canadians appear to have strange eating habits—not like the habits of British or Americans, but something else.

The giantess is only 350 pounds. I don't know how she stays thin when she eats so much. (I tip the scales at 470 pounds.)

She is very polite. Her habit of looking right up at me isn't like the affected manners of pretty Yankee women. She agrees not to disagree and is disturbed by friction—good qualities for a lifetime companion.

The giantess does not know my intentions but I am confident she will agree to be my mate and share my scientific objectives. Who could refuse to make a future that will enable every American to see over the heads of foreign nations, thanks to select breeding, vitamin baths, and skull trephining? On this world tour, the giantess and I are emissaries of the twentieth century when the marvellous will be commonplace. The limejuicers will beg for the imprint of my boot and her slipper on their royal carpets. After all, our combined heft of half a ton could sink that little archipelago.

174

CHAPTER TWENTY-ONE

Shipboard Romance

(From the Route Book of Hiriam Percival Ingalls)

April 30, 1871

The giants were a knock-em-dead success at a levee on ship last night. I billed them as the WORLD'S TALLEST COUPLE, and though I am used to seeing them clomp along the deck, practising promenade steps like heavy-gaited oxen, even this heart of mine jumped at the sight of them, strolling in full costume under the huge archway of the saloon whose mahogany wainscotting gleamed under the light of gas chandeliers.

The giantess wore a gown in navy and blue yachting colours. The swags of her dress were navy, and on her head was a saucy little white yachting cap. The Big Woman has ten gowns (packed in ten steamer trunks) custom-made for this cruise by New York seamstresses. Of course, she is richer than the rest of us, thanks to her old contract with Barnum, and could have ordered ten more gowns if she so desired. Bates is a sloppy dresser, and not so keen on his toilet, but last night the big Kentuckian looked okay in a yachting suit whose navy and white matched the outfit of the giantess. (As planned.) When he stopped to doff his peaked hat, beaming with pride at the giantess who had decorously linked her arm in his, the saloon passengers stood up and gave the pair round after round of applause, knocking over the dining benches in their excitement.

Bates has more class with the giantess by his side, I'll say that for him, if nothing else, and the giantess is always eager to make others happy: Would that she spread a little happiness in the direction of H.P. Ingalls! Bad fellow that I am, I cannot put out of mind those breasts of hers, like loaves of bread hiding under scented silk, ready to be squeezed and sampled! If I had my way, she'd marry Bates for the money that could be made out of such a winning arrangement, and spend the nights with yours truly.

This is no kind of talk for a route book, so I should get onto notes about the levee. The Nightingale sang medium fine, but all her shenanigans didn't rouse the crowd as much as the appearance of Anna and Bates. This is a real feat as the Night is ordinarily a great crowd pleaser with her soprano and contralto harmonizing sweetly, one head eating and drinking while the other head reads from *Uncle Tom's Cabin* or extolls the virtues of temperance. Oh, the Night has a whole bag of tricks including rope-skipping and polka-dancing and her pitiful signature tune:

I'm happy, quite, because I'm good;
I love my Saviour and my God,
I love all things that God has done
Whether I'm created two or one.

She usually moves the crowd to tears even as they are fixated with curiosity at the ugliness of the two-headed creature, of happy disposition, running about before them. Like Cowper's Schoolboy, the Night's audience always have "Blamed and protested, but joined in the plan, shared in the plunder and pitied the man."

How's that for poesy? Would you like it Anna, my dinosaur lady? Shet up Ingalls! If I get into that again, I'll need my head read! Anyhow, I suppose I have underestimated the impact of a giant couple on the ordinary mortal. All to the good. Of course, the levee was a clever piece of work, and done in three parts like a minstrel show, the first section being the Night singing, the second being the giants promenading, and the third section being an operetta about North American politics written by myself, Bates, and the giantess, by title "Olympian

176

Love Call." I will run through the second half for the benefit of the route book:

Right off, Bates prevents the riff-raff in the crowd from pestering the giants with questions, i.e., "Will you be able to lead a normal life in regard to producing children, Captain Bates?" asks a so-called gentleman as soon as the giants stop their promenading and prepare to chat to the audience.

"Will you, sir?" the Captain roars back. "I am of supreme confidence that I am normal in every aspect of manhood, and hope you can say the same for yourself!"

At this, the gentleman slinks into his seat, not to be heard from again. Bates is good at scaring the willies out of people even if he is full of hot air and a coward to boot.

Next Bates gives a short history of giants, and throws in five minutes from his lecture on the SURVIVAL OF THE MEDIOCRE, in which he advises us that although large critters spoiled things for themselves by growing horns and small brains, in the future Brobdingnagian beings will be streamlined monsters. Then the giant finishes off by reciting names of historical giants while the giantess stands at his side, listening dutifully.

"Aegaeon, Aegir, Alifanfaron, Amarant, Antaeus, Ascapart, Atlas...," Bates bellows. "...Cormoran, Cottus, Cyclops...Hyler, Hymir, Jotunn..." and so on "...Magog, Mimir, Morgante...."

"Where is the giant Stormalong?" the giantess suddenly interrupts after Bates has done with the S's. "So very à propos on our sea voyage."

Bates gives her a funny look but she goes right ahead: "Stormalong! The giant who had to fold back the hinged mats on his giant ship to let the moon pass.

"And who caused the cliffs of Dover to be white. Stormalong! His sailors had to soap their rocky sides in order to let his huge ship slip out of the British channel...."

Hereupon a few of the Brits in the saloon cheer and the giantess bows. Then she turns to the big Kentuckian with a coquettish smile.

"Don't think I am trying to upstage you, partner," she says saucily while Bates swivels his head to gauge the reaction of the crowd. "Oh no!" she says. "Why would I need to compete? After all, I am five inches taller than you!"

The crowd chuckles. Bates glowers and she plunges on with the list of giants: "... Saint Christopher, Samson, Scanderberg of Albania ... Topham of London. ..."

Then I totter in on stilts, wearing black face like a Christy Minstrel and an orange bow tie. The audience hoots. I look a sorry Jim Crow with my blond chops and tarred face. Okay. Then I introduce the "Olympian Love Call," and for a joke fall off my stilts into Bates's arms and the giant catches me and holds me like a baby calf, hamming it up by glancing at the ceiling as if he expects another minstrel to fall into his lap.

Following is the text of "Olympian Love Call," as sung by the three of us, a hasty bit of versifying but not bad considering the short time we had to compose it. Per usual, the giantess and I did most of the writing as Bates is a lazy oaf.

INGALLS' VERSE WARM-UP

Anna, your bridegroom
is looking up from his cities
smiling through his smoke-stacks
and wearing a ginseng root in his teeth.
See, the colossus
is the man for your dimensions—
a hill-billy gone citified
a clay-eater among carpet-baggers
his head in his seaboard helmet
is a glittering trophy
his eyes are like machines
whirring at the stars
his frost-free eyebrows are splashed
by river light
washing milky wonders out of Brooklyn
his cheeks are like mockingbirds spooning
in cup-shaped nests
his teeth are corn niblets strung in a cement
    setting

his neck is an invigorating waterway
wrinkled with your winds
your mountain man delights in your hills and valleys
and no ring of perma-frost
dirties his Kentucky collar.

Anna, like the hummingbird
who hears her mate
over 3,000 miles
you'll be stopped
short by his old
Rebel yell.
He's staked out your womb, Anna.
He wants to make hay in your summer storms, honey.

Night after night,
you'll shine
his parade helmet
and undress for his box
of goodies, his common
innovations, his gospel
of self-help

when his rivers
have run away
and his great plain
a mirage you shall
spread your western
cordillera under his Pacific
shank.

You are his lacuna
and he's the big man
who will be your stage-door giant.

O come up
from your level
interiors and get
this over in the Love Canal
the garden is going, going gone—

THE KENTUCKY GIANT'S HYMENEAL

I will speak my will to Anna
that she will lie down
and tip south her giant womb
all by herself
she is the giantess next door
her name shall be
my all-American girl.

Take me in, New World Wahine
through your untapped vagina
to more mountain-rimmed gardens
where hot and cold airs
run together and averages
mean nothing.

Your eyes are like the future
gazing down on me.
Your head is the Far North
your neck—the long wolf's throat to the sea
the Near North is your shoulder
draped with trade staples and immigrants
who will learn to boast
of your bitter winds and thousands
of unproductive acres
your breasts are cod canneries
a continental refuge
for America's old head
your belly is a topped up
basin
fenced in by fir
and river valleys.

Come from your diversity, promised one.
Hurry down from the Canadian shield—
leave behind our inland tubs
from the Rocky Mountain trench
and from the Maritime shallows

180

from the zinc bars and spud flats.
You are my stolen limits
an eyeful of possibilities—
a half-strung boulder choker!
How infinite are your granite goods!
How vast you are my love, how vast—
your eyes behind your snowdrifts
are legends of mineral wealth
your hair like a flock of bison
streaming down Mount Rundle
your teeth like a caribou-herd
easily made domestic
by tundra and where trees end
your fresh ice casts
off igloos and no floe
is the same size.

O beautiful mass!
Your lips are the north-west
passage waiting
for underglacial submarines
and your words are the wind
I can't see
if you yourself do not know
the ugly duckling you wear
around your neck
follow the trail of frosty
arpents I will blast
from your rock necklace.

You are as remote as the white
whale on your Labrador coast
but there's no platitude
in your sweeping womb—
the grass triangle of pleasure.

The scent of your breath
is the fragrance of gas
and oil

your essence flowing
without restraint
into my appealing fist.

You will fall down
and invite me
your skin dripping sap
over my coffer knobs.

Let me in to our central concern,
the long sleeping space.

You are a sunflower
in Arcady

a white pine
among sumac bushes.

How propitious your roped slippers
your west arches spanning orchards.
I will kiss the demi-Eden
between your toes
and polish your gleaming nails—
the reflector of a dying mountain
where crystal waters rush off.

Beloved—I will rise up
in your empty heights
and plunge through your
regions of softwood
to the end of your Atlantic
depth once more
your grass bowl
will be exotic
with tropical life

our densities differ
but volume on volume
She is greater than me.
O Anna, *you* are the American Dream.
My will shall grow in your void.

ANNA'S ANSWER TRUE

What? Bury my polar
cap in your southern
past and thaw my icy
tongue in your adolescent
fountains!

I do want to spring up
chewing April strawberries
and June melons but who needs
to be scourged by your bulk?

I'll pull the continent
about me to stop you
from making more of yourself—
The Wisconsin could freeze
your grasping hand up my skirts
before you respect my rights
(let alone learn to acknowledge them).

I'll be damned, Martin,
if I'll be crammed
on the seat of your
imperial fantasy.

The world knows
we have an eternal engagement—
but I'm not the sort of giantess
who gets laid
for one or two silly visions.
Such is the heart of your fresh-water virgin,
Sons of America.

We stop singing, the clapping is wild; all except the Night are
pleased since the Night has a hate-on for Bates. She calls the
Captain a "mint-juleper" because she thinks he's a southern
plantation owner. Well, her nickname flatters the giant who
comes from hill-billy stock. Anyhow, as soon as the applause

183

dies down, the Night storms into the centre of the saloon, one head wailing, the other head scolding, and she whacks Bates on his chest with a guitar. The passengers go crazy with joy, thinking it a bonus tacked on to our program, and the giantess tries to add to this impression by putting her arms around the Night and Bates and bowing as if they were doing an encore. Bates is mad as hell, but the giantess takes his hand and leads him out of the saloon. Later on I hear her telling the Night the operetta is a political conceit, put on for show-biz reasons, and that there is not a whit of truth to a romance between her and the Captain. I don't think she's telling the truth as from here I have to say the big woman looks like she is very much enjoying Bates's attention and the reaction of the crowd, which is considerably favourable to the notion of giant hearts a-flutter. So there's no need to worry. I have a good feeling she is going to marry this big lummox.

CHAPTER TWENTY-TWO

The Living Pyramids in Liverpool

(From the Diary of Anna Swan)

May 2, 1871

Last night I dreamt I was the *City of Brussels*, and Martin the captain, declaiming to all my gross tonnage, displacement, and overall length. As he talked, I sailed, on my back, too close to the wind—into the eye of disaster. I tried to speak but out of my lips came only a doleful tune from Chrissie's guitar. My lecture voice deserted me, though I begged it to return.

This morning, as we docked in Liverpool, the dream faded in my excitement over a new land unfolding. I am through with the mudsills. I will never again perform in New York, and if the British like me, I will make London my home. Meanwhile, Ingalls registered us at the Washington Hotel on fashionable Lime Street. For sport, I have been dallying naughtily with the idea of shocking the reporters and medical men at our reception tomorrow by discussing female complaints. Those pale, searching faces with whiskered chins and notepads on which they busily scratch away at incidentals, would blink in horror at the mention of inappropriate lactation, or amenorrhea. If these misfunctions failed to startle the gentlemen of the media, I could announce that the fluid I pass daily (equalling 50 bottles of ale) is a pittance compared to the waste a Liverpudlian sprinkles on the streets here! (In public view too!)

Of course, I am too polite to embarrass others with tales about female weakness. I will smile encouragingly as if I believe truth lies in the facts the press compile and tell them I rise at 11 a.m. and do not cork my brows or use white paint known to cause eruptions, dizziness, and blindness. I will tell them also I am against false ears made of India rubber, and that exercise, such as croquet, is the best cosmetic for pinking a woman's cheek.

May 3, 1871

I entered the hotel reception room with my usual talk on gianthood in mind, toe first in my lilac reception gown. I wear it to all new occasions because I believe it brings me luck and this morning I politely ignored Ingalls' little critical look that seemed to say, "Not your old brocade again." Martin walked beside me in military fashion, with fully extended instep and knee, his chestnut head, hip and back erect. I took impossibly small steps in my silk boots so my crinolines wouldn't flare out and upset drawing-room furniture but on impulse, entering the semi-circle of reporters' chairs, I pivoted and my skirts flew in a show of energy, knocking the notepads off knees in all directions.

I then stood stock still, letting the dress fold in about me, and opened my mouth to recite to the press of Liverpool my customary prattle at public interviews.

My lips parted, and no sound came out, so Martin spoke:

"My wife-to-be is unquestionably the tallest (and liveliest) woman the world has ever known," he said. "I hereby offer $10,000 to any of you who can find me a larger woman."

The press corps stirred with interest. "Larger or higher, Captain?" a reporter asked in a loud, piping voice.

"Taller, undoubtably. I have no interest in a mate I cannot wrap my arms around," Martin continued. I spotted Ingalls, who sat to the left of the circle, looking excited. (For somebody who claimed to find me attractive, he does not seem bothered that I am going to marry another man.) When Martin finished announcing our engagement, our agent rose and thanked the reporters for meeting with the LIVING PYRAM-IDS.

"I choose the above caption for no other comparison can

186

convey a just idea of their majestic vastness of proportion," he bellowed. "The awe-stricken eye gazes with amazement upon a couple that seems to be the incarnation of the famed Colossus of Rhodes. The Captain, a man of magnificent physique and unusually handsome face, which beams with intelligence and kindness, asks any of you with further questions to meet him downstairs in the men's smoker."

The reporters trailed out behind Martin. I frowned at Apollo. Who else but the AUSTRALIAN MOUTH would call me a block of sandstone? A stone Anna—walking and talking with a stone Martin in the manner of ancient menhirs?

Ingalls came up and took my arm.

"You needn't look unhappy with my spiel. I have to publicize the two of you, don't I?"

I wanted to argue and then I remembered I had lost my voice. Ingalls thought I was fooling. Not till he saw me in my suite wearing a cloth dipped in vinegar about my throat did he understand I have laryngitis. Ingalls has never seen me without my lecture voice, and I am equally bewildered. I trust it is one of those minor problems which seems to turn up right before curtain time.

Will I truly go through with marriage to a southerner who spends all his spare time investigating the history of giants? It seems so. I am a creature of show business, after all.

There is something, however, I will not do. I will not sit in a chair and let Martin remove my shoe so the largest man in the audience can put his foot in it. Nor am I going to rise and say at our levee, "Ladies and Gentlemen, you're most obedient." Let Martin do the amateur theatricals. Let him put his foot in it.

CHAPTER TWENTY-THREE

Martin's Jihad

(From "A Tract Towards Continual Anatomical
Wonders")

May 29, 1871

London. I gain kudos wherever I go. In the paper, yesterday:

"Captain Bates is a fine, manly fellow, a native of Kentucky, about 7′8″ in height, and thoroughly well-proportioned. He is active and muscular, and during the American war fought on the Confederate side, and was on more than one occasion severely wounded. Captain Bates has a frank and open countenance; he is highly intelligent, and he has not a trace of that stupid stolidity which is so frequently seen in the giant of the caravan."

Naturally, the giantess was not mentioned with the degree of enthusiasm awarded me. The limey scribbler referred to her "Herculean proportions" (a peculiar way to describe the charms of my bride, I judge it), and made a lot of how-de-do over the darkeys and their brown skin, glossy, curly hair, and brilliant pearl-like teeth. The Limeys are not used to seeing Nigras in the flesh.

Yesterday, I postponed research into anatomical wonders and escorted the giantess on a stroll through St. James Park. The London grass is already green and I picked hyacinths and tulips out of a park bed and gave the nosegay to the giantess. She has lost her voice, and is obliged to indicate her feelings by a certain arch of the brow, a melancholy tilt of the head, or a series of sad exhalations of air.

188

For discussion, she scribbles on a notepad with a quill pen, and I confess her little airs make me quake with carnal excitement. I cannot believe my luck in meeting such a biological find! A pity the weather did not reflect my amorous mood. The sun, behind a rolling grey cloud, was dimmed to the sheen of a spring moon in Kentucky, and the giantess and I kept our heads dry under an umbrella I borrowed from the doorman at our Park Lane Hotel.

The limeys are rude staring s.o.b.'s who hurl insults on the street. Several times I had to tell some pipsqueaks who asked how the climate was up there to get off their knees and find out. Wait till the limeys learn I am taller than every one of the colossi on display in their palaces and museums! They will look smart when I prove the *Americanus* a superior breed!

The giantess and I also perambulated to Trafalgar Square. The giantess admired the sixteenth-century architecture of the government buildings sprawling about us and scribbled me a notation:

"Martin, I belong among these civilized people who have the sense to design on the grand scale."

I could not share her excitement over pieces of stone. So what if the limeys have older buildings than we do? I pray she will show the same reverence for me when I debunk the height claims of English giants.

We stood among the bubbling fountains at the base of Nelson's column, looking up at the stone homunculus atop his pillar. He towered 162 feet above us who look down on the limey head and I asked: "Monument to monument, my dear, do you think I have the old warrior beat?" Anna wrote back: "Martin, you should be grateful to appear small in the eyes of your God!"

Tomorrow we are going sightseeing with limeys, all top-drawer. They are Mr. and Mrs. Henry Lee and Doc Buckland and his wife. Lee is the scientific editor of the London gentleman's magazine *Land and Water,* and the doc is a surgeon to Her Majesty's Lifeguards. The medico is impressed by my interest in British giants and has promised to show me some. He says he is always ready to act in the service of science.

June 1, 1871

My investigation began two days ago when the giantess and I met the Lees and Bucklands outside our hotel.

"Have you heard of Chang, the CHINESE GIANT?" the doc asked me. "This Foochow fake claims to be nine feet! At present, he is out of favour with the Queen for scribbling Chinese characters at his shoulder level on the Royal wallpaper!"

I let out a rebel yell and then told Lee to give me his opinion of the height of this giant who the newspapers say sits on a jade throne with the oriental dwarf Chung Maw at his feet.

"Chang wears a mandarin cap and thick-soled shoes to make him taller, but from what I saw he looks to be your height, Captain."

"Pah. Believing is seeing," I said with a proud glance at the giantess. "All orientals are runts."

"I do so admire your khaki suit," said the doc's wife. "Military fashions are popular for giants, aren't they? Dr. Buckland and I saw a giant, a Mr. Joseph Brice, in the uniform of a drum major of the French Imperial Guard."

"Seven foot eight! A manly fellow like you," Lee said.

At the Tower of London the yeoman warders in their Tudor courtsuits stared respectfully at me and banged their pikes to acknowledge my Confederate uniform. I cracked a few jokes with the s.o.b.'s, then ascended the tower steps with the giantess. The doc had to struggle to keep up, but he wanted to point out the suits of armour, so I let him show me the legends I was going to vanquish.

"Ah, Captain, here is the armour of Og!" the medico said and barked at a limey guard who took it down in a hurry from its brackets and handed it to me. Og's suit is the largest of the suits of three medieval giants, Og, Gog, and Magog, who guarded the Tower of London. It is composed of steel bands linked in a way that allows for bodily motion.

"Og used to relieve himself out of this window, Captain," the doc said. "It is said he did it even during state executions."

190

"The big limey officiated at lynchings?" I asked in surprise and the doc nodded and drew a finger across his throat to indicate a beheading. Then I thrust my legs into the suit and put my head into the helmet, inserted my arms into the sleeves and tried to straighten my body, but could not do it.

"Oyez! Oyez!" the doc announced. "The armour is too short for Captain Bates."

"The helmet and foot pieces are a little large," I told the astounded party. "Your limey must have been a monstrous fellow in breadth and width, but not more than 7'3" in height."

The next round was at the British Museum. The skeleton of Murphy, the ENGLISH GIANT, hangs there. It is suspended by a wire inserted at the top of the skull. The doc suggested having it unhooked but I shook my head and rolled up my sleeves. "Pray leave it swing, doc," I said. "I will go this alone." I brought out my measuring tape and the doc announced Murphy was only 7'7". Either the system of measurement has changed or the height of giants was exaggerated in those days too!

The following morning the doc and I took a train from London to Manchester and visited Chang, the CHINESE GIANT, on exhibition there. The giantess wanted to tour Westminster Abbey, so she stayed home. I bowed out of seeing that dump. No rivals lie there! Only dead jousters and their dames!

When I first entered the hall, I noticed Chang had on the high headdress and thick-soled, wooden Chinese shoes the doc had told me about. He was seated, but my appearance quickly induced the wiley Chinaman to stand and be measured like a man. Back to back with me, the nine-foot Foochow fake was exposed. West topped East by three and one-half inches! I next visited Warwick Castle and examined the armour worn by Guy, Earl of Warwick. Guy is said to have been 9'3" high. On measuring his armour, the doc found he was all of five inches shorter than me. With my contests behind me, I am flushed with triumph and ready to meet the limey queen tomorrow.

191

CHAPTER TWENTY-FOUR

Victoria en Passant

(From the Diary of Anna Swan)

June 2, 1871

We met Queen Victoria today. Martin wore his new dove-grey ditto suit and I, the one-thousand-dollar satin and lace gown from Barnum as well as a white silk scarf to protect my ailing throat. (I was still *sans mot*.) Chrissie and Millie had been to see her earlier in the week and helped me coach a wise-cracking Martin on forms of address. "The English Amazon," as he calls my Queen, will *not* do! Nor is he to address her son, the Prince of Wales, by his nickname "Bertie" or pat or slap the back of his royal person. (Prince Albert can't stand to be touched, according to court gossip.)

The Queen's Household Cavalry came on horseback to our hotel to accompany the stagecoach—medieval figures whose uniforms made them look like knaves on playing cards. We rode in drizzle down the pink mall to Buckingham Palace. Martin fidgeted and made a show of stretching his legs in the carriage. He said the royal coach was too small. I was comfortable on ermine cushions and ignored his remarks about the cracks he spotted in the oak panel. He said he had ridden in better-made vehicles at home.

When we drove through the gold-tipped gates, Martin stuck his head out the stage window and bellowed at the sentries standing like wax dolls in their guard boxes: "Long live George Washington!" I bristled and Apollo snapped: "Take it easy, Captain. Do you want us to end up in the Tower?"

192

Martin quieted down as we entered the throne room. It was of miraculous length and blazed with light from cut-glass chandeliers. At the far end, sitting on a dais under a scarlet canopy, was a tiny, melancholy figure. She looked as small as a child in her widow's gown of black lace. Arm-in-arm, Martin and I did our promenade step down the immense room. Apollo followed behind. Eventually, we reached her carpeted dais. She smiled wanly, without opening her mouth, and adjusted the fluffy, white widow's veil that fell down her back and shoulders, as if its weight was too heavy. Then she tapped a black fan, clasped in her chubby, jewelled fingers, against her forehead, and stared at us in a distracted way.

"How is your employer, my dear friend, Mr. Barnum?"

"Mr. Barnum is well," Apollo replied. "But it is I, Judge Hiriam Percival Ingalls, who am sponsoring the giants in London."

The little monarch looked at Apollo coldly. "A pity," she said. "Nobody can match Mr. Barnum, can they?"

Apollo frowned and Queen Victoria gazed at me. "I wish a private audience with the giantess. Few men, with the exception of my late husband, interest me."

Apollo and Martin walked away nervously. At the end of the hall, they stood and bowed. Victoria waved at them adamantly. "Off you go, like good boys!"

Slowly, the monarch rose and walked down the carpeted steps. Although I had realized she was short the moment I saw her seated on her throne, I wasn't prepared for the shock of seeing her standing next to me. Why, she was tiny, a miniature monarch whose ruched widow's cap stood no higher than my thigh!

She didn't appear to notice the difference in our heights. She smiled widely at my knees, and exposed, for the first time, two rows of small, stained teeth. The decayed smile made her look extraordinarily vulnerable, and I suddenly felt protective of the small, regal being who after all was just another normal.

"Did you know that in this very room Tom Thumb was attacked by my King Charles spaniel?" she asked in a pleased

193

voice. "And would have been eaten too if dear Albert hadn't saved the day. How? you might ask. By shooting the spaniel with an arrow." She glanced at my knees mischievously. "A blunt-tipped one, of course."

Together we strolled down a long hall, passing Martin and Apollo, who sat stiffly on tall, rose-coloured chairs. They stood up at attention and Victoria swept me by them with a frosty look.

"I don't like men much, do you?" she asked loudly. "Too excitable. But necessary for cabinet posts"—she smiled at my knees—"and the manufacture of children. . . . Of course, my Albert was a God!"

She directed me to the Music Room, and once inside, her social chatter stopped and she locked the enormous doors, gazing at me with troubled eyes. I smiled back, but I was perplexed by her manner. The chandeliers, with their rainbow prisms, began to make my eyes ache, and I wished for a chair but I remembered no commoner was allowed to sit before she did. I felt transformed again into an awkward Nova Scotian farm girl who couldn't manage an entrance without knocking over an armchair.

Meanwhile, Victoria climbed the piano bench and seated herself on top of the grand piano so her head was level with mine. Then she took my white, gloved index finger in her fat, child's hand and sighed. "You have such a kind face; I know I can trust you," she said in a desolate tone. "I need your assistance." She sighed again and squeezed my finger. "Will you help me, Miss Swan?"

Her voice sounded so despairing that I could not help nodding my head. Then she smiled that pathetic brown smile and I felt sixteen feet tall instead of a mere eight. Back in New York, I had resolved to take no responsibility for the normals. Resolved? Sworn on all that was dear to me! Yet my resolve melted in the presence of the sad little queen until it seemed no more than a selfish whim of mine that I longed to toss away. Of course, I would do whatever the head of the realm asked of me.

The monarch dropped my finger and removed her tiny,

high-heeled silk boots. For a moment, she swung her bare stockinged feet exultantly in the air and then she stopped, looking annoyed at herself, before turning to gaze deep into my eyes.

"Miss Swan, I am lost without dear Albert to guide me. How can I manage the greatest empire the world has known when my intelligence is no bigger than my freakish size?"

She stared mournfully at me. "I believe you have noticed how small I am? Only 4′8″. That is no height for a queen. Why, I am a midget! If my people knew how I am riddled with imperfections, they would display me in one of Mr. Barnum's sideshows."

To show I disagreed, I shook my head from side to side and she answered by nodding hers up and down. Then she began to strut back and forth across the top of the piano in a curious, jaunty gait which I think she mistook for the stroll of a sideshow performer. In any case, I knew she was displaying herself to me and the action was so self-deprecating, I felt deeply touched. Indeed, without her heeled boots, she looked even shorter. Finally she asked in a sad voice if I would ring a gong by the door. I obediently applied a mallet to the arcane leather instrument and two menservants appeared, carrying in their arms immense wooden tongs of the type that are used to help ladies put on their crinolines.

"If you oblige me, history will be kind to you," Queen Victoria said.

For the first time, I wondered how I was to help her. The monarch was staring at me again in the distracted manner she had exhibited in the Throne Room, and I had the unpleasant sensation that I had ceased to exist for her as a person.

Slowly, she lowered herself from the piano and then pulled off her widow's cap. She took a tiara out of a nearby commode and settled it on her head with a resolute look.

"Miss Swan, this is to please me—not humiliate you," she said.

She nodded at the menservants and they bowed before her. Then they advanced towards me, their tongs raised like the feelers of an immense praying mantis. I stepped back in fright and bumped into one of the myriad navy blue and gold columns that ringed the circular room. I did not know what to do. One part of me wanted to flee while another part felt obliged to serve Her Majesty who appeared in distress. I looked at Victoria for an answer, but she ignored me and stared blankly at her minions. They had pried under my gown and now lifted the hoop of my crinoline high in the air until the tops of my five-foot-long legs were exposed.

I looked down in horror at my open-worked silk stockings. On a whim, I had chosen the purple-striped pair, so *à la mode* in London, and not the white ones that ladies wear over a pair of silk stockings so as not to unduly expose the leg. The latter would have been more suitable for a royal audience and now I was revealed as the brazen female I knew myself, in my heart of hearts, to be.

For a second, Victoria's down-turned little mouth twitched, as if she was amused by my underpinnings, and I opened my lips to appeal to her but no sound came out. Then she frowned, as if I was a balky child, and began to march towards me, in a stately fashion. Beside me, her two servants waited, backs erect, tongs held like drummer's sticks against the froth of my raised skirts.

When she was a foot away, Victoria cried out: "God save you, my dear child!" Then she ducked her spiked head and walked in a slow and leisurely fashion through my legs. *En passant,* she paused to study the archway of my poor pelvis and my long legs trembled at the thought of her solemn little face regarding my enormously baggy drawers which consisted of two separate sections gathered at the waist and open at the crotch.

Walking out the other side, she looked back and winked and I realized her little person was convulsed with merriment. "I'm glad to see a giantess wears fine linen like other ladies," she called. "But I would recommend flannel knickers for our poorly heated buildings."

Chuckling, she walked to the door and there she smiled in the jolly manner of a well-fed British matron who had no more on her mind than the dishing out of treats for her grandchildren.

"Miss Swan, you have amused me and thus done the Empire a great service.

"I will make certain you are well rewarded for helping to dispel the Coburg melancholia that has afflicted me and my Saxe-Coburg relatives."

Then she nodded to indicate our audience was at an end, and after unlocking the doors, strolled out, no, almost skipped off, so light-hearted did she appear.

Immediately, the servants dropped their tongs and my skirts crashed to the floor. For a moment, I reacted as if nothing had occurred and stared blankly at the servants who had started to chat about the weather, employing the convenient euphemisms of "mists" and "sprinkles" which the British use to avoid the pessimistic ring of "rain." It struck me that I should be angry with the little queen. She had used me like the Lilliputian king who had ordered Gulliver to stand while the Lilliputian armies marched through his legs.

Yet I found myself smiling wryly over her childish antics. I knew she bore me no more malice than she would a tall redwood through which the Californians drive their buggies.

Just then, the door opened, and a maid pushing a tea tray entered, followed by Martin and Apollo.

"How did it go?" Apollo asked.

One of the menservants winked at me. "The Queen was enchanted with your giantess' good posture and polite manners," he said. "She envies tall gels, she does."

"You were a royal hit then, Anna," Apollo bowed.

The two men looked at me proudly and I immediately burst out chuckling. I must be the only subject that could perform such a duty for Her Majesty! Should I stitch on my cotton drawers the motto used by marmalade manufacturers and whisky merchants—"By appointment to Queen Victoria"? Apollo and Martin stared in amazement; however, I knew they wouldn't believe what had happened so I shrugged mysteriously and continued smiling.

On our way out, the menservants showed us to the spot near the ballroom dais where Angus McAskill had pressed his heels into the carpet.

"Wasn't he the one?" the servant winked. "Ruining Her Majesty's rugs."

I saw two half-moon shapes on the red wool in the middle of the second stair.

"And done nineteen years ago," the other servant added.

"But *she* won't have the holes touched. Says she wants a token of the strongest, tallest, stoutest man that ever entered the palace."

"I understand your Queen favours Highland stock?" Apollo chuckled, referring to Victoria's notorious attachment to her Highland servant, John Brown.

"The brawer, the better! The good woman took up her husband's opine over the superiority of the Scottish race," the servant said and smiled.

Martin walked up the dais and stood on the second stair. He jumped up and down next to the imprint of Angus's boots. Apollo and the servants laughed and walked over to see if the giant had left a mark on the carpet.

"Not even a dint, Captain!" Apollo teased.

"That's because you haven't looked close enough, Judge," Martin roared. He took Apollo by the collar and turned his head down towards the floor.

Martin's competitive game annoyed me. Suddenly, I wished Angus was alive. He, of all beings, would know I wasn't exaggerating my bizarre audience with Queen Victoria. He would nod sagely, thinking it made perfect sense.

CHAPTER TWENTY-FIVE

The Royal Marriage

(From "A Tract Towards Continual Anatomical Wonders")

June 18, 1871

The future of the American gigantis is secured for yesterday Anna Swan and I were made one. The limey Queen did not attend. She does not make public appearances because she is mourning her husband, Albert, who died ten years past. The little monarch has declared me the "TALLEST, STRONGEST, STOUTEST MAN" to enter Buckingham Palace and therefore sent me congrats and a bag of Imperial loot. I was awarded a gold watch whose dial is as big as a saucer. The giantess also received a gold watch and a clustered diamond ring. (Anna seemed out of sorts—perhaps because the watch is smaller by a tad than mine. However, the sovereign is known to admire large males.)

The nuptial ceremony was performed by an old friend of the giantess', a six-foot-three Nova Scotian named Rupert Cochrane, now a reverend at St. George's, Hanover Square. Lee, the science editor of *Land and Water*, was my best man and Dr. Buckland's wife was a bridesmaid. Ingalls, my runty manager, gave my bride away. The darkies wanted to be in the wedding party but I told them to sit with the congregation and bought them blue face veils (popular with the London gals).

The giantess and I are monarchs of the prodigious North American community. Our offspring will mean more to the world than the issue of a limey prince. Mankind has arrived at a crossroads. America must giganticize the human species or mankind will devolve into shrimpy land animals. To paraphrase the frog scholar Descartes: I am a man of great stature, ergo, I am a great man.

The hymeneal event that will save our species from mediocrity took place at St. Martin's-in-the-Fields, a famous cathedral in London's theatre district. It is frequented by those of us in the acting profession. I looked posh in a blue coat, white waistcoat, and grey trousers. The giantess wore a white satin gown and a circlet of orange blossoms on her red curls to symbolize the virgin's triumph over fleshly temptations.

There was a second reason for her choice of orange blossom. Because the orange tree is an abundant fruit-bearer, modern brides believe the flowers will bring fertility. I trust my bride will be fecund. Judging from her wide hips, she looks to be a good breeder.

The ceremony was impressive. I was calm even though it was a job to avoid the two hundred yards of satin train washing against my ankles. There was a little botch-up with the ring. Someone overestimated the proportions of my bride and made it too big. So she let it slide to the floor after I stuck it on her finger. I heard a limey or two gasp in the oak pews but I paid no heed and retrieved the ring and put it on the giantess' thumb. Who was smart enough to notice I stuck it on the wrong digit? Then the giantess (who had a bad throat) wrote "Yes" and "I Do" on her notepad and the big woman became mine.

"There must be less to life than this, my dear," I joked to the new Mrs. Bates while we stood shaking hands with our guests. "Look yonder at the square and see how puny the limey warrior is now!"

The giantess smiled at my joke about Nelson's head and, like me, was astonished to see how crazy the limeys were acting. Hundreds of them swarmed below us on the square and the London bobbies took pokes at some of the s.o.b.'s standing in the path of our carriage.

We couldn't make our way to the vehicle so the Reverend suggested we go by foot to our new digs which are half a block from the cathedral on Craven Street. Anna tells me it is an historic locale. Benjamin Franklin resided at 35 and the German poetaster Heinrich Heine lived at 32.

And now the LIVING PYRAMIDS will occupy No. 45 which is decorated in the Turkish style. The walls of our new home are a remarkable orange colour and are spotted with lime crescents and stars. We have genuine cloth-of-gold cushions on velvet settees plus a second-floor bedroom with a balcony overlooking Craven Street. The bedroom walls are painted to look like the gold curtains of a sultan's tent. The giantess is partial to this room and calls it "trompe l'oeil drapery."

We found the Judge and the impresarios Smith and Boxby getting soused with the Lees and Bucklands. I quaffed a few ales and then hurried the giantess out to our carriage which the doc had decorated with a collection of old boots, shoes, and slippers.

The giantess had a case of virgin's nerves so I entertained her by reading from Black's *Picturesque Guide.* I amused her in this way long after we boarded the ferry and she settled down and sat still as a mouse at the prow of the boat while her wedding skirts flapped in the breeze. I held the guidebook at chest level like a mountain preacher and my Kentucky bass drowned out the wails of the infants inside the ferry cabin and resounded across the Thames, which is not big and mighty but about the size of a Letcher County crik and gives off a god-awful stink on account of pollution. (In summer, they say the limey parliament sits early to avoid the stench given off by the Thames during midday heat!) Limeys sauntering along the foot-paths by this filthy trickle stopped to hear my oration and yelled "Hencore!"

The giantess was very interested in Black's description of our lodgings, the Star and Garter. The inn is a favourite watering hole for royal bigwigs like Louis-Philippe and the dead limey penman Charles Dickens.

Halfway to Richmond, a young couple came on deck, carrying the infants who had been kicking up the fuss. The pair had five between them. The father, a frail-looking limey, told me he hoped the air from the Thames would soothe his young'uns. I told him he didn't have a hope in hell as the river smells were enough to knock over a big man like myself. The limey said "Quite, quite!" but pointed out that the open air was not as foul as the air inside his cabin. The poor s.o.b. looked like he didn't have a dime to his name so I slipped him a shilling note with one of our pamphlets on the LIVING PYRAMIDS. Then I handed one of his screaming babies to the giantess and told her to stop its noise-making.

She held it in a back brace of her long fingers and in no time the little thing was quiet. "Well done, little mother!" I said and the limey and his wife had a chuckle.

Our appearance at the Richmond dock caused a ruckus. Obviously nothing happens in this burg. The parade of drivers leading their horses around pot-holes on the road by the dock stopped dead to stare at us and limeys trailed out of the shops and yelled remarks. I read louder than before as I did not want my bride to hear the insults made by those s.o.b.'s who are famous for being a nation of starers. I even read as we puffed along a country lane looking for transport. At last, a dray stopped and drove us up a steep hill outside the town and there we beheld the inn, as grand as a nobleman's château behind iron gates. The view is very fine; it looks down on the Petersham meadow where the Thames makes a large bow. The giantess was exceedingly pleased, but her nerves were shot by the time we unpacked so I did not press my suit last night. Tonight I will test the waters and see if her maidenly fears can be laid to rest in my robust arms.

CHAPTER TWENTY-SIX

The Star and Garter

(From the Diary of Anna Swan)

June 17, 1872

This morning I let the KENTUCKY GIANT into my life and already I wish to be out of his. I confess: I am afraid of the big southerner. Of course, it is hard for me to meet tall men and Martin is one of the few males in the world who is big enough to be my husband. But the giant and his blustery manner unnerve me. I miss Angus. I sense his presence, and hear his hollow voice rumbling: "Stupid lass, see the mess you've got yourself in!" Well, you Great Know-It-All! Perhaps I need a disastrous act like this marriage to shock me out of my grief for you!

Oh dear. Conversations with the dead on the day of my wedding. I am becoming hysterical. I must not panic. Anna Swan, I can hear Momma's voice pipe, talk turkey to yourself! You married Martin Bates because you are fond of his company and you share his interest in travel and gracious living. You are not afraid of any man. Not you, who stands five inches higher than him in your stocking feet. From a distance, he displays authority, but at close quarters, Martin is Martin, every inch a common American! A hill-billy who lost his temper in the cathedral and threw your ring onto the floor when he realized it had been made too large for your finger! A fine girl like you wouldn't do a thing like that! Imagine him in his long-johns and laugh. . . . Ah, living voices this time. But that is the trouble, Momma. I do not wish to picture him thus.

Fortunately, nobody but myself and a reporter from the

Daily Telegraph saw Martin's tantrum. When the media creature shook hands with us outside the church, he politely
referred to Martin's "moment of panic."

"A giant may get used to being eight feet but marrying an
eight-foot woman while idlers gawk is enough to flummox
any old cock," the reporter said. The amiable fellow went on
to compliment my congenial manners and made no mention
of my laryngitis. That I could manage my train with dignity
seemed to satisfy him that the new Mrs. Bates was a remarkable person. (Perhaps the wedding ceremony is designed for
women like me who are too shocked to comment on the
upheaval of their lives.)

My panic started to build after the service when we stood
outside the cathedral, chatting like monarchs in the June
sunshine while the entire city of Westminster lay at our feet.
How Barnum would have liked our vista! I wished the old
showman was with us and not travelling in the American mid-
West with his circus. If only his jolly potato face had popped
out of the crowd to enjoy with me an event after his own
heart.

As we escaped down the passage to Craven, I spotted a
diseased pigeon on the stones ahead of me. The bird tottered
with fear at the rustle of my wedding train which, at the
height of its propelling power, can knock over a man. The
lecture voice sprang to my tongue and I would have cried out:
"Martin! You oaf! Watch your footing!" But I said nothing and
the giant's farewells thundered in the spring air. I managed to
pull in my train to save the bird from smothering but when I
glanced back, its shabby grey feathers were stained brown
from a rain of Martin's tobacco juice.

My heart sank, and by the time I cut our cake I had a bad
case of nerves, made worse by the lapses of taste around me.
(When one is dumb, one sees.)

Chrissie and Millie, giddy with stout, falling over themselves in a polka.

Apollo's long fingers crawling over Mrs. Buckland's robe
like a rash.

My own nervous curiosity about Martin's baggy, sweat-stained trousers. . . .

The giant was inebriated and the journey to Richmond interminable. After we arrived at the Star and Garter, I left Martin in the hands of a porter and rushed unhappily down a perpendicular lane to the Thames. Brown cows with shiny pink noses and delicately fuzzed behinds grazed in the meadow; a few fishing scows sat moored by a bow in the river.

I was alone—aside from the cows slowly lumbering towards me to stare—and free to make my own small dramatic gesture. Everyone was happy except me. The wedding pleased even my Yankee-hating parents who wrote to congratulate me on landing a man as big as myself, particularly since the civil war had made marriageable males as scarce as hens' teeth.

I began to walk briskly through the meadow, wishing my corset would allow me to run and tumble until I had rubbed myself free of my heavy, satin garments. Columns of light fell on the tame countryside. I tramped this way and that among the munching animals who slowly moved aside to let me through.

I heard a rip as I cleared the herd and I looked back to see a cow tramping on my train. Then I heard a hum, like a hive of wasps, and gazing towards the river I saw the men on the fishing scows shouting at me. Their little arms waved crazily and a few of the scows were drawing up anchor so they could sail closer to the show I was making on the Richmond meadow.

I looked down again and saw my gown was torn. My train was gone and my white kid slippers bore yellow stains from the wet grass. I had not a second to lose. The men, frantic with excitement, were jumping onto the shore and wading through the river towards me. So I made a 180-degree turn in what was left of my vast skirts and swiftly ascended the hill.

I was out of breath by the time I reached our honeymoon chamber which turns out to be a shabby cubicle facing the wall of the hotel stable. Villagers hereabouts are reputed to pay a sovereign for the privilege of looking through the window of this hostelry but I suspect the Star and Garter's heyday is over and Martin and I have paid a packet for another over-rated British inn. (Just my misfortune to be at a historical spot when the interesting personalities have come and gone.) We have only one piece of modern furniture: the factory-made four-poster bed on which I found Martin sprawled. He lay diagonally on it, still in his wedding clothes. He had on his yellow gloves and his size sixteen cavalry boots and he was snoring. One look at the man whose wonder-world I am fated to explore, sleeping with a saliva drool on his lips, and I began to weep, sobbing into my ripped crinoline like a child. (When one makes a theatrical gesture, it is difficult to tell where the drama of hurt leaves off and genuine pain begins.)

Oh-oh! Martin has disappeared. From the bed behind me, I mean. While I've been writing, he's gone. . . . Where? I have read too many tales of horror about bridal nights. But where is Martin? I am aware I have on a silken chemise and a jet hairband.

Ten minutes later. I was sitting here, at my toilet, when suddenly, a hand from under the pleated skirts of the table grasped my ankle. I stopped brushing my hair and sat perfectly still, the way small dogs come to attention for their masters. Stocky fingers tightened their grip.

"What is the one thing I have that is bigger than something of yours?" a voice rumbled at my feet.

I sat, powder half smeared on my cheeks.

"My nose," the voice said, and Martin crawled out from under the table and brushed himself off. Then carefully, he raised himself off his knees and put his sausage-shaped fingers on my shoulder: a caress. He studied my face in the mirror before he disappeared, apparently to change out of his wedding suit in the watercloset.

"Glad you can take a joke, dearest," he called from behind the closed door.

Am I frightened? Do not be addle-pated. I, the BIGGEST (you know the rest) am larger than the KENTUCKY GIANT. I will pin on my waterfall of curls two inches higher than usual and lace up the violet satin boots with three-inch heels. Then I will take his arm, and with a firm look, descend the stairs to dinner. Husband, do you hear me?, I am bigger than you. . . .

June 18, 1872

Martin did not lay a finger on me last night. Instead, the giant sawed logs beside me, reminding me of the honk of Canada geese flying over the Cobequids. It was strange to lie beside him and smell the tobacco odour which exudes from his massive frame. It made me long for Angus and his cool candle-wax smell.

This morning Martin ordered for me at a window table in the hotel's pavilion room. We ate three courses of victuals, topped with strawberries and clotted cream in the hotel's high, domed dining room. It has a ceiling of ground glass from which hangs a massive gas chandelier. Martin noticed me eyeing the room and flushed with pleasure. "Not bad, is it my dear?" I looked away and saw, down the slope to Richmond meadow, a huge, white object. It was my wedding train, fluttering from a thistle bush. Martin followed my gaze but his vision is worse than mine and I was relieved to hear him break into exclamations about the quiet charm of the English countryside.

After breakfast we strolled in the Richmond Lanes, and Martin broke off a reading from Black's to make a confession about a former sweetheart—an army captain's daughter whom he had nearly married during the civil war. I didn't know how to respond so I wrote carelessly:

"And how tall was your paramour?"

He gave me a smug look. "Five feet."

Five feet! Close to half my height! I had been right to suspect his attraction for the captain's favourite, Miss Milling-ham. Perhaps my physical person—in secret—revolted him.

When Martin took a nap this afternoon I found myself staring at his size-sixteen boots. Again, the chant began to bang in my cerebral parts: Bigger than you, bigger than you.

207

Eventually he sensed he was being watched and opened an eye. He patted the bed beside him but by the time I had removed my underpinnings, he was asleep again.

Now he is very much awake, and I am with my bridegroom in our honeymoon chamber, unable to think because my skull is drumming with my hymeneal refrain: Bigger than you, bigger than you. Martin stands by the door to the watercloset, hesitating. He wants a sign. Should I raise my palms upward in the attitude of an Indian fakir? Scribble "Come hither" with my quill pen? Perhaps it occurs to him that I have not spoken a single word since I landed in Liverpool. He looks nervous. He sighs and begins to undress. I avert my eyes.

Bigger than you, bigger than. . . . My fingers, I see, are shaking. This is an extreme reaction. It is not as if I am to lie with Cyclops. I sit writing in my diary before the dressing table, as wound up as if I am about to spiel. Martin moves closer and insinuates his frame between myself and the lamplight.

I won't be impolite and gape at his nakedness. Even a monster such as Cyclops was half angel. . . . Or was he the son of Poseidon? A brother of Antaeus who couldn't be killed as long as he touched the earth and the son of a mother who sealed her one-eyed son in a volcano. . . . I am not certain when, perhaps when the flood drowned the angels. . . . Martin, I am bigger than you, do you hear me? He was buried alive, this Cyclops who commanded virgins to touch his dripping flesh. . . .

In the glow from the wall candle, I can see Martin's face moving closer to mine. . . . Cyclops deserved punishment for binding women with the tail of a dragon, and with his mouth, the shape of hell, burning on the skin, disfiguring with kisses. . . . I look up; I will speak to Martin whose black hair is lit like a dark halo around a planet. . . . My lips part slowly: I will speak against the blue light from his eye pouring into my interior. Martin, I will not walk backwards, in obeisance, to the bridal bed, first on tiptoe, then on the base of my heels like a witless maid. Your mate cannot be extinguished by the air you puff at my eyes, or by your bitter smell which has backed me into a far corner of myself so I am a light scintillating in an empty body...your huge eye may look down into my shadows...my skin may crawl with you, monster man, and my hair stand on end, but I, the BIGGEST MODERN WOMAN OF THE WORLD, will not undergo an eclipse of the spirit.

June 19, 1872

"Clotted cream and strawberries," Martin instructed the maître d' in the pavilion room. Martin was pleased. He chewed and spat into a flowered spittoon by our dining table. He was swanky, sitting opposite me, in his braided jacket. Captain Bates with the Mrs. He was less confident in private. When he knew I saw him without his trousers, he bounced a little on the balls of his feet and gave me a sheepish look. A well-this-is-me-and-nothing-can-be-done-about-it glance. The way a baby's eyes slide off when its mother removes its dirty breeches, trusting it will be attended.

I could do nothing but gape in astonishment. A small nub of purple bobbed from the centre of Martin's enormous frame. The organ was no longer than a baby's.

The giant blew out the oil lamp then and grabbed me to him as if *l'amour* was an extension of anger and not an emotion in its own right. Suddenly, Martin threw back his head and uttered a bleat-like cry. "God damn this whang to hell," the giant roared. "Anna, my trouser worm is a regressive ramrod that does not do justice to the great animal frame you see before you."

His moustached face crumpled, and he began to pound his fists on the bed, but his voice was meek.

"Are you going to leave me?"

Before I knew it, I heard myself say, "Martin, I will look after you."

He sighed gratefully, placed his dark head on my bosom, and soon was fast asleep.

I stared at the ceiling in shock. Was there something wrong in my preference for tall men? First, Angus had no idea how to

209

pleasure a woman, and now I have a giant husband with the equipment of an infant. I felt sorry for myself, and even sorrier for Martin, sawing logs beside me. To improve my spirits, I reached down and played with my silken folds until a rain of perspiration drenched the bed sheets and I had to blow on the bed linen in order to dry it so Martin didn't awaken and see me hot-eyed and panting.

In a few days, after we have had a chance to grow accustomed to each other, I will show him how to please me.

CHAPTER TWENTY-SEVEN

House Party at Windsor

(From the Route Book of Hiriam Percival Ingalls)

June 30, 1871

London, pop. 2,362,000.

The giantess is going over well with the royalty here. First the Queen takes a shine to her and sends her baubles and now Albert Edward, the Prince of Wales, is inviting her to his parties with the fast Marlborough House set. (I suppose the Prince is interested in Bates too. The southerner has flair. It's only when you get to know him that you find out he is an arsehole.)

Anna met the Prince at a private reception by His Highness at the Masonic Hall, June 21, 1871. The Prince was accompanied by the Grand Duke Vladimir of Russia and Prince John of Luxembourg. This trio of gents strolled in gay spirits, wearing light suits and Homburgs because they were going up to the Henley Regatta that afternoon. The Prince is a handsome buck with a full beard and the saddest eyes I ever saw (bedroom eyes, the ladies here call them).

Likely, his hang-dog look is on account of that old bird his mother who won't let him be involved in running the show. He is thirty years old, five years older than the giantess, and one of the richest crown heads in the world, but the Prince has got nothing to do except go to the races and chase women because the Queen doesn't think he is serious enough for politics.

Of course, he is married but his set don't care if the wives play around once they've provided airs to carry on the family name. Anyhow, the Prince's carryings on are appreciated by the Brits who are sick to death of the little Queen. Victoria has to be crazy as a coot. (Nobody with a full deck mourns a husband who's been dead and buried for a decade.)

All of us liked the Prince right off. He was very considerate and told us to excuse his "gadabout gear" so we wouldn't feel shy because we were over-dressed for the occasion. Anna had on an evening dress of white silk, with a garland of roses across her big breasts and a handsome cone-shaped skirt. I was proud of the big woman who looked as good as a Brit queen, standing there beside Bates in his cavalry get-up, those fake medals of his shining like real ones on his chest and shoulders. I was all fancied up, too, in a white shirt and riding jacket.

"I can see why Mama was impressed by you, Mrs. Bates," the Prince said to Anna. "You have a very understanding face."

The giantess went very red and I was surprised because she is not one to be shy with famous personages; to tell the truth, she revels in their attention. I guess the Prince's very considerable charms were having their effect on the big woman.

"I think you should visit the palace more frequently," the Prince continued. "Perhaps your influence will help the Widow of Windsor."

The giantess blushed again and, excusing herself with a curtsy, moved away to stand by Bates.

"Have I been too forward, dear lady?" the Prince called. "I hope not, for I hope we can become good friends."

Meantime, Bates put his arm around Anna and puffed cigar smoke down at the little Hanoverian.

"My wife is very shy," Bates said. "Don't pester her, Your Majesty."

The Prince laughed as if the giant's remark was a big joke and the giantess looked like she wanted to hide somewhere. (I expect the Brits let Americans get away with things because they figure people like Bates don't know any better.) In any case, Bates didn't worry the Prince at all and he complimented the giants on their foot size when we left the hall. It was raining (no surprise here) and the London streets were muddy so you could see our prints on the road. There were Bates's great clodhoppers and Anna's size-thirteen slippers in a mess of average prints. Well, His Majesty was fascinated. He and his entourage placed their own feet inside the marks of the giants and oohed and ahhed. Then the Prince shook our hands and told us he had enjoyed our company immensely and would make sure we were invited to one of his house parties in the country. We are excited over being entertained by royalty and Bates is telling anybody who asks that he is "a buddy of Bertie's." Bates is an ignoramus. I hope he don't ruin our weekend with the Prince, but the giantess tells me with all the confidence in the world that she will make the Captain look smart.

September 10, 1871

Windsor, pop. 2,147 houses and
12,272 inhabitants
We were a party of nine today in the Royal Train on the way to Windsor Castle. Yours truly (H.P.I.), the giants, the Prince and his pals, the Bucklands, and the Lees. The Prince's wife, Alexandra, didn't come. The Prince says she spends this time of year visiting her relatives in Denmark.

We sat in a coach decked out like a parlour with a real fireplace, reading lamps, and pots of ivy on the side table. (The walls of the coach are padded to cut down on noise from the wheels of the train.) The Bucklands sat at the back of the saloon, playing backgammon with Mrs. Lee. I sat on a huge leather sofa, squished between the giantess and Bates. The Prince and Henry Lee sat across from us in leather armchairs. The Prince seems fixated by the big woman. He never took his eyes off Anna's face although he spent most of the trip talking to Lee, a London nabob who tried to entertain the Prince by making jokes at the giantess' expense. (I don't like Lee very well.)

It was a sunny day and us inside the coach were sweaty in our clothes. Lord knows, the harvesters outside our train must have been having a hot day's work. We passed a small family of

213

them walking alongside a field near the train, a sorry lot of paupers they were, too; the mother had on no shoes, the little girls were dressed in rags like gypsies, and had sun-burnt faces and scrawny bodies that showed they didn't get enough. The giantess looked concerned and asked the Prince about them, and he said: "I haven't the slightest idea how the poor buggers survive. But an Englishman always manages."

"At least, they're better off in the fresh air than down in the mines," I told the giantess who smiled at me as if I had said something funny. Then Lee started bothering the giantess by asking if she would let him prove a learned point: that all women—no matter their height—had ankles equal in circumference to their wrists. Lee poked at the hem of her skirt with his walking stick and the Prince told him to "desist" but his big sad eyes looked kind of curious too. To get away from Lee, the giantess rose and walked down to the loo which is the biggest watercloset I ever saw. It is almost as large as a regular train coach and has two washbasins side by side so the Queen and her servants don't use the same water. Well, I got up to go too, and Bates woke up from a snooze and wagged his index finger at me for disturbing him and then dozed off again before I could tell the big lout to hush up. Just as I was waiting for the giantess to finish, the door flew open and the big woman jumped out in a state of excitement and her vast bell-shaped skirt knocked me into the lap of Mrs. Buckland. The ladies in the coach screamed and I scrambled off and went inside the loo to see what was the problem. There, under the Queen's basin, folded in a ball, was Dr. Buckland! "The lads put me up to it, Judge," he says, and I wondered if he meant the Prince but was afraid to ask. The giantess gets more than her portion of undue attention. Then Dr. Buckland got to his feet and in a moment was so polite that I couldn't believe he was the same gent who spied on the giantess as she took a pee! The doctor is a frail-looking man with pince-nez. He went back and apologized to the giantess and took a severe scolding from the Prince.

At the station, the Prince had his lackeys put down a red carpet for us and we trod it all the way from the train to our coaches. A welcome committee of washer women stacked bouquets of roses in the arms of the giantess and a group of farmers from the nearby environs unhooked the horses from one of the coaches and took the place of the animals in the reins. The giantess saw this and shot me an unhappy look but nobody else seemed to think it was strange for grown men to act like beasts of burden. Then the Prince jumped onto the driver's seat and beckoned to Anna to join him. She allowed herself to be helped up beside him and they looked a funny twosome, the short, heavy-set Prince and the solemn young giantess.

The rest of us had to get into the other coach. Bates didn't want to get in with us and stared grumpily at the Prince's coach until Mrs. Lee tugged his arm and admonished him: "Bertie has to amuse himself, don't you see?" Bates grunted and got in then, but he looked annoyed and I felt sympathy for the giant. Mrs. Buckland told me the Prince expects husbands to feel that he is conferring an honour on their wives if he beds them. Not very romantic, if you ask me. Anyhow, I knew Bates was burning inside and so was I. What can a bloke do when the head of the realm takes a fancy to your girl? Only pray, I reckon, that she turns the bugger down.

September 11, 1871

The Prince is pretty happy about something. He entertained us at a midnight dinner last night with tales of grouse shooting and this morning I saw him on the terrace looking very gay in a deerstalker's cap. Mrs. Buckland thinks the room arrangements must be working in the Prince's favour, i.e., that he is getting under the skirts of the giantess who he's put in the state apartments, in a suite adjoining his. Bates, meanwhile, is in a bedroom down the corridor. As for H.P.I., I've got a nasty little cubicle near the smoker, the only room in the palace where Queen Victoria lets men smoke. Apparently, the Prince fancies women like the giantess. He stays away from young girls and seeks out mature women because they aren't so indiscreet. I can't say I blame him.

215

September 12, 1871

Luckily, we have this pile of stones to ourselves as Queen Victoria is holidaying in Balmoral. Or else there would be hell to pay. (The Brits are crazy people—all pomp and circumstance when they are sober, but give them a drink and they turn wilder than savages.) The mood got wild at dinner last night after Bates had bored the crew with his yap about giants. The nine of us, including the Prince, sat at the end of the banquet table in the Waterloo Chamber. The Prince sat at the head, naturally, and looked very sullen. The giantess sat by his side and I sat by the giantess. Bates sat across from the big woman and to the left of the Prince. Well, the big oaf droned on about victims of hormonal excess as if anybody there gave a hoot about a dead dinosaur! Pretty soon, Dr. Buckland and Henry Lee, who were squiffed on sherry, started rattling the silverware and jumping up and down and asking impertinent questions like, "Just how wide is the waist of your giantess?" Bates ignored their remarks at that point, and chatted to the Prince but His Highness was quite restless and impatient with all of us. His mood made everyone uncomfortable, even nervous I would say, as it is generally known the Prince can't stand to be bored. So Lee tried hard to entertain him and the Prince never told him to stop, not even when Lee jumped into the lap of the giantess (with a wink at the Captain) and took Anna's hands and linked them in front of his belly. Lee did this just as the serving girl came in with a tray of salads.

"Do you approve of my new sofa?" Lee asked her. "I ordered it from the colonies." The serving girl clapped a white-gloved hand over her mouth and dropped the silver tray she was carrying. Anna blushed furiously, and grabbed Lee by the collar and lifted him off, but the Prince never said anything, just sat, staring coldly at all of us as if he wished we were somewhere else. He acted the same way during dessert— which was bread and cheese and mustard and cress—meant to clear the palate for after-dinner drinking. Lee was quite tight by then and told the Captain to shut up about giants because

216

he wanted to give an historical talk on the Order of the Garter. The Prince frowned but didn't interrupt and Lee bowed to him and got on with his story. He said the Order was started when the sweetheart of one of the old Brit kings dropped her garter at a dance and the King picked it up. Because his lackeys laughed, the King got mad and said, "Shame on you for thinking the worst!" Then Lee said the King told the knights he would make the garter so important they would all want to wear it and he started the Order of the Garter and made good his word along with the motto *"Honi soit qui mal y pense."*

At this point, the Prince interjected: "I heard this tale at my nanny's knee," he said. "Why are you boring me with it now?"

"Because, Sire, with your permission, I'd like to suggest that you found a new order," Lee replied.

"A new order? For sherry-tipplers, you mean?" the Prince asked.

"I propose *l'ordre de la pantoufle fourrée,* if the giantess will kindly hand over her slipper," Lee pronounced.

The ladies giggled and put their gloved hands to their pretty white throats and the poor giantess just sat next to the Prince looking stunned. Slowly, she shook her head.

"Henry old cock, I'll retrieve it for you," Dr. Buckland said and dove under the table in search of her foot. I wish I could say I helped her but it was Bates who put a stop to it. The giant walked over to where she sat.

"How about a southern army boot?" Bates drawled and put his foot on the doctor's rump. The head and shoulders of the man were under the tablecloth. "It would be a fine honour for a fine old cause." For the first time that night, the Prince smiled. The doctor did look a fool. Meanwhile, the giantess stood up, very regal-like, and sailed out of the room. Her heavy footsteps made the wall paintings shake and some of our party tittered, but the big woman handled herself pretty well in my opinion. The Prince looked mad as blazes since nobody is supposed to leave a party of his until he says so, but he didn't send anybody to fetch her back. Maybe he felt just as mad at himself since he can't seem to get in the good graces of

217

the giantess. (I don't like the Prince so well as I thought. And I think this should be the last of our royal levees. They are too hard on the giantess.)

September 12, 1871

A sin has transpired! All mine, too. I have erred in the worst way against the giantess who has had a bad enough time of things here at Windsor Castle. To be sure it was she who came to my room. How she managed to squeeze herself down the narrow corridor past the smoker I do not know, but when I retired last night, I found the big woman sobbing on my bed. As soon as she saw me, she started to wail and asked if I thought she was unhinged because she was beginning to see people here as vegetables that needed to grow. On a stone branch near the castle yesterday, she said she sang "a growing song" to old and young heads marching in rows on the road going into the new town, and people had stopped and looked at her as if she was mad. Did I think she was mad, she asked again, and I said definitely not although I warned her that she'd better get a grip on herself because we're guests of the Royal Family. At that, she cried harder and said she was discouraged with the Brits who are polite on the outside but cruel underneath. She told me she felt like a performing monkey for people who live inside a fairy tale and don't understand anything except their own humiliations. On the first afternoon, when we arrived, the Prince showed her to her bedroom which had gold-painted furniture, a bed with a crown on its canopy, and a marble fireplace big enough to keep a horse in. On the pillow of the bed was a pair of high-heeled boots in violet satin. (The Prince had got one of his flunkies to measure the giantess' prints that day at the Masonic Hall so his own shoemaker could fashion her a pair of giant shoes.) The giantess said she had never seen any shoes so beautiful! They were lined with quilted pink satin and had high embroidered tops that reached up to her mid-calf. Well, she was overwhelmed and told the Prince she wouldn't accept such a gift and he laughed and said nobody else could fit her shoes. So she wore them that night to the midnight supper and the Prince was very pleased, and all went swimmingly until tea the next day when the Prince stepped out from behind the firescreen in her bed chamber as she was sipping her cuppa and tried to make love to her. Then she told him she considered him very handsome, but unfortunately she only liked tall men. (Can you beat that? She said the next king of England was too short for her.) The Prince laughed, a bit hysterical, she thought, and then he sat down and got more and more melancholy and started to tell her all about his family and how the old queen blames him for his father's death. She was sad to hear about that and she patted his hand and tried to cheer him up and then he started kissing her bosoms and she had to bodily remove him from her person and then the Prince begged her forgiveness and said he had misconstrued her reactions and he has been in a bad mood ever since. Apparently, she went for a walk on the palace grounds after Dr. Buckland and Lee were rude, and when she went up to her bedroom, there was the Prince again, sitting in her chamber by the fire and staring at the pair of giant boots which she'd left on a bedside table. She said she saw a tear rolling down his whiskered cheek and he looked so sorry for himself that it scared the daylights out of her. She went off to find Bates but he was in the men's smoker so she came up to see me. She said it was true that she didn't fancy short men and that she'd tried to let the Prince down easy but that he had such a case of self-pity she didn't think even she could look after him, and she always figured she could make most normals happy if she tried.

She next confided a fantastical story of the Queen walking under her petticoats. The giantess exaggerates so I don't put much stock in that tale. But her story about the Prince may be true. I saw with my own eyes those boots that night at supper and Anna is a fine piece of flesh although she's on the large side. She has quite strong powers of sexual attraction, for a freak.

Then the giantess told me her marriage to Bates was a mistake. She said the giant was impotent (and wouldn't give her pleasure) but it was too late to do anything, she would just have to make the best of it because she didn't believe in divorce. Then she told me the wildest thing of all. She said she felt responsible for the big lummox. He suffered more than people knew, she said. I said a bully like Bates doesn't suffer; he is too pig-headed; and she got a bit vexed and told me if I was taller I would get a better view of things. By and by she calmed down—and then, what do you think? She fell asleep. In the bed of H.P. Ingalls.

Just when I was going to tell her I was considering quitting the troupe on account of Bates—who is enough to drive any promoter loony—she conked out! Ingalls, you bad boy, I said to myself, she said she doesn't like short men so here's your chance. Opportunity only knocks once. So I pulled up those skirts of hers until they covered her face and crawled inside her crinoline hoop which looked to be the size of a bear trap. As I uncoiled the rod, I swear I saw her spread her legs. But she was out cold, so how could she? Anyhow, I did my damnedest and she didn't move a muscle. The skirts fell off her face during. After, I just lay exhausted on her stomach, looking up at her chin about two feet above me. The heat inside her and the pull of her muscles . . . made me feel I was being sucked into a volcano that was about to go off. I wanted to be dragged all the way in, and Lord, with her, you'd think that was possible but my trunk wouldn't fit . . . not even inside the hole of a giantess. The rest of me stopped old Ingalls from disappearing. The urchin ran into hisself, so to speak. Finally, I roused my brain and went back to tell Bates that the giantess had been hysterical and fallen asleep and why didn't we just leave Anna in my room for the night, and I would sleep somewhere else. Bates gave me a funny look, a little ashamed I would have to say. The giant then said he was going to take the giantess away in the morning as he thought the limeys were being s.o.b.'s. And he also told me he was going to stay up all night and guard my bedroom in case the Prince tried any funny business. I am glad the giantess does not know about the liberty I took with her. I am so wicked. And me her agent too. It is a good thing she is a freak and does not have sexual desire.

CHAPTER TWENTY-EIGHT

Touring the Provinces

(From the Route Book of Hiriam Percival Ingalls)

December 2, 1871

Edinburgh.

What a journey! The giantess spewed out one side of the mail coach and the Nightingale out the other during our trip north. Usually only the Nightingale does that nasty trick: I didn't expect it of the giantess. I helped her to the odd sip of barley water while Bates fanned her face. When we ate our lunch in the coach, I noticed the other passengers looking at us as if we should do something more than just eat, but what could we do to help the ladies in our cramped seats? At least we arrived safely in "Athens of the North" as this burg is called and found comfortable lodgings to rest in before the performances at Waverley Hall.

I am worried about the giantess, who continues to feel poorly during our week's run here. Bates keeps her on a busy schedule, taking breakfast at 8 a.m., dinner at 12, and supper at 6 p.m., and in between their shows at 3 p.m. and 8 p.m., off the pair go—on sightseeing expeditions up towards Arthur's Mount or down to the gardens on Prince's Street where the Captain does his best to limn the sidewalks with chewing tobacco.

The giantess is eating next to nothing: She says she can't keep her food down since the coach. She sits at the breakfast table sipping tea while Bates puts away smoked beef, pancakes, and honey in the comb. The Nightingale makes little gagging sounds behind his back so Anna and I will laugh but the big woman will not take up a campaign of mockery. When Bates is finished, he picks up a Scott novel and begins to read and she listens with a kind face.

I didn't realize how seriously her health has declined until rehearsal when I tried to teach her to do the schottische—not the five-step dance done by the Nightingale, but the easier version in ²/₄ time. She isn't what you'd call quick on her feet but she has always been able to master basic steps after a bit of coaching. Yesterday, she couldn't seem to learn to slide her feet from side to side on the count of one and two.

"Look, Anna—it's simple," I said. "Slide the left foot sideways on to the X I've chalked on the floor and count one."

"Like this, Apollo?" she asked. Her face was eager and I felt like a monster when I had to make her do it over and over.

Bates, per usual, wouldn't do what I said—he hardly moved and did a kind of shuffle with a sullen look—always on the wrong beat. I couldn't believe how hopeless they were and I could feel my anger rising.

The giants received warm reviews for their last show at St. James Hall but the interest in freaks is declining and in another year the English will be weary of staring at a huge man and woman walking up and down and answering questions. The Nightingale has added to her repertoire, and the LIVING PYRAMIDS need new material unless they want to be has-beens by the time we return to London. I pointed this out to Anna, who started to blink back tears. I kept talking about what a good opportunity they had to rehearse a new act now we are playing the sticks.

"This is a professional company and we must keep professional standards. Do you understand, Anna?" I said. I give my notes to her because there is no use correcting Bates who always has an excuse ready. This time it was not a good idea to ride her so hard—she had trouble smiling and looking agreeable during the 8 o'clock show. More is the pity because we would get a bigger crowd if she would perk up a bit.

The theatre is on Waterloo Place—a busy crossroads with nice cobbled streets and immense square stone buildings with colonnades. She causes quite a stir walking down the street here on her way to work.

Weather a thick fog, 49° - 34°; population 197,581.

January 2, 1872

Glasgow.

Colonel A.J. Bates, brother of the Captain, has joined us, and he and I have been having a fight over the management of the giants. I have had to give him the title of business director to settle things. He is a quarrelsome fellow with a chest-long goatee and is half his brother's size but possesses the warring Bates spirit. He claims I provide amenities for the giantess: fizzed drinks and pillows for her back, and won't cater to the Captain's whims on the road. He is right, of course. I find it difficult to be unbiased about Bates when he clomps into reception rooms wearing Anna on his arm with his boor's smile.

The projection of the giantess' voice has been a problem since we came to London and I have had to be at her all the time to speak up. A whispery voice drives an audience crazy, particularly because in her case they are so anxious to hear what she says.

Every now and then one of them asks her about her love life with the Captain and she just stands beside him, looking dignified and happy until the questioner feels a fool. She is putting a good face on things.

This morning she fell down a street embankment when she and I tried to catch a horse tram. She couldn't get up by herself and I had to ask some passers-by to help me get her into the tram. The poor giantess was embarrassed and apologized to me all the way to our theatre which is in the Trades Hall on Glassford Street.

The review runs from 2:30 to 5 and from 7:30 to 10. I did not ask her to do the evening show with the Captain on account of her mishap. She must conserve her strength if we are to finish the tour. We are to be in Greenock on January 8th and Stirling on the 9th. We had Christmas in Edinburgh and I

223

gave each member of the troupe a raise in salary of 2 shillings. (The Night complained as I only counted her as one and said she deserved four shillings but I held out against her pressure tactics.) The giantess and the Captain presented me with a historical novel by Sir Walter Scott, *The Heart of Midlothian*. I do not share their love for this wild land and would have liked a more personal gift from her.

I think she wants to talk to me about the night at Windsor Castle but there is no chance as Bates is always hanging around like a bad smell. What a pickle I am in—fancying a lady giant who is married to a giant ogre. Have mercy on my soul, Infinite Being.

Weather continues foggy. Pop. of Glasgow, 550,588.

January 8, 1872

Greenock.

The giantess sick again, on the Glasgow and South-West Railway. I had to request a stop so she could visit the woods and the conductor made a fuss as they do not normally halt the train for nature's duties on an hour-long ride. The Captain cleaned up her mess in the railway car without one complaint and when she came back on, he put his arm around her and she fell asleep on his shoulder. I suppose he cares about her in his way.

How can she stand the ogre near her? They are always together, talking about old monuments and battles while the Nightingale and I play rummy in this God-forsaken place.

At the train station, the mayor met our party and presented us with a sailing ship in a bottle. (On account of ship-building being an industry here.) But the townspeople are not welcoming. I've had trouble with folks staring through the windows when we are dining, so the troupe takes meals in its rooms.

The pop. is 57,141. The weather damp. As the inn-keeper told me: "It always rains in Greenock, except when it's snowing."

January 9, 1872

Stirling.
The weather has broken and our troupe went up to the castle
after the afternoon reception at Argyll's Lodging. When I had
had enough of the old stones, I went off to find the giantess.
She was standing up on the battlement gazing down at a flat
plain where sheep grazed, wearing one of her ever-so-mysti-
cal expressions. I stood with her, glad to have her to myself
for a few minutes when suddenly a deep voice bellowed
behind our backs.

"Ingalls, you runt—let us duel for the honour of Mrs.
Bates's company!"

I must have jumped eight feet. I turned around and there
was the Captain in a suit of armour far too small for him. He
told us it had belonged to the ancient Scots warrior, Robert
the Bruce, and the ticket-taker had let him try it on for twice
the fee of our admission ticket. I keep thinking Bates knows I
have been to bed with the giantess. But how could he? Even
the giantess don't know.

On the way home, I had the last laugh. Our coach stopped
so the giant could go for a call, and he ended up on a small rise
where highland cattle were grazing. One of the big hairy
brutes started to charge and the Captain took off like a shot.
The sight of his bare ass flying over the hill did my heart good
and it's safe to say he'd worn off some of his huge breakfast by
the time he made it back to the coach. The giantess seems
better.

Pop. 12,014.

January 12, 1872

Perth.
From Stirling to Perth on the Caledonian Railway, a 35-mile
trip. The giantess fainted after reception here, and I woke up
in the middle of the night, my teeth chattering, not from cold,
though I have no fire in this room, but from a horrible

225

nightmare. I dreamt I was in a stone cell at Stirling Castle with some of my old acts from my days as a promoter for Robinson. In the dream, the LION BOY is ripping me to pieces with his mangy fangs, and his monkey drops down from a window sill and fastens its teeth to my *avoir dupois*. The HUMAN SNAKE—in a vest of chainmail—is coiling round and crushing me when the giantess walks in and commands the things to leave me alone. Then she blows a whistle and I realize it's my turn to go on. I follow her up a shadowy passageway and notice she looks about the size of a normal woman. There's nothing unusual about her and I see it's me the warders are staring at so I ask the giantess for a mirror and she takes one from a little purse and gives it to me with a worried look. I look in and see a hairy ape face with deformed lips and a wide, squat nose. There is even hair on my forehead, and I have two rows of teeth in each jaw. I am so ugly I want to die, then I look down and see breasts poking through my suit vest. Dear God, I am a woman. The dream ends here and, of course, it makes no sense. I am being influenced by the creepy atmosphere in these parts. Worse, I have the sniffles continually and all the troupe is sick with ague and complaining. I am eager to leave this kill-joy country where it is always cold and raining.

Pop. 23,507.

January 15, 1872

Dundee.

We are not opening here. The giantess has collapsed. She fainted again on the ferry between Dundee and Tayport. By the time we reached town, it was obvious she couldn't perform. The Colonel has changed his tune and is saying it's my fault—that I drove the big woman too hard. (I don't believe there's anything worse than going on the road with a group of excitable actors who are no more grown up than children and I am the one who has to look after them.) I am fussed about the health of the giantess. The Captain took me aside and told me she's quite a frail female despite her great size. He is worried too and suggested she leave off performing for a time. My sniffles are worse.

Pop. 86,532.

January 18, 1872

Edinburgh.

The giantess is in the hospital for a rest. It could be said her condition has made a mess of the big woman for the calm face I went to find in the sick ward regarded me with a frightened and guilty stare. She was lying on her back, exchanging sips from her medicine bottle with another patient. At my approach, she put away the elixir and asked one of the strange white-garbed nurses with a veil trailing down her back to bring me a spot of tea. I remarked on how pale and exhausted she looked, stretched across three cots, and she went right to the point.

"Apollo," she said in a low voice. "I am pregnant."

"Do you know who is the father of your baby?" I asked, pretending innocence.

"Don't you?" she returned. I jumped and looked off out the window towards Edinburgh's spook castle to collect myself.

"I told you Martin is incapable," she added gently (almost protectively, I thought).

She looked right at me and I couldn't avoid her eyes. So I said nervously, "Maybe a ghost got you in the family way."

"A ghost?" she looked stupefied.

"You heard me. A ghost from one of those Scottish ruins you and the Captain like to rummage in."

Right away she began to weep. "You do not look like a ghost to me, Apollo."

I couldn't believe my ears. Oh lord, what if this Tasmanian sinner is the father of a freak?

"I knew what you did at Windsor," the giantess said, smiling wanly. "I only pretended to be asleep."

"You knew?" I asked in a weak voice.

227

The giantess nodded. "I wanted you to make love to me. I am unhappy with Martin."

She wept very hard. "And now I am in a fix. Oh Apollo, what am I going to do?"

Her face looked waxy with fatigue so I poured her some barley water I'd brought and told her I'd figure it out. Just lay low, I said, and don't tell the Captain. Well, she agreed and the next thing I knew she had fainted. A nurse whisked me out.

I met the Captain in the hall and shook his hand as if I hadn't a care in the world. He stormed in to see her—but he was turfed out too and we walked back to the hotel, chatting about the damp weather like old friends and all the time I was thinking, Lord God, what if the Captain knew!

I have a lovely head cold and I am having nightmares again; this time of a giant baby with a featureless head and the giantess trying to stick my face on it. I say to hell with that. I am going to keep the paths of H.P.I. open. If the baby is normal, Bates can say it's his. If Anna gives birth to a giant, I'll claim paternity. It would be an easy matter to prove Bates was impotent. Then the big woman would be free of him and we'd live off what I'd make exhibiting her and the kid.

CHAPTER TWENTY-NINE

Great with Child

(From the Diary of Anna Swan)

February 2, 1872

I have laid abed at Craven since our return to London two weeks ago, agonizing about what to do. I am in the family way due to a whim of mine to be a fly on the ceiling at Windsor Castle and observe the invasion of my body by a normal. (I have not had much satisfaction from the love-making of giants. Particularly, Martin who avoids discussion of a sexual nature and hasn't tried again to consummate our marriage because he doesn't want to risk failure.)

The love-making was not planned. I went to visit my agent to complain about my treatment at the hands of the Queen and the Prince of Wales. For a nation that would fit inside a Canadian lake, the Brits are an arrogant people. It was a relief to unburden my unhappy feelings to Apollo whose bedchamber was an attic room at the end of an interminable, icy, and creaking corridor. And no sooner had I sworn that I would never entertain in England again than I fell asleep.

Some moments later, I was re-awakened by a pleasureful sensation in my privates and I felt the start of the downward undertow that reduces all of me to a dwarfling tremor. I opened my eyes and there was Apollo bouncing against me as if I was a vast flesh trampoline. I suppressed a smile at his mischievous face, flushed a tea-rose pink under a flying mane of yellow hair, and closed my eyes again to feign sleep. It felt so nice I wished him to continue but I thought it best not to be overt. (Victorian men are a mysterious species: They expect women to be uninterested in the physical and are easily frightened if we express enthusiasm.) I opened my eyes once more and was astonished by the look of joy on Apollo's face as his shadow danced on the gas-lit walls of his tiny bedchamber. (To think I could give another being so much pleasure!) And when at last he wailed "Holy Mary, Mother of God," and his dandelion head roasted the skin of my breasts, I was moved by his gratitude. I hardly noticed that he had not satisfied me. Instead, I rejoiced that my big self made a fellow human so happy.

All too soon, he buttoned up his breeches with a distracted air and I glimpsed a massive instrument of the same beautiful rosy colour as Apollo's face. Then he kissed my forehead and tenderly tucked the shabby linen about my thighs.

Ahhh! I do not know why I have preferred men taller than myself. It is silly to seek symbols of superiority in males. I have been as guilty of sloppy thinking as the normals who think the male is strong in all areas because he has strong muscles. What nonsense! A hole is not less than a rod; it is merely different, and it is a grave mistake to mythologize biological facts to prove that one sex is better than the other.

In fact, there is much to be said for short men like Apollo who complements my size instead of doubling my impact. Martin does not put me in proportion: When the two of us enter a room, we look as if we are going to take it over.

I am digressing from my predicament which is a serious one. I have told Martin I am suffering from nervous exhaustion but I will not be able to conceal my condition from him much longer. Apollo has promised to come up with a plan and I have asked him to visit me tomorrow. I am certain he will have an answer I have not considered. Dear Apollo, he is more clever than he lets on.

February 3, 1872

Apollo came today after I sent Martin off to shop. The giant was glad for an excuse to go. I suspect my errands are a pretext for Martin to loaf in Trafalgar Square where he picks fights with other out-of-work actors. Martin is rambunctious these days, arguing his theories on whoever comes into his hearing, starting with me in the morning.

"Giants have always been the underdogs of history, my dear," he burbled this a.m. as he stood in our bedroom doorway, holding a breakfast tray while the light behind him winked off the edges of his burly frame.

I listened wearily and waited to hear the departing clunk of his boots on our tiled entranceway. There is a *je ne sais quoi* quality about Martin that does nothing to inspire me, despite my efforts to find the swashbuckling young cavalry officer I once saw in him.

To make certain he was truly leaving I peered from behind the front curtain and watched the giant set his jaw against the drizzle. He unfurled his umbrella and shot a missile of tobacco over the iron railing and into the bedraggled ivy in the box by our gate. Then he was off, marching past the awe-struck street performers who give Craven the atmosphere of a country fair, one of his giant arms holding his brolly, the other swinging free in case he had to manhandle a passer-by.

The rough-voiced men with baskets of daisy roots stopped yelling their wares and gazed in awe at Martin's back which is as wide as a keystone arch. The street acrobats, wearing spangled shorts, stopped somersaulting and tossing coloured balls; children stopped whacking badminton cocks; and the barrel organ of an old showman who plays beneath my window every morning was silent.

As soon as I saw Martin disappear up the hill near St.-Martin's-in-the-Fields, I stepped out onto the small, grilled balcony off our front parlour. The showman caught sight of me and bawled through his speaking trumpet:

"How are you today, luv? Here's a bit of 'Shoe the Donkey' to liven you up!"

He ground out his Irish jig; the pedlars cheered and the acrobats tumbled faster and faster until the children brought the show to an end by pelting the performers with badminton cocks.

On impulse, I threw my head back and began to sing that

231

dear old Brittish ditty "Take Me Back to the Land Where I First Saw the Light." The showman laughed and pumped his organ in accompaniment. I have not been on stage since we toured through the provinces and there is nothing like the approval of an audience to make me feel alive.

Apollo called out "Bravo!" from the street below. A feeling of relief overcame me at the sight of his square frame. I rushed to the door and scooped him up in my arms.

"You're smothering me, Anna," he said in an embarrassed tone.

Apologizing, I set him down and led him hurriedly up to the Turkish parlour. There I served tea and wept about the mess I was in while he hissed reassuringly, curling and uncurling his long fingers about a new pair of dice. He wore his plaid trousers and a new top hat which he lay on the floor alongside a hickory walking stick, according to the custom of gentlemen callers. I wore a *Godey's* gown for his benefit. It was in two shades of apple green, and a myriad of dark and light green bows marched down the front of my skirt whose hem was edged with ruched lace.

"So what you said in Edinburgh is true," Apollo remarked when I stopped crying.

"My condition has been diagnosed and I suffer the tell-tale symptoms—nausea, fainting...," I replied. "Of course, it was a task for the doctors to detect a fundamental change in a mass like mine. For all they knew, I could have been great with child since I was twelve."

"You sound bitter, Anna."

"I am frightened because of my circumstances. Yet I'm also pleased to discover that I can conceive like other women." Apollo stared in surprise.

"I assumed my freakishness meant I would be abnormal in the child-bearing parts," I continued. "This had been the opinion of most doctors."

"Of course, you are pleased," he said. He looked grave and I realized he'd adopted his "play the politician" manner, a style he normally used with theatre-owners.

232

"It is good you feel proud of yourself because there is no other recourse now."

He studied me solemnly and I realized he wasn't going to deliver me from my troubles. We had no relationship which could be the basis for raising a child. There was nothing for me to do but have the baby and say it was Martin's.

"I know there is no possibility for us to be together," I said (and wondered if I truly wanted that to be the case). "But don't you wish to have your rights as a father?"

"As long as I am your lover, I don't care who is the kid's dad," Apollo said.

"What shall I tell Martin?" I sighed. I knew the news would hurt the giant who tried to pretend he was not sexually inadequate.

"Anything you wish. It don't matter now."

Apollo rattled his dice thoughtfully. "It's up to the Captain to decide how he's going to handle being a cuckold."

At the word "cuckold" I began to weep again. Apollo patted my hand.

"It's going to turn out all right, Anna," he said. "After the kid's born, we'll make up for lost time."

"You don't want to be my lover now?" I asked.

"But you are pregnant." Apollo moved his hand away and stood up. His pale green eyes regarded me with alarm. "It wouldn't be right, Anna. A man don't touch a goddess who is bearing fruit."

I felt a stinging blow to my pride centre which on me is located at the nape of my neck, safely hidden by masses of my red curls. He does not want to be the lover of the BIGGEST MODERN WOMAN! He does not know how fortunate he is that I find him desirable? I rose and coldly looked down at this popinjay dressed in the garish trousers of a Bowery tough.

"I am weary of your chatter," I said sternly. "Go!"

An astonished Apollo grabbed his umbrella and fled down the stairs. As soon as I saw the small of his back, I changed my mind and hurried to the second-floor balcony.

"Apollo, come back!" I cried. It had started to drizzle.

Drops began to plaster my hair against my forehead. Below, umbrella-carriers scurried for shelter. I yelled again and this time Apollo turned round and his face convulsed as if he took me for a ghost. He stood frozen by our street sign which threatens to persecute "tippers of rubbish."

Alas, dear diary, I was like a mechanized figure in a cuckoo clock that forecasts the weather. Because no sooner did I call to Apollo, the sunshine man, than I saw Martin, the rainy-weather man, marching up the opposite side of the street, his massive head and shoulders looming above the umbrellas. The giant's face was shiny and wet from the misty drizzle and he chewed tobacco, swivelling his head from side to side to dispense the loathsome juice.

Martin tramped in a straight line up the hill to 45 and did not notice Apollo stumble away down Craven, one arm raised to cover his face as if my darling had received a blow to the head.

Martin spied my rain-soaked form. By now the dark green dye had seeped through and stained the underskirt of green plaid. Martin's jaw fell open. ·

"Anna! Get inside! You'll catch a chill!"

A crash below shook the eight-globed chandelier in our Turkish parlour (Martin does not know doors can be closed lightly) and in a moment the giant was on the balcony. I do not recall him putting me to bed, as he says he did, only a shameful feeling of helplessness as if I could be as weak and boneless as a pollywog. I awoke just an hour ago, troubled with uneasy dreams. The most vivid one I include here:

THE NIGHTMARE OF THE BIGGEST MODERN WOMAN

I was running from the Prince of Wales in the Great Hall at Windsor Castle when I heard the worried voice of Apollo. I turned to see his square torso cutting through the columns of moonlight that spilled on a vermilion rug almost as wide as New York's Broadway. His appearance in my moment of need made me feel strong again. Strong? Magically potent! The power of the little people was with me and the growing sap pounded in my veins, just as I'd felt it do when I was a child, singing to Poppa's vegetable garden.

"Touch me, Apollo. Do you understand?" I cried. "Touch me and your head will reach the clouds!"

Apollo grabbed the hem of my gown and instantly his hand grew larger than the Prince whom he picked up in his rapidly growing fingers and hurled against the wall. The Prince sailed through the state portrait of his mother, Queen Victoria, leaving behind a star-shaped hole. Then Apollo's block-like form shot up and exploded through the painted escutcheons on the palace ceiling.

I rushed out to Home Park and found Apollo, enormously swollen, standing in the rubble of Windsor Castle. One of his mile-long feet rose out of a battlement strewn like a column of toppled shillings across the Wedgwood green lawns of Home Park. His other foot stood arch deep in the dank Thames. His shoulders were as broad as the English Channel and his head blotted out the sun. Fronds of his golden hair waved in the breeze like hempen sailing ropes.

As he took out a comb of ancient oak trees to tidy his locks, he spied me, standing by his ankle.

"My dwarfling," he said. Immediately, a breeze, sweet with the odour of pumpkins, flattened me. But he snatched me up with his index finger and thumb and kissed my head with his long-as-sea-serpent lips. Then he placed me in the left-hand pocket of his colourful organ-grinder's shirt.

"My babykins," he boomed as I dove to the woollen depths of the pocket so I wouldn't be buffeted by winds from his mouth.

"My marvellous midge," he roared. "We will elope to Gretna Green because I am crazy about your crushable little arms and legs—ah, helplessly, hopelessly enslaved. I swear I will never let you go for fear harm might come to my fragile fairy girl."

Then off up the west coast strode Apollo, me no more than a flea on his chest. Just past Manchester, I grew out of his pocket so he placed me like a child on his shoulders. In the Lake District, his footsteps began to plod and I looked

down and saw my own legs dangling in the water. I slid off
his shoulder but by the time we reached Carlisle I was a head
bigger than he. In Dumfries, he came up to my belly button.
In Gretna Green, he was thigh high and the minister
wouldn't marry me to a man who was disappearing before
my eyes.

"Help!" Apollo said in a baby-boy voice, so soft I had to
crook my head to hear him.

"Here I am," I said, and he jumped into my arms in terror
at the roar of my voice. Then I rushed off to Edinburgh to
consult the best of Scotland's medical opinion. But the doctors in Auld Reekie said science would do nothing for my
incredible shrinking man. So I hid a baby-sized Apollo in the
prickly gorse on Arthur's Seat, but the hawks circling overhead and the dogs panting after the strollers on the sweetly
rounded volcanic mound drove him mad with terror.

He started to cry and, to amuse my thumb-sized sweetheart, I began to wrap shearings of sheep's wool around the
civic statues and monuments in Edinburgh's graveyards and
public squares. It made him giggle to see the stone figures
standing on the tops of columns smothered in fluff but he
was shrinking fast so I spiked Sir Walter Scott's monument
with a two-deck horse bus that had discharged passengers on
Princess Street and set a handful of smoking trains to chug
uselessly on Carlton Hill and balanced a royal yacht on the
top of Nelson's memorial tower. . . . I thought I saw a laugh
dimple in my love's cheek but he was shrivelling to the size
of a blossom among the gorse's yellow flowers. So I dammed
the Firth of Forth with my foot and my love smiled but his
voice was so feeble I had to blow away the screeching hawks
to hear it.

My breath knocked over the walkers who rolled down the
treacherous slopes of Arthur's Seat and snagged in the
heather but I didn't care. I had to amuse my fading lover so I
threw the bleak sandstone streets of Edinburgh's old town as
far as the Kingdom of Fife and then when Apollo made a sad
little face at my ferocity I rebuilt the Scottish capital, chim-

ney pot by gold-painted chimney pot. Then Apollo disappeared and I jumped on top of Arthur's Seat to find him but I couldn't distinguish him from the earth. My little man had gone—from a detail in the landscape—to seed.

No offence to my Druid foremothers, the *bean-grugaches*, but there must be more to being a giantess than pretty views. I could see as far south as the pollution-blackened factories of Leeds and as far north as the Rosencratztower in the Norwegian port of Bergen. Yet I had no playmate. I began to jump from Carlton Hill over to Ben Loman and back again to Arthur's Seat, stopping to carve a heart with "A.S. L. A.I." on every old historic hilltop I felt like. What else could I do to take my mind off my dreadful loneliness?

February 4, 1872

Martin has been told of my condition.

Yesterday he squired me to the London, a venerable fieldstone hospital in the east end of town. He was very nervous.

"Move your butts, you filthy loafers!" he bellowed at the porters standing about the stone porch of the hospital.

The porch was crowded with barking dogs and patients lying on stretchers waiting to be announced on the telephonic communicator at the door. Two men immediately rushed down the steps carrying a stretcher which is standard treatment for all cases coming in to the hospital.

"You idlers!" Martin roared. "My wife requires five men—not two!"

A moment later Dr. Buckland and his apothecary appeared on the porch.

"Hello Bucky!" Martin bellowed. "Mrs. Bates is under the weather!"

"Not to worry old chap," the doctor replied. "We'll fix up the little woman in a jiffy."

The porters tied together three stretchers and I was tilted on my back, my feet aimed at the sky like a swooning maharani. A procession of men, led by the doctor's apothecary, who carried the surgeon's box of instruments, transported me into the hospital.

At the door of the receiving room Martin paid the sweating hospital porters and the doctor sprang to my side like a polite dance partner. The little man escorted me to his chilly examination chamber, directing a stream of court gossip at me. His chat stopped once we were inside, where he led me in austere silence through a sequence of formal positions—our bodies intersecting at odd angles, his head on my chest, his fingers tapping messages on my spine and, at last, tickling the entrance to the wonder-world between my thighs.

When I rejoined Martin, I reeked of the doctor's shaving lotion. Martin nervously unrolled himself from a couch in the physician's office and waited for Buckland to speak.

"Captain, there are some things we don't know about the animal frame," Buckland said. His face looked purple from exertion. "But I have had no difficulty ascertaining the problem here."

Martin looked at me in alarm.

The doctor chuckled.

"Mrs. Bates is expecting a little one in June."

Martin sank back onto the couch, working his plug at a furious rate. I stared sadly at his shocked face. Dr. Buckland chuckled again and nodded to the apothecary, mistaking Martin's bewildered reaction for the surprise of an expectant father. The apothecary handed Buckland a bottle of French brandy.

"Captain," Dr. Buckland said, "let us drink to the great event, shall we?"

Nervously, I picked up a slender tube sitting on a cabinet top. It was a polished flute-like instrument, the size of a wooden vase. I blew into it without thinking and it made an odd squealing noise. The doctor poured Martin and me a glass and then smiled at me in condescension. "I see Mrs. Bates has found the foetal stethoscope. Would you like to listen to your offspring, Captain?"

238

The doctor took the stethoscope from my hand. He pressed it against my body, and demonstrated how to detect the infant's heartbeat. Martin offered his ear to the tube with a stupefied look. I had a strange impulse to smile, but levity was not *à propos* so I concentrated on the saddest thing I have experienced: Poppa's mutt, Bark, dying of pneumonia.

Martin put the instrument aside with a frown. "I can't hear a sound, Bucky."

Dr. Buckland made a fussing noise and put his ear to the stethoscope. "There it goes. Splendid. From the rat-a-tat-tat tempo, rather than a pitty-pat-pat—I'd say it was a boy."

"Will Anna be able to carry a child without a hitch?" Martin asked.

"Yes, Captain. Her organ of life is in a fine creative state."

Martin continued to look startled. "Creative?" he mumbled dully.

"Ahh—Captain," said the doctor, throwing me a sympathetic look as he nudged a brass spittoon in Martin's direction. "First, try to consider the uterus along the lines of its twin—the brain." Dr. Buckland made a helpful gesture, indicating a basket shape with two curved handles. "After all, it is triangular in shape and daringly complex."

Martin chewed and spat more slowly and suddenly dared to look directly at me. I avoided his eyes.

"Of course, it has not nearly the number of surface considerations as the organ of reason," Dr. Buckland continued, "and although capable of creating a human being, the uterus cannot legislate a government. Yet, Captain, the land of our birth lies within its pale walls. We must respect the terrain for what it is—down to the orifices of tubular follicles on its inner cloth, the *arbor vital uterina*, the tiny—oh, very minute—oblique columns like tree branches proceeding to the light at the end of the southwest passage."

"Captain and the Mrs!" Dr. Buckland concluded, draining his glass. "I pray for a *lusibus naturae*!"

We left Dr. Buckland's office and walked to a stone bench in the hospital garden to digest the news. Martin sat—elbow on knee, chin cupped in hand—staring at the withered chrysanthemums in a stone urn by his foot. It was wet with moisture stains. Finally, the giant spoke.

"Who is the father?"

"I cannot tell you," I said, "but the father wants nothing to do with the baby."

Martin grunted and continued to gaze sadly at the dead flowers. I covered his hand protectively with my long fingers.

"Martin, you are the legal father. Why do we not continue so?"

He looked at me in surprise. "You want me to be the pop?"

"You would make a good father," I said (not without certain qualms).

Martin bowed his head and began to sob. He did not try to cover his face and tears dripped off his huge nose and ran down his chin onto his polkadot cravat. I squeezed his hand and the giant groaned and put his head on my shoulder. For a long time he rested against me, weeping. I sat dumbly staring at the bleak little garden, watching tiny clouds of mist move off his convulsed face into the damp air.

To be candid, I am frightened to be a mother. But I am LARGE; I will handle it.

May 22, 1872

I, the BIGGEST MODERN WOMAN, gave birth to a record-breaker at 4:23 a.m., May 19. A female child who, at 18 pounds and 27 inches, is the largest female ever to be born. Hear ye! Hear ye British mothers, fathers! Announcing the arrival of the BIGGEST BABY GIRL IN THE WORLD! Call her the B.B.G.W. . . . I do not wish to go on with this bitter spieling. What point is there in producing a champion who does not live to see the record she has set?

Alas! My darling girl was stillborn. I have no memory of her face as the chloroform kept me senseless during her birth. The drug was recommended by Queen Victoria in a gloomy note:

240

Dear Anna:

My daughters speak of the pride of giving life to an immortal soul, but I think much more of our being like cows or dogs during childbirth; so imbibe the powder of forgetfulness and wipe your poor mind clean of such moments when our inferior nature becomes so very animal & unecstatic. Victoria, Queen of all the Britons, Defender of the Faith, Empress of India.

Labour began when Martin was out on an errand. The skies had cleared and all London walked the streets in celebration. The Brits are a nicer race when the sun shines, and even Martin looked amiable strolling out the door *sans parapluie*. Despite my bloated 550 pounds, I heaved myself out of my down bed and crept to the window to see the sunshine. I opened the pane and waved at the old showman. As the merry noise of his barrel organ floated up to me in the spring air, I heard an earsplitting ping in my lower depths. Suddenly, there was a rush of falling water. On the street below, unbrellas sprouted like mushroom caps. A few bystanders craned their necks to investigate the mystery of rain on a cloudless day, but most pedestrians acted as if they were experiencing a spring shower and hurried down Craven with their shoulders gloomily hunched. Only my Cockney serenader stood his ground and stared up at me in alarm, moisture dripping from his blotchy red face.

To my astonishment, I began to giggle flagrantly. My waters had broken! I wished to shout to the showman but laughter rendered me speechless. So I removed one of my drenched slippers and inserted the key to our lodgings in its toe. Still giggling, I leaned out over the railing and threw the flat, flimsy object in the wildest arc I could, hoping the showman would not think me mad. For a moment, the slipper hung over the showman's head—a dainty pink cloud—before my fellow artist reached out and grabbed it.

"Make way! Make way!" his speaking trumpet bawled. "A damsel in distress."

So it happened that the fierce-voiced showman and another bystander, a pedlar of daisy roots, were my escorts for my final call to the London. They conducted me, in a mule-driven dray, along the congested streets and then through the noisy confusion in the Hospital halls to an ominous private room.

I pen this now in the hospital garden, the same courtyard in which Martin wept a few months ago. Today the urns are filled with tulips; the balmy air roils with purple doves. I toy with the notion that I am holding my child against my swollen and leaking breasts. She is perfect in every respect—as large as a bulldog with pink, pouched cheeks, sweet hazel eyes, and a mop of glossy curls.

But I do not believe in Victorian sentimentality. My daughter is dead. Dr. Buckland, in a top hat and silk cravat (fresh from dining with the Prince at Marlborough House), delivered her.

"There will be no Derby bundle in your case," he said—he meant the clothes left for new babies by the hospital's charity dames, the Lady Almoners. He turned and went out.

Martin came in with a downcast mien. He said Dr. Buckland has asked him if we will give the dead child to the London Hospital to use in research on the causes of growth in giants. I said yes, and then wept as if I had swallowed a weeping pill.

There is talk among the hotel staff of "the Bates baby." Martin looks pleased to hear this term. "Not only was the loss of our baby a tragedy for the wife and I," I heard him say to a nurse today, "it is a grave setback for the development of our species." The nurse gaped at Martin and nodded as if she believed him. The giant has been kind, and far more loving than I have any right to expect, doing and saying all that he can to make me feel that I have not failed although that is exactly how I do feel: female and flawed. I could aid neither myself nor my child during her birth which marks the end of life for me here. I do not like the aristocratic style, and I have no further wish to be a European celebrity. I want now only to return to America with my husband.

CHAPTER THIRTY

Apollo Goes to Australia

(From the Route Book of H.P. Ingalls)

June 2, 1872

I went to visit Anna in the London today to talk her into exhibiting the giant baby but the floor matron advised me that the giantess was in chapel. I was disappointed but I know the big woman likes her prayers. It is better to let people put the pieces back on their own anyhow without friends and relations to worry them. Of course, I feel terrible for the giantess. I hate to think of her crying every time she sees a child which is what the Night tells me. It is too bad Anna is overgrown when she is so thin-skinned. A freak can't expect to have normal things happen to her.

Then the nurse told me the Bates had donated the baby to the hospital museum so medical students could study her. I didn't think Anna would allow something like that to happen without telling me. And I thought, Ingalls, you're going to kidnap that child and show it on your own without Anna or the Captain to bother you. So I rushed over to the museum. I had a job getting past the reception girl but finally I made my way down to a basement room in the old stone building and found Dr. Buckland taking notes in front of a cabinet lined with jars. The doctor tapped a large glass vessel (a sixteen-gallon kilderkin) and said *"Voilà le monstre Bates."*

What did I see but a big yellow baby girl curled up and floating in the jar. "Ingalls, that's your kid," I told myself, "dead and pickled." I began to tremble and couldn't hardly make sense of what the doctor was telling me about preserv-

243

ing fluids. I was shook up because it looked so pitiful. Plus, I haven't been a father before and I didn't know it would feel personal. The doctor thought I was interested in his talk because I was gaping like a fool so he went on explaining that *she* (your daughter, Ingalls) would turn bluish-black from a blood component called haematin and then turn grey like the things in the other jiggers. He said the meconium in the fluid had dyed her yellow at the moment.

While the doctor yapped on, Bates walked in. The giant looked like he had heard the speech before and when he saw me, his face creased with condescension.

"This is not for popular exhibit, Ingalls. Only the interests of science are appreciated here."

I left at once, my teeth clenched. I didn't like seeing Bates and the doctor meddling with my kid. Maybe it is a good thing the giantess has wasted an exhibit opportunity. I would feel funny having my flesh and blood gawked at by nasty-minded strangers. God damn. You are a bit of a softie after all, H.P. Ingalls.

August 23, 1872

Scarborough, pop. 24,259.

My troupe drew four thousand people to the matinée at the spa here, and the saloon in the Grand Hall was packed during the evening performance. For the sticks, that's unusual. Fras Goodricke, the spa manager, said touring companies from London just come up for a matinée as the audience here is small and if you do two shows you get the same number as if you had put on one. Our act proved the exception! Of course, it was part of a Grand Midsummer Gala event which featured English music-hall stunts like Professor Brownes's ride out to sea on a lighted bicycle as the sun vanished behind the red cliffs of the North Riding coast, and a firework display by a Mr. Brock.

The giantess seems to have recovered from the death of the baby. She looked handsome in a watered silk gown the colour of plums. Her sleeves were shaped like bells and she twirled a

244

plum parasol. She has asked me to lunch with her tomorrow. She says she has told Bates we have important business to discuss so we can be alone for once to talk over "recent happenings." All to the good, I say. I am lonely for the giantess.

August 25, 1872

Yesterday was the best day and the worst day in the life of H.P. Ingalls. It started when the giantess and I ate a lunch of cured pork at the beach. It was hot and we were eating under a candy-striped awning to get a sniff of breeze. All of Scarborough was on the shore with us. Pedlars offered children rides in wicker baskets that hung from the haunches of sand burros and bathers ran through the white puffs of foam. The giantess had on a straw bonnet and an enormous padded navy water costume with yachting hose in navy and white stripes. (Trust her to wear the latest!) My own costume was not so elegant—just wool trousers and a long-sleeved sweater that made me hot and itchy.

Well, I kicked off my bathing shoes under the table and buried my extremities in the sand. Mid-way through lunch, I spied under the table two mounds of sand where the striped stockings of the giantess ended. Then I saw a small circle of pink protruding out of the sand. Aha! Her big toe! I leaned over and touched it and the giantess said "Oh my!" in a pleased tone. Then I pointed to my feet and she looked down and saw my square toes wiggling in a friendly fashion at her hills of sand.

Well, she giggled and lifted her toes out of the sand and waved them back. Sand dribbles fell from her extremities and I saw her feet completely nude and they were just beautiful! Long and slender jobs, not like my blocks of wood! Anyway, I danced my feet close, and what do you know, Joe, I lifted them up and placed them on top of hers.

Just as we were getting on so well, there was a bellow behind us.

"All aboard, Anna!' And Bates emerged from a haze of

bleached ocean colours, leading a horse-driven bathing chariot. Heads under tented canopies turned in his direction. He
was carrying the knobbed cane he flourishes during his
promenades.

"Time to take the waters!" he roared. The giantess put on
her navy bathing coat and rose and I leapt to my feet and
inserted myself between the big woman and the wooden
contraption. The driver was an old woman in a knitted shawl
and cap who stared at Anna.

"You can't let her go, Captain. Anna can't swim," I said.

"Judge, quit your yapping." The Captain pushed past me
and helped the giantess up beside the driver. "A dipping is
doctor's orders."

I began to yell. "Anna! I beg you don't go! Do you want to
drown?"

"Apollo!" she said in surprise. "Are you worried about
me?"

She climbed into the wagon; the team lurched about and
sprinted towards the sea. The giantess' bonnet fell off. She
turned and called to me for help so I started running across
the tide flats. Bates came lumbering after, bellowing and
waving his cane. At the water's edge, I caught up and snatched
the bridle of the leading horse. The old woman began to
scream at me and I was too busy screaming back to see Bates
approach. The shock of his cane coming down on my back
knocked the wind out of me.

"You no-good meddler!" Bates barked. I turned and there
was his ugly mug two feet above me. He shot his foot at my
head. I ducked. He kicked again, but this time I grabbed his
boot and held it to my shoulder so the big oaf danced like a
heron on the crowded seashore.

Bathers started to laugh, and the bathing chariot took off
again, crashing through the waves on the sand bar with my
giantess.

I sicked the town constable on Bates and went back to the
beach to wait for Anna. Beyond the breakers, I saw her driver
extract a gaffing pole out of the back of her wagon and
indicate to the giantess that she should descend. Well, Anna

246

staggered to her feet and climbed down the ladder into the sea. I could not believe my eyes when I saw the waters close over *her* head. She must have stepped into a tide hole. At last I saw Anna's head bob up and the lunatic driver helped the big woman back into her wagon.

The old woman stuck her gaffing pole into the spot where Anna went down and I realized she was doing some kind of measuring of the giantess. My poor big girl. Everybody wants to use her. The next thing I knew, the bathing chariot was racing towards me in the surf and I was able to lead the team in.

"You'll be fined for this!" I yelled at the old woman but she just drove off the moment Anna got out, waving her gaffing pole at me.

"Anna, I thought I'd seen the last of you," I said.

She began to cry and said I was very kind to worry about her. We both felt happy to be together and I bought her some water ice and the two of us took off towards a remote section of the cliffs. We didn't say it out loud but I knew we were going to be romantical. Soon the red roofs and domed pavilion of the spa disappeared and she and I were watching our shadows walk ahead of us in a hot, bright world. Behind a jut of rock, I fell to my knees and began to stroke her toes. I tugged each piggy, and brushed off the grains of sand.

"What tiny darlings," I whispered to them. "What eentsy-weentsy babies. So neglected! So overlooked!"

I peeled back the striped hose on her leg and stared at her ankle bone. It was the size of an ostrich egg. I bestowed an ice-cream kiss on its protuberant shape. Then I peeled the hose back and kissed my way up her extremity. Soon my arms were around her knees.

"Pity me, Anna," I said, and the big woman sighed and stripped off her enormous wet suit and lay down on the sand. We're all the same height lying down, aren't we? That's what I said to myself as I stood and surveyed the immense female bulk stretched before me. I gaped and felt the most awesome responsibility at approaching something so trusting as a naked woman. Ingalls, get a grip on yourself, I said. She expects you

247

to know what's what. So I shucked my duds and, without thinking, buried my head in her privates. Holy Mary Mother of God, I kissed her there until rivers of sweat ran down my brow and the sun burned a hole in my back.

Just as my energy ran out, she arched off the sand and her whole body quaked in a mountainous seizure, like she had taken a painful blow to the belly, only it wasn't pain. It made me feel happy to see her smiling face above me so I continued to kiss her like that and she shook and quaked about thirty times I'd say and I was amazed to think she would respect me enough to do me the honour of letting me make her feel nice and, when I entered her, her thighs were wet with my tears. Lord Jesus, forgive me!

Afterwards, Anna asked me if I found her normal and I said in every respect and also I told her I was accustomed to her height and it was only when we were with others that I noticed she was a fair-sized woman. Then she wept quite a bit and said she had always fancied herself the pleasure-giver but she saw now that she had been wrong and if she liked to please me it would follow that I would like to please her. (And I thought, it was goddamn lucky, Ingalls, you took the dive, and then I thought, no, not lucky, smart. I'm not such a bad fellow after all.) Anyhow, I was feeling very good when all of a sudden she looked startled and asked, "Apollo, where's Martin?"

I buried my face in her breast, which is at least five handfuls big, and said, "The local constable put him away for disturbing the peace."

Right away, she lifted me off her stomach and stood up and began to dress.

"Apollo," she said, "I must deliver Martin from jail."

I got mad at how worried she sounded and jumped up, drawing myself to my full height in front of her. She stared down in surprise and moved around me. I planted myself again in her path. I did this a few times until she sighed and snatched me up and placed me on a high ledge of rock and plodded along the sand towards the pavilion.

A few seagulls dove and soared around her head and I

hollered and hollered but she kept going so I scrambled down the ledge, doing up my fly buttons, and ran after her. I caught up with her at a vendor's booth and tried to block her path again.

"Do you have to take such big steps?" I asked in a furious tone. She looked down and her face was very sad and then she said, "Don't be jealous, Apollo. It's you I love."

I stared up, my mouth open. I couldn't believe my good fortune. She loves you, H.P. Ingalls: she is telling you that herself. You! A nothing, who stands no higher than her waist. Well, I reached up and kissed her long fingers.

"My darling girl," I said, very choked up. "I never thought a decent woman would care for the likes of me."

"You are a fine person, Apollo," she smiled. Then she picked me up and puckered her lips and we smooched. Next thing I knew, she'd put me back down on the sand.

"I am bound by law and duty to somebody else and must honour my obligations," she told me. "So far, I have not tried very hard."

I snorted. "For God's sakes, Anna. You take duty so seriously."

Then she said, "I can't help it, Apollo. That is the way I am."

She wouldn't listen to any more of my complaining and walked off to help Bates while I stood, watching her go and feeling very bad. An hour later, I saw her in the tearoom at the spa. She didn't know I was spying on her and she was listening with a kind look as Bates ordered a sassafras blend.

"The tonic will purify your blood, my dear," the grinning oaf said.

I wanted to barge in and tell Bates that I cared about the giantess, but the pair of them looked so suited to one another, sitting there as man and wife, that I knew Hiriam Percival Ingalls hadn't a hope in hell. This evening, the big woman sent a note up to my room, confirming my worst fears.

Darling Apollo [She always calls me by my old museum nick-name which nobody uses any more]:

I am writing to tell you that I think it would be easier for all of us if I dismissed you as my agent. I intend to retire in any case. I am twenty-seven, wealthy, and bored with show business—the faking up from a valise, the camaraderie before the slump on second night, and the obligation I feel to make each show live in the memories of staring normals. (Behind its romantic nonsense, what is the theatre except a business?) I am also ashamed that I have been unfaithful to Martin and I wish to make it up to him by attempting to live a normal married life. Perhaps I am doing my duty out of guilt and will regret my decision. I cannot say. I should have told you this during our marvellous afternoon together but I could not bring myself to mar our time alone. Only you know all you have been and are to me. THE LONELIEST GIANTESS IN THE WORLD.

So it's off to Australia for H.P. without so much as a goodbye.

A TESTIMONIAL BY CHARLES DICKENS
ABOUT THE PROFESSIONAL GIANTESS

I first saw the Canadian giantess at the American Museum during my tour of the United States in 1867. She performed in the amphitheatre with another colonial, a black gentleman named Goshen. The giantess was uninspiring; neither she nor Goshen possessed the training required by British theatre. When we met backstage, she expressed a desire to do Shakespeare and said she was hoping to play Lady Macbeth in a Brooklyn theatre.

I excused myself and withdrew. (Why does every inept foreign actor feel compelled to do our great author?) Goshen's main talent was the length of his arm muscle. Therein lay his popularity since North Americans worship a cult of size. Seeing that they have little else to admire, I suppose they have a right to make the most of nice-tempered apes.

A giantess like Miss Swan is likely a short-lived aberration.

In 1868 or thereabouts I saw her singing with a British midget in Vauxhall Gardens. She wore a lavish blue bonnet and cape. Exposure to the British Music Hall seemed to have improved her timing. Inadequate training may have been the reason her employer, Mr. Barnum, had her tour the British Kingdom.

She can thank me for making her immortal as "the particularly tall lady" singing at the gardens in my *Sketches by Boz*.

TESTIMONIAL BY CHRISSIE AND MILLIE SMITH
(THE TWO-HEADED NIGHTINGALE)

We were on the road with Annie Swan when she got engaged to the giant Bates. Annie was twenty-five years old and had no husband. So Millie and I could see it coming. He was a mean customer. On our cruise aboard the *City of Brussels*, he talked Millie into swallowing a tobacco plug for a lark and both of us sat in the privy all day as a result. And us in steerage where there were only two toilets for one hundred passengers! It made us vomit (both heads at once) and the steward didn't know we were show-biz personalities and told us to clean it up. It was terrible enough down there, sleeping in old wooden stalls with immigrants who were going home to Europe because their dreams of a new life in America were kaput. We got meat at night and pudding on Sundays but what good is food when you can't eat on account of the smells from the dirty linen and the boat rocking.

Annie was a kind lady. She had the captain move us to her stateroom. It had oilcloth on the tables and Turkey rugs on the floor. Our manager, Judge Ingalls, didn't lift a finger until she intervened, and then told everybody we were poor travellers who treated him like Apollo-Fetch-It.

Of course, we were at Annie's wedding, a high-society affair in a great church, and we visited the giantess in the hospital when she lost her child. I'll never forget her in the hospital garden, crying to break your heart, and feeding love-birds with bread she took out of those big puffed

251

sleeves of hers. Then she got dropsy of the chamber pot, a
diabetic complaint. It was diagnosed while we were in Ger-
many entertaining relatives of the Kaiser. That got Bates on a
diet kick. One week he had Annie eat nothing but grapes,
and the week after that nothing but bananas. He turned the
routine of the château upside down with his orders. No
French sauces! No pigeons under glass! No ornamental
dishes! The chefs were scared to death. Bates invited the
household to watch Annie "feed" (his word), and everybody
would rush into the chamber where Annie lay under a down
comforter on one of the fancy canopied beds and goggle at
her while she spooned down raw liver, or whatever Bates
decided would cure the dropsy. She was too tired to speak
and only nodded at the German folk whose triple chins
shivered when they talked their funny language. Bates used
to shout out a daily bulletin on Annie's health:

"The giantess winked at me over her chop! The direction
is up!"

Our hosts would make happy sounds and applaud. They
were good folk and eager to please us. One time they took
us on a goat hunt in the Alps. And Bates ate the picnic food
while they were off firing musksts at leaping mountain
creatures.

The giantess stayed at home and didn't perform. In the
evenings, Bates lectured and Millie and I submitted to a little
experimenting by a committee. This was an exercise to demonstrate where it is that Millie and I share nerves and plumb-
ing. Bates or some German prince would shake Millie's hand
real hard and I would register no reaction. Then the experi-
menter would step on Millie's toe and I would say "Ouch!"
because I feel everything that happens to her below the
waist. Then we were escorted to a watercloset rigged up in
the middle of the room—a box seat decorated with dolphins
and mermaids—where we would pass urine from the same
hole.

Crowned heads always paid extra for our committee demonstration. I never told the giantess about it. She was too
much the lady. Old troupers like Millie and me—we don't

252

give a darn. Of course, the Judge had gone to Australia by then and we had no manager to pay so it was all the more for us.

In May 1873, Annie and Bates and us sailed back to America. We were glad to get back to this side of the Atlantic. Millie and I sang "Rock My Soul in the Bosom of Abraham" as our steamship sailed past Fire Island into New York City bay, bringing God's children home to the land of the free.

Everything Christina says is the almighty truth—M.

PART FOUR

The Giants of Seville

CHAPTER THIRTY-ONE

Buck-eye by Adoption

January 3, 1872

A letter to my daughter, the BIGGEST MODERN WOMAN OF THE WORLD (to be opened on the event of her first child):

During your birth, I thought I was dying and although I knew the Saviour was waiting for me, I cursed Him for delivering a girl monster into our hands. Bitter thoughts kept me from speaking; I would not look at your father, obliged to fetch the midwife in the blistering August heat. She came too late with boxes of baby clothes from the rector's daughter. Of course, her "half-a-dozen-of-everything" was too small for you. What good were tiny shirts and nighties on a babe I could hardly hoist over my shoulder? So she set you, naked, except for a nappie made from your father's shirttail, in my arms and said how sweet your face was.

I had no milk and she said I must in order to feed a baby the size of a six-monther and your father told her to hush up—oh, those sharp raps of his with the back of his hand—and asked me "Is this my daughter, then?" I lay stony-faced and he kept repeating his question, and when he saw I was still in my "trance," he addressed the words to you, more as a statement.

I know you will not hold my behaviour against me, Annie, as life is about to offer you the LARGEST HAPPINESS there is. (Lofty words, but so true.) I did want you, just as you and Martin are looking forward to your LITTLE ONE. I talked turkey to myself when Alex went out; we Grahams have common sense, you can say that for us, and Alex didn't mention my selfishness once he saw I'd come round. I used to wish before David, my last and twelfth child, that children came out of our armpits, or some more suitable part than that other place, but enough said.

I should tell you Uncle Geordie told me *before your birth* the little people were bringing me a *bean-grugach* they'd found in a pine grove. In the old country, *bean-grugaches* are women of large size and intelligence (like you, dear) who are looked upon with respect. I know young people don't believe in the *sithichean*; you like to feel the clink in your purse. But Uncle Geordie had the *an da shealladh* and he wasn't wrong about you or the train he saw crashing through the forest, with its headlights burning up the darkness, before no train tracks were there, or invented.

Some days I think I have not been a good mother and I worry my habits have pained you: I see the bad in things first, which is my disposition (and not yours), but I cannot help it if I like to find the flaw in a piece of goods before I buy. You Annie, you give people, first of all, your passion which seems a backwards way of doing things.

It is not the *safest* way, nor one which is always kind to you, so watch you do not let the weak take advantage of your sweet self. (You are not as strong as you appear, Annie.) I trust Martin appreciates you and is proving a charitable help-mate on the threshold of your new course together. (Judge Ingalls hinted at something about a peace bond put on Martin. Pls. explain in your next letter.) How I wish I could take your future sufferings and pains on my shoulder, but your father says I brood on morbid things when I should be resigned to His will. So let me stop here and remember I am standing strong and protective behind you, affectionately the MOTHER OF THE ONLY GIANTESS IN THE WORLD. P.S. Hubert Belcourt was kind enough to write this down for me as you know I did not learn the art of penmanship. He is a nice midget, always eager to hear of your doings.

October 24, 1873

Dear Momma:

Your letter, with the news of my new brother, David, moved me very much. I received it in New York this May after our Atlantic crossing aboard *The City of Antwerp* and have carried it with me ever since. I had special need of it during our homecoming tour which has proved unsuccessful. Modern audiences expect curiosities like us to sing and dance as well as actors in the professional theatre companies which have grown up in the East during our absence.

All of which brings me to my news about Seville. By now, I expect you have received my letter about the baby, but do not know anything about our decision to build a giant house in the Ohio hamlet of 900 souls which I have been living in since late August.

Momma, it is a very unlikely place for somebody like myself to choose as a home. It may be the most typical little town in the world so it can lay claim to some kind of superlative. Barnum would find a way of making its ordinariness sound exotic, but I have no interest in doing that. I am eager to experience everyday reality. After my years on the road, the normalcy of a place like Seville appeals to me. What better antidote to show business could there be than a farm in Ohio—the strong, the steady, well-balanced heart of America? My old tutor, Miss Beasely, once told me that Ohio is the most average state in the Union because its prosperous blend of agriculture and industry encourages a moderate strain in its people.

So you see I am ideally situated although, knowing you, you probably wonder why I didn't come home to New Annan. To answer that, I need to tell you how we came here. It was only twelve weeks ago that Martin and I were travelling through the Midwest doing barn shows with Dad Bideman, a barker whom Martin knew from his old days with the Cincinnati circus. A barn show is a step down from the type of exhibits we worked in before but entertainers can't be fussy if they are not in demand. Certainly, Martin and I would like better work. Needless to say, we were in low spirits and beginning to expect failure wherever we went when we signed up with Bideman—a sure omen with an actor that the time has come for a retreat from public life.

That was our state of mind the day we were travelling south down the "pike" which is the name for the old stagecoach route running from Cleveland through the central part of Ohio. We were part of an entourage that included the CANADIAN HERCULES, Louis Cyr, and his mother, a six-foot-two Québécoise who carries twin bags of oats on her shoulders for reasons I will explain shortly. Louis is described in his handbills as a QUEBEC SAMPSON who could have routed the British on the Plains of Abraham. In person, he is shy and eager to oblige and very much under the thumb of his English-hating mother.

That day I sat on the floor of Bideman's spring wagon, my legs stretched out in front of me, my back against a steamer trunk. Feathers, Bideman's boa constrictor, lay curled in a bulging heap beside me, half-entwined around one of Martin's cavalry boots because the snake had taken a liking to him. Martin, meanwhile, sat above me on the trunk, holding my English parasol over my head in order to fend off the fierce Ohio sun. The farmland was sweltering despite the lush green of the tobacco fields and wooded hills which are as bumpy as the teeth on a dragon's back. Both of us were perspiring heavily as giants are inclined to do. We had dressed warmly that morning in Cleveland, fooled by the breeze from Lake Erie into thinking a cool day lay ahead.

Martin was miserable in the habitual costume of the well-travelled gentleman—black suit, black felt hat, and long frock coat. And I was suffocating in a lemon-yellow walking dress whose sculpted side panels resembled the wings of an insect. Louis' music was a further annoyance. The young strongman lay beside me on the floor of the wagon in a skin-tight black tunic, his eyes popping with exertion as he sang an anti-English song. Louis' mother had placed her sacks of oats on his chest to increase the power of his lungs and chest muscles. She'd made him sing in that position five times since we'd started out and Louis' patois was beginning to grate heavily on my nerves. The song is a parody of the English anthem (which I include here in English for you):

> English plum pudding
> is a delicious dish.
> Somewhat thick.
> Plum, plum, plum, plum.
> One prepares it with
> a pound of dry raisins
> and the fat of beef kidneys
> and then an egg!

As you can see, there is nothing offensive in those childish verses. I was insulted by Louis' assumption that I was under the influence of British royalty and would be annoyed. But he seemed to think he was performing a daring act, and his mother's smug looks at me as she clapped and beat time from her seat on the

260

cage of Bideman's pigeons indicated she thought it was a bold thing for Louis to do.

Suddenly, Bideman whirled around and glared down at Louis.

"Shut up your caterwauling, Frenchie. We're in America now and nobody speaks that lingo here."

Then he turned off the hot and dusty road and drove down a shady street that reminded me of the roads in New Annan. The air under the arching stand of elms and maples was cool and spicy with the country odours which in Ohio are a mingling of manure and lye soap. Louis stopped his singing and his mother rolled away the sacks from his chest so he could sit up and see where we were. I slowly unfolded myself and climbed up on the steamer trunk beside Martin who was putting down my sunshade.

We passed a long string of clapboard houses with the front porches and eye-like bay windows you see in most towns in Eastern America and then the wagon rolled over a suspension bridge strung across a stream-fed ravine and we found ourselves in the centre of a rural hamlet in which any stranger is easily visible.

"Welcome to Seville—my hometown," Bideman cried. "Where everybody can truthfully say he has a competence and something to bestow."

Martin and I exchanged an amused glance at Bideman's turn of phrase.

"You're a native of these parts, Mr. Bideman?" I asked.

"My folks are pure Buck-eye. They descended from the Pennsylvania Dutch who settled Medina County with the Connecticut Yankees."

"You mean your people come from the land of the tulips?" Martin asked.

"Nope. Dutch comes from Deutsch. See Cap? I'm German."

"Well, I'll be," Martin grunted. "What's 'Buck-eye' mean?"

"The settlers of Ohio were called Buck-eyes after the buck-eye tree," I said. "Its soft wood is ideal for putting up log cabins in a hurry."

"My dear, why must you prove you know more about my country than I do?"

"You should be flattered. I'd be over-joyed if you knew anything about mine."

"Hush, my big beauties," Bideman chuckled. "You don't want to make a bad impression on the Seville people. See?"

Meanwhile, old men yelled at us from benches in a small park and pedestrians before a respectable selection of small shops and offices turned to stare. Louis stood up behind Bideman, waving and blowing kisses at the townspeople. Chuckling, Bideman pulled up in front of a brick inn overrun with ivy and he and Louis distributed handbills to a pack of children waiting on the mud street for something to do.

Then the pair tacked up a banner to the hotel pillars which read: SEE THE WORLD'S TALLEST COUPLE AND THE CANADIAN HERCULES AT BIDEMAN'S BARNSHOW, AUGUST 20, 1873.

A few minutes later we turned down another street lined with the same arching maples and drove up to a large, two-storey clapboard home with the same eye-like bay window and front porch. The home stood on the edge of town, beside a graveyard, and looked badly kept compared to the other homes in town. A few straggling four o'clocks grew in the muddy lot which was surrounded by a half-built clapboard fence. In front of the house stood a line of dead saplings that must have been planted there to become part of the natural arbor we had just driven through.

Our barker leapt down and led the wagon along a footpath to the back of his house and I was surprised to see a crowd already waiting for us. They swarmed across the back lawn and onto the tobacco field which stretched in waves of green behind the house down to a creek shaded by primordial maples. Young people sat on the roof of Bideman's rust-coloured barn and in the branches of a crab-apple tree near his back stoop.

A group of men in straw hats like Bideman's and long overalls were seated on a tobacco wagon, drinking from tubes attached to strange glass beakers which they held in their hands.

"Dad, the air here smells like wine," Martin boomed as we lumbered down from the wagon.

"It's the breeze from Lake Erie," Bideman replied. "Dry, loamy soil in these parts too. Good for tobacco growing."

"Hell, who wants to grow that old weed? I'd have Durham cattle—the finest herd in the county if I lived here. Plus draught horses of the Norman breed."

"And a dream home built to our proportions. With a giant piano so I can entertain our neighbours," I said.

Bideman waved at a farmer on the tobacco wagon. The farmer was a fox-faced man with a full beard of orange and red and wore a suit of long underwear without trousers or shirt.

"Virgil Shook—you scoundrel! Is that 'baccer you're smoking?" Bideman yelled.

The farmer grinned and hoisted aloft his primitive hookah. "None other, you old booze hound," he called back. The man pointed to two women sitting on the stoop of the house next door.

"Why don't you go and kiss your woman who's been waiting with Cora for you to come back."

The woman, whom I took to be Bideman's wife, looked about 55 years of age. She had a kind, owl-like face and had her arm around a girl who was suckling a baby at each breast. The girl was beautiful in the style of a *Godey's* fashionplate: dark, curly hair, small, straight nose, and rosebud mouth. I gaped at her as if she was a member of an exotic species. She blushed and ducked her head behind the other woman's shoulder.

"Don't hang back, Frannie," the owl-like woman chuckled. "Dad's home to claim you after all and you thought he'd cleared out for good. Didn't Virgil and I tell you he'd turn up like a bad penny?"

She plucked the babies out of the young mother's arms and pushed the squealing girl in our direction. Grinning, Bideman strutted over to his child-bride (who stood no higher than his armpit) and scooped her up against his protruding abdomen. I watched intently. Ah. So that was how it was done. Effortlessly. As if the female was no heavier than a child.

The girl laughed and kicked in Bideman's arms and I peered at her fluttering feet which must have been eight sizes smaller than my own. Mrs. Bideman ceased kicking and gaped back, astounded by my freak size as I was by the enigma of her normalcy. Now, Anna, I told myself, she is another human being like you. Be careful you do not treat her like a symbol as the world often treats you.

263

"Who are the foreigners, Dad?" she asked, and I was startled to realize she meant us.

"The Captain and his lady, Frannie," Bideman replied. "They were married with the blessing of Queen Victoria. See? The British monarch gave them two fine watches as wedding presents. There's the Cap's watch hanging off his belly. Mrs. Bates has hers tucked inside her jacket pocket."

Martin and I obediently pulled out our gold watches which we wore on long pearl chains and dangled them above the head of Frannie Bideman.

"Ooooh! They're as big as saucers," she said, reaching up a tiny hand towards mine. I moved closer so she could touch my watch and she shrank nervously into her husband's chest.

"Anna's nobody to be scared of, Frannie," Bideman laughed. He took my watch and gave it to her and she turned it over in her tiny hands as inquisitively as a child.

Bideman set her down and asked the other woman, Cora Shook, to show me the privy behind his tobacco barn. When I reappeared, I found Martin chatting to a bespectacled photographer who was setting up his stand. Louis posed in front of the camera in his black tunic, flexing shyly as a dapper man wearing a long cape called out the circumference of Louis' chest and biceps. A group of farmers listened, some smoking water pipes while others hawked tobacco at Bideman's yellow pigeons pecking in the gravel.

The birds flew in the air as I drew close and the men's heads turned towards me. Their sunburnt faces showed no embarrassment as they boldly looked me up and down. I smiled at them like an adventurer trying to befriend the natives through a momentous effort of good will. The man in the cape hastily extended a hand.

"Who else can it be but the lady giant?" he chuckled. "I'm Dr. Beach and your husband has just been telling us all about you. To the best of my medical knowledge, giants have never given birth to giants before."

He paused and inhaled a pinch of snuff from a box in his vest pocket and I felt myself in the presence of a local eccentric with a flair for theatrics resembling my own.

"I would very much like to make medical history again," I said, avoiding Martin's eyes.

"I hope you will, tall lady," Dr. Beach replied gravely. "You come from the North, don't you, like Mr. Cyr? Do you speak French too?"

I laughed. "I am a Blue-nose from Nova Scotia and I do not speak French like Louis who comes from Quebec."

"Is it Nova Scotia or Quebec which is a state in our great land?" Dr. Beach asked.

"Both," snickered one of the men beside the little doctor. Louis' bullish face reddened. He spoke rapidly in his home-made French which was as incomprehensible to me as Chippewa but I nodded my head to indicate I was on his side.

"We are a country of two nations," I said. "And we are not part of the American empire."

The ability to function without a national consensus in the Canadas is a mystery to the Yankees who cannot fathom a system that isn't modelled on theirs. The Buck-eyes stared in puzzlement. Suddenly, Louis flung up his arms in a dramatic gesture of exasperation. He took my hand and tucked it under his arm and I felt for the first time the fabulous muscled breast which had grown strong under his mother's bags of oats. Louis smiled. "The Americans, Annie. They'll never understand."

At that moment, Bideman lifted the bull-horn from his neck and addressed the milling crowd.

"If I can have your attention, friends, the giants will show you how they can shuffle those great legs of theirs."

He nodded at us and we executed a few clumsy steps of the schottische in Bideman's backyard. Then we paused and I leaned against Martin to catch my breath and the farmers cheered, thinking we were done.

"It doesn't take much to please these s.o.b.'s," Martin hissed in my ear.

Bideman held his calloused hands above his head to stop the cheers.

"That's the dance show for today, folks. The giants need a rest. But because you've been nice to 'em, they're going to answer a few questions."

Bideman hitched up his trousers and walked over to where Martin and I stood panting under a large buck-eye tree. He threw his arms around the giant's waist in a mock-hug and craned his neck skyward to bellow on his bull-horn:

"Have you big lugs any objections to giving me some statistical dimensions?"

"We are both 7′ 11½″," Martin grinned. "I measure 62 inches around the chest, wear a No. 26 collar and a No. 9 hat. Mrs. Bates' longest finger measures 5 ¾ inches; her wrist is 9 inches around; and from her wrist to her shoulder she is 44 inches."

"How long is she around the waist?"

Martin laughed and stretched his arms up to the boundless Ohio sky. "From the way I measure it, I can't exactly say but I should judge about so far."

The crowd chuckled and pressed close until we were waist-deep in friendly Sevillites. Their open manner is refreshing after the self-conscious air of us backwoods Blue-noses. They are farmers who belong to a nation that has known few defeats and we come from a land which prides itself on surviving.

I patted Martin's ample stomach. "A good thing we don't have to measure this, my dear."

The country folk roared with laughter. Personal remarks at Martin's expense are always a crowd pleaser because the remarks relieve the fear people feel when they gape at a giant man.

"Where are you two from?" somebody called.

"Mrs. Bates is from Nova Scotia and I hail from Whitesburg, Kentucky," Martin replied.

"We don't like southerners in our neck of the woods," another farmer cried.

The mood of the crowd changed and Bideman planted himself in the middle of the muttering farmers.

'By Jesus, I know we sent 113 soldiers and one nurse to the front, but the war that turned brother against brother was over ten years ago. See?

"And if a Union man like me—who as you all know did his time in Libby Prison—if a vet like me can say it's time to bury the hatchet—well, it's time to bury the hatchet."

He rubbed his sweating forehead and glared at the crowd.

"Anybody here going to say different?"

The crowd was silent and Bideman grinned. "Good. Now we

can get on with the event you came to watch: The Canadian Strongman holding Shook's draft horses to a standstill.''

Bideman put his megaphone to his lips: "Ladies and gents of Ohio, you see before you in the flesh the CANADIAN HERCULES who stands 5′ 10 ½″ and weighs 315 pounds and has a chest circumference close to 60 inches. . . .''

The Seville audience gasped and Louis snatched the megaphone out of Bideman's hand, and with a look of inordinate pride, finished the roll call of measurements:"*Jambes*—33 inches, *faons*—28, *biceps*—24, *avant-bras*—19, *taille*—45, and *cou*—22.''

His delight in his size was so disarming that the crowd laughed and cheered the burly youth, before he was done.

Louis lowered his bulky head and motioned for silence. "*Mes amis,*" he said in a soulful voice. "*La force—c'est un cadeau de Dieu.*"

He smiled at his mother who stood by the cattle yard where Dad had Feathers on display for 5¢. "*Ça n'est pas la force pour la force—mais pour la félicité de tout le monde.*"

Louis began his curious and touching warm-up exercises. First he carried five fence rails from one side of Bideman's yard to the other. Then he performed two hundred deep knee bends with a sheep on his back, murmuring encouragement to the animal who baaed each time the strongman bent his swollen legs. Finally, he fell fifty times on his stomach without using his hands. Then he walked smiling over to the pair of percherons which Virgil Shook had led out into the yard and stroked their noses. Solemnly, he assumed his strongman stance—each beefy arm bent in a V-shape around the harness straps of the giant horses which stood eighteen hands high, his beefy fists clasping the reins. The crowd cheered and excitement mounted. Next to me, Martin chewed hoggishly— spewing juice out of first one corner of his mouth, then the other. Bideman rang a firebell.

The percherons refused to move.

Bideman consulted with Martin while the audience milled uneasily about on the lawn. Martin walked off and re-appeared carrying a midget named Tim Delaney on his back. Martin and Delaney waved at the crowd, and people smiled and waved back.

Once more Bideman rang his firebell. Once more the horses didn't move.

This time Bideman walked out with Feathers wrapped about his shoulders and arms.

"We paid to see the snake. Where's the show?" a Sevillite demanded.

Martin grabbed the firebell. He walked up to the percherons whose ears flattened at his approach. The giant glared at the beasts and rang the firebell under their noses. Again, nothing happened. Martin shouted at them, "Goddamn glue pots." The giant took aim and kicked the nearest horse on its hind end.

Louis dropped the reins and seized Martin by his collar. "*Maudit anglais*! You do not harm dumb animals!" He picked Martin up and whirled the terrified giant about his head like one of his mother's sacks of grain. Martin bellowed in alarm and Bideman called to me anxiously as I stood with Louis' mother in the shade of a maple tree: "For God's sakes! Do something Anna!" I nodded and took the megaphone from Bideman. My lecture voice rang out:

Dear Friends, Family and Children of Ohio: I, the BIGGEST MODERN WOMAN OF THE WORLD, will sing a tune in honour of Louis Cyr, the QUEBEC SAMPSON, who does not want unwilling horses to disappoint you and who has consented to perform this astounding human back lift of 550 pounds, instead.

Attention shifted to me and I threw back my head and sang Louis' tiresome tune which I'd heard so often that day:

> *Le plum pudding anglais*
> *Est un excellent met*
> *Un peu épais.*
> *Plum, plum, plum, plum. . . .*

A pair of muscled hands grabbed my waist.

"No Blue-noser makes fun of the way I speak," Louis snarled. Up I went in his clenched mitts—higher and higher until the strongman held my 450 pounds at arm's length above his head. The Seville people cheered wildly, for Americans adore a well-staged conflict, particularly if it has anti-British overtones.

(Here I must stop, for my wrist is aching. I will resume tomorrow.)

Dear Momma:

It is the next morning. I have had a meal of cocoa and chipped beef and I feel ready to go on.

In Louis' arms, that day, my body went limp. I suddenly felt heavy with exhaustion. The strongman staggered and we collapsed together falling forward towards the crowd who scrambled to get out of our way. I awoke on a tobacco wagon, piled high with golden-green stalks, under the scrutiny of dozens of worried female eyes. I was on my back, surrounded by the women from Seville who had pulled me into Bideman's tobacco-drying barn. Above my head, tobacco hung like scalps from the ceiling rafters and the air was sweet with fermenting plants. The women wore crooked, self-satisfied smiles which I didn't understand.

Then Cora shook bent down and whispered in my ear: "The curse of Eve is upon you, Mrs. Bates."

"Yes, the curse. It's the curse," another woman next to her muttered.

I hadn't heard that word, Momma, since you used to tell me the reason for your belly-cramps, talking low so Poppa wouldn't hear. The word made me nostalgic, and I wished I was waking up by your hearth to a cup of spruce tea instead of far away in Ohio.

Cora said she had noticed blood stains on the back of my gown when I went into the privy but was too shy to tell me. (I did not notice that my menses had spotted my dress. Indeed, I didn't notice the state I was in although it explained the gloomy mood I had woken up in that day.) Immediately then, I sat up and felt my skirt behind me and sure enough the panels of silk were damp. My monthlies had come, taking me, as always, by surprise. I do not know why this is so, Momma, as I can predict with some accuracy when it is due. Yet each time it comes as an unexpected wonder. Ordinarily, I feel relief and a sly pride that the cycles of my body are working as they should. But that afternoon I felt a bitter despair. It made me think of my baby whom my body had betrayed and I began to weep and inwardly curse the irony of a female physique that paid lip-service to creation but had failed to perform the act with any competence. The women thought I was sobbing over the shame of a stained gown and began to murmur

269

sympathetically. Then the Seville doctor came into the barn followed by Martin and Louis who wept loudly and fell to his knees before a hay pile and begged my forgiveness. I told Cora to reassure him I bore him no ill will and then the doctor listened to my heart beat and looked into my eyes and did every manner of thing except examine the part of me issuing the life-giving fluids that had soaked down through the tobacco leaves beneath me by the time he was through. He pronounced me to be suffering from "female weakness" and prescribed Lydia Pinkham's Vegetable Compound, a bottle a day, due to the size of me, and complete bed rest. Afterwards, Louis carried me into Bideman's home whose interior revealed the barker's eccentric character even more than the dilapidated exterior. The downstairs consists of three rooms, a kitchen, a central parlour, and a small side parlour which Bideman calls his cigar factory. Feathers and the yellow pigeons are housed in the parlour. The room smells of pigeon dung and fleas jump onto your arm when you pass through it although it is not something I like to do as I have to stoop to keep my head from hitting the ceiling. Upstairs there is a loft and several bedrooms.

The house is run by Cora Shook. She is Dad Bideman's sister and one of those remarkable pioneer women who a Frenchman named de Tocqueville said are the reason America is strong even though American men seem not to know it. Cora talked her brother into marrying after he got a seventeen-year-old girl from town in the family way. Cora looks after the babies since Frannie is so young and manages Bideman's cigar-manufacturing business here in the house. (In the winter, the small parlour in which I am installed is used as a factory for young boys who hand-roll cigars with the strange wooden devices I see cluttered about me on the table and floor.) Cora is also a mid-wife and well-versed in female business. Thus she has fixed me up on a bed of their/ tobacco leaves, mimicking the practices of Indian women who she says used to go to a special house during their monthlies and sit on beds of moss, chanting songs and prayers to celebrate their female powers. The nerve of Indian women priding themselves on their bodies pleased and amused me. Why should we not celebrate the blood-letting upon which everything depends? Why should you, or any of us, Momma, refer to it as an affliction, although, I admit, I don't look my best when it comes. In any case, I have grown fond of my strange mattress. It was a necessity during the fourteen days and nights when I bled as if the inside of me was emptying out, wrapped in sheets arranged so my bottom was bare against the plants. I have also become very fond of Cora who has hourly changed my bedding and waited on me as faithfully as you used to do in New Annan, when I was suffering growing pains.

Meanwhile, Bideman has cancelled our tour and Louis and his mother have returned to Quebec. Martin has taken a room at the Seville Inn and I will join him there when I am feeling stronger. We have purchased 160 acres just east of town, beyond Mound Hill Cemetery. We have spent many pleasant afternoons walking through our stretch of farmland and maple woods which is not much different from the other farms in Guilford Township but seems to me like a sublime place. Yesterday, we had a picnic lunch on the lawn while about us leaves fell rustling from the crab-apple trees and crickets chirped in the grass.

The farm is in the country and yet it is close to town and will be easy on the horses. Martin is pleased with it and full of ideas about what to build after we tear down the old house which is too small for our purposes. He feels, as I do, that we have happened by chance on the ideal retirement spot. The only concern he has about Seville is its anti-South sentiments. Since I last wrote, Martin has become an abolitionist. He met a black preacher on board *The City of Antwerp* who gave him *Uncle Tom's Cabin* to read and the book has changed his thinking. Martin has decided he identifies with black people. They are a minority, just as freaks are. I don't know whether this will matter to the people in Seville. Bideman says not; he says they possess a battalion mentality and don't really like blacks any better than people in the south. But he thinks they will accept us once we have made our home here and shown them we would like to be part of the community. I hope he is right.

The town has been kind to me. I'd forgotten how people in a small community rally to help those in trouble. It is a fine thing and I admire the Sevillites for doing it. On my second day, the theatrical Dr. Beach arrived carrying a plate of liver and onions which he said his wife had cooked because she thought I needed iron to cure my anemia. He deposited it on my sheeted lap and said: "I have lived with women all my life so I know about these things." I chuckled because he blushed as he made this formal declaration. Like most men, he is shy on these matters. The next day, he visited with his wife, a tall, bulb-shaped matron who stayed on after the doctor left and confided that she disagreed with her husband's diagnosis that I was sick because my womb was draining my mind of its mental faculties. She was certain it was nothing so sinister and suggested the August heat may have caused my monthlies to be profuse. Then we had a confessional conversation in which we both admitted we bled more in the summer than in the winter and then she got up to leave and politely shook my hand. Her opinion has been shared by the other women who came, bringing fried chicken and grape pies for me to eat. Some of them confessed to Cora that their menses arrived the day after mine. Cora says one bleeding woman brings on the monthlies in other females close by and because I am so big, I may have caused all the women in Seville to spill over together with the blood of creation! If only I could be like them and have children. I long to make a history the way women have made history since time began but there is little chance I will have another baby. The doctors in England said the strain of the first birth on my giant womb meant another conception would be unlikely.

So now I see I have written twenty pages to your two and must stop before my wrist breaks. Thank you for your kind words in your letter. I smiled over what you said about Uncle Geordie. A *bean-grugach*? I thought only Poppa believed in the fairies. To me, you are a sober trainer of conscience who has risen to the rank of supreme magistrate during your hard life in the backwoods. And how I have missed you this past year! There is nothing like the death of a child to make a daughter long for her mother. YOUR ANNA IN SEVILLE.

P.S. I have enclosed a nightgown to keep David warm in the chilly autumn nights in New Annan. It is odd to think you gave birth so close in time to me.

P.P.S. I don't know what Apollo meant about a peace bond on Martin. Explain to me another time.

CHAPTER THIRTY-TWO

Normal is as Normal Does

June 20, 1874

Dear Momma:

I have not had any word back from you since my last letter. I know this is not unusual, considering the postal services in the backwoods, but please write and let me know how things stand with you up in New Annan.

I, for my part, have had my hopes dashed since my last letter, although in many ways what happened was no surprise. I know rural folk are intolerant about individuals who do not adopt country ways. Farmers have a hard life and they want everybody in their community to be the same so the chances are greater the group will pull together and survive.

Yet after the novelty of our stay wore off, Martin and I have been treated more unkindly than any stranger would be in New Annan. The Buck-eyes are friendlier than my people, but they are more pugnacious too and think nothing of displaying hostility when they feel like it. Here they seem to feel difference is deserving of ill-treatment. The two merchants over-charge us and the men bait Martin because of his size. We are the most foreign of foreigners which is the word people here use to describe any stranger, even inhabitants of the next town.

The effect on Martin has been unfortunate. The giant has become belligerent and bad-tempered and I find myself cast in a new part. Anna, the entertainer, has been replaced by a wifely manipulator whose sole purpose is moderating the behaviour of her husband. I stare at this substantial female head smiling inquisitively above a torso gussied-up with wide Cluny lace and Bohemian garnets. I feel I am acting out America's relationship to the Canadas. Martin is the imperial ogre while I play the role of gen-

273

teel mate who believes that if everyone is well-mannered, we can inhabit a peaceable kingdom. That is the national dream of the Canadas, isn't it? A civilized garden where lions lie down with doves. I did not see the difference until I married Martin. We possess no fantasies of conquest and domination. Indeed, to be from the Canadas is to feel as women feel—cut off from the base of power. Oh Momma, I am finding housewifery difficult. Why didn't you tell me it is more work than being a spieler?

My first tea party fared badly. I held it in mid-June, a month after the last board of clear, yellow pine had been nailed in place on our giant home. Curiosity seekers frequently drive by to gawk at our two-storey clapboard farmhouse which, from the front, resembles a white wedding cake. It is flat on top and divided into two tiers by a front veranda garnished with spidery Italianate trim. It sits overlooking the country road on a sloping lawn dotted with spruce and fruit trees.

Shortly before the party, I walked out onto the front porch to wait for my guests. Martin followed me out, wearing his old Confederate uniform which I had not seen him put on since his shows as a bachelor in New York. He took out his Moroccan measuring tape and dangled it before my eyes. "Back to back," he said. "For the Bates Olympiad."

"Very well," I replied. "But be quick about it." You know me, Momma, I enjoy being measured. It is particularly rewarding with Martin since he hasn't come close to my 7′ 6″ as he hoped when he finished his growth last year. Despite his claims to the Seville people, he remains two inches below me without his boots. With his boots on and me in flats, he manages to look a shade taller. He is certainly heavier even though he has lost most of his baby fat and weighs well over 500 pounds.

"You know my contests are just for fun, don't you, Anna?" he asked after he'd put away his tape. "I am proud you are bigger than I."

"You just need somebody to look up to."

He chuckled and threaded my arm in his and I wondered if we were visible to the buggies I noticed crawling along the country road. From that distance, we would have looked like a miniature

bridal couple posed on the first tier of wedding cake. Martin spotted the buggies and gaped in disbelief. There were fifteen in a
long line that stretched all the way down to the cemetery. "Is that
another party of rubber-necking Buck-eyes?"

"It's the Ladies' Aid Society from the Baptist Church."

"I didn't know you belonged to that group of tongue waggers."

"I won't be asked to join when they see what you've got on," I
joked.

Slowly the buggies made their way up the dirt road, the front
section turning in one motion down the circular drive which
ended at our curing shed. In a few minutes, the driveway was
jammed with horse-drawn vehicles. The drivers climbed down and
then, in columns, like ants, the women marched over our lawn
and gathered by the foot of our veranda. My welcome smile
sagged because I knew as soon as I saw their expectant faces that
they had come to inspect the house and gossip about its extraordinary features, not to see me. I may as well have been a tour guide
and as I stood on Martin's arm, I suddenly heard Apollo's deep
voice in my ear, spieling:

Step right up, ladies for a tour of the giants' dream home. See
this amazing North American box whose front section has four-
teen-foot ceilings to accommodate giants while the back half
has ceilings of nine feet for people of normal size. For just 10¢
you can have a cup of tea and wonder at the scale of the
immense rooms which will make you believe you have stepped
into a fairy tale. Be sure not to miss its special features as fascinating as the treasures of the giants in *Jack and the Beanstalk*: a
kitchen table that stands 2 ½ feet from the floor at one end
and 5 feet from the floor at the other in order to seat giants
and those of normal stature; a study hung with giant bones
(where Captain Bates researches historical giants); and the couple's extraordinary 8-foot-wide by 9-foot-long bed. Our last
stop is the borning room—the side parlour which people in
these parts use to birth their babies and show their dead. The
door of this interesting chamber is large enough to let a giant
coffin through.

275

I had no time to continue my fantasy-spiel for an argument broke out over Martin's uniform. "What's that you have on, Captain Bates?" Mrs. Beach asked.

"The glory of the South," Martin chuckled.

A murmuring started up on the lawn.

"I'm not going to a party at the home of a rebel," somebody cried.

"Oh—go on," another voice said. "It's worth it to see the inside of the house."

"My husband uses the uniform of the Fifth Kentucky Infantry as a costume," I replied.

"I hope he isn't making fun of us, Mrs. Bates," Mrs. Beach continued. "Many of us here lost sons and husbands to the South."

Cora Shook marched to the head of the throng. She looked oddly formal in an old Zouave dress of cuir-coloured percale that had been popular in the 1860s. I hadn't visited with her for a month and I was pleased to see my old friend, smiling up at me like a kindly owl.

"Dad Bideman asked the Captain to wear that suit this morning to meet a circus promoter," she said loudly so everyone could hear.

She turned and looked at Bideman who was climbing down from a buggy carrying a crate of cooing pigeons.

"Isn't that so, Dad?"

"What are you gals fussing about?" Bideman set the birds down and smiled at the unhappy women. "The Cap's had enough headaches in Seville over that gol-darn thing."

Bideman winked at them. "Of course, if the Cap weren't such a bull-headed Southerner, he'd have no trouble with this town."

"The more I see of you unfriendly Buck-eyes, the more I think the South deserved to win," Martin chuckled.

"Well anyhow," Bideman grinned. "We beatcha." He picked up his crate good-humouredly. "Come on now, Cap. Stop fooling with the ladies. We've got work to do."

Martin ambled down the steps to join Bideman and the women moved slowly onto the veranda and into the farmhouse. They appeared uncomfortable and stood in the front parlour gawking nervously at the high ceilings and huge doors made out of panels of rare wood. The parlour is in the sombre style I favour. Its tall windows are hung with velvet curtains, roped apart by tasselled cords so the inner curtain of Nottingham lace is visible against the pane. Giant Louis the Fourteenth chairs stand in conversational groupings near huge console tables that support Dresden vases sprouting ostrich feathers. On the north side of the room is my piano, constructed for me on 36-inch stilts. Near the piano is a custom-made Sibley rocker from Nova Scotia and the enormous pine chest in which Martin and I keep our theatrical costumes. There is a fireplace with a mantel of imported Italian marble but a woodstove is the chief source of heat: its pipes run overhead into the other rooms of our farmhouse.

The women seated themselves in the large furniture, suppressing embarrassed smiles as I poured tea into giant Spode cups. Not until I had filled the cups did I realize my mistake and then Cora came to my rescue, going off in her matter-of-fact way to the kitchen where she managed to salvage a Wedgwood tea service of normal size from one of the unpacked crates of our belongings. Anybody would have been fortunate to have such an ally, but even she couldn't save me from the disaster that was to come. I think the truth is the women were glad to help me when I was in trouble and they could look down on me, but when they saw me standing before our grand farm house in an ivory tea gown, they felt envious and there was very little I could do to convince them I wasn't the snobbish doyenne they imagined me to be. Perhaps I should have worn one of my old gowns and tried to look like them but I felt I would patronize them if I didn't act like myself.

As soon as the tea was served they began to quiz me about the house which is constructed in a series of box-like structures that slope in declining height from the front parlour to the laundry room and wood box at the back.

"Why are the ceilings high at the front end and not at the back?" asked Mrs. Beach. She was sitting on our giant Turkish divan. Five women sat alongside her, balancing cups on their knees in the polite manner while their legs dangled above the floor.

"We saw no reason to waste space on the living quarters of our cook," I said. "We needed to cut costs anyhow—the pine used in the frame had to be brought from the West by boat and we under-estimated the cost of transporting it."

"That's thrifty of you, Anna," said Cora and nodded at the other women to encourage them to make admiring noises.

"You have servants?" asked Mrs. Beach. "Can't you cook and housekeep?"

I blushed hotly. "No. I have never had time to learn. When I am on the road, I perform three times a day."

"It must be easy work standing around so people can gape at you," giggled Frannie Bideman.

Cora looked at her sharply and there was a sudden hush in the room.

"Show business is hard work," I replied. "But it is certainly not as difficult or as important as the work of raising a family."

The women eyed one another and said nothing.

"Do you know anyone who would be interested in coming here to cook?" I smiled nervously. "Martin has asked his sister to come up from Kentucky, but she is too busy with her own family."

Again nobody said anything and I realized I had bewildered them. First, I had shocked them by flattering their disparaged pro-fession and now I had offended their pride by suggesting they might be my employees. I suddenly felt terrified for I wanted them to like me, and I realized if I didn't reach them that after-noon they would never accept me as a friend. Just then a prepos-terous appeal popped into my mind and it was all I could do to restrain my lecture voice:

DEAR SEVILLE SISTERS: I am 28 years of age and sound in mind and body although I have more body than mind (430 lbs. of body to be exact) but that's true of all of us, isn't it? Please overlook my fancy ways and recognize me as a member of the stoical sorority who endures in silence the pain and discomfort involved in populating our planet with a stamina that would outstrip any soldier. YOURS IN GOD, ANNA BATES, THE GIANT CHURCHWOMAN.

Momma, do you see my difficulty? I cannot stop myself from spieling even when I want to be down to earth. I should never have tried to be an Ohio housewife: I belong on stage. Meanwhile,

278

the uncomfortable moment in my parlour was shattered by a commotion in the barnyard.

"It's the sheriff and the town musician, Chuck Roughton," somebody said. The women flocked over to the window, standing on their tiptoes to see out. Then footsteps echoed in the kitchen and Martin and Dad Bideman burst into the parlour.

"Excuse us, ladies. Can Cap and I join you?" Bideman asked breathlessly.

I glanced at the men with dismay. Their trousers were smeared with yellow dye. Martin smiled at me nervously.

"I'm just thankful it's not bird do-do," the giant muttered. He strode to a cupboard and took out a cloth and a bottle of turps which he handed to Bideman.

"Tidy me up, will you, Dad?"

"We've been dying birds gold," Bideman said.

He began to scrub Martin's trousers in front of the startled women.

"My husband pays more attention to his menagerie than he does to his tobacco crop," I said, trying to make light of an ever-worsening situation.

"Mr. Bates runs a zoo?" a woman asked.

"Captain, ma'am. It's my old military title."

"The Cap and I own a boa constrictor," Bideman added. "You should see the Cap handle the critter."

"I saw your snake at your barnshow last year, Mr. Bideman," said Mrs. Beach. "It tried to swallow my daughter's dog."

Bideman grinned. "Feathers wouldn't do that. She only likes rodents. See? But listen: We're going to be holding another show. Maybe you ladies would like to join in?"

There was another commotion at our front door and the Seville constable walked in carrying a billy club.

"Good day, Mrs. Bates. Cap. Ladies," he said. "I expect you know what I'm here for."

"I have not the slightest idea," I replied.

"You don't?" The constable looked uncomfortable. "The Captain must have forgotten to tell you about the fight he had this morning with Chuck Roughton."

"That Union weasel," Martin said.

"Mrs. Bates, the Captain pretty much smashed up Berry's barbershop over a crack Roughton made." He sighed deeply. "The Captain was lathered up for a shave and telling Berry he planned to ask St. Peter for a peep into hell when Roughton piped up: 'Never mind, Captain. We think you'll get more than a peep.'"

"Martin felt angry about that?"

The constable looked at his feet. "Your husband took a bad razing about that Reb's suit he's wearing before he lost his temper at Roughton."

"I see. Are you here to press charges?"

"Not exactly. Berry wants to ban Roughton from playing the mouthorgan for his customers and Roughton says he'll put a peace bond on the Captain if that happens, so I came to see if you would pay the damages and maybe Berry and Roughton will change their minds."

"I'll pay for one broken shaving mug," Martin said. "The one that says Capt. M.V.B. Bates."

"Of course, I'll pay for everything."

"Thank you, ma'am," the constable said. "And Captain, I'd appreciate it if you'd take it easy on the town. There've been problems since you folks came to Seville and my chief is talking about making me work full-time. I'm only on evenings now."

"Are there more fights I don't know about, Constable?"

"A few, ma'am. Yesterday, the postmaster complained the Captain spat tobacco in his face."

"The little Buck-eye made me wait until he served the last customer," Martin said.

"If you didn't lean over the wicket and grab your mail, he wouldn't serve you last," Bideman chuckled.

"Keep your nose where it belongs, Dad," Martin snapped.

The constable gazed nervously towards the door. "Anyway, thank you ladies for tolerating the interruption. I think I'd better go out to Roughton now."

"Roughton's here?" Martin bellowed.

"He's in the buggy," the constable said. "But listen, Captain, if there's any more trouble, Roughton will slap a bond on you."

"Why, I'll tar and feather that lying skunk," Martin said.

The giant pushed his way through the frightened women and stormed out to our yard. Screams sounded outside, and from the parlour windows, I saw Martin chase a terrified Roughton across the lawn. Then Virgil Shook emerged from our barn and began to chase Martin with the fork.

The constable and I rushed outside as the three men ran off into the field behind a corn bin.

And so ended a typical scene, Momma, of the Bates's farm life in Ohio. But the tableau was not over, not yet. There was more to come, indeed the saddest part followed immediately after for as I turned to go back to the farmhouse looming up behind the spruce trees I saw Cora Shook come out onto the side veranda, looking very nervous and upset. I hardly heard her when she told me not to go back into the house because I was feeling so angry and ashamed about Martin's behaviour and even guilt for I can't seem to stop myself from feeling responsible for controlling him, foolish as this may be. Cora took my hand and whispered that she had tried to stop "her" and I nodded and said it was all right, thinking she had meant to say "him" for Martin. Then I walked past her up onto the side porch and suddenly I stood dead still. Through the parlour window, I saw Frannie Bideman standing on my tall piano stool wearing an old Victorian corset of mine which had been stored in the pine costume trunk. She had on one of my old feather hats and was making a show of sticking her nose in the air as she held the garment with its stiff, bulbous bosoms about her like a wooden barrel. The Seville women were giggling and talking. Then Frannie unhooked the corset, tossed it to a sea of hands below her, and jumped down so somebody could lower an old petticoat of mine over her head.

This crinoline is made of steel and resembles a cone-shaped cage. At that moment, I raised my arm and rapped on the window.

"It's her!" Mrs. Beach cried. The women turned and gasped at me standing behind the glass and Frannie Bideman stared out through the steel struts of my petticoat like a terrified child, the top of her frilly lace bonnet protruding above the narrow waist of the undergarment.

"They don't mean any harm, Anna," Cora said in a gruff voice. "They were curious to see your costumes."

"Oh. So they are interested in the stage?" I said, smiling mechanically for I was too shocked to feel any emotion. "I should have guessed. Perhaps they would like some mementoes to take home."

Cora stared up at me and I swept past her into the parlour where the women were now hastily putting my belongings back into the costume trunk. I told myself that it wasn't a desire to hurt me which had compelled them to go through my private things. It was their fascination with show business. Then I made one final futile gesture which again only served to illustrate the gulf between us. I walked over to the trunk and retrieved a stack of old photographs of me at Barnum's. "I would have shown you anything you wanted if I'd known you were theatre aficionados," I said. I began to autograph the pictures and pass them out. The women stared wordlessly at the tintype of me in the plaid dress I'd worn the day I met Apollo. Then, one by one, they made excuses and left.

All, that is, except Cora Shook, the woman who has been a friend to me since I first came to Seville. She was angry with her friends and said they were too close-minded to appreciate me. She said they acted like hypocrites when I told them I needed household help because most of the women took on girls to cook for the hands during heavy periods of work on their farm. I wept then and told her I was used to normal people rejecting me and explained that even my own mother had been horrified when she first laid eyes on me. (I know you did not feel that way for long.)

She told me she would have accepted me from the start if I'd been her baby and the next thing I knew she offered to come and stay in the back wing when I needed her. I was glad to accept her offer and she is staying with me now. It is ironic that I, who like to think of myself as a benefactor, should need somebody to depend on. However, I am not as strong as I look and I am grateful for her help.

In any case, it seems I am doomed to feel a kinship that few can recognize. Suffering makes me understand my connection with the small irascible beings who share this earth with me although my size—the thing that brings my suffering—keeps us apart. Meanwhile, I take comfort in knowing that by facing my weaknesses I find my strengths. For I am certain, Momma, that to be a freak is no different than to be human. YOUR ANNA.

August 20, 1874

Dear Annabelle:

Your father and I are coming to Seville next month. Maggie (the second Maggie born in 1853) took sick with consumption last winter and I have had my old hands full, with no time to write. I am bringing her with me in the hopes the Ohio air will act as a tonic. Your father says there may be better doctors in America, but you know my feelings on that score. It's all fads and foolishness what goes on down there although I am prepared to stay as long as you need me. Your life sounds troubled, Annie, and I would have no value to this world if I didn't do what I could to help you out. YOUR LOVING MOTHER, ANN.

P.S. Thank you for the nightgown. I should have told you in my other letter that David was born January 10, 1871, and died May 5, 1872. That's five out of twelve already gone.

CHAPTER THIRTY-THREE

The Verdict of the Supreme Magistrate

April 30, 1875

Dear Anna:

I couldn't speak my mind to you in Seville. Many times it was on the tip of my tongue to tell you what I thought of *him*. It is the custom with us Grahams to give our opinion of the new mate once the newlyweds entertain their kin. So it is fitting that I speak. Yet it troubles me for what I have to say is not the kindest thing. I had my heart set on liking him when we met ye at the station November 25, the Yankees' Thanksgiving day. I recall it with some pain. We were shivering in the chilly wind, huddled together for a wee bit of warm. Neither of ye recognized us. (Your eyes are bad and you hadn't made us out yet from the crowds waiting by the locomotive. And he had no idea we were of such small size.)

You looked so grand, Annie! A great, refined lady in a long cape and fur-trimmed parasol! I had my troubles remembering you were my own. Then you rushed over and picked me up in your long arms and kissed me and I knew my Annabelle was inside that grown-up woman. Then I heard a roar and I saw a dark, overgrown man waving at us and spitting tobacco in the shadows. My heart sank as he made his way towards us. So this was your Martin? Maggie huddled against me in fear and your father shook his head to warn me not to say anything.

"Do I behold the great clan Swan?" he shouted as he shook our hands off, laughing and throwing back his colossal skull so it travelled from a point over his belly to some distant, amazed star. (You'd think Annie, with everybody joking about his size, he'd guess how we felt when he made jokes about ours.)

Well, I said I was glad to meet him on this side of the ocean as I

284

used to worry he might ne'er bring you back from the old country. Then he said, "Ann, no European lodgings would fit sovereigns of the flesh like Anna and me." And patted me hard on the head. (Isn't that just like an American? One minute they call you by your first name like they're part of your clan and the next—they trample all over your toes.)

So didn't I ask if ye had considered locating in a palace, trying not to smile. And he said, without comprehending my droll jest, that the two of ye felt tightly housed abroad, like all our kin before they set out for the New World.

"One wrong move and we could have extinguished the million puny universes we found about us," he said, spitting a great wad of tobacco on your father's boot. The folk nearby turned their heads to stare. I blushed over the spectacle he was making of us and then the station master came up with our trunk. Your father tried to lift it and he laughed to see Alex struggling. He told him to stand back and let a man do the job, and he threw the trunk into the back of that big buggy of yours like it was nothing. (Your poor father.) Then he asked us what we thought of your appearance. Did you look healthy? he meant.

"I don't know how to describe the change in Anna. Budding? Blooming? The bairn looks fit," your father said.

"You must be a good caretaker, mister," I said.

He claimed the fresh breeze from Lake Erie had worked the cure on you and I said I hoped living by an inland lake would help our Maggie. Then he said ye'd put Maggie on a diet of raw liver. And I said no bairn of mine would follow an American craze. And your father looked cross and told me nobody wanted to talk politics. So Maggie piped up that it didn't matter what she et because the world was coming to an end on Dec. 22, 1885. Well, the pair of ye started back as if ye could have been knocked over by a feather. Your father and I are used to Maggie. The consumption has given her religion and a good thing too. (You never saw her naked body, Annie. No breasts at all, nipples like a man, and a horrible sunken area over her left lung, like somebody pushed her flesh in with their hand.)

Maggie may have been a little fanatical but she didn't sit up in trees wearing a white gown and looking to the east like the screwballs in the Boston states. She minded her P's and Q's because I brought her up to believe in manners, unlike Yankee folks.

Anyhow, autumn is a bad season for consumption and Maggie began to cough standing out there in the cold. So you took off your cape and wrapped her in it and he lifted us small folk aboard with a great many chuckles and ill-mannered jokes about our bantam weight. He started to tell us his opinions of the royal homes ye stayed in but as soon as we got past the last house (I remember it had an old corncob hung on the front door—a time-honoured Yankee custom, you said) a snow storm started up and none of us let out a peep of sound. The snow came down so thick and fast he couldn't see the road. I felt a sense of foreboding with the wind howling and Maggie crying as she bounced up and down in your lap. Your father felt it too for he took my hand and kept his eyes away from him who was yelling at your Clydesdales and lashing them with a great black whip which looked like it belonged to Lucifer himself. And I wasn't wrong either although the horses found our way to your grand farmhouse. For you know what came next. Maggie opening her mouth at your dining table after she'd climbed up on the stool you placed for her on a giant chair. And looking at me very helpless as if she wanted me to stop her from doing something shameful. Meanwhile, your servants from Seville were running in and out with turkeys and fresh sausage (more food than your mother has seen in a lifetime) served on plates as big as platters. And he was toasting General Lee and telling us that President Grant was the wrong Yankee to be sitting down to turkey in the White House that Thanksgiving. And I looked at my Maggie and I knew before I saw the blood pour out of her mouth that it was going to happen although I sat dumb like the rest of ye and watched wave after wave of crimson fluids spill onto her laced dress front.

After that, I knew she'd be underground in three months, just as the Halifax doctor told us. The same one who fed her raspberry vinegar and had her bled with leeches. And didn't she expire after Alex went back about the barn that burnt down ($600 we lost, plus hay, grain, and mowing machine) and didn't we bury her in March in the Baptist cemetery near your farm? During her funeral service, all I could think was that for three months I'd lived with your husband cheek-to-jowl and I didn't like him any better than I did when I had my first look at him. I despised him for his ill-mannered ways as I sat between ye in your giant pew, his big, booted foot sticking out in the aisle as he shoved a monstrous gum wad of tobacco into his ugly cheek. Then he started hawking it, bit by bit, into his spittoon. Nobody else in the church had their own spittoons and I don't know why he thought he could be different except maybe he felt the minister would be scared to discipline him like the other members. Oh, he acted like he owned the house of God, while you were an example to the congregation, kneeling on your prayer bench, your good head bowed in prayer. I am so proud of you, Annie. Do you recall the text the pastor chose for our Maggie? "In the culture of fruit, flowers and vegetables, we rejoice to see them engaged." I squeezed your hand every time the Baptist man said words like "elegance of her person" and "delicacy of her table." I knew before I saw your house that you would have made a model home to encourage model behaviour. And so you have too. (I believe us females instill moral values in those around us if we dress proper and run the world as a refuge from the wicked ways of the world.) And I know you believe, like your old mother, that a woman should modify her man. As adverb to adjective and adjective to noun—as your father puts it. And I know too you have tried to influence him with our Blue-nose values of decency, order, and moderation. I saw you frown at him when he drove too fast to the cemetery. And poke his side when he spat on Maggie's grave before the undertaker shovelled the first spade of dirt onto her coffin. I cursed him then for I felt he'd won a battle with me. He'd got one Swan under Ohio soil and he'd get another before he was done. Because he's running you into the ground with his problems, Annie. I saw it with my own eyes. You think you can civilize an American. But you cannot make over one like him who takes no responsibility for his bodily juices, who dispenses the evil-smelling weed wherever he pleases and stands with his hands in his pockets and stirs his coffee so the spoon hits the side of the cup. He also neglects his farm chores and spends his days at the carnival man's when he should be on the homestead helping you. His instincts are *all bad* and no matter what you do, your man will

287

never learn. He's like all Yankees—out for himself and the devil take the rest. I don't know why you take their side unless you have become one of them yourself. And him the worst of the lot! He has the whole town talking about him. Do you know the things they say in Seville—and he is one of their kind?

Do you know they say his family are hill-billies who live dirt cheap on a Kentucky boonpork, feuding and killing and mating with one another like baboons?

Do you know they say he never was an army captain?

Do you know they say he deserted the war after a minor foot wound?

Do you know they say he helped his family hang five men down there in the Kentucky hills?

Do you know they say he's had ten peace bonds sworn out on him?

Do you know they say he keeps a pair of duelling pistols in your barn?

Do you know they say he hides behind your skirts?

Do you know they say if it weren't for you he would have murdered one of the Seville people long ago?

Do you understand, Annie? Your man is everything a sensible body should hate and fear. Well, the Yankees will get their comeuppance one of these days. Their lawless country will fall apart and then men like him will be sorry. YOUR MOTHER, ANN.

May 30, 1875

Dear Momma:

Martin has no secrets from me. He grew up poor like us Swans in Colchester County and it is not his fault that life was rough in the backwoods of Kentucky. But he struck out on his own and gave up their primitive ways. As for the gossip you heard in Seville, why do you take the word of intolerant people before your daughter's? The men here bait Martin. They mock him to show how patriotic they are to a dead cause instead of trying to see the good in him.

And furthermore, I am still a Blue-nose even though I don't share your contempt for the Americans. I believe it's a waste of energy to go around predicting the collapse of such an energetic people. The world hasn't heard the last of them. Americans have their faults but they possess the courage to be themselves while Blue-noses like you sit on your verandas, ridiculing the world beyond their doorstep. If you weren't so rule-bound and narrow-minded, you'd notice Americans are a Goddamn lot more lovable than most peoples elsewhere. Yes Momma, I am blaspheming. I am tired of your provincial prejudices and your mean-spirited fault-finding. Don't you realize how boxed-in your critical ways make those around you feel? There is nothing so defeating and limiting as to be with somebody who spends their days looking out for bad in others. Who will ever be able to meet your standards? Not Poppa who is spared your scorn because he is too meek to take himself seriously. And not I. As a wee one, I used to feel fearful when you repeated your rollcall of human failure: Foolish Jacques Belcourt—he prided himself on a kind nature and neglected his wife, Sophie; foolish Marybelle and Isabel, Hubert's sisters, who hated their father for his insensitivity and yet thought of nothing but marrying. . . . I lived in dread of the smallest misdemeanour placing me on your list. Well you may put me on your list for all I care. You belong there too although you don't know it: self-righteous Ann Swan—she fancies she loves other people when what she does is look down on them. YOURS, ANNA BATES.

CHAPTER THIRTY-FOUR

Anna's Big Dilemma

September 17, 1876

Dear Momma:

I have wanted to avoid correspondence with you for a long while and the same must be true of you. A year has gone by, and I have had the chance to assess our quarrel (which I truly regret) and my anger with you is gone. Indeed, I think of you fondly and often, particularly as the maples are turning red and yellow in our back-woods. Do you remember the melancholia you used to experience at this time of year when you had to exhibit me and face the jeering multitudes you couldn't control? (By the way, I shall soon go on the road again. Martin and I have accepted an offer from a circus promoter named W.W. Cole who claims his show is exempt from the coarseness permitted in most tent exhibitions. His circus is one of the first to visit Western mining towns by train. It is small compared to the scale of an empire-builder like Barnum who has managed since I worked for him to achieve more success with his travelling circus than he'd had with the American Museum.)

And so I come to the point of my letter. I must be as honest as I can because you put your finger on a painful truth as mothers are inclined to do at the very time when their daughters are frightened and won't listen. You see, behind my fierce manner lay a sea of fears as deep as your own. If only you knew how many hours I have spent wondering if I am wasting my life living with Martin! Not because, as you so harshly put it, his instincts are bad, but because I am sick of my wifely role and yet unable to behave any other way with my husband. I do not know if he or the insti-tution of marriage provokes my behaviour. Because it's a mistake

290

for wives like me to take on the role of civilizing their mates. Why should I be my husband's divine conscience when the job develops my character while he remains the same as before? In any case, I dislike my condescending schoolmarm's voice as I administer the punishment he seems to beg for like a naughty boy. I am not the prim matron I hear leading him through soulful conversations to show him where he has erred or the wide-eyed sunny smiler who bestows praise when he performs a Christian act such as offering his gold watch to divert the two-year-old Hay wailing in the church pew behind ours. I am not exempt from unkind or selfish acts and I do not live in a circle of virtue that shuts out a universe of exiled men. I am Anna, an imperfect being.

At times, I suspect the worst of myself. I think my maternal chiding must come from a misguided pride that I am the only one big enough to understand him. Or is it simply practical? Certainly, looking after Martin is the best way I've found of feeling useful in a world of limited choice for the female. For whatever reason, I am becoming bitter about our marriage and discouraged by a private conjugal matter. (I cannot go into this: I feel treacherous to be even hinting at it to you.) Unfortunately, I dread the prospect of circus life and so does Martin. An hour ago, as we took our tea in the kitchen with the Shooks, Martin lost his temper at Virgil because the farmer asked if we would be in a sideshow. "We are not circus people, man! We are entertainers who give special appearances on request. And we don't move our butts for less than $20,000 a season!" Virgil's eyes popped. I know Cora will say nothing but tomorrow Virgil will talk and our salaries will have the merchants charging us twice the price the locals pay.

As I write, Martin is pacing dispiritedly up and down before the big doors of our barn in an effort to calm himself. The weary hunch of his shoulders is familiar. He is unhappy here (although he likes the countryside like me) and I am miserable. My life has taken a wrong turn and I am uncertain about how to mend it. Would you think me wicked if I left him? YOUR ANNA, WHO IS SORRY FOR OUR WORDS OF DISCORD.

291

November 1, 1875

Dear daughter:

I deserved your words of ire. There is no good that comes of listening to a worn-out old woman who just gave birth to her last bairn three years before. My trouble is I see how those about me would benefit from instruction and cannot get it through my thick skull that it is better to keep mum. I am sorry my ways cause pain. Meanwhile, I do not ken what you should do about that man. You will have to make up your own mind in your own time. And I am sure my Annie will do what's best. God sees what a good woman lives in that big body of yours. My prayers are with you. MOTHER.

CHAPTER THIRTY-FIVE

A Surprise Visitor

One December afternoon, as I looked out the parlour window, I saw Apollo walking down the country road. A light snow was falling. He was carrying a carpet bag and a baby monkey dressed in a velvet jacket and a pill-box hat. I rushed outside onto the cold veranda, blushing over the ferocity of the tremors in my bottom storey. Apollo saw me and began to run and leap through the snow, shouting in his deep, booming voice.

"Anna! I heard you had died!"

He raced up and grabbed me around the waist, resting his head against my abdomen with a relieved sigh. The monkey leapt to my shoulder and held its hairy fingers across my eyes.

"Nothing vanquishes the BIGGEST MODERN WOMAN," I said in a solemn tone that didn't reveal the excitement surging through my animal frame. "Who is blindfolding me?"

"Oh, that's Bijou. A present for you. Am I welcome, Anna?"

"You are." I smiled as the monkey's fur tickled my cheek. "I thank you for your ape."

Apollo laughed. "She likes you, Bijou, you lucky fellow. Now let's be serious for a moment, shall we?" Apollo took two railway tickets to New York from his pocket and waved them at me. "I've come back to get you. Will you run away with me, Anna?"

"And leave Martin?"

Apollo nodded. "I am not happy without you and you are not happy with him." He eyed me shrewdly. "Your life in Seville isn't working, is it?"

"No." I bowed my head in shame.

"Ah! I knew it! I knew it!" Apollo shrieked. He leapt up and down on the snowy porch. Then he thrust the tickets into my hand. "Keep them while you decide what to do." Apollo grinned. "I'm giving you a week to decide."

Although I tried to act sedately after Apollo's arrival, I walked about with my head in the clouds. Apollo's timing was uncannily accurate. I was desperate to put down the burden of wifely help-mate and anxious for the world to open up again. In 1876, I had turned 30, the age for casting out ghosts, and I was still too young to know the way to make an unwieldy structure like married life suit myself. However, my problem remained. How was I going to allow myself to leave Martin?

CHAPTER THIRTY-SIX

The Giant Ménage

Each morning, I rejoiced to see Apollo at the short end of our kitchen table, holding his soft-boiled egg in a napkin to eat it in the correct style while his barker's voice boomed out stirring tales of the new life that could be made with the circus in Australia. Martin, the homebody, looked so pathetically oafish at the high end, that I could not bring myself to admit what I had decided. I stared at him guiltily, wondering if he guessed how uninspiring he looked munching through breakfast courses of peas, oatmeal grits, baked potatoes, and vegetables which Cora served up on our giant Spode china.

Meanwhile, Martin's proprietary interest in me increased. He stayed home instead of dallying at Bideman's and hung over my shoulder in the evenings, watching Apollo and me play double solitaire with my enlarged deck. On the sixth day of Apollo's visit, I resolved to talk to Apollo and beg for a postponement to his question. It was a cold and windy Ohio night. I sat in my Sibley before the parlour woodstove, wearing my winter coat for extra warmth. My cheeks still glowed from an afternoon skating expedition to Chippewa Lake. Martin stood behind me, while Apollo sat across from me on a cushion, dealing our cards in fluid motions onto the piano stool which we had employed as a table. With each remark from Martin, the corners of his bull-frog mouth drooped further.

"Be quiet, Martin. Or leave us in peace!" I snapped.

The giant grunted and heaved himself into the most fragile of the Louis the Fourteenth chairs. It was my favourite and the one chair in the house that was too slight for Martin to sit in. Grim-faced, I said nothing. Five minutes passed and then Martin groaned and heaved his boots onto the wall. I put down my cards.

"Martin, you're getting stove black on the flocked wallpaper!"

The giant swung his feet down with a triumphant look. See Apollo, his look said, I have Anna's attention. Then up to bed he went, spitting tobacco juice as he climbed the stairs to wait for me in the bedroom. Apollo and I played on. Overhead, the giant's footsteps began to pound back and forth across the bedroom floor. I threw down my hand.

"It's no use, Apollo," I said. "I'm going to retire."

"And your answer, Anna?"

"I'll tell you in the morning."

Apollo uttered a tragic little sigh. I felt his eyes on my silhouette flaring against the wall like an immense, inverted pagoda. I said good-night and then went to the kitchen to fetch a nightcap of buttermilk. On my way back, I heard a whisper from the borning room.

"Anna. In here."

I stopped on the first step of our winding stairway and Martin called out above: "What's keeping you, my dear?"

The whisper came again. "In here."

"I've spilled my buttermilk, Martin," I hollered. "I'm going back for more."

I peeked into the borning room. Apollo was stretched out there on a day bed, a look of appeal on his whiskered face. He wore a pair of longjohns and his fingers were moving rapidly up and down a quivering tube of flesh.

I advanced shyly.

"Oh Anna." Apollo sighed as I seated myself on the floor beside his cot. "My big girl likes me, after all."

He rose and stood on his bed so my head was level with his waist. I wrapped my arms around him and pulled him close. Then wonderingly I rubbed his silky member against my cheek and kissed its trembling head. Ah. Its flesh was lengthening before my eyes.

"Apollo," I murmured. "I am making you grow." He nodded, eyes closed. Sighing, I opened my lips and received his quivering organ whose new dimensions inspired in me a thrill of dread.

"Anna! Where are you?" Martin suddenly roared from above.

"I'm on my way up," I called, hastily releasing Apollo. Trembling with guilt, I rushed from the room and marched upstairs.

Martin was waiting for me in the bedroom, smiling in a strained way. He wore a nightcap and nothing else. A purple nub of flesh dangled between his thighs.

I blew out my oil lamp.

"Always the perfect lady, aren't you, my dear?"

He lumbered towards me and began to fumble with the hook of my gown. In the mirror of our armoire, two huge, white creatures toppled onto the mammoth bed. One pressed against the other and uttered a bleat-like cry. Martin's spasm of love was done. I rolled over and stared at the wall.

"Is anything wrong, beloved?" Martin asked in a worried tone.

"Martin, you needn't deny me my pleasure."

The giant looked at me as if I had three heads.

"What pleasure?" he asked.

My eyes travelled downwards.

"Woman, all's not normal in that department." He gave me a grave, pitying look. "Hasn't Dr. Beach had a talk with you?"

I shook my head.

"Well, the doc is a little shy. Anna, I wish this was not true, but he has apprised me that large women have difficulty achieving physical release. The sensational impulse takes too long to traverse the network of nerves in their physique." He paused meaningfully. "If you were smaller, your frame would register the impulse."

"And why is that not true of you?"

"What do you mean, Anna?"

"The speed of the impulse travels like lightning in your case."

A devious look appeared on Martin's face. "Ahhhhhh," he said softly and looked away for a moment. Then he turned back with a condescending smile. "Ask Dr. Beach and he will tell you what applies to women has no relation to the workings of men."

I frowned and turned away. A few minutes passed. Martin sat up in bed and stared at me with fear in his dark blue-black eyes.

"Anna, I have omitted the rest of Dr. Beach's talk."

"What could be left for that man to say?"

Martin began to sob. "He asked a specialist down from Cleveland and the other medico confirmed that I am hypogonadal."

"I beg your pardon?"

"My dear, I am not capable of manly spending. I have the undeveloped organs of a child and the quivers of pleasure I feel will never aggrandize into anything more than what I experience now."

"Oh Martin. How sad." I put my arms around him and pulled him close. "And yet I suspected this was the case."

He wept louder. "Despite my great affection for you, there is no way the lesser part of me can bring you happiness."

"Why not?"

"Dr. Beach told me the female impulse can only be released by a large [he made a sad choked noise] and erect male member."

"Martin, you don't believe that country bumpkin."

"He is the expert, my dear."

"Martin, I know what gives me pleasure. Look. If you rub me here [and I touched my sweet spot] you can make me dizzy with joy 100 times a night."

Martin averted his eyes from my bottom storey. "Anna, please do not make up tales to save my pride."

I studied Martin in dismay. Was I a freak in my sexual responses? Impossible.

"In any case, Anna, I will subject you no longer to my shameful displays of failure. I am renouncing carnal activity from this day forth."

The giant dried his eyes and smiled meekly. Poor Martin. I felt sorry for him and yet—I could not endure a union without sexual love and the prospect of children. A moment later Martin was snoring in my arms. Stealthily, I lifted his heavy skull off my chest and put it on the pillow where it belonged. Then I flew downstairs to the borning room and Apollo and I spent the night disproving Dr. Beach on the subject of the sensational impulse in large women.

Nelvana's Nordic Regulator

Apollo wanted us to leave at once but I convinced him that we should wait and elope after the season with W.W. Cole had finished. Then there would be no need to break our contract with the circus promoter who had sent an advance of $10,000 as a token of the value he placed on our act.

Meanwhile, Apollo was sworn to secrecy until I found the courage to tell Martin. We met in the borning room after the giant fell asleep and life in Seville passed by uneventfully. Then, one afternoon in January, we returned from a shopping trip to town on our ice sled and found our farm occupied by the Thumbs. The midgets had brought with them a patent medicine purchased from a Canadian Eskimo whom the General had befriended during a reception at the home of the Governor General in Quebec. The medicine was named after an Inuit goddess called Nelvana, the daughter of the northern lights which are a common spectacle in skies over the Canadian Arctic. The Thumbs were impressed with the nutritious qualities of the tonic and hoped to amass a fortune selling it to the American public.

The midgets were in the barn when we drove in, fuelling up a woodstove near the stall of Martin's stud horse, Young America. Tim Delaney, Seville's shortest man, had found them the stove and he sat on a hay bale watching the Thumbs brew a demonstration batch.

Martin swung open one of the immense terracotta barn doors which had been made seventeen feet high to accommodate Martin's head when he drove out the home outfit. Sharp February sunlight drenched the steamy interior of the barn and our long shadows billowed across the hay-strewn floor. Young America whinnied nervously.

"Look out! It's the Captain!" Delaney cried.

"Why, you little s.o.b.'s!" Martin bellowed. "You're making a mess of my barn."

Thumb came forward, wearing a medicine man's top hat with a band of crimson silk. He was twice as plump as I remembered him and dark pouches under his eyes made him look dissipated.

"Captain! Mr. Delaney has encouraged us to take the liberty of testing our new nostrum," Thumb said.

"Don't worry, Bates. We're going to cut you in on the profits," Lavinia said, winking at me. She looked plumper too, but had aged less than her corpulent mate.

"Is that true, General?" Martin asked with a grin.

"Of course it is, you big oaf!" Lavinia replied.

"We need investors in our secret potion," Thumb added. "Visionary individuals who see the possibilities in a normalizing tonic."

"You might talk me into investing in a normalizer," I said. "But I won't drink it."

"Oh Anna. There you go having to remind everybody you are the tallest here," Lavinia said.

"What's Nelvana's? And why won't you drink it, Anna?" Apollo asked, strolling into the barn and winking up at me. I smiled giddily. (The BIGGEST MODERN WOMAN is in love, I thought.)

"Nelvana's Nordic Regulator—a new self-improvement tonic for the Yankee nation," Thumb said. "Not to be confused with cosmetic elixirs such as Egyptian Regulator Tea, the product that brings graceful plumpness to flat-chested girls, nor with Rengo medicine which turns fat into muscle for overweight men."

"If you are too tall, it will make you shorter," Thumb continued. "If you are too short, it will make you taller."

"Of course, it is not a panacea," Lavinia added, her black eyes flashing. "It will cure only catarrh."

"Of which there are many forms," Thumb said. "Catarrh of the lungs (consumption), of the intestines (enteritis), of the heart (heart disease), of the skin (measles and boils) and, of course, catarrh of the growth organ."

"Not to mention catarrh of the common-sense organ," I teased. "A social ailment of the American people."

"There's no money in a regulator, General," Martin said. "People in our great land just want to get bigger."

Thumb shook his head and his chipmunk jowls, now the size of a fat beaver's, quivered indignantly.

"You're behind the times, Captain," he said. He climbed up on a hay bale and unfolded a long embossed scroll. Then he thrust his hand into his shirt (just as he used to do at the Museum) and he began to read:

DEAR FRIEND: Drink Nelvana's Nordic Regulator and be the height you desire. Brewed by the Eskimo savage from the crystal waters of the Arctic streams and the bark of mighty Canadian pine, Nelvana's secret potion is now extensively used on midgets and giants in African and Indian institutions, hospitals and asylums, and is prescribed as a morphic regulator by the medical faculty in many parts of North America. The elixir seldom affects any two people alike. Beginning its work as soon as it is in the mouth, Nelvana's eliminates all catarrhs as it goes circulating through the system, ending with the demise of catarrh of the growth organ. Soon you will thank Nelvana for making something that has reached your weak spot. Recommended dosage: one teaspoon for a man, two for a horse. Nelvana's Nordic Regulator is prepared in Bridgeport, Connecticut. Price $1; six boxes $5. Sent by mail in the form of bottles, also in the form of lozenges, on receipt of price. All letters of inquiry promptly answered.

Then Lavinia ladled the brilliant canary yellow liquid in the vat into six glasses of heavy English cut crystal. She handed them to us and smiled a glittery show-business smile.

"Bottoms up, girls and boys," she said, draining her glass. Thumb, Apollo, and Delaney tossed theirs back and I took a sip of the lemon sweet cordial and then another. "Delicious, Lavinia," I smiled.

Martin stopped mid-slurp, his moustache yellow from the elixir, and made a disgusted face.

"By Jesus, this bile is crapola," he spat on the barn floor. "Give the poison to pipsqueaks."

With our midget guests underfoot, Apollo and I decided to change our nightly rendezvous from the borning room to the barn loft.

Thumb and Lavinia darted out from behind a giant chair or popped up from under a giant table (which they could walk under with ease) when I least expected it. The loft was quieter; Martin seldom came into the barn and Virgil Shook was an unobservant farmer. The Thumbs were still a danger; they ran in and out of the barn supervising Tim Delaney whom they'd hired to manufacture the nostrum.

We met there on Groundhog Day, February 2. According to a North American superstition the groundhog leaves its burrow on this date and returns underground for only six more weeks of winter if it is sunny enough for the animal to see his shadow. There was no sign of sun on Groundhog Day in 1878. It was grey and overcast and so cold the ground squeaked underfoot as if the earth hurt to be stepped on. We hoped the cold would keep the midgets inside the farmhouse. Alas! No sooner had I sat down on an ice-cold hay bale and pulled Apollo into my lap than we heard the high-pitched chatter of the Thumbs on the floor below. Apollo jumped up and squatted down, peering through a crack in the floorboards. "God damn those stubborn dwarfs," he hissed. "They're starting up another batch of Nelvana's."

Moments later, clouds of hot, lemon-flavoured air rose up and filled the loft. Apollo and I stared helplessly at one another.

Lavinia's shrill voice floated up to us:

"Mr. Stratton, you know I am a Temperance woman and I say Mr. Delaney is not putting in so much as a drop of whisky."

Thumb scoffed. "All patent medicines are stiff as a highball, Vinie. Why even your Lydia E. Pinkham's Vegetable Compound is cut with alcohol."

"I never use Lydia E. Pinkham!" Lavinia said.

"Then who guzzles the carton of empty Pinkham bottles I throw out every week?" Thumb snapped.

"Liar! You are the drunkard in our family."

There follows a yelp of pain from Thumb and a metallic clatter of falling pots. A familiar acrid smell wafted up through the loft floor.

"Fire!" Apollo hissed. He jumped to his feet and yanked my hand. I retained my calm and stood up. (I rise to a crisis. Angus would say it is my Highland spirit coming out and perhaps that is accurate. I know how to meet the peaks and chasms, but the long, flat spaces in between, those I find harder than I can tell you. . . .)

"The bale crane. We can lower ourselves to the ground from the hay window."

Apollo's eyes popped. "You know I'm terrified of heights, Anna!" There are times when a giantess has to do what a giantess has to do. So I gathered up the squealing Apollo and made my way through the hay bales to the window. Virgil Shook appeared through the barn door below.

Soon a lazy river of yellow syrup spilled out into the snowy yard. My nostrils quivered. The odour was spirits. Lavinia and Delaney raced out. Thumb came next, his head down, his portly torso rocking in the sailor-like walk of midgets as he trudged through the steaming snow that was quickly turning to yellow ice. Suddenly he stopped and looked up. Our eyes met and Thumb's fleshy visage furrowed in disapproval. Then the midget turned and ran along the path cleared among the snowbanks into the farm house.

"The midget's seen us and gone to spill the beans!" Apollo cried.

"Our plan to elope will be spoiled," I sighed. "Thumb has never liked me."

I put Apollo down wearily. A thin fume of smoke hung over the loft. Under my feet, I heard Virgil overturning the last vat of syrup onto the hay which had caught a spark from the woodstove.

Then Shook left and we climbed down from the loft, too worn out to talk. Apollo drove in to town and I walked morosely through the snowbanks back to the farm house. Martin came in from town, driving the home outfit, and noticed my glum look.

"No sign of spring, is there, my dear?" he called. He wore his black frock coat and a brown fur cap with huge ear flaps—an untied string dangling from each flap.

"The groundhog missed its shadow," I called back. "It's winter for ten more weeks."

Martin nodded and took the team into the barn. I walked uneasily through the kitchen and into the dark hall. The giant house was silent except for a creaking noise in the parlour. I stood still and listened.

"Don't you try and avoid us, Anna Bates!" Lavinia's voice called. "Mr. Stratton and I want to talk to you."

I peered nervously around the door. For a moment, I saw nobody in the huge room. Suddenly Thumb cleared his throat and I looked down and saw the pair of them glaring up at me about a foot from where I stood. Lavinia bobbed slowly up and down in a child's rocker painted with frogs and butterflies that Momma had sent me in the event that I had a second child. Thumb stood behind her, his hand thrust into his shirt.

"Why is Apollo boarding here with you and Martin?" Lavinia said icily.

I walked in and sat down heavily in my Sibley rocker.

"Apollo prefers to be away from the hurly-burly of the city. Besides, I require his advice on financial matters."

"Your agent gave up a prosperous business in New York to handle your investments?"

"Yes."

"Aw, honey. He's milking you."

"A con man like the Judge wouldn't be out in the sticks if he wasn't up to something," Thumb agreed.

"And what does Martin think about it?" Lavinia asked.

"Whatever he pleases," I replied. "He's living off the earnings from my investments, just like Apollo."

"Anna, are you supporting Bates too? Tell Vinie all."

"Martin hasn't had the same good fortune with his stocks as I, Lavinia," I replied coldly.

"How about the Judge? Another unlucky soul?" Lavinia said.

"Apollo has doubled my money while he's been on the farm. That should interest you. I doubt if much else does."

"Money interests everyone. No need to be hoity-toity with your friends, Anna Bates," Lavinia retorted.

"I expected more humility from an adultress," Thumb said.

I stopped rocking. The creak of Lavinia's rocker resounded in the room.

"And what are you accusing me of?"

"Mr. Stratton saw you spooning with Apollo this afternoon."

"He was hugging her by the neck," Thumb said.

"I tried to lower him from the hay sling so we could escape the fire. Or do you not remember the disaster you started, beaver-jowls?"

Thumb jumped towards me and Lavinia grabbed her husband by

his coattails and pulled him back. She patted his quivering cheeks and winked at me to indicate that she and I understood men were fragile creatures who needed to be coddled.

"Honey, we know why you're having a romance with the Judge." She smiled knowingly. "Domestic life—what a bore! Marriage doesn't hold enough adventure for women like us who possess a strong animal vitality." She tossed her dark head and looked adoringly at Thumb to show she meant no insult to him.

"That is why Mrs. Stratton and I will never retire from show business," Thumb squeaked. He brushed his thinning hair out of his eyes and tried to look friendly.

"We thought it best not to tell Martin," Lavinia went on. "We're sure you two giants can patch it up."

"With a little extra work you may achieve a relationship as happy as ours," Thumb added.

Lavinia blushed and squeezed her mate's hand. "The idea is to aim high," she said.

I rose to my full height and glowered down at the midgets.

"Just who are the two of you?" I retorted. "The moral guardians of Middle America—the very people who look down on us as freaks?"

I took a step closer to Thumb. "How dare you give me a talking to—you sanctimonious shrimps!"

I reached down and grabbed at Thumb who scampered off and slid under the Turkish divan. Angrily, I turned on Lavinia and tossed her rocker back and forth until she squawked in terror.

"Enjoying yourself, are you, Mrs. Stratton?" I said as her screams grew louder. "I trust you find the air sweet in Ohio? Please don't let Martin's belches at mealtime affect your digestion! Is the child's crib you're sleeping in comfortable?"

Lavinia leapt up and ran off around the piano and Thumb raced after her.

"Thank you for your sound counsel, dear friends!" I shrieked as their forms disappeared out the parlour door. "Tomorrow you shall have more of my time! As much as you want! Feel free to ask more personal questions! To probe my intimate secrets!"

Then I sat back down in my Sibley and had a giant cry. I saw us through the Thumb's eyes—three bumbling players in a domestic triangle. The vision depressed me. My life was a cliché—a farce acted out on an Ohio plain where the marvellous was diminished by the perception of those who dwell within material reality. And I was a prisoner in the thin dimension of ordinary life, looking for a way out.

The first container is the house.
The first sensation is the rustle of the body
dancing to fill it.

The self is the second container.
The second sensation is the round-up body
sighing in a hand-built stockade.

The body is the last container.
The last sensation is the self dying
to be as big as all outdoors.

CHAPTER THIRTY-EIGHT

The World's First Shrinking Giantess

The Thumbs said no more about my relationship to Apollo and stayed on the farm, brewing their patent medicine. One March morning, on my way to meet Apollo, I made an unsettling personal discovery. It was one of the spring days in Ohio when the sun burns your face. The earth was starting to show through the snow on the rolling fields, and down the county road some farmers stood in a honey wagon, tossing forkfuls of manure onto the ground, believing winter was done. My shadow seemed to stretch past the farmers and their wagon and loom towards Seville, darkening the clapboard homes of the pugnacious Buck-eyes whose failure to accept us had been a sore blow.

Outside the barn, I paused to feed a carrot to Young America who whinnied when he saw me and poked his head out his stall window. I stared at the loins of the stallion, daring the mesmerizing pink snake to slither out of the velvet case on his belly and astound me. Nothing happened; the horse only rolled his eyes and I entered the barn going through a door that had been specially cut inside the towering seventeen-foot doors to let Virgil Shook pass in and out without bothering to open the bigger doors. The small door was an inch taller than Martin so he could use it too. It was too small for me to enter without ducking, but nobody expected me to spend time in the barn. Inside, I stopped. Was I addle-pated or had I just entered without bowing my head? I lifted up my gown and strolled back out into the sunlight whose reflection off the snow almost blinded me. Then I strolled back through the door into the barn. No tucking of chin to chest, no curling of shoulders was required. I could sail through freely.

I walked back out through the door, certain this time that my head would knock against its lintel. All my life I'd lived with the fear that I might start to grow again, but the possibility of shrinking

307

had never been a worry. Again I cleared the door with no trouble.

I began to rush in and out while Young America whinnied and knocked against his stall. There could be no mistake: I was shorter than the doorframe which had once obliged me to duck. I broke into nervous giggles and clambered up the rickety loft ladder to tell Apollo. He lay unclothed at the bottom of a shiny mountain of hay, carefully anointing his quivering instrument with Anti-Child Roborant (a sperm-killing oil which Dr. Beach had prescribed). He let out a shriek when I slid down and landed on top of him.

"More informal these days, aren't you?" he said grumpily.

"Get dressed," I commanded. "Come and measure me."

I climbed back up the hay hill and then down the ladder again and into the farm house to find the moroccan leather measuring tape which I knew Martin kept to verify his stature. My drowsiness was gone. A titillating dread had cleared my brain. I tried to understand it as I rattled the drawer of Martin's campaign desk, my fingers more clumsy than I ever remembered. Was I pleased by the prospect of shrinking? I quivered nervously. No, I was not!

Back in the barn, I found Apollo hitching up his trousers near Young America. He stared at me in shock as I strode towards him, waving Martin's tape. Then I settled my back against the reality of Virgil's door and stood ramrod straight so I wouldn't cheat—not even the smallest bit. I heard the chalk make a gravelly little squawk on the red wood. Apollo solemnly gauged my length from the floor to the white smudge.

"Seven foot three," he boomed.

"Apollo, my height is $7'6\frac{1}{2}''$. Do you understand? I'm shrinking."

I picked him up by the lapels of his brocade jacket and held him level with my head.

Puzzled, my lover peered into my face. Then his bull-frog mouth expanded in a grin. He kicked himself free of my hands and landed on the barn floor with a little hop.

"It's Nelvana's. It's made you shrink, Anna. Oh my big girl, what wonderful news this is!" he said, falling to his knees and raising his arms to the sky in a gesture of gratitude. Suddenly, I felt uneasy. Of course, any man with a giant girlfriend would prefer her to be shorter. But I thought Apollo cherished my size.

Beaming, he leapt up and pointed to the chilling mark on the wall.

"Anna, think of all the afflicted women like yourself who would like to be shorter than their men. Think of the joy Nelvana's would bring to their world by removing two, three—in your case, twenty-five—inches that interferes with your femininity."

"Apollo, I am not certain I wish to be small and insignificant," I blurted.

"Well, I doubt if you will go down to 5′5″ but something under six feet might be very nice," he replied.

He rocked back on his heels and threw himself into my arms, wrapping his legs around my waist.

"Something under six feet? Apollo, I'd be puny."

Apollo laughed and began to kiss my neck. A fresh wave of dread made me feel depressed. Did Apollo mean it? His grinning face said he did. He tugged my left breast to indicate we should go up to our love nest.

I climbed the ladder, frowning at Apollo like a mother carrying her child off for a thrashing. Down below Young America reared and squealed and the stallion's lonely cries increased my dread. I felt an uncivil desire to drop Apollo, but the ligaments in my forearms trembled at the thought of his torso sailing down to the barn floor and I continued skyward.

In the loft, the March sun slid through the cracks in the barn panelling, warming the hay, and lighting up Apollo's comely blond head. I stared appealingly into his eyes, wanting him to say he'd been jesting. Instead, he snuggled into the hollow of my chest—jiggling my breasts on each side of his head.

"Apollo, would you really like me better normal size?" I asked.

He looked up, a breast flattened against each ear. "Let's concentrate on pleasure now, shall we?"

"I have to know."

He chuckled and his head vanished beyond the curve of my belly, and settled where it was accustomed to settling.

"Don't you want to be one of the diminutive females our age idealizes, sweetheart?" he hissed from below.

"Only if you would like me that way," I replied.

309

He chuckled and kissed me wetly. "I like the thought of you standing on your tiptoes to kiss me."

"So you mean yes?"

"Yes, I mean yes, Annie. Now be quiet and enjoy yourself—like you always do."

Apollo's tongue beat a tattoo against the bulb of flesh at my giant centre.

"Don't you want to shrink, Anna?" he whispered.

His tongue worked faster.

"Say it, Anna. Say yes."

"No."

"Yes."

"Um. . . ."

"Yes."

"Apollo? I've already shrunk."

"That's my big girl," Apollo chuckled.

Following our evening meal, Martin sank down beside me on the giant chesterfield and gave me a worried look.

"My dear, the Judge tells me you have shrunk," he said.

Apollo unfurled Martin's handsome tape and dangled it before our faces.

"Back to back, Anna, so the Captain can see for himself."

In a daze, I stood up with Martin. The giant made a great many nervous huffing noises as we squared off. Apollo uttered an astonished whistle.

"She's still got you beat, Captain," he said.

"You fool, Judge! Anna was always four inches taller."

Apollo hissed thoughtfully. "Well, it's only one now."

"Only one?" Martin roared in surprise. "Only one, Judge?"

Apollo clapped Martin on the small of his back and winked at me. "Only one."

Martin gazed at me in alarm. "My dear, you must stop drinking Nelvana's. I don't want a short woman for my wife."

"Apollo would like me something under six feet," I said.

"A foot or so less would be nice. But no shorter. We still want our Anna big. Right, Captain?"

"I don't want Anna to shrink, Judge," Martin said. (I had never been fonder of my mate than I was at that moment.)

"Now, now, Captain. Like all females, Anna is eager to use a beauty aid that makes her more feminine." He lifted up my hand and brushed it with his bull-frog mouth, and I recoiled ever so slightly.

"You wouldn't want to stop her from being happy?"

Martin shrugged and looked at me but I only stared back at him blankly.

"I guess what she does is up to Anna," Martin concluded.

"Thumb feels, and I agree with him," Apollo continued, "that a regulator which makes tall women short will turn us all into patent medicine millionaires."

"And tall men?" I asked in a hollow voice. "What does it do for them?"

"Nothing, Anna. Why should it?" Apollo grinned.

"Obviously no man would be up to the opportunity of becoming the world's first shrinking giant," I said listlessly.

Martin looked startled. Before he could reply, the Thumbs entered, carrying a tray of champagne.

"We don't need the Captain when we've got Delaney," Thumb said.

"Delaney?" I asked, still baffled.

"That's right, Anna Bates," Thumb said. "The Judge here tested Tim this afternoon and found he has grown three inches."

"And Mr. Stratton has shot up one inch in the last month," Lavinia added. I gazed dully at my short guests. So the medicine was potent enough to affect midgets too! Well, the damage was done: I was three inches shorter except that I didn't feel any different than I did before. My eyes were still level with Martin's forehead and the heads of normal people still swam somewhere in the vicinity of my chest and waist. Of course, on somebody as large as me, it would take more than three inches before I'd notice a difference.

That night, my shock and terror were reflected in a dream: Martin and I, our arms threaded, waving gallantly at the bespectacled little Seville photographer as we posed on the front porch of our giant home. I was clearly taller than Martin by half a foot and smiling the self-satisfied smile of the Ohio gentry. Apollo stood nearby, his head at my breasts. A bejewelled Thumb and Lavinia held hands under Apollo's elbow. As the camera clicked, I drooped

311

and dipped below Martin until Apollo was a yard higher and the top of my red head was level with Thumb's ear. The curiosities shook with uncontrollable laughter while I stared into the lens of the camera like a dead woman.

CHAPTER THIRTY-NINE

Accidents at the Zoo

Every morning that week, Apollo marched Delaney and me through the melting snowdrifts in the yard to measure us against the chalk marks left on the terra cotta doors of the barn from the day before. And every day, a less perceptible gap appeared between the two chalk lines. Apollo noted the measurements in his old route book like a mariner charting the tide levels.

March 9, 1878—7′2⅞″, a new low for Anna.
March 20, 1878—7′2½″. On her way to breaking the seven-foot barrier. Good work, Anna!

My mood plummeted with my decline and Delaney's soared until I couldn't stand the sight of the Seville dwarf who began to call me "my great, big, beautiful doll." In church, I prayed, "Please Lord, bring me no closer to earth," while Reverend Cather grinned foolishly down at my kneeling form. Whereupon I would silently vow not to touch another drop of the nostrum and my resolve would last until the next assignation with Apollo. Then he would make love to me so wildly and proclaim his delight in my new femininity so ecstatically that I would forget my dread and the next day I would drink my daily bottle of Nelvana's as if I couldn't get enough of the patent medicine. As my dependency on Apollo increased, his need for me lessened. Instead, he spent hours with the Thumbs discussing plans to market Nelvana's.

At the end of March, just as I hovered above the seven-foot mark, the Thumbs left for Bridgeport where they intended to start a factory of Nelvana's Nordic Regulator. Apollo was a partner in the enterprise and he agreed to sell the medicine during our circus tour, using Delaney and myself as contented customers.

I felt unhappy and stopped drinking the tonic—in secret, so Apollo wouldn't know—but the medicine had started some bizarre, unstoppable reaction in my genes because Apollo's measurements showed that I was continuing to shrink.

On April 10, W.W. Cole opened. Despite our beneficent salary, our lectures were just another sideshow next to Hernando, the HALF-MAN, and Schoobie, the frightened PINHEAD, who worried his thumb through a circle of fingers each time he saw a female. Three times a day Martin and I had to walk between the STEAM MAN and the GAUCHO HORSEMEN OF THE PAMPAS in the opening procession around the three rings of the big top. And three times a day Martin plodded through a spiel at the sideshow booth while I hung on the giant's arm, imitating the strong and silent females that are favoured on the frontier. His spiel bangs in my mind. "Seville? One of the friendliest towns in the Midwest. An ideal retirement spot for Kentucky planters like ourselves."

On a moonless June night, after Martin fell asleep, I slipped out of our Pullman coach for a rendezvous with Apollo in the Monster Music Car. Apollo had bribed its driver, Dan, to park the crimson vehicle near the train instead of in its usual spot with the menagerie wagons which make up the part of the circus known as the *Zoo*. The Music Car was drawn by four camels and guarded by Bowser, a small terrier who made a nuisance of himself by barking at the sea-lions during the opening procession under the big top.

"Bowser should fight the lions and get it over with," Apollo hissed as Dan retrieved the terrier by the sea-lions' slime-coated aquarium. "Then Anna!" Apollo's huge mouth yawned a grin, and he held up two entwined fingers: "Every night, like this!"

As I tiptoed over to the Music Car, Bowser suddenly hurtled out of the shadows and clamped his jaws about my kid boot. Apollo appeared at the door of the wagon in the clown suit he wore for the evening show.

"Kick him with your other foot," he hissed.

"I can't." I cried. "I'll lose my balance."

Cursing, Apollo leapt down and shook the dog free. Then he yanked my hand so I lurched closer to the vehicle. Bowser jumped after me, barking savagely. Immediately, shouts broke out and lights came on in the sleeping train. Apollo ducked inside the wagon and flattened himself behind the bass fiddle.

At the sound of the commotion, Bowser turned and ran towards the train. Martin suddenly emerged out of its door in a robe and sleeping cap. The giant looked sleepily into the darkness. Frowning, he raised his arms out to the sides to protect the noisy crowd of performers gathering behind him. Then he spied me. His mouth dropped open and he reeled back as if I'd struck him. A wave of guilt and sorrow made my knees tremble. Suddenly, Martin chuckled. He grinned at the blinking curiosities who were too frightened to advance further.

"Take a good look you poor s.o.b.'s and go back to bed. It's just the missus out for her evening constitutional."

In our Pullman, the giant didn't quiz me. He put on his wire-rimmed bifocals and began to scribble on a piece of paper, chuckling appreciatively at what he was writing. A few minutes passed and then he cleared his throat and read me a sample paragraph:

The circus community was awakened last night by a tall stroller who walked out of the Stygian darkness, little knowing she would give Bowser, the camp watch-dog, the fright of his life. The mutt, whose vigilance knows no peer, awoke Schoobie, the PINHEAD, who beseeched manly Captain Bates to determine the cause of the ruckus. Imagine the surprise of the fearless giant when he discovered the intruder in their midst to be his wife and partner in their act—the TALLEST COUPLE ON EARTH.

Martin regarded me eagerly over the half-moons of his spectacles.

"Not bad for a cub reporter, is it my dear?"

I gaped stupidly at him.

"I've been appointed editorial assistant of *Big Top Bulletin*." The giant smiled. "It cuts down the research time for my tract, but I have always liked to chase fire engines, you know."

I continued to stare at him and he shifted uneasily.

"You don't like it, beloved?"

"Ah...eliminate 'Stygian.' It sounds too literary."

"My dear, a word like 'Stygian' will give the *Bulletin* class."

Martin chuckled. "Let me see. Have I covered the essentials—who, why, where, when, and how?"

"And what," I said.

"Yes, what. Now my dear, don't interrupt the muse so I can finish my story."

I watched Martin nervously. Would he continue to be a hobbyist after I had gone? I saw him chatting with the town loafers in Seville's park: a gaunt farmer shivering in the autumn breeze. The image troubled me as I turned on my back and fell asleep.

The Thumbs' shipment of Nelvana's Nordic Regulator arrived a week after this incident. The circus had stopped in one of those small Colorado mining towns that disappear as soon as the gold is panned. Apollo unpacked the bottles in the cook's tent while I sat across from him, too morose to speak. Apollo's tasselled Hessian boots rested on top of my quilted slippers in a secret proprietary gesture. Ordinarily, it gave us both comfort. Martin sat beside me, reading the *Big Top Bulletin* to Delaney.

"There was a happening three days ago which cast gloom over the usually merry atmosphere," Martin boomed. "Little Bowser, only a dog, is dead."

I looked at Apollo. For three nights we had met without hearing the terrier bark.

"Bowser had one fault and that was his hate of sea-lions," Martin went on. "His keeper put the dog in their cage and said Bowser would have to have it out with his enemies. When the keeper returned, Bowser was found floating in the water in the tank. . . ."

I rose from the table, pleased to feel Apollo's boots falling off my arches.

"Dan wouldn't do a thing like that. I know who made a gladiator out of an innocent terrier."

Apollo jumped guiltily.

"Did you place a wager to see how long Bowser would last?"

"Anna, the Judge didn't hurt Bowser," Martin said. "Dan was fed up with his dog stopping the parade."

Apollo swore that was the case. Nevertheless I felt angry for the rest of the day which was spent setting up the medicine display. Apollo had put together a comical and arresting booth. On one side of the booth, a circus artist had drawn a cartoon of me holding a long scroll which proclaimed: NELVANA'S—THE NOSTRUM THAT LENGTHENS THE SMALL AND SHORTENS THE TALL. In the sketch, a jolly Tim Delaney sat on my shoulder (in the old style of Commodore Nutt) swigging from an olive-green medicine bottle. A caption above Tim's head exclaimed: "I'll meet you on the way up, Anna." A tall, wooden wall stood next to the booth; Apollo had painted on it our changes in height since the first day he had measured Delaney and myself. Huge, crimson numbers rose and fell in two columns on the board. The one that recorded my shrinkage ended at $7'\frac{1}{4}''$; Delaney's column ended at $3'11\frac{1}{2}''$.

Our booth was at the end of a crowded and muddy lot between the opera house and a beer garden. The atmosphere reminded me of a Nova Scotia fair. Bearded miners and dandies from the opera house mingled with ranchers' wives and girls with bare shoulders. At the edge of the crowd, beautiful courtesans sat listening in open carriages. Apollo ran through a short spiel and when he was satisfied that even the drunks were listening, Apollo handed the megaphone to a blushing Delaney who began to speak:

DEAR COWBOYS AND COWGIRLS: For fifty-two years, previous to drinking NELVANA'S NORDIC REGULATOR, I was a martyr to small manhood. I stood $3'7''$ and felt so ashamed of my masculinity that I would only work at night at the blacksmith shop in Seville. I daily got sadder and believed with all my heart that I was a poor excuse for a male and deserved to die. Then I discovered NELVANA'S, an old and secret remedy of the Canadian Eskimo. After three months of getting into the NELVANA habit, I was a quarter inch higher and today, at $3'11\frac{1}{2}''$, I am proud to be a man. If any of you doubt the truth of my story, contact Mr. I. Davison, Druggist, Seville, Ohio. He knows my case very well and would verify with me (if only his wife would allow him to join the circus) the truth of this wonderful cure. YOURS IN MANHOOD, TIM DELANEY.

The crowd cheered and it was my turn. Apollo took the megaphone from Delaney and handed it to me.

DEAR CIRCUS FOLK AND FRIENDS: I, the BIGGEST MODERN WOMAN OF THE WORLD, am in the throes of a glorious plunging, a miraculous reduction of flesh that will shrink me into the zone of feminine perfection. All my life I have longed to be a dainty beauty who could promenade with my head nesting in the crook of my escort's arm. But I was 7′6 ½″—too large for a real woman. Why, I could not be picked up and carried across the threshold like a normal bride nor could I wear the elegant heels of the ladies of fashion! Today, thanks to NELVANA'S NORDIC REGULATOR, I have shed an unsightly six inches and will continue down until I am 5′5″. I urge the tall girls like myself in the audience to try this nostrum for it is true (based on my experience) that small women have more fun. It is thrilling to decline! What could be more generous and unselfish than to watch the body get smaller so you will please the eyes of others? How breathtaking, how stirring to see the inches fly off! Oh, ladies, the joys of descent are more profound and private than the cheap, giddy thrills of ascent. YOURS IN WOMANHOOD, ANNA BATES.

Cowboys threw their hats in the air and a yelling mob surged towards me. Most of them were women, not tall women, but women of all shapes and sizes. Even the courtesans in the jewels and ostrich feathers rushed out of their carriages and began to scream confessions of dissatisfaction with their physiques.

"Yoohoo giantess! I am too tall too!"

"Will my man love me if I shrink?"

I stood in a daze. Their eagerness was astonishing. Why did they want to shrink when they would look so nice big? Then the irony of my situation struck me. I, who had defeated gravity for 32 years and who took pride in every inch of me, I had been as gullible as any thrill-seeking sideshow customer and allowed Apollo to convince me that I wanted to be shorter.

Apollo motioned Delaney and me over to the board. The dwarf trotted up to his column, impatient to see his progress, while I ambulated over to mine, pondering my discovery. I faced the crowd blankly; Apollo measured and thrust me aside so everyone could see the new mark.

The crowd roared and saw my chalk line at the crimson seven-foot figure. The line for Delaney read four feet.

Apollo picked up the megaphone again:

"Ladies and gentlemen, this is a record-breaking day for both the giantess Anna Bates and the dwarf Tim Delaney," Apollo spieled. "In honour of this occasion, bottles of Nelvana's will be given away free to the first ten customers."

The women descended on the booth, grabbing bottles and plucking at my skirts. I could stand it no more. I rushed away from the stand, pushing through the mêlée until I found myself in the zoo near Dan's wagon. I slipped inside and hurled myself on the floor near the bass drum.

I was too annoyed with myself to cry and sat in the darkness cursing my own stupidity. About twenty minutes later there was a tap on the door and Apollo's whiskered face thrust itself into the gloom of the wagon. I burst into sobs.

"Apollo, I don't want to get any shorter," I cried. "And I hate being a mere seven feet."

Apollo stepped inside, his bull-frog mouth wide open.

"Don't you see? I don't want to shrink and if you loved me, you wouldn't want me to shrink either."

Apollo's eyes suddenly filled with tears. "Oh, my poor big girl," he said sadly. "You aren't shrinking."

"I've lost 6 ½ inches! You measured me yourself."

He shook his head; his chin sunk to his chest.

"I fooled you into thinking you were shrinking, Anna. Virgil Shook adjusted the barn door because the Captain complained it wasn't high enough to keep him from hitting his head. Nobody but me knew Shook had it fixed."

"What about the receding chalk marks?" I asked angrily.

"I redid them every night so it would look like you had shrunk but you never lost an inch."

"And Delaney didn't grow either?"

"No."

"How could you lie to me Apollo?"

"Anna, I never wanted you to shrink. I always liked you big. Your body has fed and loved me. A woman who can do that for a man is the best there is."

"That's not what you said before."

"I lied. I don't even notice your height." He paused. "Except when we're around other people."

"Why did you do it then?"

Apollo stared at the ground. "I have spent your circus salary, Anna."

"You have what?"

319

Apollo sighed. "I gambled away the salary Cole paid you and I thought I could make it back with Nelvana's."

He looked at me fixedly. "I knew you wouldn't put up with shrinking for long."

"Do you think I'm going to run away with somebody who tricks me like that?"

Apollo shrugged his shoulders. "You are never going to run away with me."

"What do you mean?"

"It's against your mythology." He sighed. "Anna—the big protector. If you didn't look after the Captain you'd think your life was meaningless. You aren't happy unless you've got a burden to carry on those great shoulders of yours. Of course, you whine about your situation, but I realized you were stuck with that oaf when we were on the farm in Seville."

I thought this over wonderingly. "Why didn't you tell me?"

"You wouldn't have listened. Anyway, you freaks never let go of your own mythologies."

He pulled out a pair of dice and rolled them on the head of the drum. "It's all you've got."

"And how about your mythology?" I asked, wanting to beat him about his whiskered face.

He gaped at me. "I don't have one."

"Ha! You are the worthless carny that nobody loves so it doesn't matter if you break their trust."

"My big girl never stays mad," he said imploringly.

"Well, this time I do." I stood up to go.

"You can't leave me, Anna!" he cried and leapt through the air and tackled me about the knees.

"Keep your hands off me." I grabbed him by the seat of his ballooning clown suit and hurled him with all my might at the brass instruments of the circus band. There was a cacophony of brassy noise and Apollo lay slumped on the floor. For a moment, I thought I had killed him and I leaned forward to see what my quick temper had wrought. Suddenly, he rolled over and groaned and lifted up his arms, asking to be picked up.

"Oh Apollo. That was wrong of me," I said. A tear rolled down my cheek. "But I'm going all the same."

"Anna! Stop! I love you," he cried.

I stepped sadly out of the wagon and didn't look back.

The next day, the booth was dismantled; apologies were made to the crestfallen Delaney and the remaining shipment of Nelvana's was sent back to the Thumbs. Martin was relieved I hadn't shrunk and so was I.

For the next month, I ignored Apollo's desolate face in the opening procession. And at night, when he tapped on my train window, I rolled over and went back to sleep.

On our way back east, Martin woke me up in a hotel room in downtown Fort Worth.

"You should be the first to hear this, beloved," he said quietly.

"Oh, is it hot off the press?"

He nodded with a solemn face. "Death claimed another circus favourite last night—Judge Ingalls, manager of the giants. While sleeping under a heavy wagon, H.P. Ingalls was run over and killed. His body was found by a circus employee, cut in two pieces by the wagon wheels. A bottle of rum was found near the corpse. . . ."

Martin put down the paper. I began to sob. Killed! Like a razorback injured by a circus wagon as he lay on the ground, sleeping off a drunken night.

Martin cleared his throat. "It was the Judge you were sweet on, wasn't it?"

I nodded, the tears streaming down my face, and the giant put an arm around my shoulder.

"The ladies always liked that little s.o.b.," he said. "But I didn't know you did until I read the Judge's route book."

I stopped crying abruptly. "When did you do that?"

"When we were abroad. I hated the bugger. Then I saw how happy you were to see him again and I figured you had a right to what I couldn't give you."

The giant spat nervously on the floor. "And by God, Anna, I wanted an heir." He reached for my hand and kissed my fingers. "Who was to know it wasn't mine? Didn't you want another child after the first one died?"

"You wanted me to sleep with Apollo?"

"You know, I have dreamed of founding a dynasty of giants." The giant hung his head. "Is that so terrible, beloved?"

"It is not what I would have hoped," I said coldly.

"What would that be, my dear?"

"To spend my life with a man who suited me. Instead, I've had to accept what each one of you had to offer as you came along."

Martin smiled. "You are romantic, beloved. None of us are big enough to meet your expectations."

He chuckled bitterly. "An odd remark for me to make, isn't it my dear?"

"It is more intelligent than usual," I said cruelly.

"Isn't that a little harsh?" Martin shrugged his shoulders. "I love you and so, ah...did the Judge, God rest his soul."

Martin frowned. "If you want to leave me, I will understand, my dear."

He released my hand and lumbered slowly out of the room. A dynasty of giants! Martin had wanted me to make love with Apollo! He'd given me up to somebody else because he dreamed of a race of supermen! As long as nobody knew that he was impotent he didn't mind another man fathering his child. He'd abandoned me for a silly dream and now his substitute was dead. It was a bitter revelation. And so it was Martin's turn to experience my anger. I rose early to avoid him and went to bed late, marching well behind him in the opening procession, and looking away when he glanced back—the girl aerialist perched on his shoulder.

Apollo was buried in Dallas, Texas. The tents were unfolded on a fine old lot, and the receipts from the booths selling red lemonade and peanuts went to the cost of his funeral. The dismal event left me weakened and miserable.

All this happened in the last week of September. On October 2, in Charlottetown, North Carolina, I discovered I was pregnant. My anger at Martin vanished. The news felt redemptive—mythic in its proportions of wit and tragedy. I had not lost Apollo. He was with me, after all. And if my body did its job, would not leave me again.

CHAPTER FORTY

The Giant Birth

The snow came late in December 1878. It fell in clouds and buried Seville, staying as high as the windowsills of our farm house. Day after day, blizzards transformed Martin's barn into a remote and ghostly shape that looked as out of reach as the town from the coal-fires of our farm house. When Martin went into the Seville restaurant for morning coffee, he returned with hair-raising stories about missing farmers whose corpses would have to wait until spring, when the snow melted, to be found.

My labour began the morning of January 15.

Cora and I stood at the kitchen window watching Virgil Shook stagger through the wind and snow with feed pails for the animals.

"Don't get caught between the house and the barn!" Cora yelled. Then she put the kettle on the woodstove so she could have tea ready for Virgil when he returned. Martin sat at our end of the kitchen table reading the *Cleveland Plain Dealer*. He wore a pair of bifocals on the end of his nose and the reading glasses made him look domestic and cozy. I was standing on the curious wooden dolly which Virgil had built: It allowed me to be rolled through the rooms of our home standing upright and holding onto its rails. I had gained 100 pounds during my pregnancy and was too heavy to lift myself up or down out of furniture, too heavy even to walk. My arms and legs were swollen with fluid and my thirst was unquench-able. I had to sleep sitting up in bed to keep my lungs from congesting.

My body was in danger of obliterating me—it had grown vastly global in the final month. I felt out of touch with the huge, bloated Anna in the mirror but my alienation at least gave me freedom from responsibility. That morning when the first pains resounded through my gargantuan belly, it felt as if the labour was happening to somebody else.

"The baby is coming," I said, smiling dreamily as I doubled over, holding my arms across my stomach.

"Captain, her pains have started—her labour has started!" Cora cried in alarm.

Martin heaved himself up from the table and then the kitchen was in an uproar: Martin bellowing for Virgil to fetch Dr. Beach, Cora bellowing at me to go to bed, and Virgil bellowing across the snow at Martin to mind his tone. My dolly's wheels squeaked and spun and Martin pushed me through the dining room, past the bust of Homer and into the borning room which Cora had made ready for the birth. The room was very cold. I shivered miserably as Cora wrapped me up in my plaid bed shawl. The snow blew violently against the window, blanking out the rolling Seville landscape, sliding through the cracks in the wooden wall and spilling onto the floor near my bed.

None of us had anticipated that I would have my babe on such a bitterly windy day and there was only an overhead pipe running from the parlour stove to supply heat.

So Cora ran in and out, bringing extra blankets, while I lay trapped like an animal and helpless to stop the process my body had begun. Martin ran in and out too, until I lost track of him and Angus trudged into the room. His beaver hat was in his hands, his head and shoulders were covered with snow, and his freckled face was half-frozen in a case of ice. He moved his lips and whispered, "Anna."

Suddenly, I stopped shivering. Indeed, I stopped moving at all. Civilization lay nearby, as close even as the fingers of my long and swollen body could reach, but I could not find my way out of my frozen universe.

In the vicinity of my left ear I heard Cora's voice: "Relax, Mrs. Bates! Now push! Again! Push! Relax! Don't stop! PUSH! Lean on the pain! Not enough! Relax! PUSH! AGAIN! PUSH! Come on! A big push for the Captain. . . . ''

The door of the borning room flew open and in came a snowy, caped figure who brought with him the odour of rubbing alcohol. It was Dr. Beach. "Gidiup, Mrs. Bates!" he cried. "That's a good girl! Now whoa, whoa!"

The babble was short-lived, and a quiet fell, like the private silence of winter. The smells grew vague and I heard my own words,

"I'm sorry I'm so large, Doctor," drop off a distant cliff into a white sea that resounded with the far-off roar of glacial floes. The rubbing-alchohol smell came closer again and vanished again, and I remained, like my large relative, the BLUE WHALE, relegated to cold waters and, for that infinite moment, frozen fast inside a cresting wave.

"Her abdominal muscles have collapsed and the baby's stuck inside her," a new voice announced. The voice spoke the truth. I couldn't move to bear down, and I lay as eerily still as the waves of my deathly sea. I could not even feel the child trapped in my giant vagina. Is this how the normal female goes through birth? Disembodied from the physical self which is the arena of action? Surely not. Yet that is how I felt as the doctors struggled between my spread thighs.

For three days, I lay in the Arctic slumber. In the afternoon of the third day, I looked down to see the doctors between my legs yelling in dismay as gallons of my birthing waters broke over their astounded faces. Then Dr. Robinson extracted an arm of my poor babe from the depths of me, and both men pulled the rest of it out with a kind of bandage slung around the protruding arm and shoulder. Dr. Beach had his foot up against the bed to give him leverage and Dr. Robinson was sweating in exertion or terror—I know not which.

My exhausted son emerged—a true giant in his physical proportions from the looks of him—and I held him up to show Angus but Angus was gone. Then I clasped him to my leaking breasts, grateful he was not stillborn.

All babies look fragile, I know, so incompetent and defenceless are they against us larger creatures. Still, Babe appeared to me extremely weak despite his astounding size which Dr. Beach informed me would make medical history: length 30 inches, weight 23 ¾ pounds, breast circumference 24, breech 27, head 19, and the feet 5½ inches. His nose and cheeks were badly squashed from his three-day journey out of me but the doctors thought he looked like Martin—and he did, in a sad and crumpled way.

There was something sickly about my son. He was too worn out to suckle or cry. And after Martin handed out whisky and cigars (as triumphant as any paternal father) and Cora had wrapped Babe up in a sweet blue silk robe and put him down for a sleep in the custom-made crib near my bed, I felt a heavy dread.

So while the snows blew I slept fitfully with Babe beside me in the borning room, reaching down to feel for the wisps of breath issuing from his mouth, and brooding over the way he barely moved beneath my anxious hand.

Eleven hours after his arrival, the photographer that Martin had sent for stumbled into the borning room. The storm was over and sunlight illuminated the drab little room, but my mood was fearful as the local fellow set up his tripod near Babe's crib. He was the same bespectacled and formless little man who had worked at our sideshow and he complained sourly about the trouble he had protecting his equipment as he waded through the snowbanks to our farm house.

When he saw Babe, he stopped his grievances and chuckled. Then he leaned over Babe's crib and tweaked his cheek. Martin loomed over his shoulder—a smirking, fatherly phantasma. Suddenly the photographer stood bolt upright, as if my mate had walloped him from behind. He peered at me through the blazing sunlight.

"Your baby's not breathing."

"What are you talking about, man? My son is asleep," Martin bellowed.

"Bring Babe here," I commanded.

The photographer obeyed, carrying Babe in outstretched arms as if my child was a diseased object. Before I could hold him, Martin snatched Babe from the photographer and began to count his fingers and toes.

"See! Alive and perfectly formed," the giant thundered at the frightened photographer.

"I won't photograph no corpse," the photographer said.

I began to weep for I saw that Babe wasn't moving in Martin's arms and his tongue lolled slackly out of his open mouth. Martin stopped shouting and meekly brought the inert child to me. I cradled him to my breast and sent Martin to fetch the doctors sleeping upstairs.

"Will you take a picture of my child?" I asked. "It will be my only memento of him."

The little man shuffled and blushed and softly said yes and then replaced Babe in his crib for a formal portrait. The doctors rushed in with Martin at their heels as Babe was posing for posterity.

"That's it son. Watch the birdie," Martin roared. The doctors, meanwhile, swarmed about the crib.

"Captain Bates, your son is dead," Dr. Robinson said finally.

"Passed away just moments before," Dr. Beach confirmed.

"My son is perfect in every aspect," Martin yelled.

He shook his fist at the doctors and photographer and Cora brought in Virgil Shook who was carrying a pitchfork and together the crowd chased my broken-hearted mate out of the borning room and into the kitchen where Dr. Robinson convinced Martin to let him administer a sedative. I lay in the borning room with Babe, glad to have him to myself for the last time, and felt resigned. His death ended Martin's dream for a giant race and dashed my hope that finally, someday, I might have a connection with this odd world into which I'd been thrust. Yet, for all that, it was just as well for Babe that he had died.

The doctors admitted Babe had genetic difficulties. Dr. Robinson said his sex was uncertain as he possessed an unformed male organ on his outer body and might have had female organs inside. Martin wished the death record to say "male" but the doctors refused and pencilled in "sex unknown" under the cause of death.

I've included here the doctors' reports which were published shortly after the birth in the medical journal *Pioneer Medicos*. Typical of the profession, which too often leaves patients in the dark, the reports contained much information that was unknown to Martin and me.

Dr. A.P. Beach: I arrived at the giants' home at noon, January 15, 1879. I had never been inside the house before. The giantess had come to my office at East Main, and asked me to arrange a delivery at the farmhouse with the cook, Cora Shook, in attendance.

The house was quite a showplace. It was a sprawling white clapboard building. Handsome outside and in. I particularly recall a stove in the kitchen, a round, swollen contraption with claw feet and a statue of Martha Washington on top. There were ostrich feathers everywhere. On the mantel and sideboard.

327

The giantess was sitting up in bed in their borning room when I came in. Tilly had taken me out in the sleigh. It was a blustery winter day, and the cold had froze my whiskers so the giantess told me to bide by the stove and get warm.

"You're spread out like a week's wash, aren't you girl?" I said. She lay across two double beds pushed together to accommodate her. I was glad to see roller towels were tied to the bedposts for the patient's convenience during labour.

I sent Cora off to make a hot milk sedative so I could have a little chat with the giantess. A woman shows her true nature in childbirth. Her personality has to rise to an inordinate challenge, the greatest in the life of a woman, and by the first stage of delivery, I can tell whether she is going to succeed at child production.

"Your body is throwing down the gauntlet, Mrs. Bates. Are you going to pick up the glove?"

She whispered she was a little apprehensive. She wanted to know if I thought her size would cause problems and I said the edema was unfortunate, but I had some of Lydia E. Pinkham's Vegetable Compound (for female weakness) which would restore balance to her bodily fluids.

"I'm sorry I'm large, Dr. Beach," she said when I began preparations for the ordeal ahead.

Here are the notes I made for my report:

January 16, 12 noon. A sudden change in conditions. Took a sighting and found pains had worsened. Patient was complaining of two contractions at once—the echo effect. Recommended a sponge rub to midwife to freshen patient's spirits. Just as upper torso adapts itself last to shock of submersion in icy water, head & mental equipment of mother need time to adjust to birthing. Patient gripped roller towels and promised to do her best. Can't get dilation reading. Overwhelming quantities of dropsical flesh. Vagina may be as long as 22 inches. To get exact measurement exceedingly tricky.

January 18, 4 p.m. Rupture of membranes soaked goatee and vest during per vaginam examination. (Lucky vest not the embroidered silk done by wife.) Fluid on floor by bed. Very slippery, almost treacherous. Told midwife to watch her footing. Estimate 6 to 8 gallons of fluid—increase a result of edema. Patient distressed when I slipped during a sighting. Intense pain of contractions has tired patient.

5 p.m. Another sighting. Foetal head stuck in vagina. Recommended castor oil as interior lubricant. Patient exhausted from 3-day labour and ignoring midwife's attempts to coax activities from her huge abdominal muscles.

5:30 p.m. Husband and friends returned from town through bad snowstorm only to be sent back out to telegraph for help. Labour has ground to a halt as muscles of abdominal wall have relaxed over foetus. Quite a conundrum. Dr. J.D. Robinson coming from Wooster.

9 p.m. Robinson a tall, unlikeable chap. Refused to believe me when I said baby's head had broken my wooden forceps. Very tired from attending patient, and coldish. Got sniffles and chills from wet garments. Robinson going to try his forceps. Robinson says vagina is 13 inches according to his calculations with calipers on exterior wall of abdomen. I'm convinced it is 22.

9:30 p.m. Robinson and I had a toddy and consulted. His forceps got a grip on something but fearing mutilation, he didn't pull. I made list beforehand: a milk pan under mother to induce baby, castor oil douche, coaching husband to call to his offspring to come out. Robinson by-passed my suggestions and said bandages. Robinson at me all the time about washing my hands to prevent child-bed fever. Said my cologne is giving him headaches. We are going to pass a bandage over the baby's neck and try to pull the child out.

11 p.m. Head almost born, but shoulders stuck fast. Husband wept in parlour. Worst case in Robinson's and my career.

January 19, midnight. I tugged down and to the side with bandage. Robinson did the reaching. Bracing our feet vs. bed, Robinson got his hands on giant baby's arm. It came out first. Midwife hid eyes of patient so patient wouldn't see dangling purple limb. Hand and fingers size of a 10-month infant. More exertions brought forth rest of extraordinary American. Largest in nation and possibly world! Delivered Ohio. Weight 23 ¾ lbs., height 30 inches, breast 24 inches, foot 5 ½, head 19, breech 27. Patient and baby exhausted after labours of half a week. Small argument with Robinson about vagina size. Took short cut over the ice on Chippewa River. Bates said snows too deep up that way, but got through, thanks to Till who keeps away from deepest snowbanks. Showed wife ruined vest. She said, "Honey, doctoring in these parts is never dull, is it."

Dr. J.D. Robinson: Everything about the small, caped man who met me at the door of the Bates estate conspired against my confidence. He smelled of perfume, not a good portent for a country doctor who is in a position to take a nip or two.

No adequate preparations for the birth had been arranged although Beach had plenty of warning and should have secured a bed in Wooster for the poor woman who suffered a great deal throughout. My heart went out to her as we did our best to keep up with an event that went beyond our control, and Beach made an impossible situation worse with his jokes about skating over the floor after the waters broke. As if a woman in her state would be amused.

I blame premature exertion for the delay in the second stage of labour. Beach had the mother bear down before she was ready, tearing her cervix. I didn't point this out to Beach who had already kicked up a fuss about who was going to write up the birth. I said I had no intentions of stealing his thunder. Beach also claimed her vagina was 22 inches. A woman that developed is unimaginable. (Average length is 2½ inches along the anterior wall and 3½ posterior aspect so Beach is fooling himself if he thinks it is more than 12 p. and 7 to 9 a.)

The infant could not live in its condition. It was of uncertain sex, showing a poorly formed exterior male organ indicating the likelihood of female organs in the interior. The mother had diabetes mellitus and her condition may have been passed on to the child, whose fabulous size could have been the result of the disease, and not gigantism.

The Bateses wanted to bury it as quietly as possible. She was very concerned about the sex of the child and I said she must reg-

330

ister it as indeterminate. I think her husband told the newspapers it was male.

I did not tell her any of my diagnosis. The infant died from collapsed lungs. I passed the word to Beach about Mrs. Bates having diabetes and he promised to look into that possibility. She has a strong character and I congratulated her on her extreme effort. She was very low. She felt she had let the side down with her muscles collapsing in the second stage of labour, and asked me about "emblem fatigue" which I took to mean worry about suffering an aneurysm. I said I didn't foresee a problem with blood clotting and was sure Beach could prescribe something for her condition.

We buried Babe beside Margaret in the family plot in Mound Hill Cemetery, Seville. The undertaker dug a grave twice regulation size, foolishly imagining a baby that had sprung from my body must have been adult size. I was too exhausted to attend the winter burial but as soon as I felt strong again, Martin took me out to the cemetery so I could put a sprig of wintergreen on my child's grave. Icicles dripped from the eaves of the farms, and the thaw had reduced the snowbanks at the side of the road to dirty, sunken shapes. It was obvious spring was inevitable. I wore mourning clothes—a black cashmere cloak with a matching black cashmere muff. Martin had on a fur-lined gentleman's coat and his brown cap with the huge ear flaps.

At the cemetery, we met Cora Shook and Virgil. They were putting a wreath of carnations on Babe's grave. Cora nodded sadly at me as we approached and then she and Virgil climbed into a spring wagon and drove away.

At the cemetery, Martin paced up and down, his spurred cavalry boots banging the ground. I stood by the grave, my mind on Babe. Then across the rolling plain of farmland, I saw a chorus of giants—oh, rows and rows of dancing giants, each row taller than the one before, ascending from the snowy tobacco fields up into the March sky, jubilanty defying gravity. I pointed them out to Martin and he stopped marching about and stood gazing up at the sky.

Then he put his hand in mine and we drove home from the cemetery in a consoling silence.

331

Babe has been dead nine years now. In that time, we didn't perform. The people in Seville thought we didn't because we were rich enough and didn't need the money, but that isn't the truth. We tried twice more with W.W. Cole in 1879 and 1880 and it was exhausting for me. After the performances, I felt sick and weakened. Babe's birth and death wore me out. I am becoming weaker each day. Gravity is beating me and proving what Angus once told me—giants die young.

Following Babe's death, Martin and I stayed together in the manner of married couples who are inseparably wedded by the geography of their souls. Babe's death confirmed the bond between us and sometimes we think he is with us so we leave a third chair.

And so I come to the end of the Real Time Spiel in which all the diaries, testimonials, and devices that I've inserted to entertain you are done and my conclusion is known. To me, life is a performance and all moments are dramatic. (I believe this is a characteristic of show biz people.) Yes. I have made my bed and I have to lie in it, as the Blue-noses put it—that nation of scoffers who don't understand the need to dance up to the aurora borealis. Yet I am content. I will leave these memoirs for Martin to amend and publish when I have joined Babe as I do not have much time left. I have accepted my destiny. I was born to be measured and I do not fit in anywhere. Perhaps heaven will have more room.

Anna Haining Swan Bates 1888

EPILOGUE

Ann Swan: It wasn't only Uncle Geordie but the rest of the family who felt my girl would not live long and I knew it as a true prophecy. A babe who stood taller than her mother seven years from birth was destined to cross the river of death first. Anna declined in her sleep, on Sunday, August 5, 1888. The obituary which *he* wrote himself for the *SevilleTimes* said it was a peaceful declension. He often said things lacking truth so I had my doubts until the doctor took me aside at the church and whispered Anna slipped into a coma 18 hours before her death Sunday at 2 p.m. There was no pain. In the little man's opinion, heart trouble was at the back of it.

He held the funeral up until we arrived Thursday the 9th. It was a sad day for me. I hadn't seen her for ten years. My last child was born in '72, David, so I was tied up with him and the others of whom six are left out of the twelve. It broke my heart on the last visit to see how mean *he* was and selfish with her and that's what crushed her spirit because she was always very healthy for a giantess.

Do you know people in Seville wrote Alex after Anna was gone, appealing for funds because *he* wouldn't pay his debts, even living off her money. He was a bully and it was too bad for all concerned he didn't get put in his place. He counted on her to put oil on troubled waters and, out of the goodness of her heart, she protected him.

I had no complaints about her funeral fixings except for the monkey. Her manager, Ingalls, had given it to her as a pet and *he* was keeping it on a chain at the end of their driveway. It kicked up a racket during the service. Oh the poor thing was in disgraceful condition by the time we got there. The flies had et the fur off its head and neck. I hear he didn't look after his big Durham

333

either or the boa constrictor. The snake died when it got its fangs caught in a horse blanket. I can't feel sorry for a hideous reptile but it shows *his* character.

I had to hear second-hand she was dying. Hubert Belcourt read in the papers somewhere she had lost ninety pounds and was looking frail and sickly. Why he didn't look after her better I don't know. He never knew how lucky he was to have a woman that nice. She was dead at forty-two.

I remember her the morning we left by coach for New York. With her auburn hair and delicate white skin, she could hold her own with the best of the Yankee ladies. Her father and I were proud at the way she had grown. Maybe if she hadn't married so young, at 23, she would have found a better provider.

I blame myself for making her feel money was important. We were poor when she was wee although we are enjoying the rewards of our labours now. Then her father said not to meddle— she had found one as big as herself. I never was with her long enough to discover if her heart was happy after she went to live down there. I have a sad notion she got used to living in a fog. She has always had a romantic nature. I figure she was searching in her quiet way for some means of getting him to show respect, as if anything she could do would make the slightest difference to a swaggerer like that. My poor child. She wouldn't accept that he was hopeless. He did give Lizzie (Liza) many of Anna's jewels and dresses and the gold watch you wind with a key. Anna left us money too—$500 apiece for her dad and myself and $7,500 to be divided between what's left of her brothers and sisters. He could have cheated us so I should be grateful for small mercies.

Another sad thing was her dead bairn. She would have made a good mother. I should know. I taught the BIGGEST MODERN WOMAN OF THE WORLD how to love.

Cora Shook: I knew Anna Bates for fourteen years. I used to cook for her during threshing and don't think it was easy working in a house where everything was above my reach. I'd look at Virgil and shake my head.

It was me who did the mid-wifing for her second child. The

doctors botched it. If they'd had good instruments, the baby would have lived, I know that much. No human should have to suffer the way she did. Before it came, her ankles swelled up and some days her legs were too swollen to get off her bed. One morning, she slipped on the puddle of ice in the barnyard and I had to fetch the Captain to get her upright. She looked like one of them ocean turtles on its back. But she never would complain. It's true she left me $500 in her will. Some of the Seville people will tell you I only worked for her because she was rich but that's wrong. I would have helped her no matter what she paid me because she was as dear to me as my own daughter, born a mongol idiot and died a day later. Dr. Beach said her death was a blessing only I'd have accepted my baby at any price. She'd have been Anna's age if she'd growed up.

Virgil Shook: We used to be known for growing tobacco. Then after the Bateses moved here everybody thought of us as a circus town. My wife liked her but I ain't got a good word to say for Captain Bates. He spit his tobacco at me and I had to carry a pitch fork to protect myself in case he lost his temper. Then he used to make the field hands wait in a big line-up while he got their wages. He kept the money in a drawer of a commode behind a screen in the kitchen so the men couldn't see how much he had. He'd tell lies about how brave he was in the War. And the men would wait and wait and finally, the Captain would have a good laugh and say "Here's your chicken feed, boys." I didn't blame them when they got mad. I guess any man who would take on the Captain had a lot of guts. Now when I read in the papers about what an upstanding member of the community he was, I say to myself, you don't know the Captain like I did.

Frannie Bideman: Dad knew the Captain but I never got to know her. She was too grand for the Seville people. We were all right to have as servants but she lived in a different world. She was a celebrity and we were no better than dirt under her feet.

The Captain was more down to earth. You could have him over to tea and not worry about getting out the good china.

Martin Bates: My wife was long-headed as well as long-bodied—the top of the crop of American womanhood. Her early history in New Annan, Nova Scotia, saw many hardships that contributed to the wells of understanding I drank from throughout my life.

I was the youngest son of noble Kentucky landowners, John W. Bates and Sarah Bates, and fortunate to enlist for the Confederacy as a private in the Fifth Kentucky Infantry C.S.A. on the 15th of September 1861.

The toll of duty in one so young captured the respect of the woman who permitted her history to blend with mine. Anna was a shy, retiring person whose main interest was to stay behind the scenes and improve her mind. I credit her conservative nature with our happy tempers. Hers was as bright and sunshiny as a May morning.

My wife had an impressive funeral. There was a crowd so I was obliged to hold a 4 p.m. service on our front veranda. People sat and stood in the barnyard. The procession of carriages extended the distance down the county road from the farm to Mound Hill Cemetery.

I held a fine memorial service the following Sabbath at the Baptist church. The Rev. Ashley took for his text Mark XIV:8th: "She hath done what she could." I draped our pew in the best crêpe and where she used to sit I placed five bushels of white petunias, her favourite flower. P.T. Barnum and other bigwigs were there. P.T. admired the life-size female statue I put over Anna's grave in Mound Hill Cemetery.

The only foul-up was the casket manufacturer in Cleveland. He thought the telegram with my darling's measurement was a mistake and sent a regulation box. It tood three days to get the proper container. I have ordered my own chariot in advance so nobody will be able to botch the job for me when my time is up.

With the exception of the loss of my offspring, our life was blessed with uninterrupted felicity. To be sure, we had little disagreements. Anybody could put the touch on Anna for dough. She let mortgage claims over town without calling them when we had to go three years on the road to cover our own costs. She willed the task to me of disposing her claims and I made certain the bums scrambled to get the money they owed her.

I am often asked about my hope for a new race of giants. It is true I foresaw myself and Anna as the first in a magnificent dawn of the evolutionary process. But she was not able to fulfil my plan, and I don't carry a grudge over her weakness. It isn't the blueprint one draws on the slate but how one beats down the path that will count with the Great Judge when the final curtain falls. I was privileged to live with the one God made for me. You, my friend, will be blessed indeed if the same opportunity is given to you.

Dad Bideman: The Cap was a real Southern gentleman, see? He worshipped his lady. Had her on a pedestal. I mean the giantess could do no wrong as far as the Cap was concerned. Every day, he'd flip their cook, Cora Shook, a silver dollar and ask her to bring the Missus a bottle of that fizzy water. Course, his politics didn't go down in town. The boys couldn't stand the Cap, but he had a good side if you knew how to treat him. He loved children. He used to put our babies in his stovepipe hat when he came to visit and there was nothing he liked better than to walk the whole bunch of them down to the candy store to buy them sweets. The Cap had a sense of humour too. I remember having many a good laugh with him.

There was the time the visiting minister came to the Baptist church for a revival meeting. The Baptists have a funny way of doing things, see? They make people walk down into a big hole in the altar floor that's full of water and then they baptize 'em. Well, the visiting minister called up the Cap because he thought he was standing up and volunteering when the Cap was kneeling. So the big son of a gun marched up to the altar and walked down the steps into the hole of water like he believed. By gee, it was a sight. The Cap was too tall to be submerged so he stood eye to eye with the minister who was so nervous you could see his hands shake as he poured the holy water over the Cap's head. The minister realized his mistake, see? But he wouldn't admit it and he called out to the congregation and asked them to say "Hallelujah" for their brother and the whole church fell to its knees and asked the Lord to have mercy on the Cap's soul. I guess the Cap had a good joke on the town that day.

Then if the big bugger didn't move in and become one of us

after she died. The Cap was lonely after Anna departed for the hereafter and, at the turn of the century, the Cap married Lavonne Weatherby. She was a preacher's daughter whose pumpkin pies won first prize at the Baptist church. She made Cap undergo a physical examination to see if their marriage could be consummated, see? I told the Cap it was too much to ask of the man you love and the Cap agreed but he went along with her. Lavonne bossed him good. She made him stop chewing his tobacco and I reckon he thought he had to do what she said because he was living in her house.

You see, the Cap sold his farm and all his belongings except for his marriage bed after he took up with Lavonne. And he moved into Seville. She had to cut a bigger window in her house so his bed could get into the place. Lavonne wasn't pretty but she was a clean, tidy-looking woman. She wore her hair in a pompadour and she stood five feet in her stockings. I can tell you the pair of them made a funny sight walking down the street to church.

Well, the Cap lived in town for nineteen years with Lavonne. He was here for the big storm in 1913 when the water came up to the windows of the Seville barbershop. He was old and sick by then and spent the day talking to the town loafers about Anna. I have a snap of him leaning on a big wooden cane in the park. He growed his moustache long and his hair was white, see? And he didn't look like the Cap any more. I reckon he just wanted to join Anna. Because he kept his coffin of ornamental brass in the barn down the street from our house. Right up until he died children went to that barn and played in the Cap's box. On the day of his funeral, it stuck out the back of the hearse.

The Cap died sometime in January 1919. I was sorry to see him go. But maybe he was happy because he had been acting peculiar. Before he died, he told me his second wife was feeding him poison. See? The Cap believed that Lavonne Weatherby and Dr. Beach had ganged up on him and were trying to kill him. Isn't that the funniest thing you ever heard? A little thing like Lavonne doing in the Cap! I told the big so-and-so he was getting senile if he thought a pint-sized female could bring a man his size to his knees.

When he was on show in the funeral home, all the men in town went down and had a good look at the Cap's privates to see if they were up to the rest of him. I didn't join 'em but the story is they weren't. After he died, Lavonne Weatherby had to go on welfare because the Cap didn't leave her any money. I always figured he was making a mistake marrying a short woman when he had been so proud of Anna's height. And I guess in the end the Cap thought so too.

Lavinia Warren: Everybody has an act and Anna's was manners. During the old days at Mr. Barnum's museum I thought she was trying to upstage me with her fancy airs. But for twenty years I never knew her to take advantage of me. In our business, that's rare. Then General Tom Thumb died July 15, 1883, and she went out of her way to help me. She knew I was worn out after my last three years with Barnum and Bailey.

Tom Thumb and I hated circus work, like Anna did. No class. Our employer, Mr. Barnum, posed us with a baby and sold our "family" portrait at 25¢ a piece. I looked down on Mr. Barnum. He gave us beautiful presents like the rosewood bed, but he called me a dwarf. I am not a dwarf. I am a small woman—a midget.

But I didn't care about the baby. Anna did. She wrote Mr. Barnum and complained about subjecting me to humiliation. Anna wanted a child very much. (Me, I have no use for children. My sister Minnie, who is an inch or two taller than me, died in childbirth with a five-and-a-half-pound girl.)

I am a career woman from start to go. Tom Thumb understood. No other man has, not Count Magri, my second husband. I moved into films, and when midgets went out of style I ran my own businesses, like our general store in Middleboro, Massachusetts.

Nobody can make Lavinia Warren throw in the towel. Tom Thumb was the same. We made up to $100,000 a year together. My husband liked money and he knew how to spend it. We had a sailing sloop, jewels, pedigreed horses, a country house. Tom Thumb was buried with Masonic colours and 10,000 came to his funeral.

The funeral left me up to my ears in debt but I went ahead with the life-sized granite statue of Tom. It sits on a 40-foot marble shaft in Mountain Grove Cemetery, Bridgeport. Tom commissioned it. He liked quality.

I had a few pieces of property and about $16,000 when I went up to Anna in Ohio to think things out. I remember Bates getting me at the train station and Anna sitting quietly in the buggy. She looked tired until she saw Bates carrying me and then her face lit up. I had my first ride down those country roads with Bates cursing and whipping his team while I bounced on the seat. Anna held my suitcases so they wouldn't fall off.

Their home was a showplace. Anna was a pope in taste. I slept in a crib she had had made for her baby. It had silk sheets. My room had velvet curtains and wallpaper right from London, England. Anna carried me up every night and tucked me in. She took care of me and then I took a troupe on the road and met Count Magri. We married two years after the death of Tom Thumb.

I never went back to Seville until long after she was dead. Not until after the Captain was dead. It was in May 1919. I was passing through with the Count, my second husband. The next day we travelled on to Cleveland. It was raining when we left and I made the Count stop at the cemetery. Then we saw Anna's stone monument. It was smaller than Mr. Stratton's but very nice. Bates had put it up with the inscription from Psalm 17, verse 15: "I will behold thy face in righteousness. I shall be satisfied, when I awake, with thy likeness." The Captain is buried at the statue's feet next to Anna's baby and her sister. Then we left and drove by the Bates' farm. Normal people were living in it. We didn't drive in. The weather was still bad and the Count wanted to press on. He said he'd heard enough about the giants of Seville.